To Redeem a Rake
Heart of a Duke Series

Copyright © 2016 by Christi Caldwell

For more information about the author:
www.christicaldwellauthor.com
christicaldwellauthor@gmail.com
Twitter: @ChristiCaldwell
Or on Facebook at: Christi Caldwell Author

For first glimpse at covers, excerpts, and free bonus material, be sure to sign up for my monthly newsletter!
Printed in the USA.

Cover Design and Interior Format

© KILLION
GROUP, INC.

To Redeem a Rake

Heart
of a
Duke

THE
SERIES

USA TODAY BESTSELLER

CHRISTI CALDWELL

Other Titles by
Christi Caldwell

THE HEART OF A SCANDAL
In Need of a Knight—Prequel Novella
Schooling the Duke
Heart of a Duke
In Need of a Duke—Prequel Novella
For Love of the Duke
More than a Duke
The Love of a Rogue
Loved by a Duke
To Love a Lord
The Heart of a Scoundrel
To Wed His Christmas Lady
To Trust a Rogue
The Lure of a Rake
To Woo a Widow

LORDS OF HONOR
Seduced by a Lady's Heart
Captivated by a Lady's Charm
Rescued by a Lady's Love
Tempted by a Lady's Smile

SCANDALOUS SEASONS
Forever Betrothed, Never the Bride
Never Courted, Suddenly Wed
Always Proper, Suddenly Scandalous
Always a Rogue, Forever Her Love
A Marquess for Christmas
Once a Wallflower, at Last His Love

DEDICATION

To Rory

*From the moment, you were born, you were a fighter.
You fought to do everything that came natural to most: eating, drinking,
crawling, walking. Gifts I once took for granted, you showed me were
great miracles. Eight years later, you are still a fighter. Do not let a single
person ever tell you that you cannot do something. Let no one limit
you. Trust that no dream is unattainable, not only because we're at your
side…but because of who you are.*

The sky is the limit.

Miss Daphne Smith's story belongs to you.

ACKNOWLEDGEMENTS

Daphne and Daniel's story was one that was very close to me for personal reasons. As such, I am forever grateful to Louisa Cornell for being the first person to read it and help me bring forth the vision I had.

PROLOGUE

Spelthorne
Surrey, England
1801

WITH THE BLAZING SUMMER SUN filtering through the trees, Miss Daphne Smith accepted the ugly truth. She was going to die here.

Even the excruciating agony shooting a path up her leg wasn't distraction enough from that inevitability. And it would be no one's fault but her own.

Draping an arm over her face, she attempted to lessen the glare of the sun's rays still burning her face. It produced the kind of heat that a red-haired girl could feel cooking more freckles. That mocking sun. That blasted, showed-itself-too-late ball of agony in the sky.

Another shuddery sob slipped from Daphne's lips and she closed her eyes, willing back the pain. Yes, she was going to die here, in her favorite copse, after having been expressly forbidden from coming—would Mama and Papa even know to come look for her? Panic filled her. Why *would* they come, when they'd threatened to take away her mount if she disobeyed them and visited this place? They would know there was nothing she loved more in her ten years than riding Ginger.

And she'd gone and ruined it all by setting out in a rainstorm to chase the rainbow.

"You silly girl." She brushed the back of her hand over her tear-stained cheeks. Now, she'd never ride again.

Her left leg throbbed all the more. Shoving onto her elbows, Daphne peered at her foot. Nausea twisted in her belly at the ghastly bend of her leg. *Why does it look like that?* Thrusting aside the fearful question, she bit hard on her lower lip and made one more attempt to stand. She wiggled onto her belly and pushed onto her right foot. Then she placed a tentative weight on her left. Another cry spilled past her lips and as several wrens took off in a noisy flight from the trees above, Daphne crumpled to the damp ground, landing hard in a deep puddle.

With her nose caked in mud, she lay there. The feel of the wet ground was cool on her cheek as her tears blurred with the earth. *Blasted rain.*

She rolled onto her back and glared up at the cheerful sun. The same sun that hadn't made a single appearance in nearly six days, except for early that afternoon. And then there had been the rainbow. And the promise of fortunes at the end of it. And well, everyone in Surrey knew they needed fortunes—even if Papa would never, ever dare admit to it. But Daphne knew. She'd been so convinced of it that she followed that brightly colored prism.

Now, she was going to die for it. She'd die alone beneath the oak, not even able to touch her fingertips to her rolling brook. Even her horse had bolted off and abandoned her.

Tears seeped from beneath her lashes and poured onto the muddied earth. Her cheek itched and she focused on that slight discomfort, for she wouldn't have to fix on the agonizing pain of her foot and leg. Sniffling, she turned her head and stared into the near distance. The pristine surface of the lake she'd first learned to swim in rippled as a faint breeze stirred the trees.

"Stupid s-sun." Daphne whimpered as she moved her left foot and then something glittered in the light. Her heart kicked up a beat and she stretched her hand out. Her fingers collided with the cold press of a rusted guinea. Her fortune? She wrapped her hand around the coin with a jagged lightning-like scratch down the middle of King George III. *This* had been the treasure?

A branch snapped and she went motionless, not taking her gaze from the lake. Salvation had come.

"Daphne?" Oh, no. *Not* Daniel. Anyone but Daniel. He was forever teasing her about all the scrapes she landed herself in. "Is that you?" Except... His voice, usually so full of his boyhood confidence emerged hesitant.

She sniffled and brushed the back of her hand over her leaking nose. "D-Daniel."

Then, who else had she hoped would come to this spot, other than Daniel Winterbourne, the Earl of Montfort's son? He was the only person who loved these grounds more than she did. So much so, that he'd ordered her from them too many times to count when she'd been a small girl of five because they would one day belong to him. By the time Daphne was six, he'd realized she was not going anywhere and certainly not because he, a silly boy, had demanded it. Since then, they'd struck a truce and shared the lake and every other part of the countryside when he was here.

Well, they had, until her parents had forbidden her from coming.

"What are you doing on the ground?" he called from several paces away.

"Looking at the m-mud." Her attempt at sarcasm was ruined by that tremor of pain. She'd sooner die here alone than let any boy see her in pain, especially Daniel who was always so good at *everything*, so she rolled onto her back and shoved herself up onto her elbows.

The brush crunched under his boot steps as he came forward and then stopped abruptly several feet away. His fishing rod slipped from his fingers and he gasped.

And she would have preferred his mocking her for not being as skilled a fisherman or rider as he was than that soft exhalation. Daphne's lower lip quivered and, for the first time since she'd raced over that fallen trunk in her quest for fortunes, breathed the great fear aloud. "Is it...*broken*?" She peered up at him. Almost thirteen, he was so very tall. Many more inches taller than herself. He was always so confident. Where she'd rolled her eyes at him in the past, now she wished him to be that same kind of confident.

Instead, his cheeks turned white and his eyes rounded.

Tears swelled in her eyes once more. "It *is* broken, isn't it?"

Daniel blinked several times and then sank to a knee beside her. "I...it...I think it is."

A single tear slid down her cheek. Followed by another. And

with his faltering confirmation, she forced herself to truly look at the limb. Jutted unnaturally to the left, her leg was impossibly turned. And no matter how much she willed it, no matter how much pain she endured, she couldn't get it straightened.

"Don't," he said gruffly.

She angrily slashed at her cheeks and then winced. After countless moments lying here, the sun had scorched them. "Just go," she cried softly. "Let me die here." Daphne flopped down on the ground and draped her arm over her eyes. That way, she didn't have to see how Daniel kept looking at her ugly leg and swallowing loudly.

"How long have you been here?" he asked with so much concern that Daphne suddenly wished she'd been less bothersome to him over the years.

"I don't know. I left the schoolroom a-at ten." Her governess was, no doubt, nipping from the decanter, as she often did whenever she had a chance to imbibe.

Daniel's frown deepened. "It is nearly one o'clock." And in an un-Daniel-like manner, he flicked his gaze around the copse. "My brother would know what to do." Alistair, the future Earl of Montfort, the proper young man who had earned the respect of all in the county. Mama and Papa always said some lady would be lucky to land him as a husband.

She, on the other hand, if she had to marry a miserable boy, would far prefer one who rode and spit and fished—like Daniel. Not that she wished to marry Daniel. Or any boy. "Well, Alistair is not here. *You* are." And another thing she'd never dare admit… She was glad for it. As much as he'd always teased her, this was Daniel. Her *best* friend. Her *only* friend, really.

Daniel gave a jerky nod.

"W-Will you go for my papa?" she whispered. For the truth was, she'd rather give up riding Ginger before dying here. And certainly, not dying here alone.

Daniel shook his head. *No?* He'd surely not leave her to die here. "It will take too long," he said, his frown deepening. "I will help you home."

"Y-you will?" He'd told her time enough when she'd been stung by a bee two years ago what he thought about girls and tears. Still, his offer brought another round of tears.

Daniel puffed his chest and gave a nod. "I will. Mirabel is tethered a short distance from here."

Together, with some struggling, he managed to get her upright and onto her right foot. Looping an arm at her waist, he caught her weight against him and guided her slowly through the muddied copse. With every jarring movement, her belly turned, until she feared she'd cast up her last meal. Stars danced behind her eyes and she blinked them back.

Daniel stole a sideways look at her. "Chasing treasures?"

She nodded unevenly; the pain too great to speak through. Of course, Daniel would know that.

"Did you find it?"

Daphne thought to the rusty coin in the front pocket of her dress. "Yes." She braced for his teasing, but he said nothing.

They reached Mirabel and after untethering his mount, Daniel swung astride. He held a hand down for her and Daphne reached up… Her leg crumpled under her.

She cried out and his mare danced nervously. Breathing heavily through the pain, she glanced at the ground. "J-just go ahead. G-get my papa."

Indecision raged in his brown eyes and he glanced about again. A moment later, he dismounted and retied Mirabel's reins to the juniper. He bent and carefully scooped her into his arms.

Daphne swung her gaze up to his. "Wh-what are you doing?"

Daniel flexed his jaw, appearing more like his always serious brother, than the boy of twelve who'd long-lived to tease her. "I am bringing you home."

Her heart tripped a beat. It was at least a mile to her family's property. The grounds were muddied. The hills were high. "Y-you cannot."

Anger filled his eyes. "Because I'm not Alistair?"

The village might adore Alistair for being so perfect, but when their families joined for dinner parties and picnics, he didn't do anything fun like tease her, or even talk to her. And she'd never, ever seen him fish at her copse. How could she truly trust a man who didn't swim or fish? "I am too big, Daniel," she said practically. After all, she *was* ten now and was everything logical. Except for the part about disobeying her parents and rushing about the estates.

Daniel firmed his mouth and then started forward. With every jarring step, she swallowed down nausea. "Does it hurt?" His breath emerged raspy from his efforts.

Daphne nodded against his chest, burrowing close. She buried her face into him, not wanting to see his mocking eyes.

"It will be all right."

Startled, she swung her gaze up. His gaze was trained forward and sweat beaded his forehead. He shifted her in his arms, stumbled, and then quickly righted them. "D-do you really believe so?"

He hesitated. Even through the pain she saw it. But then, he nodded. And she knew he lied. Another sheen of tears blurred her vision as her mind ran amok with fear. "D-do you think I'll ever ride again?"

"Of course." Uncertainty filled those two words.

"No, I won't," she cried, her voice shaking. "I'll never swim again. Or curtsy. Or dance." What was she without her legs? A sob tore from her.

"You don't like to curtsy or dance," he said, wrinkling his brow.

"Yes, but mayhap someday I'll want to. What if I do want to marry and can't because I can't curtsy or dance?"

He grunted. "Well, I don't want a wife who can curtsy or dance. I would much rather have one who rides and swims."

Her heart caught, soared, and then promptly slipped to her broken leg. She would never ride or swim. Even as she didn't *wish* to marry, if she did, it would be to a boy who wanted her to fish and swim.

Her shoulders shook from the force of her tears and Daniel hugged her closer. He didn't promise any more that it would be all right, but just let her cry, without making fun of her. That was when Daphne knew—she would love him until the day she died.

A long while later, they neared her family's property. Daniel faltered and, gasping, shifted her in his arms.

"You can put me down, Daniel."

"I am not putting you down," he said angrily. With steely determination in his eyes, he resumed walking. Not another word was spoken between them until her cottage home came into view. In the distance, she spied Papa climbing astride his mount. His gaze caught on them and then his cry went up.

Daphne quickly looked to Daniel. "Thank you." She reached

between them and withdrew her single guinea. "I found my treasure today," she whispered. "I want you to have it."

He rounded his eyes. "You are giving it to me?"

She nodded and stuffed it in his pocket. "It is yours now."

Daniel hesitated. "You're certain?"

"I want you to have it."

"I can't—"

The excruciating agony of her twisted limb sent tears to her eyes. "You *have* to take it."

Daniel gave a reluctant nod and shifted her in his arms. "If you ever require your treasure back, Daphne, I will return it."

Through the pain, she gave him an arched look. "A person honors their word and I told you it is yours."

Her father galloped into the clearing and interrupted the moment. "Daphne," he cried. Dismounting, he raced forward and wordlessly plucked her from Daniel's arms. "Thank you so much, Daniel. I cannot ever repay you," he said, his voice shaking with emotion.

The young boy squared his shoulders and nodded.

She bit the inside of her cheek at the agony the abrupt movement had on her foot and leg. Papa rushed to his mount and handed Daphne over to Daniel, once more. Daniel held her close. "It is going to be all right, Daph," he vowed and then helped her astride Papa's mount.

As her father guided her home, she peered back at Daniel. Now, with him gone, there was no distraction from the pain. Coldness stole through her and blackness plucked at the edge of her conscious.

She blinked and tried to retain the light, fixing on him in that same spot, staring after her. Daniel erroneously believed her gift had been the treasure she'd found at the end of the rainbow. What he'd failed to realize was the truth—*he* had been the true treasure she'd found.

Just as he would be for the rest of her life, when they fished and swam and rode reckless around the countryside, together forever.

And even through the pain, Daphne managed a smile.

CHAPTER 1

April, 1819
Spelthorne
Surrey, England

MISS DAPHNE SMITH WANTED TO sit. *Desperately*. From the corner of her eye, she covetously eyed the seat in front of the immaculate rose-inlaid desk.

Mrs. Belden, the headmistress at Mrs. Belden's Finishing School, transferred her gaze from the sheet in her hands and peered down the length of her nose. "In three months, nothing has changed, *Miss* Smith." In a dismissive manner that sent panic spiraling in Daphne's breast, the woman set aside the list of references and slid them across the desk.

With the assistance of her cane, Daphne limped forward. "My references are honorable ones," she said resolutely. "I ask you to please reconsider." Again. She despised the faint shake that hinted at her desperation. Then, when you were a crippled spinster of eight and twenty years, without a living relation to depend on, and even less funds to survive through the years, that is really what one became—desperate. How she despised a world where there were so few options for women.

The headmistress took in the drag of her left leg and her frown deepened. Yes, for in a world where Society valued utmost perfection, particularly of the physical sort, Daphne would never, ever be anything but broken. The tap of her cane served as an ever-present damnable reminder. Her skirts, at least, hid the mangled, ugly truth everyone knew. "Miss Smith," the woman began, carefully removing her spectacles. She folded the pair and rested them on her desk. "How many times have you come to speak with me?"

"Five." That was if one did not include the time she'd approached the headmistress in the village for an "accidental" meeting.

"Six," the greying woman corrected. "One of those times I was in the village on a matter of business."

Daphne curled her hand over the head of her cane. Yes, well, a woman who was tasked with the care and deportment of the most revered ladies in the land *would* have a head for such precise details. How had she been reduced to hoping for employment in this stifling place? Shoving aside that useless self-pitying, she attended the headmistress.

"Since that time, what experience have you had in working with the nobility?"

She flattened her lips as a damning silence stretched on.

"And why has no one hired you?" Mrs. Belden continued, relentless. The woman could have taught Genghis Khan a lesson on ruthlessness.

However, when one was ridiculed and mocked through life for being a cripple, the harsh words of an old headmistress, though frustrating, otherwise rolled off a long-stiffened spine. "There are concerns as to my ability to move freely with children," she said evenly. But not all people were of Mrs. Belden's ill-opinion. Some had confidence in the capabilities of women with disabilities.

The much-read page inside the clever pocket sewn in her dress burned hot. It was that scrap that had brought her before this miserable woman.

"Tell me, Miss Smith," the woman asked while folding her hands. She leaned over those gnarled interlocked digits. "If you were to serve a lady eager to be rid of a chaperone or companion, how would you expect to keep up, hmm?" In truth, Daphne's interests in employment moved far beyond those flawless ladies Mrs. Belden now spoke of. Rather, it extended to women, flawed and imperfect, striving to make their place in this world, the same way she now did.

The muscles of her lower leg tightened. With the aid of her

cane, she shifted her weight. "I expect if they are your esteemed students, Mrs. Belden, then there would be no worries of those young ladies daring to defy propriety and decorum," she delivered evenly.

Mrs. Belden froze. "Are you being insolent, Miss Smith?" she sputtered.

Oh, blast and blazes. The last way she'd secure employment was by insulting the headmistress. "Not at all, Mrs. Belden." Daphne spoke in the smooth, modulated tones her mother had once believed her incapable of. Once again, desperation allowed a woman to draw on otherwise absent skills. "You have a revered reputation and work with noble students. As such, I do not doubt their unfailing devotion to the lessons learned here." Dull, miserable lessons on how to sit, stand, and how not to speak.

Then, it said something to the state of her own sorry existence that she'd so crave a post at a school where young ladies' souls went to die. Alas, experience with young ladies being required for future employment and the families in the area unwilling to hire a woman with a disfigurement, Daphne would trade her soul for proper references. References that would ultimately mark her as qualified for the work she truly wished.

The headmistress pursed her lips, bringing Daphne back to the moment. "Miss Smith, I am not cruel. I do appreciate the impossibility of going through life as a cripple."

Fury stirred and Daphne bit the inside of her cheek hard. *Do not say anything. Do not say anything.* Not everyone felt that way. Most did. But there was one woman who believed the contrary…

"However, the young women I hire are of respectable origins."

As the daughter of a late, impoverished member of the gentry, Daphne had been born into respectability. But respectability was not nobility. And when there were no funds involved, her value was even less to the world. "My origins are respectable," she interjected when the woman took a moment to breathe in her perfunctory enumeration. "My father was a member of the gentry." Sadness stuck in her chest at the never-distant thought of her late papa.

"An *impoverished* one," Mrs. Belden added, drumming her fingertips on the surface of her desk in a grating rhythm.

"But *respected* nonetheless." The challenging words slipped out before she could call them back.

The older woman winged a frosty eyebrow upward. "But not respected *enough* for another respected family in the county to offer you employment."

Despite the agony eating away at her leg from standing motionless for so long, Daphne remained still. She'd rather be slayed where she stood than allow the headmistress to know the mark she'd landed.

In a surprisingly magnanimous show, Mrs. Belden released a long sigh. "This audience you've been granted is far more than I would allow most women, Miss Smith." How very fortunate for her. Daphne tamped down the bitter smile. "It is due to your birthright and circumstances that I have been as patient as I have."

"Thank—"

"However, I will insist, once more," she thumped her fist once on the desk. "Unless there is a remarkable change in your employment history, one that includes direct employment in a noble household and glowing references, there is no place for you here as an instructor."

A humbling entreaty hung on her lips and then died there. Even with the panicky fear that kept Daphne awake well into the early morning hours, she would never do something so pathetic as to beg.

A knock sounded at the door.

"Enter," Mrs. Belden called out, looking past Daphne's shoulder.

The creak of the opening door filled the room. How singularly odd that such a flawless establishment should have hinges that needed oiling. "Mrs. Belden, Lady Alice…" At that familiar name, Daphne whipped her head around. The young woman's gaze slid to her. "The young lady's belongings are nearly packed, however," again, she looked to Daphne. "His Lordship has yet to arrive." The young woman's voice contained the smooth, emotionless tones demonstrated by all the ladies fortunate enough to find employment.

The headmistress nodded. "That will be all, Mrs. Ludecke," she said brusquely.

A moment later, the door closed, once more creaking on its hinges. Mrs. Belden wasted no time in launching into her diatribe. "Please let me make myself clear, Miss Smith, lest you waste your time." Again. "Unless you have clients of noble birth and references speaking to your diligent effort on those ladies' behalf, there is no place for you in this school. Now, if you'll excuse me," Mrs. Belden said, impatience in that polite, empty request. "I have a matter to attend to." Then in a dismissive gesture, the woman picked up her spectacles, perched them on her nose, and returned her attention to the notes in front of her.

The headmistress' students. Those cherished young ladies with their still-living mamas and papas, and laughter. They had no worries over what happened when a woman officially ran through her meager funds left. And worse, the distant male relative who'd brought her displacement.

A lump formed in her throat. A hungering for her own loving parents. The only people who'd seen beyond her disfigurement.

"Miss Smith," Mrs. Belden snapped, jerking her into motion.

Daphne limped over to the desk. With her spare hand, she grabbed the handful of respected names—friends of her departed parents who could serve as a character reference, but wouldn't do more than that; like hire her for their cherished daughters. "Mrs. Belden," she said flatly. Useless page in hand, she lurched across the room. Her neck burned with the woman's stare.

Yes, one who'd committed herself to instructing ladies on the effortless way with which to glide over marble ballrooms would never look with anything but revulsion on a woman who moved like a lame pup just learning to walk.

When she exited the room, closing the door behind her, Daphne did not break her stride. Instead, she marched ahead at a brisk pace that strained every last muscle and ligament from her ankle up through her knee, and higher up to her thigh. Sweat beaded her brow and she dusted the back of her forearm over it.

If her limp appalled Mrs. Belden, she would, no doubt, find a lady perspiring as a punishable offense. Not all were as ruthless as Mrs. Belden, however. For the men and women of all stations who viewed Daphne and the other imperfect girls and women as useless to Society, there were those that believed in their capabilities.

With her spare hand, she dug out the single, neat scrap she'd snipped from an old copy of the *Herald Gazette* and scanned the page. Even though she'd read it enough times that she'd burned the words on her mind.

The Marchioness of Guilford, founder of Ladies of Hope, a distinguished institution for girls and women with disabilities, seeks the most experienced educators and doctors as candidates for work with those living within the institution. Only those with a belief in the ideology and principle of the establishment, as well as experience and glowing references will be considered for employment. It promises to be unlike any other respectable institution for ladies, etc, etc...

Daphne gripped the edges of that sheet so hard, her fingers turned white. The same hope that had filled her since she'd first read of Lady Guilford's held her motionless. There was a place. A place that existed for women of all walks and ages where they were valued. A place where only the best, most qualified were hired for the people who called that institution their home. Alas, her hopeful query to that distinguished proprietress had been met with a gracious, if perfunctory, declination on the merits of Daphne's lack of experience. She rested her cane against the wall and, through her gown, kneaded the muscles of her thigh.

Society was a riddle wrapped in a conundrum. To obtain honorable work, she required experience and references. And yet those gifts that would grant her security could not be earned *without* experience or references.

Marriage was not an option for a woman such as her.

With fiery red hair and too many freckles, she'd never be considered a great beauty but even as such, had she the use of her limb and a modest dowry, she could have married a respectable gentleman. Not that she *dreamed* of marriage. Not any longer. She'd long ago come to appreciate the perils in giving her affections to a gentleman.

Now, a woman of nearly eight and twenty years, she yearned for a control of her own future. She dropped her gaze to the page once more, with a sigh, and stuffed it inside her pocket. Opportunities, however, were limited and far and few between for cripples.

Shoving aside useless self-pitying, Daphne grabbed her cane. She took one step, when a hushed conversation from the closed door across the hall reached her and halted her forward momentum.

"...Lady Alice is certainly not the first lady who... Lady Clarisse Falcot—"

An inelegant snort cut off whatever words that employee now said of Lady Clarisse. "This is entirely different. This is not Christmas." Not wishing to listen any further on the instructors' gossip about the students who attended these hallowed halls, Daphne resumed walking, when the next whispered words halted her mid-step. "She is being thrown out."

Thrown out? Of Mrs. Belden's? Lady Alice, the Earl of Montfort's sister—Daniel Winterbourne's sister—would be… Her mind raced—sixteen. Mayhap seventeen years of age. What offense found a lady dismissed from finishing school? She furrowed her brow. Though once best friends with the girl's older brother, Daphne had only a few interactions with his much younger sibling.

"Nor is Lady Alice Winterbourne Lady Clarisse Falcot. But each lady's brother is rumored to be something of a rake."

At that, Daphne frowned. Yes, years ago Daniel had gone to London and made quite a splash on the scandal pages through the years for the reputation he'd garnered as rake.

"…What manner of brother forgets his sister?"

She covered her mouth to stifle a gasp. He'd forgotten Alice?

"…One who is deep in dun territory," the other woman replied.

Most of the ladies who attended Mrs. Belden's were lofty nobles who'd either little interest in having a daughter or sister underfoot or a lack of funds to hire the proper governess. Her frown deepened. In Lord Montfort's case, it appeared to be a mix of the two.

Annoyance with the boy she'd once called friend stirred. Then, they'd not been friends for many, many years. Not since his mother had died. What use did noble sons, set to inherit an earldom, have need of a crippled lady without noble connections? *Especially* a noble son of whom she'd once, as a young girl, thought to marry and live happily with forever and ever. What a bird wit she'd been.

"…They say he's returned from a wicked party he hosts in London…"

Daphne gave a disgusted shake of her head. The village had been set on its ear four years earlier when carriages of courtesans, widows, and whispered-about rakes and rogues had arrived for a hunting party at the young earl's estate to do more than hunt at his now severely crumbling estate. Scandalous gossip of the particular *feasts* enjoyed by the gentleman in attendance had spread throughout the village that still set Daphne's ears to burn.

It would seem, by the young instructors' gossip, that those parties hadn't ceased, but rather their locale moved.

"…I also heard…" The door suddenly opened and Daphne stumbled back as the two young women's gazes landed on her. Shifting her cane, Daphne forced a smile, and resumed her trek down the hall.

As she made her way by, her skin pricked with the always familiar, open stares. Looks she'd grown accustomed to through the years. After all, crippled ladies were an oddity in a world that valued flawlessness in every way for women. Even with that, even knowing people ogled and pitied and talked, her insides twisted. No person wished to be the object of pity.

Daphne reached the front foyer and a servant came forward with her cloak. Balancing her cane against the front of her skirts, with some difficulty she struggled into the worn wool garment. The same servant spared a glance at the aged fabric and then rushed to draw the door open.

The cleansing spring air filled her lungs. She paused on the front step, focusing on the familiar comfort of the country air. Fixing on that prevented her from thinking of returning to her small cottage that would soon be turned over to a distant relative whom she'd never even met.

Laughter trilled around the immaculate grounds and she looked wistfully to the young ladies with baskets on their arms as they snipped and gathered gold and orange chrysanthemums. She paused and appreciated the beautiful simplicity of that act. One she'd performed so very many times as a girl alongside her mother.

When had she snipped a bud for the pleasure of it? Since her father's passing eighteen months earlier, her life had moved on, driven by survival and necessity.

"Miss Smith, is that you?"

Daphne whipped her head toward that excited call. The abrupt movement caused her leg to buckle and she steadied herself with her cane.

Several ladies giggled, earning a quiet rebuke from the instructor attending them. Basket in hand, Alice sprinted over with an ease and agility Daphne would have traded a sliver of her soul for. "Oh, Miss Smith, it is so wonderful to see you."

Daphne smiled and attempted a curtsy, her body screaming in protest. "My lady—"

The young lady with flawless cream skin and golden ringlets

made a sound of protest. "Oh, surely after all these years you might still call me Alice." She followed her insistence with a beatific smile that dimpled her right cheek. "Though I am hardly the child you so graciously held in your arms when my Father passed."

Sadness filled her breast. "No, you are not." How deeply and how very quickly the Winterbournes had been shattered. With the death of Alistair, the eldest brother and heir, the family had slowly and methodically crumbled until they were mere shadows of the family they'd once been. Then, having lost her own parents, Daphne appreciated the finite quality of death and all the pain it wrought. "I should allow you to return to the other ladies," she said with another smile.

A smattering of giggles filled the gardens. Alice's cheeks turned red and her effervescent smile dipped. "Are they staring at me?" she whispered.

Daphne furrowed her brow.

"The nasty creatures in pale blue skirts."

She slid her gaze over to the girls now staring in their general direction. Another round of laughter followed. And more chiding from the instructor. It was invariably Daphne who was the gawked at one. In this, however, the three students in blue stared baldly at Alice. Had the news that the young lady had been forgotten already leaked out? Having been the recipient of unkind glances and whispers, Daphne's heart pulled. She'd wish that ugly on no one. And especially not a girl of Lady Alice's kind spirit. "I've no doubt it is me who's earned their unkindness this day," she reassured.

"Lady Alice," the instructor called, the stern underlying edge hinting at disapproval.

"That is lovely of you to say," the girl said softly, ignoring the young woman in hideous brown skirts. "But it is me. I'm being turned out and Daniel forgot me."

Daphne opened and closed her mouth several times. Over the course of her life, she'd cursed Daniel Winterbourne, the Earl of Montfort, numerous times. As a girl, when she should have never uttered those scandalous words. Then years later, after he'd disappeared from her life. And then after that, when she'd read and seen the manner of man he'd become. Never had she cursed him more than she did in this instance. "I am certain he did not forget you."

The lie slid forth easily.

"That is kind of you to say," Alice murmured, fiddling with her basket. "But the instructors have been less than discreet."

Daphne's fingers curled reflexively on the head of her cane. No, for all Society's dictates on politeness and proper discourse, most people were not careful with their words. They belonged to a Society that was a backward mirror image of itself.

"Lady Alice," the instructor called again.

Blatantly ignoring that sharp command, the young lady waggled her eyebrows. "Though, one of the benefits of being tossed from finishing school is you really don't have much of a care as to what your former instructors have to say." They shared a smile and then the troubled glimmer returned to Alice's pretty brown eyes. "If you'll excuse me. I should return, at least until they determine what to do with me."

"It was lovely seeing you again, Alice," she said softly.

The young lady nodded and then with slow, reluctant movements, rejoined the small group of assembled ladies.

The spring wind tugged at Daphne's cloak as she started down the stone walkway. With each faltering step that carried her away from Mrs. Belden's and toward her temporary home, her frustration and fury grew, blending together in a potent mixture that fueled her awkward, lurching movements.

And not for the first time since she'd broken her leg and discovered the truth of the ugly in the world, resentment consumed her. Anger at a world where women were subject to the whim and whimsy of distant relations. Negligent brothers. Unkind ladies. Even unkinder headmistresses and temperamental peers.

Ultimately, she would be tossed out of her cottage. Her prospects limited. Her funds even more so. Terror licked at the corner of her consciousness, threatening to consume her, and she forcibly thrust it aside. There would come a time to lament her circumstances and panic over her future later.

Daphne shifted direction and began the long, slow march away from Mrs. Belden's and away from her cottage to the largest, sprawling, if now crumbling country estate in Surrey. No, she might not be able to help herself this day, but there was something she could do for Alice. In helping the young girl, Daphne would have *some* control. If she could not save herself in this moment, she could at last protect another.

Firming her mouth, she continued the trek to the Earl of Mont-fort's.

CHAPTER 2

THERE WAS NOTHING DANIEL WINTERBOURNE, the Earl of Montfort, wanted more after an exhausting night of lovemaking than mindless sleep.

And never was that truer than after his evening with the naughty, insatiable, and more than anything, tempting widow, Mrs. Stillwell. Mrs. Stillwell, whose Christian name might have or might not have been mentioned. Either way, it eluded him. It mattered not.

A satiny soft caress whispered along his naked chest. "Surely you do not want to sleep, my lord." That voice marred by desire, purred in his ear.

"Actually I do," he drawled lazily, his arm stretched and bent above his head. Countless women believed they mattered more than others. Believed themselves more inventive. More passionate. Those egos prevented them from seeing the obvious truth—they were all the same. All fools who'd somehow deluded themselves into believing he was a man worthy of an extended affair.

The young widow dragged her nails around his navel and he flinched at that cold caress sharp enough to draw blood.

Forcing his eyes open, he winced as the sun pierced the crack in the curtains, blinding and bright, and devilishly unwelcome. "Have a care, sweet," Daniel said tightly and captured her wrist in a hard grip.

The voluptuous beauty pursed her mouth. That tightening around her slightly too narrow lips gave her a pinched look that showed a woman who was no longer in the blush of her youth. "I expected far more interest from a gentleman with your reputation," she said, shrewish in her determination.

He stretched his arms. Nothing repelled him more than clingy interest from desperate ladies. "I had you and now I intend to sleep." Then he closed his eyes, dismissing her.

The persistent widow ran clever fingers up the inside of his thigh and his shaft stirred. "I see you are not as immune to me as you pretend," she breathed teasingly against his ear and then closed her palm around him.

What the lady failed to realize was after more years than he could remember of availing himself to the pleasures of women who were equally wicked to his own licentious self, she was just another warm body. He could respond to her soft touch and efforts to arouse, but she was no different than any other. There was no emotion; there were no feelings or sentiments beyond the gratification of two like beasts sating mutual desires.

Daniel shifted quickly, startling a gasp from the widow, as he brought her under him.

"I see you *are* interested, after all," she said triumphantly, lifting her lips to his.

He lowered his mouth to claim hers—

RapRapRap

The beauty in his arms frowned.

"Go away," Daniel bellowed. The handful of loyal servants who remained on knew better than to interrupt him—particularly when he had a woman in his bed.

Mrs. Stillwell spread her legs and he positioned himself between her welcoming thighs.

RapRapRap

"My lord," his ancient butler interrupted, "you have a visitor."

"There is no one I'm expecting," Daniel said impatiently. His man-of-affairs was not due to discuss the increasingly dire state of Daniel's finances until next week when he returned to London. Mayhap it was an irate husband? "Tell him to—"

"It is a *lady,* my lord," the butler said on a loud whisper. "It is—"

"Splendid," he called out. He really didn't require a name. "Show her in." Mrs. Stillwell giggled.

A long pause stretched out, and then: "Uh...she is not *that* manner of lady, my lord."

Then he was otherwise uninterested. "Let the lady know I am not receiving visitors, Haply." One's proper reputation was safer with the Devil himself than Daniel Winterbourne.

The widow in his arms stroked his back and arched her hips in invitation.

"The lady insists, my lord. Demands a meeting." Demanded a meeting? His curiosity stirred. But for a spot in his bed or the exchange of sexual favors, women didn't demand anything of him. "Insists it is a matter of urgency." He had long since become immune to the undercurrent of disapproval in a person's words. Yet, to Mrs. Stillwell's cry of protest, he rolled off her frame and sprawled on his back.

He may be a rake with no morals, but even he would have trouble sustaining an erection with the same butler who'd teasingly chased him around this very household as a child carrying on outside his chamber doors. Daniel dragged a hand over the day's growth on his cheeks. "I will be down shortly," he called out and reluctantly swung his legs over the side of his bed, settling his feet on the cold floor.

"Should I show her to the parlor, my lord?"

Bloody hell, Haply and his temerity. "No." He climbed to his feet and gathered his wrinkled breeches. "Leave her in the foyer." Mayhap she was one of those naughty ladies offering payment to be debauched by him. He'd never bothered with virgins, regardless of their hot eyes and eagers hands. Regardless of what had brought the woman here, she wouldn't be staying long. Daniel stepped into his pants, tugging them up.

"Is there anything else you require, my lord? A visit from your valet?" Poor Haply. He'd even less hope of curtailing Daniel's outrageous ways than when he'd attempted it years earlier.

"Must you go?" His now forgotten bedpartner pouted, rolling onto her stomach, so her lush buttocks were on display.

"We're done here, sweet." Daniel returned and slapped her sharply once on the arse, eliciting a squeal. "Haply?"

"My lord?"

"Have Mrs. Stillwell's carriage readied."

"As you wish, my lord."

Her mouth fell agape. "You mean you do not plan on returning?

We were—"

"We're done here," he repeated. And with her sputtering and shrieking after him, he started for the front of the room.

"You are heartless, my lord," she pouted.

"Indeed," he agreed, not bothering to look back as he pulled the door open. And it was folly for any person—man, woman, or child—to believe he was in possession of that organ.

Stalking down the halls shirtless and in his bare feet, Daniel made his way to the foyer. In the hall, the truth of his circumstances glared back with a mocking potency. The dire state of his finances. As he walked, he took in the faded satin wallpapers. The frayed carpet.

Yes, his last and latest attempt at financial survival was a failing mine he'd won in a lucky game of hazard, had proven little help. And he, who was emotionally deadened in every way, felt something deep in his belly: panic. It sat there like a pit in his stomach, needling and niggling.

A familiar painting momentarily froze his steps and he stared at the heavy gold-framed portrait. A bucolic setting with twin boys, identical images of the other for all but their eyes, and a smiling papa with a hand resting on each of his sons' shoulders. The smiling golden-haired mother, her eyes alight and vibrant. That moment, forever captured a lifetime ago.

It was the easy smile of those twelve-year-old boys memorialized on that canvas which held him frozen. Real and joyous...and alive. That moment in time, may as well be fiction for how long it had been.

...I cannot hold on any longer, Alistair...I'm so sorry...

His own sobs from long ago echoed around his mind, making a mockery of the last joyous family tableau captured. Daniel gave his head a disgusted shake and moved on from that portrait. It should have been sold long ago. The gold frame would have fetched enough coin to make it worth the sell. For some reason, it had escaped him. He'd rectify that. Eventually. He'd speak to his man-of-affairs during their next meeting.

For now, there was still the meeting with his mystery visitor. She was a lady, whom according to Haply, was "unlike that lady"... as in every woman who entered Daniel's home and came to his bed. He reached the top of the stairs and, making his descent, he glanced around the spacious marble foyer. His gaze landed on a figure hidden inside a hideous brown cloak. That fabric was antithetical to the fine silks and satins donned by his lovers.

"Madam," he greeted, icing that single word with an edge of steel. "If you are here with hopes I'll debauch…"

The woman shoved her hood back and he froze with his foot suspended. There was nothing that a man would remarkably note of the lady being any grand beauty. She wasn't. Her crimson hair, pulled back tightly at the base of her skull, accentuated the sharp angles of her heavily-freckled face. But there was something *familiar* about her. *Too* familiar.

Surely exhaustion and too much liquor the evening prior accounted for seeing a girl from his past as a grown woman before him now. Then the lady collected the cane resting against her seat and struggled to stand. His lips parted in shock. He swung his gaze to her face. It had been countless years since he'd seen her or spoken with her but the green eyes, freckled face, and wooden cane all marked her identity. "Daphne." Surprise pulled that word from him and he struggled against the onslaught of long buried memories. Of a carefree past, of laughter and happiness and—

"Lord Montfort," she greeted curtly.

…I won't call you 'my lord' or 'lord anything'…you're just a boy and I'm just a girl, so we're equals, and this is as much my lake as it is yours… That long ago recollection of her, hands on her hips glaring at him from beside the brook, whispered around his mind, until now, forgotten.

Her large, emerald green eyes snagging on his chest and her cheeks blazing the same shade of red as her hair, she dropped her gaze to the floor to his naked feet. She gasped. Then she glanced up at the mural painted on the ceiling. The tense lines at the corner of her mouth belied her casual perusal.

A hard half-grin tilted his lips. This absolute lack of artifice was foreign to him in the life he now lived. The Daphne of his youth would never have done something as innocent as avoid his gaze. Then, time changed them all. "Daphne Smith," he drawled. As soon as the name left him, he arched an eyebrow. "Or are you now a Mrs…?"

"I am no Mrs.," she said tightly.

When had she become this staid creature? A peculiar regret

stirred for the girl she'd been. "A shame." He stretched those syllables out in a husky whisper, in a bid to elicit some Daphne-like response.

She cocked her head and then slapped her spare hand over her mouth, glowering over her long, gloveless fingers. "My lord," she scolded with far more impressive sternness than any of the tutors he'd suffered through as a boy. "I understand you are a rake, but I daresay even you draw the line at attempting the seduction of a childhood friend."

He tamped down a grin at that show of spirit. "You would be wrong." In a deliberate bid to further unsettle, Daniel folded his arms at his naked chest. "In the ten years since we've last exchanged words," he said in lazy tones, "the rule of seduction expanded to include all." He followed that up with a wink.

The lady narrowed her eyes.

A loud commotion sounded from the landing above, calling their attention up. Mrs. Stillwell, golden tresses disheveled and gown wrinkled, stormed down the stairs.

If Daphne's cheeks burned any brighter, she was going to catch fire. When was the last time he'd so much as exchanged a single word or greeting to one of those innocent creatures? Then, this wasn't just any innocent creature. This was Daphne Smith, whom he hadn't seen in *thirteen* years and he didn't care what she thought of him. Or he shouldn't. And yet, with Daphne frowning on as his lover from last night made her appearance, his ears went hot. Surely he was not…*embarrassed*? He thrust aside the preposterous thought.

Mrs. Stillwell paused briefly beside Daphne. "Miss Smith," she greeted in cool, polite tones.

"Mrs. Stillwell," Daphne returned punctiliously.

For, of course, even in matters of extreme discomfort and slight scandal, ladies recalled the rules of propriety. With a last pout for Daniel, the plump woman stormed through the door that a diligent Haply pulled open.

As soon as he'd closed it behind her, the older man stalked off, after a bow in Daphne's direction. A twinkle lit the old man's rheumy eyes. She favored him with a wide smile that dimpled her cheeks, softening her features and momentarily transforming her.

Daniel cocked his head. By God, Daphne wasn't truly ugly. She was—

Frowning once more. Her sharp features drawn into a smooth mask of disapproval, she flicked her gaze up and down his largely naked form. "Thirteen."

It was his turn to tip his head.

She thumped her cane and glanced about. "It has been thirteen years since we've spoken. Not ten." A sad, wistful expression stole over her face as she took in the discoloring left by paintings that had long since been sold.

Daniel shifted, unnerved by her obvious disapproval. "I did not expect you'd be keeping track, love," he said with forced nonchalance. He was a heartless bastard, but long ago they had been inseparable friends and her opinion had once mattered more than his own parents'.

Again, Daphne whipped her gaze to his.

Daniel took several slow, predatory steps forward, closing the space between them. He more than half-expected this new Daphne Smith to retreat. Then, he'd underestimated her too many times in their youth.

She rooted herself to the floor and angled her chin up. "I'm hardly one of your doxies." Doxies? "I'm here because of Lady Alice."

He furrowed his brow.

"Your sister, Daniel," she snapped, the sharp ire in her tone stripping his name from her proper lips.

His favorite part of a woman was her mouth. A man could imagine and receive so many wicked pleasures from a woman's mouth and learn just as much. Never before had he noted Daphne's lips. Then, the last time he'd seen her had been in black mourning attire, when she'd been a girl of fifteen. Now, he appreciated the bow-shape to the plump flesh. The—

"*Aliice,*" she spoke slowly as though talking to a lackwit and effectively killed his improper musings. "You do remember your sister?" she gritted out.

By the downturned corners of that same mouth, the lady was furious. Then her frigid tone and furious eyes were proof enough of that. "I know who my sister—" He froze and his mind ran through a meeting several weeks ago. A letter received from his uncle. Cutting off funding to Alice's finishing schooling at Mrs.

Belden or Mrs. Biden's, or whichever Mrs. B's Finishing School had been one more expense cut. Bloody hell. The whole bloody reason he'd been forced from London to the countryside.

"I trust you've remembered to collect her?" Like an elderly Society dragon, Daphne again thumped her cane on the floor. The sharp staccato echoed around the space.

"I remembered," he groused under his breath.

Some of the vitriol faded, replaced by a wistful glimmer. "You were always a rotted liar. Go get her, Dan—*my lord*," she quickly substituted. She drew her hood back into place and then gave him one final reproachful look. "And I suggest you put a shirt on."

Haply materialized, sliding from the shadows, and rushed to pull the door open with a speed befitting a man many years his junior. Daphne's words of thanks were met with another grin from the old servant.

She paused on the threshold and then angled her head over her shoulder. "Oh, and one more thing, my lord. With your reputation of charmer, I expect you can at least pretend you didn't forget her."

"What do you know of my reputation, love?" he called after her.

Daphne snorted and without another glance, took her leave.

CHAPTER 3

🙙N THE WHOLE OF HIS thirty years, Daniel had never been without words around ladies. Widows and debutantes. Dowagers and women of the demimonde. Words flowed freely.

Until this very moment.

His sister sat on the opposite bench of his carriage. Her arms folded in a mutinous pose, Alice had a hard look he himself would struggle to emulate on her face.

"I didn't forget you," he blurted. And generally, he was a good deal more effortless with his words than that.

Alice narrowed her eyes all the more. "I didn't say you did." Some of the tension went out of his shoulders. A gent never knew how to speak around a sister. Vastly different creatures than the ladies one took to bed. "However, by those words, I expect that you very much *did* forget me."

Apparently, Daphne Smith had been incorrect. He'd been wholly unable to muster a sufficient charm to at least pretend he'd not forgotten Alice. If he were capable of feeling guilt or remorse, then this would certainly be one of those times. Long ago, he'd ceased to care about anyone's opinion. Such a weakness only opened a person up to pain and he was quite good without any emotion.

Daniel reclined in the torn seats of his conveyance. Had the carriage ride through Spelthorne ever been this long? Tugging back the curtain that was in equal disrepair to the seats, he stared out at the passing hillside and yawned. God, he despised the country.

The shameful wagers, scandalous affairs, and abundant widows of London all beckoned. The only break from the tedium of a long summer was the naughty party he threw annually; those orgies that had earned him the deserved reputation of rake and scoundrel and every other nefarious word that could be handed down to a gent. At one time, the ill-opinions of others had chafed.

…You're a sorry excuse for a son. It should have been you… His late father's booming voice thundered around his mind and Daniel forcibly thrust back that hated reminiscence. With time, that paternal disapproval had mattered less and less, and Daniel had taken an unholy delight in becoming an unfeeling rake.

A rake who… A rake who…

He peered out the window and then rubbed his eyes. Alas, the sight reminded him. With a sigh, he shot his hand up and rapped once on the roof. The carriage lurched to a sudden stop. His sister went flying forward and caught herself against the side, landing with her face pressed to the window.

"What…?" Alice narrowed her gaze on the willowy creature limping along the road, with the aid of her cane. She cursed soundly with an inventiveness most gentlemen would be hard-pressed to rival. "You forced the lady to walk," she lambasted.

"I didn't—" his neck heated as he almost inadvertently confirmed his sister's earlier supposition. Nay, he hadn't *forced* Daphne Smith to return on foot. He'd simply failed to realize that the lady was absent a carriage. The ladies he kept acquaintances with rode in fancy barouches and elegantly sprigged vehicles. And they certainly didn't walk. Daniel shoved the door open and cupped his hands around his mouth. "Daph—oomph," he paused to glower back at his sister.

"She is a lady." His sister's stern rebuke was better fitting a leading Societal matron and not the young woman about to make her Come Out.

Daniel sighed. He'd not debate the history and length of friendship between him and Daph—Miss Smith. Miss Smith, who still continued her onward march. He searched around his mind for the long ago details about the girl he'd called friend. She'd suffered a nasty fall and shattered her limb. Had the lady also injured her hearing that long ago day?

His sister shoved him between the shoulder blades, propelling him forward, and he landed hard on his feet. He stumbled a bit and then caught himself. His driver made to dismount, but Daniel waved the man off.

"Go," Alice snapped.

"I am going," Daniel muttered. He quickened his stride. "Daph— Miss Smith?" he bellowed, cupping his hands about his mouth, once more. His long-legged strides easily ate away the distance between them.

Leaning her weight on her cane, the lady wheeled around and glowered. "I am a cripple, Daniel. I am not deaf."

Ah, so it was just the lady's leg. He doffed his hat and beat it against his leg. "Unpardonably rude to not offer you the service of my carriage earlier." At one time, there had been several conveyances. Well-sprigged, velvet-upholstered ones. Now, there were but two. And they were sad affairs that put most hired hacks in a grand light. All the rest, lost to too many wagers and failing estates.

Daphne shielded her eyes from the sun and lifted her head. "You do not strike me as one overly concerned with being taken as unpardonably rude."

Daniel offered her a wolfish smile. "I'm not. But I'd still offer the use of my carriage."

She eyed him warily. It was a suitable, proper response any young or old miss alike would be wise to don around him. Then she slid her gaze over to the conveyance.

"Hullo, Miss Smith," his sister called cheerfully, waving a hand.

Daphne returned the greeting, but hesitated still. The girl of his youth had cursed, spit, and skipped with equal abandon. Inevitably they'd all gone from carefree to jaded. What had resulted in her transformation? Had it been that moment, long ago, when he'd found her with her shattered limb? He dipped his lips close to her ear, his breath stirring a red curl that had escaped her hideous chignon. "You were not always so cautious."

"And you were not always a rake," she countered and his grin deepened. The lady eyed the path toward her home and then looked to his carriage. The war raging in her eyes spoke to her indecision.

"Come, my sister is present. As such, your virtue will remain safe." High color flooded her cheeks, swamping her freckles, but she remained tight-lipped. Daniel held out his arm. "What will your father think of me, if I fail to provide a proper escort home?"

She turned her lips up in a dry smile. "Given he is dead, I'm afraid I'll not have the luxury of inquiring."

He opened and closed his mouth several times. And he, who was never without the proper words and, more importantly, the improper ones, came up empty, yet again. Her father had died. A man who'd been a loyal, loving papa. Daphne would have been devastated and, yet, Daniel had not even known of her loss. If ever proof had been needed of his self-absorption, this moment was certainly it. "I'm sorry," he said quietly. Not that any proof would be required. Everyone knew the contemptible blighter he was.

"Thank you," she said softly. A spark of pain lit Daphne's eyes and he looked quickly away, horrified by that show of emotion. He didn't deal in feelings. Once he had. After a reminder given him by his miserable sire that everyone and everything he touched was destroyed, Daniel had embraced a deadened state. *Feelings* were an empty currency that held no value. And he certainly couldn't commiserate with sadness with the loss of a father. His own father had been a bastard who'd depleted the crofters and left them in near dun territory. Daniel had seen to the remainder of that grand effort for him.

"Come," he urged, waving his arm. She eyed it the way Eve must have studied that apple in Lucifer's hand.

Smart woman.

Squaring her shoulders, Daphne shifted her cane and then, pointedly ignoring his arm, marched to his carriage. He stared bemusedly after her. As one of the most notorious rakes in London, there was always an eager woman to warm his bed. Both young and old ladies sought his favors, if for nothing more than the thrill of risking their reputation. Not a single woman had rejected an arm he held out.

His longer-legged stride immediately closed the distance between them. He reached her side. Then he captured her about the waist and tossed her inside onto the bench alongside his sister.

Daphne frowned. "I can climb inside without assistance."

"I've no doubt," he muttered, hefting himself inside. The lady had always been capable of doing anything and everything. Or that had once been the case. After his brother's death, he'd seen the girl he'd once called friend less and less, until not at all. Who had she become in those years? Daniel frowned. Not that he much cared at all either way.

His driver closed the door behind them and a moment later, the carriage dipped under the weight of the man scrambling back onto his perch. Then they continued on in silence.

Which lasted but a moment.

"Thank you for seeing that my brother came for me," Alice said with a smile for Daphne.

"I…" Daphne looked back and forth between brother and sister.

"She believes I forgot her," Daniel supplied with a deliberate vagueness that came from clever prevaricating where irate husbands were concerned.

"Ah," she said noncommittally, setting her cane alongside her seat.

A blessed silence finally fell. He lowered his head along the back of his seat and closed his eyes. He was either aging or the village widow had thoroughly exhausted him. He opted to believe it was the latter. Yet blissful peace was short-lived.

"What were you doing at Mrs. Belden's?" God, had his sister always chattered like a magpie?

He yawned, again. At the quiet, he popped an eye open. Another one of those telling blushes stained Daphne's cheeks. Long ago, blushes and shifty gazes had ceased to arouse even the faintest curiosity or interest. It took a good deal more than those innocent gestures to prompt a question. Yet, he stared on, oddly intrigued by Miss Daphne Smith. Then, he had always been more than fascinated by her. As a girl who'd raced, rode, and spat, she'd been wholly unlike any other. As a woman, it merited she'd still command his notice.

The prim miss cleared her throat and then glanced down at her folded hands. Yes, she was certainly the *primmest* lady who'd ever ridden in his carriage. And she didn't fawn, flirt, or seek to seduce with her eyes and movements. "I was discussing a matter of employment."

Alice slapped a hand to her mouth. "Surely you are not going to become a *dragon?*" Daniel's sister turned horrified eyes to him and by the furious glint in their brown depths, *something* was expected of him here.

He lifted his shoulders in a slight shrug, not knowing precisely what that *something* was. Nor did he have an inclination to muddle through to what it might be.

Daphne cleared her throat. "I was discussing the possibility of a post with Mrs. Belden."

Discussing the possibility. In short, the lady had been denied.

"You cannot become a dragon." Alice's words contained an entreaty. "Your spirit will die."

By the tense lines at the corner of Daphne's downturned lips, her spirit had died long ago.

Fortunately, she knocked hard on the ceiling and the carriage rolled to a stop outside the thatched roof cottage. Daniel stared for a long, suspended moment. How many times had he played on that very lawn? Tossed pebbles at her window. He frowned. She was unmarried and, yet, she lived in the cottage, still.

"I thank you for seeing me the remainder of the way home, my lord. Lady Alice," Daphne murmured in parting as his driver drew the door open and helped her outside.

As she limped along the small rose-lined walkway to the front of her cottage, Daniel watched her stiff, jolting movements. How time changed a person. Daphne Smith had gone from a girl who could outrace him, outjump him, and outswim him…and now she'd become this tight-lipped creature.

"Her spirit is going to die, you know?"

"You said as—oomph." Alice nudged him hard in the leg with her sharp knee.

"You really owe it to the lady to do something."

Other than outstanding debts to creditors and other lords, he owed nothing to anyone, and certainly not to a tart-mouthed woman whose only hold on him were unwanted memories. "I'm not certain how you expect me to help Miss Smith." Nor had the lady asked for any specific assistance. More to the point, she'd blatantly ignored his earlier offer of aid. And furthermore, neither were there funds to, in any way, help Miss Smith, not that he was in the habit of debating sixteen or seventeen-year-old innocents.

And once more, he gave silent thanks as they reached the front of the crumbling country estate—the former great stone building gifted to the first Earl of Montfort three centuries ago. Not bothering to wait for the conveyance to come to a full stop, Daniel shoved the door open and jumped down. He started forward.

Now that he was home, he could see to a hot bath, a bottle of brandy, and some much needed rest. Not necessarily in that or—

"Ahem. I said 'ahem'."

Daniel stopped abruptly and wheeled around. His sister gave him a pointed look. And standing there at the front steps, the *cracked* steps of his estate, a dawning horror slammed into him. By God in heaven…he was going to have…a bloody sister underfoot. He'd not truly given proper consideration, or rather, *any* consideration, to the note from Mrs. Belden. Or was it Mrs. Belten? Regardless of the harpy's name, he'd not given it a thought until this very moment.

And by the slow, widening, wicked grin on her lips, his sister had recognized his growing horror. With a curse, Daniel stalked back to the carriage and handed her down.

A bottle of brandy. Yes, that was decidedly the first order of bloody business when a goddamned rake found himself saddled with a—a shudder wracked his frame—a sister. He stalked up the steps, not bothering to see if she followed, and the door was thrown open.

"See that a bath is readied," he said as he doffed his hat. He threw it to one of the few remaining footmen who easily caught it. Daniel shed his cloak next. "And have a bottle of brandy sent to my chambers." In thinking, he could have two of the very orders of business he required. He tossed his cloak to his butler and it sailed through his fingers, landing in a shuddery heap at his feet.

Haply dropped to a knee and retrieved it as Daniel started past him. "My lord," his butler cleared his throat. "You have a visitor."

Daniel stopped on the third step. A visitor? He furrowed his brow. "Tell Mrs. Stillwell I'm not accepting calls at this time."

His sister sailed through the still gaping front door.

The butler glanced red-faced between brother and sister. "Uh… it is not…" He gulped audibly. "It is not, ahem… It is a different visitor," he settled for.

First Daphne Smith and now another guest. "Tell her—"

"I'm not one of your fancy pieces, Daniel Winterbourne," a thunderous voice boomed from down the hall.

Oh, God. *Please let this entire day be a liquor-induced dream.* If it were so, he'd swear off spirits and whores and…well, mayhap not the whores, but he'd certainly give up the bottle. Or, at the very least, give it a serious consideration.

Viscount Claremont strode forward, slowly. His cheeks more wrinkled, his eyes more rheumy, and his shock of white hair thinner, but it was invariably the same, disapproving uncle. And if Daniel had learned one thing in history, it was that he never wanted a visit from his uncle.

Bloody, bloody hell.

"Uncle Percival," he greeted with false cheer. The miserable bugger had not only cut off his funds but also Alice's tuition for Mrs. Belden's.

The old man ignored him. He looked to Alice, who took in the exchange with, by Daniel's estimation, far too much glee in her mischievous eyes. God help him, she was going to be a bloody nightmare in London. "You've returned from that gloomy school, then?"

"This very moment," she said with a smile and hugged the bear of a man.

The viscount folded her in a brief embrace. "I should have cut off your tuition to that place a long time ago. And I would have," from over Alice's head, Lord Claremont glared, "if there had been some honorable nephew about to see to your care."

In the whole of his adult life, Daniel couldn't draw forth a single embrace or kind word this man had ever had for him. Not that he blamed the man. There was hardly anything redeeming about Daniel.

...*It should have been you, Daniel*...

"Your brother remembered to get you, I see," Uncle Percival observed, turning his focus on Alice. There was a question in the viscount's eyes.

Daniel braced for her to reveal the truth and then the stern lecture that would invariably follow. "Shocking, isn't it?"

Lord Claremont grunted and then patted Alice on the head. "Run along. I've words for your brother." Bloody spending. "In your office, boy," the man bellowed. If he'd not received a small fortune from his childless uncle through the years, he'd have lifted a crude finger up at that insulting form of address. Alas... Daniel eyed the top of the stairway covetously and, with a long sigh, started for his office.

The sooner he could be done with this meeting and the whole

day… the sooner he'd have to figure out what to do with a sister underfoot. A gentleman couldn't go about his rakish pursuits and his beddings if there was a sibling to care for. He slowed his footsteps. A husband. Of course. Alice would make her debut and she'd fetch a husband. Mayhap one who was plump in the pockets. His spirits lifted. There was some benefit to having a sister about, after all.

They reached his office and he motioned the slightly smaller gentleman ahead of him. Then closing the door behind him, Daniel started for the sideboard. "To what do I owe this—?"

"Your father knew what you were," Lord Claremont interrupted and Daniel froze, hovering his hand over the impressive collection of decanters.

"Are you here to speak about my *dear* departed papa?" God rot his soul. Daniel swiped the finest French brandy and poured himself a tall glass.

"Bah, time changed your father. Wretched bastard." So they were of like opinion on one matter. But then the late earl hadn't always been that way. Grief had turned his soul black and his heart empty, just as it done to Daniel. "My late sister is an altogether different story," his uncle continued.

He remained with his back presented to the often bellowing viscount and stared a moment into his glass. His mother. God, he'd not thought of the woman in… too many years to remember. All his mother's good and kindness gone with his parents' quest to bring a new child into the world—a worthy child. He turned around and propped his hip on the edge of the mahogany sideboard.

"I promised your mother I'd watch over Alice." Because when she'd been dying, in the days after her childbirth, at Daniel's young age, she'd known precisely the manner of person her youngest son was. That truth had once left an ache, now he was immune to that pain. Mayhap that was why his father had become the miserable bastard he had. He froze and forcibly quashed the remembrance of his late sire. He'd not thought of the late earl in years. Now, in one bloody afternoon, Daphne *and* his uncle forced his past upon him.

Fueled by impatience, Daniel raised his glass in mock salute. "A good place to begin watching over Alice is at the finishing school you so abruptly cut funds to."

It was a credit to his uncle's temerity that he showed no outward reaction to that insolence. "And what, have the girl remain there while you rut your way around London and host your naughty parties with coin you do not have?" The Winterbourne line had once been a wealthy one. After his heir and his wife's passing, Daniel's father had lived the life of a wastrel and pissed away a fortune.

Though, his father hadn't always been reckless. Just as Daniel hadn't always been a coldhearted rake. His brother's visage flashed behind his mind's eye.

...I can't hold on any longer, Alistair. Forgive me...

"Are you listening to me, boy?" his uncle barked, impatience lacing that query.

Daniel snapped his head up. "So is this why you've come? To lecture me at thirty years of age?"

His uncle snorted. "Bad behavior knows no age boundaries." Yes, given the company Daniel kept, there was truth to that claim. "You can drink yourself to death for all I care," he added, gesturing to Daniel's glass, as though contained within were those final, fateful sips.

"Why, thank you. I'm touched," Daniel drawled, lifting his glass again in mock salute.

"I didn't always think you were bad." That admission came as though dragged from the older man. "I believed you would sow your oats and cleanse your system of your wickedness. Instead, you only descended further and further into depravity."

Yes, Daniel had been bad so long, he was certain his soul had been crafted in the Devil's image. As a young man, his father's contempt had shredded him. As such, Daniel had reshaped himself from the weak fool he'd been. In his place, he'd resurrected barriers so he was immune to the world's disapproval and condemnation.

"I am not going to be around forever," his uncle went on, "and I'll not draw my last breath with knowing that you," as though there were another "you" in question, he flicked a derisive hand in Daniel's direction, "are the only one left to care for the girl. Your mother would greet me at the gates of heaven and send me on my way promptly to hell if I trusted Alice's future to you."

Daniel glanced over at the long-case clock, wishing the other man would get on with whatever had brought him 'round. He'd long ago tired of Society's ill-opinion. His family was included amongst those *polite* peers.

"I've eight thousand pounds left me by your mother, to go to you." That admission brought Daniel's head whipping back around. "I see I have your full attention, boy." By God, it was a fortune. Albeit a small one. But certainly enough funds to pay off the most pressing creditors and debt holders, and mayhap a fine mistress, and—

"You can stop counting those coins in your head," Lord Claremont snapped. "You won't see a pence or pound until your sister weds."

All he needed to do was see Alice married off? Life had given him countless reasons to be wary. He thinned his eyes into narrow slits. "Surely you require more than that."

The older man chortled. "Indeed. I will have your sister wed a good gentleman. Not a miserable blighter like yourself who beds any willing woman."

"I assure you, I'm far more circumspect than you credit." Only the most full-figured, inventive creatures found a place in his bed. The more scandalous, the better.

He'd not debate his uncle on the obvious truth that there were, in fact, no good gentlemen. The men who attended his naughty parties were proof of that. Daniel grinned coldly and raised his glass to his lips for another sip.

"I want you behaving until the girl finds herself a husband." The viscount took a furious step toward him, glowering. "A *good* husband. Not some bounder you're quick to marry her off to so you can get your coin." With each cool cataloguing, Daniel drew his shoulders further and further back. "I don't want a single, bloody scandal attached to your name. Not one widow. Not one orgy. Not even a mistress." Daniel choked on his swallow. "Find the girl a companion and a proper suitor, who will make her an even better husband." His uncle ticked off on his fingers. "I want your sister cultured. See she visits museums. The opera. Take her riding."

Daniel shuddered. "Egads, surely you aren't expecting me—?"

"I don't care if it's you or the bloody companion. But someone must see to the girl. You do those things and the eight thousand entrusted me by your mother is yours." There was no other accounting for it. The man was fit for Bedlam. "We're through here." He'd enter Daniel's home, disrupt the order of his wicked existence, and then casually leave? He gritted his teeth. God, the man should have been born a duke. Only a man just below royalty could manage such arrogance.

"And who, exactly, will serve as Alice's companion?" he called after him. The sooner she was married off, the sooner he could be on with his own pursuits.

Lord Claremont stilled, his fingers poised on the door handle. "My boy, that is for you to figure out," he drawled. With that whirlwind of chaos he'd brought upon Daniel's life, he stepped out.

Well, bloody hell.

"Where in blazes am I going to find a goddamned suitable companion?" he muttered, tossing back his drink.

CHAPTER 4

$\mathcal{A}$ DESPERATE WOMAN WOULD DO DESPERATE things in order to survive. And Daphne Smith would most definitely place herself in the quite desperate category.

It was the only logical explanation to account for an entirely illogical decision. For a second time in the span of a day, she made the long trek to the Winterbourne estate. A second trek, when she'd not visited these once opulent grounds in many, many years. Long ago, she'd learned to be wary of those lofty lords of which Daniel was now one. Particularly the rakish, roguish sorts. It was only because this particular nobleman had once been a friend that she sought him out, even now.

Slowing the frantic pace she'd set for herself, she leaned her weight on her cane and dusted the back of her hand over her damp brow.

Daniel was not long for Surrey. The boy, who'd so loved the English countryside and all the beautiful pleasures in living in these great grounds, had somehow lost that appreciation. Instead, he spent most of his days in London. That was, of course, with the exception of when he returned to Winterbourne Manor for his summer hunt, which Daphne had the misfortune of learning only after she'd come upon a pair of his guests at the lake they'd once loved. It was the last time she'd ventured anywhere near his property. She gave her head a disgusted shake and resumed walking.

Nonetheless, a desperate lady had little recourse. Daniel had once been a friend. Even though he was nothing to her now, he did have the title earl affixed to his name. And though she well-knew how little worth actually went with those titles, the Mrs. Beldens of the world did not. They still oohed and aahed and dropped their curtsies and eyes in deferential greeting.

Then, that was the way of their world, wasn't it? A fraction of people, a *ton* to be precise, ruled the minds and opinions of all around them.

After the infernal walk, Daphne reached the base of the stairs of Winterbourne Manor. Lifting her hand to shield her eyes, she looked up the long, long row of steps. Once she could have and would have made the trek to Daniel's property in but ten minutes. Once, she would have skipped every second step or hopped along on one leg to reach him. She settled her cane on the bottom stone stair and began her long climb. Inevitably, life changed a person. One went from being one person, capable of running—quite literally—wherever her legs would carry her to a prisoner in her now-failed body.

She shook her head wryly, the irony not lost on her. As a child, she'd required less assistance through life than a woman of nearly thirty years. That, of course, only reminded her of the very specific request for assistance that brought her here, now. Daphne firmed her lips as she finally reached the generous stone landing. Before she thought again of the folly in being here, she banged her closed fist on the door.

Silence met her rapping. She caught her lower lip between her teeth and studied the heavy panel a long moment. Mayhap, he'd already packed his carriages and been onward to London. It would hardly surprise her. It would, however, prove most inconvenient. Well, for her anyway. Having read of his scandalous pursuits over the years, she expected it would prove anything but inconvenient for the gentleman whose favor she now sought.

She knocked again. The door opened and she didn't know whether to give silent thanks or stamp her foot in frustration. The old butler registered his surprise with the flare of his bushy white eyebrows. "Miss Smith," he murmured, shuffling slowly out of the way to allow her entrance. She took in his stiff movements. Mayhap that was the inevitable fate visited upon all, albeit at different times. Invariably, they each ended up with useless legs and shuffling steps that forced one to slow and think about one's decisions.

"Haply," she greeted, offering a gentle smile for the servant who'd once obligingly chased her and Daniel around these very halls. "I've come to see His Lordship." She lifted her gaze to the sweeping marble staircase that led to the grand living quarters. "Has he departed yet for London?"

The servant shook his head. "Not yet, Miss Smith." *He is still here.* An unexpected wave of relief assailed her. A foreign response to any nobleman...particularly the roguish sort. "If you'll follow me?"

A footman came over to collect her cloak and, shifting her weight over the cane, Daphne released the clasp of the old, slightly tattered garment. She handed it over to the waiting servant.

She trailed along, taking in the threadbare, once great hall. Bright satin wallpaper where paintings had once graced the walls, stood a stark contrast to the faded, aged material. Daphne shook her head sadly at the shame of it. A family born with a wealth that should have seen their ancestors cared for through centuries, had squandered it away. And then people of her lesser station? Dependent on their wits and, now, the magnanimity of those same men who squandered away their fortunes.

They reached the earl's office and Haply scratched his knuckles along the surface of the door. A bleating snore reached through the thick wood. She knitted her eyebrows. *What in blazes?* The old servant gave her a sheepish look. Dispensing with the polite scratching, he pounded hard on the oak panel.

A loud grunt and muffled curse stretched out into the hallway. "By God, man, you know not to disturb me at dawn."

At dawn, she mouthed. How could this be the same person who'd tossed pebbles at her windowpane to wake her so they could rush to the hillside and watch the sun make its climb? Haply made another clearing sound in his throat. "You have a visitor, my lord."

"Tell Mrs. Still—"

"It is Miss Smith," the servant quickly interrupted. Cheeks flushed, he swung his gaze quickly to Daphne.

A moment later, Daniel pulled the door open, standing in his stockinged feet and *sans* jacket. "Miss Smith, we meet again," he drawled, in sleep roughened tones as he stuffed his shirt inside his breeches.

"My lord," she said evenly, refusing to be scandalized. Despite his opinion of her, she was no missish, wide-eyed virgin, given to shock easily.

He stepped back and swept his arms wide with the elegance of a lord greeting a lady in a drawing room and not—Daphne wrinkled her nose—a room heavy with a plume of lingering cheroot smoke and darkness. Squaring her shoulders, she marched, as much as she was able, inside. She jumped when he slammed the door loudly behind them.

Her heart picked up its beat as she passed a wary gaze between him and that path to freedom.

"You may rest assured, I've no grand designs upon your virtue," he said wryly, striding over to the torn leather button sofa. Daniel retrieved his jacket. She bit the inside of her cheek at his taunting words. *Do not allow him to ruffle you… Do not allow him to ruffle you…* He smartly snapped the wrinkled black fabric. To no avail. Heedlessly, he pulled it on.

"Yes, I expect a notorious rogue would have more discriminating taste than to bother with a spinster." From her thankfully brief foray into London Society, she knew the smooth-tongued earl had his choice of ladies. The passage of time had been kind to him in some ways. His tall, muscle-hewned frame had more of a breadth and width to it than the lean, wiry figure of his youth. His thick, chestnut hair tousled, a day's growth of beard on his face, he fit not at all with the proper lords of London she recalled from her too-brief foray into that miserable place. The harsh set to his hard lips and cynical glint in his chocolate brown eyes aged him in ways that time alone never could.

At her perusal, he gave her a slow, wolfish smile. "I assure you, I'd never be so snobbish as to turn a spinster out of my bed."

And just then, he proved her earlier sense of calm around him entirely wrong. Heat scorched from the roots of her crimson hair down to her toes. She fisted the head of her cane. Everything was a game to these men. A lady's heart. Her sensibilities. It was all fair game in their tedious world. "Well, I assure you," she said with a sardonic edge, "I'm certainly not searching for a rogue in my bed."

Daniel folded his arms, drawing her attention to the broad muscles straining the expert cut of his midnight jacket. "Which begs the question, what manner of man are you searching for?" he asked on a silken purr.

A snorting laugh bubbled past her lips and, with the aid of her cane, she strode to the tightly drawn brocade curtains. "Surely that is not the manner of drivel that's earned you the reputation of rogue?" she goaded as she layered her cane against the wall and opened the curtains. Sunlight streamed through the crystal windowpanes and Daniel cursed, covering his eyes.

"A rake," he muttered as she retrieved her cane and turned to face him squarely. "I've earned the reputation of a rake."

Did he find honor in that notorious moniker attached to his name? "Yes, well," she said with a flick of her hand. "Rogues, rakes, scoundrels. All really the same."

He took a slow, languid step closer, followed by another, and another. The smooth grace and elegance a black panther would be hard-pressed to not admire, until he ate away all the distance between them. Her pulse pounded loudly in her ears. "Ah," he whispered, dipping his lips close to her ear. The scent of brandy wafted over her skin. *This is Daniel. Do not be silly. He's the same boy whose nose you bloodied countless times when he'd given her pugilism lessons.* "But they are entirely different, Daphne." He commandeered her name in a silken baritone that set off a wicked fluttering in her belly. A dangerous one. One that she'd known before and had learned was the root of evil, and ruin, and pain.

It also served to coolly restore her logic. "They aren't, Daniel," she corrected, neatly stepping around him. "You are like all men who live for your pleasures, take countless women to your beds, and drown yourselves in liquor, caring for nothing or no one but yourselves. There's no difference."

Most men would have been properly shamefaced by that leveling charge. Then, Daniel was not most gentlemen. "I do not expect you've come to discuss the differences, of which there are many," he added, "between a rake and a rogue?" His smile deepened, revealing two even rows of pearl white teeth and a dimpled cheek. Everything about this man on the surface was masculine perfection. But so, too, had been the Devil in disguise in that fateful Garden of Eden.

"No," she agreed, drawing in a deep breath as he brought her round to the whole reason for her visit. "I once gave you a guinea and you vowed if I had a need for it, that you would return it. Well,

I've a need for it." She held her gloved palm out.

He eyed her hand a moment through perplexed eyes and then looked to her face. "What?" That single syllable utterance conveyed his proper bafflement.

"I did not believe you recalled—"

"I recall," he said suddenly, unexpectedly. The boy he'd been would have cherished that small treasure she'd found. The man he'd grown in to would have scoffed at the meagerness of it. Or she expected he would have.

"Splendid," she beamed, wagging her hand. "I shall take it back, then."

Daniel dipped his head, examining her for a long moment through bloodshot eyes. He whistled. "You're out of your blasted mind."

Yes, well, desperation did that. "I take that to mean you do not have it." She let her hand fall by her side.

"That would be a safe assumption, Miss Smith," he said, his tone drier than an autumn leaf.

Daphne folded her arms before her and the end of her cane knocked into his leg, coming dangerously close to—

"Have a care to not unman me, love."

For a less cautious, less jaded by life young woman, that husky endearment would have posed dangerous to her self-control and virtue. Fortunately, she was no longer a young woman. She thumped the heel of her cane on the floor. "I assume you lost it at a hazard or faro table long ago."

"Oh, no doubt," he conceded, marching over to his well-stocked sideboard with such speed and grace, a wave of envy filled her. "Though," he paused in the process of pouring himself a glass of whiskey. "It very well may have been whist."

She tightened her mouth. Good, that coin should be well and truly lost. It had represented the end of dreams she'd not yet even realized as a girl and the uncertain future that awaited a poor gentry man's crippled daughter. Thrusting aside the useless, unwanted self-pity, she nudged her chin up. "Given this unexpected," of which it was not at all, "turn with my fortune—"

"Treasure."

She tipped her head.

"I believe you once referred to it as a treasure." He toasted her with his glass and then downed it in a long, slow swallow. His lips pulled in a grimace and he set the glass down. Only to reach for the bottle once more.

Daphne stood, opening and closing her mouth. She was properly flummoxed, as he no doubt intended. "You remember that?"

He paused mid-pour of his second whiskey, blinking slowly. And then, waved her on. "You were speaking about your guinea, Miss Smith."

Yes, right. Of course. She smoothed one palm along the fabric of her coarse woolen skirts, which only brought Daniel's attention downward. She bit the inside of her cheek, hating that he should see the threadbare garments and know precisely her state. How different it was for a lord, born with a proverbial spoon inside his mouth only to throw the contents of it at the wall, and a woman who was…well, born with few options other than to marry.

"Miss Smith," he said impatiently.

"As I was saying, I've come for my coin. Which I believe we've ascertained you do not have?" She pressed him with her gaze.

"To which I already said yours was a safe assumption."

"Which means, we have a bit of a problem, then, my lord."

"Oh?" he asked, his eyes straying to the clock in the corner, a telling indication of just how concerned he was about this very problem. "And why do you not enlighten me as to your problem."

"*Your* problem," she swiftly amended. "You see, you pledged to return it and, yet, you do not have it. As such, I expect some form of payment."

Generally, those words coming from the lips of lovers portended all manner of wicked deeds and naughty delights.

This stern-faced, pinch-mouthed creature before him was most certainly not a lover. And if she was coming to him for a fortune, treasure, or pence, she sought the wrong lord. "Tell me," he said, wrapping those two words in a husky whisper. "What form of payment do you seek, Daphne?"

Where he'd demonstrated so many failings in life, he'd become an expert at reading a woman's body; the soft flush on her naked skin as she climbed toward her release. The whispery sigh that hinted at romantic musings. Or in this case, the slight tremble of too-full lips as they fell slightly agape. Proving that even an angry spinster, once a childhood friend, Daphne Smith was not wholly immune to him. A wave of masculine triumph ran through him.

Then, she whipped her eyebrows into a single, angry line. "Surely you are not attempting to seduce me?"

"Uh…" Or mayhap she *was* wholly immune. He stared on with an increasing curiosity for the woman who'd shattered his quiet not once, but now twice this week. Daniel angled his body closer, lowering his lips once more to the lobe of her ear. The faint scent of lilac wafted about him; a wholly innocent, feminine scent which he should detest for that innocence and, yet, it flooded his senses, dangerously intoxicating. "Only if you wish me—"

"I assure you, I've no desire to be seduced by you, or *anyone,*" she added, through tight lips.

"A shame," he whispered, once more, brushing a speck of dust from his sleeve. He narrowed his eyes on that recalcitrant fleck.

Daphne reached out and dusted her long fingers over the fabric. "There. Now, do attend me."

The women he favored were warm, willing, and always eager. They were certainly not those bossy, ordering creatures. Though, in this moment, with Daphne's talk of rogues, rakes, and seduction, and unintentionally suggestive words, mayhap he'd been wrong all these years. There was something quite appealing about those ladies, too.

"Daniel," she snapped.

"Yes, yes. Your pence."

"It was a guinea," she gritted out. "You promised to return it. You do not have it and, as such, some payment is necessary. I require references."

Of all the requests she would have put to him, that was certainly the last or least that would have come to mind. "References," he parroted.

She nodded.

"What manner of references?"

"Glowing ones."

His lips pulled at the corners in a rusty smile that strained muscles he only turned up in coolly mocking grins. Until this very moment. Unexpected humor filled him. "And what are these references for, Miss Smith?" he asked, swirling the contents of his glass.

"For?" It would seem it was now her turn to repeat. "I require employment," she said haltingly. Ah, her visit to Mrs. Belden's. Or Mrs. Belten's? "And my prospective employer requires references." She paused. "From a nobleman."

So his sister had been correct and Daphne sought work at the finishing school instructing proper young ladies. A slow, niggling of a thought took root in his mind. "And the word of any nobleman will matter? Including a rake, rogue, or scoundrel?"

"To this woman it will." By the crispness of that deliverance, the lady was of a contrasting opinion than this illustrious prospective employer. Then, Daphne had always been a clever girl.

"I expect I'll need to know what to write or what manner of work you wish me to endorse you for."

"I simply need a testament to my character and capabilities with young ladies." Hope filled her green eyes and small silver flecks danced to life.

He froze, momentarily transfixed by that emerald hue. Why, with those lively eyes, when she wasn't frowning and snapping, she was really quite *pretty*. He coughed and quickly downed another drink, again grabbing for his bottle. "I hardly know any young ladies who've benefited from your, uh, assistance," he said, when he faced her.

And damn if he didn't mourn the light that those words extinguished from her eyes.

"Given *your* penchant for carousing, whoring, and bedding other men's wives, I expect mustering a few glowing words on my behalf would hardly be out of the realm of what is acceptable of your character."

Of his character. The lady had rightly formed the same ill-opinion of his character and honor. Which, once more, just proved Daphne Smith's cleverness. Such a truth might have mattered to the boy who'd called her friend. That boy was long, long dead. As dead as his brother, which had left an undeserving Daniel as earl in his stead. "Reading of my pursuits, love?" he asked, stretching an arm out. Her breath caught audibly. But he only reached around her for his bottle, refilling the partially empty glass.

"Witnessing them," she clarified.

He eyed her over the bottle.

"I had a Season, my lord."

Daniel looked to her with some surprise and he dug around his mind for memory of Daphne Smith in London. "You had a Season?" A lady of her spirit and honesty had no place in that rotted place. It was reserved for men and women with black souls who'd do anything to survive. Of which she was now a member. Minus the whole black soul part.

A wry and not at all Daphne-like smile formed on her lips. "Yes, even *I*, a poor cripple, had a Season."

At her incorrect supposition, Daniel frowned. Is that the light she saw herself in? And he, who'd long ago ceased feeling anything, found himself—annoyed. Thrusting aside the peculiar sentiment, he grunted. "I do not recall seeing you in London."

"Yes, well, a gentleman so self-absorbed with his own pursuits, dancing attendance on widows and unhappily married ladies, would hardly notice something outside his own pleasures," she said pragmatically.

Long immune to anyone's displeasure, her barb somehow struck at a place of caring that he'd long believed dead. Unnatural stuff. He tossed back another drink, welcoming the burn. Yes, he far preferred feeling *nothing*. "I hardly think insulting me is the best way to attain your *glowing* references," he pointed out, arching a single eyebrow.

"I'm not here to mollify or beg, Daniel," she said tersely. Did the lady realize she'd slipped back into the use of his Christian name? And even more dangerous, how much he preferred hearing it spoken in her husky contralto? "I came for my guinea," she said, neatly bringing them round to the reason for her visit.

Daniel inclined his head. "Which we determined I've, no doubt, lost."

She nodded. "Which means you must offer me some form of payment."

He fished around the front of his jacket and his finger connected with the warmth of one coin. He paused and then, instead, extracted another.

Daphne froze, her wide eyes going to the coin in his hand and then swinging back to his face. She stepped closer eyeing the shiny, new piece. "This is not it."

No. This piece was certainly not her treasure. He waved the guinea under her nose. "I expect any coin will do."

She retreated a step, like Red Riding Hood realizing too late that the wolf was at hand. "Oh, indeed not. *My* guinea was special."

"Of course," he said dryly, earning another frown. He stuffed the inferior one back inside his jacket.

"As such, I expect I should determine the proper form of payment. And that payment is references—"

"For a job you've never performed," he cut in. It really was rotten for him to lead her along, particularly when he knew precisely what she required. Even worse, he knew he'd never been the man to offer a favor without acquiring something in return. "I will help you," he said. She continued to watch him carefully. Then, he'd long been the bounder she'd rightfully accused him of being. "But I do require something from you." A pretty blush bathed her freckles in red. "Favors which are not sexual in nature," he said lazily and the color of her cheeks only burned brighter. "Unless," he dropped his voice to a husky purr. "That is something you wish?"

"Decidedly not," she squeaked.

He quashed another smile. If he weren't already going to hell for too many sins and crimes to count, then he'd be going there now with his teasing of an innocent Daphne.

Putting aside that repartee, he returned to the matter of business. "Alice is making her debut and she requires a companion." He waved a hand. "You will serve admirably in that role. The post is yours and then so too will be your glowing references, as soon as my sister makes a proper match." Of course, with the young woman's limited options, she'd no choice. The partnership was mutually agreeable to both. Then, he'd only ever dabbled in friendships and relationships that served his interests. "We leave within three hours." He stalked over to his desk, only registering the absolute silence of the room when he'd claimed a seat. Daniel looked up.

Daphne hovered at the sideboard, unmoving, unblinking with a motionlessness that could have confused her for a statue. "London?"

Did that weak, threadbare whisper belong to the always fiery, fearless Daphne? Surely not. "I take it you did not approve of the place after your failed Season?"

She gave her head a nearly imperceptible shake in the first real hint of movement since he'd handed her his offer.

"In time, you come to appreciate it. Far more thrilling than the countryside," he said dismissively as he dragged forth a ledger to review his mounting debts.

"I cannot go to London."

At that strangled admission, he glanced up. All color had drained from her face, leaving her gaunt cheeks a pale hue. Having been born an earl's second son, he'd often moved between London and the countryside, so much that he'd developed an ease and eventual appreciation for the thrilling city. A young woman like Daphne, however, who'd left but once that she'd shared, would never belong in that land of sin. Nor did he prefer imagining her forever immersed in that abhorrent place. It wasn't for the handful of Daphne Smiths in the world. He frowned. "Then, I'm afraid I cannot provide you references." If he were most men, he'd feel a modicum of guilt for forcing her hand this way. But he was not most men. He was the rake she'd accused him of being. A man who'd taken coin to betray his friend and that was only one of the things among his immoralities.

If her skin went any whiter, there'd be no blood left in her being. "You are a bastard, Daniel Winterbourne."

"Yes," he easily agreed. "But I am a bastard whose sister requires a companion. Someone to…" He searched his mind for his uncle's specifics. "Take her to museums and the opera, and…" What did cultured entail? "And other events," he settled for.

A sound of impatience burst from Daphne's lips. "I'd make her a rotten companion," she said on a rush, limping forward with such haste, she stumbled.

"Should I include that in your reference?" he asked, another smile forming.

Daphne quickly caught herself and then straightened, speaking over his humor. "I'm not a lady. I expect you know any number of ladies—"

"Oh, I know ladies." Her shoulders sagged with relief. "None, however, that my uncle would ever deem appropriate."

The lady wetted her lips. "I'm a…." She firmed her shoulders and squarely met his gaze. "I am a cripple."

Daniel passed his eyes over her, lingering on the cane. She'd once been spry and quick. He, mayhap, was somewhat human after all, because he despised the sad glimmer in her eyes. "Daphne Smith, an old injured leg would never stop you from marching on the king's forces if you so chose. I would favor any wager with you and your limp over a gentleman without."

Her lips parted and, at the softening in her eyes, a shudder wracked his frame. Egads, he could do without any hint of adoration.

"I do not have a wardrobe," she said, this time, tentative. "I have no noble connections."

"If you are attempting to convince me of your unsuitability, you're doing a splendid job," he drawled and leaned back in his chair. "Are you suggesting I find another?" Countless years at the gaming tables had made him a master of dissembling. The truth was, he was without options, in terms of coin, and in terms of so much as knowing a single appropriate and, more, respectable, lady to serve as companion.

"No," she said quickly. Daphne searched around the room and then turned resigned eyes back on him. "Very well. I will, come with you." She spoke with all the enthusiasm and excitement of a woman agreeing to march to the gallows to face her executioner. "At the end of my tenure, I expect references and one hundred pounds," she demanded and then added on a rush, "and *one* replacement guinea, of course."

Poor Daphne, she'd always been rot at wagering. He'd have offered her five hundred of those eight thousand coming to him. He inclined his head. "We're agreed, then."

She came to the edge of his desk and stretched her hand out.

He furrowed his brow, taking in her long, graceful fingers. Fingers that conjured all manner of wicked thoughts of that hand wrapped around his length, stroking him—

"You are supposed to close your hand around it, my lord." At the mental imagery she conjured, a surge of wholly inappropriate thoughts for this woman burst forth. Lust blazed to that uncircumspect organ.

"Uh, yes. Right." Daniel placed his fingers in hers and heat burned his palm. Slightly callused and tanned from the sun, that skin was nothing like the smooth, white palms of the ladies who warmed his bed. Yet, there was strength to hers. A strength he was hard-pressed to not admire.

"We are done here, then," Daphne concluded. With a nod and demonstrating a remarkable, if infuriating, calm to his touch, she drew her hand back. She started for the door.

"Daphne," he called out, halting her in her tracks. She glanced back over her shoulder. "See that Haply has a carriage readied to deliver you home, first." Her eyes registered her shock. Then she nodded. With a word of thanks, she took her leave.

Yes, the lady was wise to also be surprised by any show of goodness in him. For in truth, there was none. All good had died long, long ago. Forcing his onetime friend to enter a world she so hated, was proof of it.

CHAPTER 5

When Daphne Smith had left Polite Society ten years ago, she'd vowed the only way she'd ever reenter their midst was if her life depended on it. Even then, if she could strike a deal with the Devil to retain her hold on living, then that was a deal she'd happily take.

In the end, she'd made a deal with an altogether different devil and ironically one that would thrust her back amongst the *ton*. A devil who'd also politely refused the use of his mount to claim the seat opposite her.

"You're not riding Satan?" Lady Alice puzzled aloud, echoing Daphne's very wondering.

Satan?

Daniel rolled his shoulders. "How could I be so rude as to forego the delightful company here?"

His sister rolled her eyes to the ceiling.

"You named your horse Satan?" Daphne snorted. "I would suggest striving for being *less* obvious in conveying the depth of your wickedness."

Alice widened her eyes and burst into laughter.

Through the mirth echoing off the walls, Daniel winged an arrogant eyebrow up. "It occurs to me you have been attending stories of my wickedness, Miss Smith."

Daphne promptly closed her mouth and redirected her attention out the window, staring out at the passing countryside, deliberately ignoring him and the intense gaze he trained on her. How empty were the lives of noblemen that they would find enjoyment in needling and baiting a lady. And in this case, a lady who'd once been a friend.

Daniel shifted his weight on the bench and that subtle movement brought their knees into contact. An unwanted heat burned through her fabric. She gritted her teeth and inched closer to the side of the carriage.

Seven hours. That was how long she'd be forced to endure the jolting, miserable carriage ride with Daniel across from her. And she only knew the precise amount because she'd counted the minutes with excitement as a girl of eighteen when she'd first gone to London. Then she had lamented the infernally slow passage of time on the return from that miserable hell.

Alice broke the tense impasse. "Have you been to London, Miss Smith?"

"Once," she murmured. "Ten years ago." Unease formed a pit in her belly. It was not that she'd despised London. She had enjoyed the thrill of the city. But rather, it was a certain *gentleman* that she despised. Lord Leopold Dunlop's face flashed behind her mind's eye. She'd never meant anything to that rogue. As such, he'd hardly remember the cripple he bedded against a wall, like a cheap dockside doxy.

Alice surged forward in her seat, her brown eyes radiating an excitement Daphne herself had been filled with years earlier. "Is it as wicked as all the gossip columns claim?"

Worse.

"I would have to defer to your brother," she murmured and then mentally cursed herself for inviting Daniel into any discourse of which she must be part.

Alice turned an expectant stare on her brother.

"Worse," he supplied, stretching his legs out once more, sending another round of that unwanted awareness. She didn't want to notice that he'd grown into this towering, well-muscled model of male perfection.

He gave her a slow, languid look. A knowing one.

Daphne gritted her teeth and attended Alice. "I expect your brother would rather you not know of the wicked end of London," she supplied for him.

"All of London is depraved," he countered, unhelpfully.

Daphne shot him a reproachful look. "That is untrue," she countered. Ladies of Hope was proof of the good in the world, still. "Some parts are not," she said lamely when brother and sister continued to stare at her.

"But most are," Daniel persisted.

Alice brightened. "That will do. I *was* hoping for wicked."

She swallowed a groan. Her charge would, of course, possess a bit of her brother's wild spirit. "There is something to be said for dull." Of course, an earl's sister didn't know the same uncertainty that came for lower-born women like Daphne.

"Yes, there is," Daniel concurred, unexpectedly helpful. "It is tedious." He followed that outlandish charge with a wink, eliciting a bark of laughter from his sister.

Daphne swiped a hand over her eyes. Could he not be a proper brother? The protective older brother who scared off suitors and showed the correct level of worry for his sister's reputation. "No, there is something safe in it. Reassuring. Comforting. Wicked is uncertain." Lord Leopold Dunlop's smug, smirking face flashed behind her eyes again. "And often dangerous," she added and thought better of it. "Always dangerous. Always," she whispered to herself, an unnecessary reminder she no longer needed. Not when her lack of virtue stood as a testament to that very fact.

She registered the absolute silence in the carriage and looked up to find the Winterbourne siblings studying her with varying degrees of interest. Cheeks heating, she shifted her attention to the window. She'd said too much. Mayhap, they'd let the matter rest and go on with their discussion on the wicked wonders of London.

Of course, that was all too much to hope for. "Do you know, Miss Smith," Daniel began. "You speak as though a woman who doth protest too much."

Her skin pricked with the curious attention Alice trained on her. "I speak as a woman who was properly warned away from scandal and not one who'd romanticize it. And given," she held his gaze, "Lady Alice's entry into Polite Society, I should think you wish her to embrace respectability and honor."

"Yes, well, I do not care if the gentleman to court me is a rake or honorable gentleman, as long as he is hopelessly in love with me," Alice piped in.

"Rakes don't love," Daniel interrupted with a jaded edge as he reached inside his jacket and withdrew a silver flask. He removed the stopper and took a swig.

"The reformed ones do," his sister protested with a frown of one who believed she knew more than she, in fact, did.

He took another sip. "Rogues may be reformed. A rake never. Find the suitable lords. A proper, wealthy duke. In fact, any wealthy gent will do. Don't go wasting your attention on anything less."

The muscles of Daphne's stomach knotted. How many believed those powerful peers made the ideal match? Most ladies dreamed of lofty, fat in the purse, lords. She had been a lady, dreaming only of love. "Think equally with your heart and with your mind when deciding on a suitor," she said quietly.

"Your mind?" Daniel chuckled, the sound empty and devoid of mirth. Oh, how changed he was from the freckle-faced boy who'd snorted and shook with laughter. "Hardly the romantic words to pass on to your charge."

"I would pass her words of wisdom," she challenged. He narrowed his eyes on her face and the dark, piercing intensity hinted at a man who could see inside a woman's head and extract her every secret. If he did, he'd have seen her unsuitability, tossed the carriage door open, and kicked her back into the countryside where she belonged.

Daniel said nothing more. Instead, he returned his attention to that silver flask.

Another thankful silence descended on the carriage. The quiet was only shattered by the rumble of the carriage wheels and the soft, evenly drawn breaths of Alice slumbering and the faint snoring of Daniel as he slept.

Daphne released the tension she held in her shoulders and rolled the muscles aching from her stiff carriage. For so long, it had been easy to put her experience in London into a trunk, close the lid, lock it up, and bury it away under her bed, to never be brought out again. That place where horrible memories and foolish mistakes were dusted aside, but never truly forgotten. For they could not be forgotten.

Now, Daniel, with his offer of employment, had forced that trunk out into the open. All her sins and follies mocked her once more for the hopefulness of her youth.

She'd been tricked by a smiling, dashing *gentleman*, far too hand-some than a man had a right to be, with the right words on his lips. She would forever live with the reminder of trusting a rogue. Or rake, or scoundrel. Because even with Daniel's semantic dance, they were all invariably the same.

Just as he was the same.

She shifted her gaze over to his sleeping form. In repose, the cynical lines melted from the harsh, angular planes leaving in their place a beautifully sculpted gentleman. The square jaw, the high cheeks, all embodied the perfect material for those great artists to memorialize in their precious stone. It was no wonder he'd become one of those lords whose favors were coveted and craved by unhappy women and debutantes eager to dance with excite-ment and danger.

For he represented that. Daphne captured her chin in her hand. He'd not always been that way. He'd been outrageously fun to bait and tease and chase. A boy with clever jests, who'd seen stags in the stars and wolves in the clouds. Then, a boy and girl invariably grew up and became the jaded figures that she and Daniel now were.

He…was awake.

Her stomach lurched as his chestnut brown lashes twitched. Impossibly long lashes that no gentleman had a right to possess. She bit the inside of her cheek. The bounder. A slow, decidedly wicked grin curved his lips up. "How long have you been awake?" she demanded on a charged whisper.

"Long enough." He waggled his chestnut eyebrows and then spoke in hushed tones. "Did you enjoy what you saw, Miss Smith?"

Daphne rolled her eyes to the ceiling. "Hardly." She was going to hell for lying.

"And yet, you stared." God, he was more tenacious than he'd been as a boy, rooted at the shore at dusk, refusing to leave until he'd caught a fish.

"I was thinking of how you have changed," she said, off-setting him with her honesty.

He opened and closed his mouth several times, like that very fish he'd inevitably prevailed to catch. The company he now kept, he'd not know what to do with honesty. His momentary lack of control receded, replaced by the smooth, cocksure arrogance that could only belong to a sought-after rogue. "So tell me *how* have I changed?" he urged.

Of course, he'd noted her earlier appreciation. She was wise and wary, but she was not dead. That was where she'd fail and she'd see the glorious specimen he'd become. "You used to smile." A glorious sunny grin that had twinkled in his eyes and matched his dimple. "I preferred when you were smiling," she added, unable to keep the regret from seeping into her musings.

He turned his lips up again, in a smooth, wolfish grin. "I still smile."

Sadness tugged at her heart. "That is not a smile, Daniel. That is an empty, dark expression that could never be disguised as anything good."

"And what of you, Daphne?" he challenged in hushed tones, while his sister slept on. "Have you not changed?"

"I never said I did not," she rebutted.

He placed his hands on his knees and leaned across the bench. Her heart quickened as all the much needed space between them faded and his nose nearly brushed hers. "At least, I can still move the muscles, Miss Smith, which is a good deal more than I can say for your angry lips and your warning to my sister to stay away from wicked and wonderful pursuits."

"They are dangerous," she said on a furious whisper.

"Do you know what is dangerous?" he rebutted, his breath stirring her lips. God help her, she was a wanton still, for she wanted to close the distance between them and know their contour and feel in ways she never had. In ways she'd never truly known a man's kiss.

Oh, God. *This is dangerous.* She closed her eyes and gave her head a slight shake. He interpreted that desperate, silent appeal for sanity as an answer to his question.

"Dangerous is never knowing pleasure. Dangerous is living with the worry of what other people think and, worse, caring about what they think, so that you lose every piece of you that is worth living. That is dangerous." He opened his mouth but his words faded and his gaze fell to her mouth.

Her too-full mouth.

No doubt the ladies who'd known this man's kiss had all been blessed with the bow-shaped ones captured in portraits and written of on the pages of sonnets. Not that she gave a jot what Daniel, or any man, thought of her mouth. Or her flawed, awkward body. He hooded his lashes and a smoky darkness filled his brown eyes.

Oh, my God in heaven, he is going to kiss me.

The carriage hit a jarring bump and tossed him against her. His chin knocked the top of her forehead and she winced as pain radiated from the point of contact. Her accelerated heart rate resumed its normal pacing.

Daniel silently cursed. "Let me see," he commanded, reaching a hand out to explore the sensitive skin of her brow.

Daphne held up frantic, staying hands. "I am fine," she assured, hastily backing away. *Other than my momentary descent into madness where I craved your kiss.*

He probed along her right eyebrow. Her useless pulse pounded all the harder. How strong and sure his touch was. And how pathetic her reaction to him.

"I'm fine," she insisted, swatting at him. Needing him to stop.

"Don't be a twaddle," he muttered, continuing his search.

...that isn't the proper use of the word twaddle, Daniel...

Her lips twitched. "That is not the proper use of twaddle."

...it should be...

Daniel briefly shifted his attention from the slight knot forming at her brow to meet her gaze. "I know," he reminded her and her heart started.

Did he recall that long ago debate between two often competing children?

He froze and then quickly yanked his hands back. "I trust you'll survive your slight lump, Miss Smith," he said, in his smooth, deep voice. One that resurrected the proper barriers where he was the rake and she the woman who knew far better than to trust the touch, words, kiss, or anything else of those gentlemen.

Yet, as he sat back in his seat and closed his eyes once more, she could not account for the regret at the brief, happy recollection that had been so quickly shattered.

By Lucifer and all his armies, he'd almost kissed her.

Which really should not set off this rapid round of panic in his chest and certainly not shock. He'd stolen countless kisses from countless ladies. And yet, this was not just any woman.

This was Daphne Smith. A lady in the truest sense. The manner of one who'd attended Sunday sermons and who, no doubt, still suffered through those infernal masses. The girl he'd swum naked with in a lake on his father's property. Who'd hurled mud at his face and from whom he'd taken a fist to the nose countless times so she could properly learn to beat a boy…all to protect herself, of course.

Except, with those long-forgotten remembrances, new ones whispered forward. Of this new, stern-faced Daphne with her crimson hair in that God-awful chignon. He tormented himself with the forbidden image of yanking the combs from those fiery locks and letting her hair cascade about them as she dove under the surface of that same lake, like a siren, luring him out to sea.

He groaned and quickly converted it into a practiced snore. The spirited woman now dancing wickedly through his thoughts looked quickly in his direction. Suspicion clouded her eyes. The proper suspicion befitting any suitable companion.

In selecting her as Alice's companion, she'd proved the ideal choice to silence even his stodgy, always disapproving uncle. Proper. Respectable. Without scandal. She fit with everything his bastard of an uncle expected of someone serving in that role. She was also forbidden, given their history as childhood friends. And with her transformation into pinch-mouthed, disapproving miss, well, there were no worries of any lusting after a servant in his employ.

Or there hadn't been. Until he'd first noted those damned silver flecks in her eyes and her lush, full mouth which only conjured even more delectable, wicked, and the word she so feared, danger-ous, images of all the pleasures he could know from that luscious mouth.

He peered through his lashes once more and found the lady directing all her tense energy to the window. The stiff set to her lean, lithe frame was a contradiction of the full-figured beauties he'd long favored. The sight of her stern face reflected back in that crystal windowpane effectively doused all lust and restored his logic.

He'd no interest in bedding an angry miss. And certainly not one who'd long ago punched him so hard in the nose, she'd driven him to cry. Humbling stuff, having been brought to tears... by a girl, no less. Yes, he quite preferred his women laughing, tempting, teasing, and well, in short, all things this harpy before him was not.

She'd not always been like this. Then, they'd all been different in many ways, before life ultimately shaped them into the people they'd become. When had her happiness died, leaving in its place the cautious creature whose breath quickened at his glance alone? Had it been long ago, after that fall that shattered her leg and the physical perfection expected of their world? Or had it come later? With the death of a parent? Or a failed Season where no match had been made?

Had those self-important lords in the market for a bride, been too consumed by the model of beauty that they'd failed to notice the lady?

Eventually, with the passing moments, her shoulders sagged and she leaned against the side of the carriage. The soft rasp of her gentle, even breathing blended with the rumble of the wheels. She slept.

His pretend bid at sleep over, Daniel opened his eyes and frowned. She'd had her Come Out and he'd been there, and not once had he seen her, or danced with her, or visited. It spoke to the emptiness of his soul that he'd been so enrapt in his own pleasures that he'd failed to visit a former friend come to London. Which would have been better for the lady, anyway. By that point, he was riddled with scandals, feared by protective mamas, and, as such, hardly the gentleman a gentile lady would either want or need about.

He told himself that. And yet, studying her in her sleep, a sentiment he'd believed long dead stirred within him. Guilt was a sentiment he thought he was incapable of feeling or even recognizing. But he'd not always been a ruthless, self-serving bastard. He'd once been very much human and capable of hurting and loving and crying. He shuddered. All mulling, pathetic emotions. Daphne might resent his absence all those years ago and judge him for the empty smile he wore, but he was far safer now than he'd ever been before.

He studied her as her head lolled back against the squabs, her face relaxed in her slumber. She'd spoken to his sister of the perils of wickedness. Her unspoken words and disapproving eyes condemning the life he lived. When in truth, he'd achieved something that she still, by her warnings for Alice, strove toward—absolute unfeelingness. He knew carnal pleasures and lived for his own material comforts.

He'd have it no other way. For the path she'd trod was a weary one and in the end, Daniel's was the safer one. The one that would see him guarded from pain and loneliness. And Daphne Smith was free to the miserable course she'd set.

CHAPTER 6

THAT EVENING, AFTER A LONG, miserably bumpy carriage ride without any volatile sparks or baiting conversations or dangerously seductive grins, they arrived in London.

The air was dank and heavy. The clouds thicker. The sky darker. The streets stank like refuse that had sat too long in the summer sun. In short, it was everything Daphne remembered it to be. And given as much as she despised this town for the memories contained here, she was never more grateful to reach a destination.

Not bothering to ring for help in changing her dusty garments, Daphne rested her cane alongside the nightstand. Her movements stiff and painful from a day of traveling, she sat down on the edge of her borrowed bed and slowly lowered herself onto her back. Closing her eyes, she stretched her arms above her head and reached the tips of her fingers toward the ceiling. A little moan escaped her lips as the tight muscles popped in protest.

Society took a crippled lady as weak. Those low expectations found women and men like her without work, living a life where they constantly strove to demonstrate their worth or, worse, found themselves shut away in a hospital or asylum. She withdrew the scrap from her pocket and held it overhead. Her eyes automatically went to the center of the page.

...Only those with a belief in the ideology and principle of the establishment, as well as experience and glowing references will be considered for employment...

To present herself to the marchioness, with neither references nor experience, and make a plea for employment would be nothing more than an appeal to the gracious woman's pity. Daphne would not be a charity case taken on, but rather a worker who'd earned a place within the respectable institution.

A knock sounded at the door and she started, the scrap of paper falling from her fingers. Mayhap it had been another door. For surely after a long day of traveling, no one would request her presence now.

Another knocking ensued. "Miss Smith, His Lordship requests your presence in his office."

Daphne scrubbed her hands up and down her face and made a small sound of protest in her throat. She'd been wrong. He would request her presence now, after a long day of traveling. Then, he was no friend to her. He was her employer and she a servant in his employ; a servant who sought to prove her capabilities, despite her injury.

"Miss Smith?" the hesitancy in the maid's query reached her ears.

With a regretful sigh, Daphne grabbed her paper and stuffed it inside her pocket. She shoved herself onto her elbows. "I'll be but a moment." She angled her body left and then right. Then, biting her lower lip, she scooted to the edge of the bed and retrieved her cane. Settling it on the floor, she propelled herself to a stand. A small cry left her lips and she crumpled against the nightstand, knocking her hip into the sharp edge.

"Miss Smith?" the maid called, a frantic worry underscoring those two words.

Gritting her teeth through the strain, she counted her breaths until she trusted herself to speak. "I am all right," she reassured. She took a step and agony shot from her foot up her thigh, to her hipbone, making a liar out of her. Pain had become such a part of her existence that long ago, she'd set aside self-pity. But still, on the occasional moment, regret slipped in that she did not move with the youthful grace she'd once known. The same languid, elegance Daniel still demonstrated with his every effortless movement. Perspiring from her exertions, she reached the door, and grabbed for the handle.

She opened it to reveal Tessa, the same smiling, patiently waiting young servant who'd shown her abovestairs not even thirty minutes earlier. "Oh, there you are, Miss Smith." The girl beamed. Her grin dipped as she took in Daphne's cane. "Are you certain, you're well? Should I tell His Lordship that you are unable to come down?"

Daphne grinned wryly. "Do you expect it would make much of a difference to His Lordship, if I had you do that?"

A little twinkle lit Tessa's lovely hazel eyes. "No, ma'am, I rather expect it might not." They shared a smile and a friendship was born. Motioning Daphne to follow, she started a path through the quiet corridors. It did not escape Daphne's notice that Tessa moved with slow, precise steps, carefully looking over her shoulder to be sure Daphne followed. "Though in truth, it might matter," the maid added belatedly. She hummed a discordant tune that Daphne vaguely recognized as *A Fox May Steal Your Hens, Sir.*

Daphne looked questioningly at her.

"His Lordship," the girl clarified. "Not nasty like the last lord me and me mum worked for," she whispered. "Doesn't yell, doesn't make his servants be quiet. So you're free to sing." Free to sing? With that, the young girl continued her humming of the old folk song, leaving her to puzzle through that slight but telling reveal about the manner of employer Daniel had become.

The households she'd entered in her last foray into London had been stiff, formal affairs, with deferential servants who avoided gazes and certainly didn't speak freely. Her lips pulled in a grudging smile. Of course, an unapologetic lord like Daniel Winterbourne, the Earl of Montfort, would rule his household with that same, free spirit.

They reached the top of the stairwell and Daphne gripped the rail. She lowered her eyes. There were thirty-three stairs, certainly an odd number for any architect or builder to settle on for those marble steps. And she only knew as much because the only thing that had gotten her through the long climb not even thirty minutes prior was that counting.

"Miss?" Tessa urged gently, springing her into movement.

If she wished to spend her days working with girls and women inside Mrs. Belden's or Ladies of Hope, she'd have to battle far more than thirty-three steps. Daphne placed a tentative foot forward and then step by agonizing step, made her way down. A small bead of sweat trickled from her brow and ran a trail down her cheek. Her skin itched and she paused to briefly wipe the moisture.

Thirty-one.

Thirty-two.

And, thirty-three, that final, odd-numbered step. Feet settled on the white marble foyer, she thrilled at that small victory and proceeded to follow Tessa down the corridor.

As a young woman ruined and humiliated by Lord Leopold, Daphne had spent years hating herself and her injury. The second son of a marquess, Lord Leopold had proven men craved proper wives who made expert hostesses and performed grand activities, like dancing or walking and only used broken, marred woman as a diversion to satisfy their sick curiosity. Regardless, she'd come to find peace with who she was. She aspired to far more than being a pretty arm ornament for a bored nobleman.

"Here we are, miss," Tessa murmured, bringing them to a stop outside a heavily paneled door. She knocked once.

"Enter," Daniel called distractedly.

Tessa gave her an encouraging smile and pushed the door open. Daphne stepped inside.

His jacket abandoned so it hung haphazardly over the back of his leather winged back chair, Daniel stood with his broad back to her, arms folded, and hands clasped behind him. He'd the look of a military general assessing his battlefield plans. Daphne wet her lips. She didn't want to notice the way his biceps strained the fabric of his white lawn shirt or the shocking intimacy of him standing before her so. In fact, it would have been far easier had he grown into one of those boring, pompous lords who padded his waistcoats and doused himself in floral fragrance. But then, if he were one of those staid monocle-sporting figures, at his age, he'd even now have a proper wife and a passel of babes. There would be no need at all for a highly improper companion such as herself.

A lady who'd proven herself all manner of corruptible and weak for a gentleman, a good deal less inspiring than Daniel.

The door closed with a quiet click behind her and Daphne jumped, casting a single, longing last glance at that wood panel between her and freedom.

"I require your help," he announced, not even bothering to

glance back.

Required help? A gentleman who commanded a room and a person with such ease, needed no assistance from her in anything. He shot a questioning look over his shoulder and she cleared her throat. "You never liked asking for help." They'd always been alike in that regard—two proud people refusing to humble themselves.

Daniel flashed her a slanted grin. It pulled at that dimple in his right cheek, transforming him so easily into the always smiling boy he'd been, long, long ago. "Yes, well, it does speak to my desperation."

She thumped her cane once on the hardwood floor. "Desperation that required my presence summoned so soon after arriving?"

"Absolutely." Either he failed to note or care about the dryness of her inquiry. Daniel refocused his attentions forward. "It's the bloody Season."

"You should not use that word," she corrected automatically, limping forward.

A rough snort left his lips. "You've used far more impressive curses than that one."

"Yes," she muttered. "But I was a child." Which wasn't entirely true, as there'd been a nasty bunch she'd strung together about the man whom she'd thrown her reputation and future away for. And Mrs. Belden. And… Yes, she was still given to cursing. She'd sooner snip out her tongue than admit as much. She stopped alongside his desk and studied the parchments laid out before him. Daphne furrowed her brow. Alice's Marital Plans. "What are these?" That was rather silly to even ask when he'd quite neatly titled the sheets.

"They're the plans to marry off Alice."

She'd found him wanting not even a day earlier for failing to ask the appropriate questions and discuss his sister's entry into Society. How very humbling to see that for her hastily formed opinion, he had put *some* thought into it. Daphne perused the pages. Two pages, to be precise. Proper Balls. Cultured Activities. Of which he'd broadly listed the museum and opera.

At her silence, Daniel picked his head up from those sheets and glanced at her.

"Uh, it is a start," she managed.

He cracked his knuckles. "It is, the only way to see that we both accomplish our like goal. She will be wed, and then I can resume my carousing, and you can…do whatever it is you care to do at Mrs. Belden's."

Whatever it is she cared to do. He'd so little interest in the woman she'd become to know her goals beyond this post or even his own sister. Her fledgling respect flickered out like a snuffed candle. "How very touching," she said with an acerbic edge.

FOR THE FIRST TIME IN the whole of his life, Daniel was filled with—uncertainty. Yes, in matters of—he shuddered—planning a young lady's London Season, he was remarkably out of his element. Particularly a Season for his sister where his entire happiness, and hers, now rested.

Interestingly, the only woman he'd turn this concern over to was the woman before him. Odd, he'd not seen her in greater than thirteen years, but how easily they'd moved into their respective roles of friends. In some ways. His gaze went to her slender hips and small breasts that would fit quite comfortably into his palms. He grinned wickedly. And not so much, in other ways.

She disapproved of his titled list.

Such an understanding didn't only come from his ability to read the subtle nuances of a woman's body but rather because this was Daphne. He knew her in ways that moved beyond the sexual. As a child, he'd long been fascinated by the pronounced vein at her temple that ticked whenever she was displeased or frustrated.

It mattered not. The lady was entitled to her disapproval or disappointment or any of those other fault-finding responses to the person he was. He'd never presented himself falsely before her as someone he was not. He hadn't done so as a boy and he'd not do it now, as a man. "Well?" he demanded impatiently, comfortably steering himself back into the role of unaffected employer who didn't give jot.

What he did require was help.

Daphne sighed. "I am thinking, Daniel."

With her attention trained downward, he used her distraction as an opportunity to study her. Drab, ill-fitting brown dress that clashed abominably with her crimson tresses aside, the lady had an incredibly long, graceful neck. An odd feature to admire in a lady. He'd always preferred a woman's hands or lips, of which hers were certainly in the kiss-worthy category. The neck, however, had held little appeal. Until now. He took in the details he'd previously not considered. The pulse that throbbed there, a marker of a lady's heightening desire. And he ached to place his lips to that cream white flesh and mark it with a faint love bite—

She glanced up. "Are you all right?"

"Quite." The lie emerged garbled to his ears.

"You groaned."

"I am sore from a day traveling." That second prevarication came out as easily as every other one he'd ever offered a woman. Or man. Or friend. Anyone really. Lying was fair game for all and ultimately necessary.

The suspicion faded from her eyes. "Yes, I understand that."

He frowned as her words only made him feel like the worst sort of rotter. Which he generally was. He was not, however, the manner of gentleman who didn't take into consideration the comforts of a lady. "Would you care to sit?"

She looked up with a healthy dose of surprise. It spoke volumes to the level of her regard—or in this case, ill-regard. Then, with the assistance of her cane, she lowered herself into his torn leather winged chair.

"Where is there to begin?" he demanded as soon as she'd settled into the seat.

"I do not know," she said, her tone heavy with impatience.

He dragged over a chair, positioning it close to hers. "What do you mean, 'you do not know'. You are a woman and you had a Season."

She pursed her lips, only drawing his lustful thoughts back to that plump flesh. "I mean I do not know," she said with a cantankerous edge that effectively killed all his improper musings. "I had *one* Season." The slight, drawn-out emphasis of that particular number was better reserved for an instructor trying to reason with a lackwit. "You had thirteen."

"It is entirely different for a gentleman."

"Even more so for a rake," she added.

"Yes, entirely," he concurred, earning a wild eye roll from the lady.

"I was being facetious," she said with a sigh.

"You were also invariably correct." The events he attended and oftentimes hosted—the orgies, the scandalous masquerades—were no proper affairs a debutante and her companion would dare attend. Unless they were bent on ruin. In which case, they most certainly *would* attend. "In your one Season, you've acquired far more an idea of what…" he slashed his hand at the page gripped in her fingers, "is expected in the launching of Alice."

Daphne set the page on the desk. "We are speaking of your sister. Not a ship." His neck heated and by God, he, for the first time in too many years, was *blushing*. "Her happiness should be your utmost priority, not the speed with which you're able to resume your rapid decline into self-destruction." Who'd have believed it possible that he, the Earl of Montfort, felt this niggling of shame turn in his belly? "Second," Daphne thankfully returned her notice to that largely empty sheet. "I didn't have a true Season, Daniel. I came in the middle of the Season and didn't have…" She brought her lips closed into a tight line.

He studied her closely, waiting for her to complete that thought. When it became apparent with her silence she'd no intention of clarifying, questions trickled into his mind. What hadn't she had? Suitors? A happy time? Something in that possibility, for the girl she'd been and the friendship they'd once shared, raised a frown. How very different they'd taken to this place. She, born for the country, he, perfectly suited for Town.

Daphne sighed. "There are certain gowns she'll require," she eventually said.

A surge of relief went through him. Of course she would know. She'd always known all. Even as he would have sooner severed off his left hand than admit as much when they'd been children. "You will see to it."

She looked at him sadly. "I spent the whole of three weeks, a fortnight and three days, in this place." Well, that was a peculiarly specific number for a girl who'd long despised math. His curiosity piqued. "I am sure you know the most fashionable modiste." He did. He'd paid many visits to Madame Thoureaux's, with inventive mistresses and their expensive tastes. "We must begin there."

"On the morrow." Daniel flicked an assessing look over her drab dress, drawing forth an image of Daphne draped in a daring ice blue silk gown that clung to her lithe figure. That dress would draw out the rich hues of her hair and the green of her eyes. A wave of desire went through him. For Daphne, the former friend of his past? A woman narrow and remarkably uncurved like the usual ladies he took to his bed. He shoved aside that shock. After all, he was a rake. "You'll require gowns, as well," he added.

Daphne dissolved into a paroxysm of coughing, that shook her frame and turned her cheeks the same red as her hair. He leaned over and thumped her hard between the shoulder blades. "You are mad. I do not require gowns."

He studied her curiously. Any and every female he'd known before her craved baubles and fripperies, trading favors to coax more from him. And she rebuffed that offering? "You very much require them," he said with wry humor that raised a frown.

"I don't," she protested.

His intrigue redoubled at her declination and he peered at her. How singularly different she was than the ladies of the peerage he'd dallied with. "Would you have the *ton* question the status and suitability of Alice's companion?" The color drained from her cheeks. Damned if he didn't feel like the naughty boy who'd kicked a pup.

"One dress," she conceded.

"Five."

She remained unyielding. "One."

By God, if this wasn't the same discussion he'd had with spoiled mistresses, only with their negotiating roles entirely reversed. He dragged a languid look over her slender frame. "Four and a peignoir."

If the lady shot her eyebrows any higher, they'd disappear into her hairline. When had she become this serious, easily shocked creature?

"I was jesting, Daphne," he drawled. "Unless you *wish* to have a peignoir." In which case, he'd have Madame Thoureaux drape her in various satin and silk beaded creations and insist on watching.

She searched his face with sadness in her far too expressive eyes. "Is everything a joke with you, Daniel?"

Actually, since his brother's drowning, everything had become a game. It had begun as a means of ratcheting up attention from his heartbroken mother and his catatonic father. Somewhere along the way, the boy he'd been had merged with another, capable of only caring for and about himself.

...It should have been you, Daniel... He forcibly thrust back that steely whisper hurled at him by his father.

At his silence, she sighed. That faint exhalation bespoke her condemnation more than any damning charges. He gripped the arms of the chair, despising himself for noticing that slight whispery sound and giving so much as a damn. "It is a grand production," she said quietly. "A lady must wear a gown of white, adorned with a train, and a certain number of feathers in her hair."

Daphne would have been lost in white. It would have turned her cream white, freckled skin a sallow shade that did nothing to enhance her earthy, natural beauty.

"She'll need to be presented at Almack's," she continued. The lady would certainly not be so methodical if she knew the improper path his thoughts had wandered. "The patronesses will decide upon her acceptability." Her lip peeled back in the faintest sneer.

Daniel didn't give a jot about what people were thinking or feeling, or anything truly that involved a single emotion. Mayhap it was fatigue from the days of travel. Or mayhap it was nostalgia wrought by her presence. "And what did they decide about your acceptability?" He should have been there. At that point in his life, he'd been a rotted bastard, but she'd have been a friend he'd not seen in just two or three years.

"They didn't much care either way." Daphne fiddled with the fabric of her skirts and smiled faintly. "I was merely permitted entry because your father arranged for it." He started. *My father.* The cold, unfeeling bastard who'd sent the family spiraling into dun territory had vouched for the lady.

"My father made an appeal," she murmured.

An uncomfortable silence descended. Daniel cleared his throat and picked up the nearest sheet. "Very well, then. A visit to the modiste tomorrow for a proper wardrobe. The following evening—"

"I expect it will take at the very least a week for gowns to be created."

He chuckled. "I assure you, you and Alice will have no fewer than two gowns each by the following day's end." Such assurance came not from arrogance but in very specific dealings with the modiste.

She shook her head bemusedly. "How very foreign it is to me, this world you live in. Where you desire something and…" She snapped her fingers once. "It is vastly different for the rest of us." She lumped herself in with an entirely different lot than the *ton*. And yet…that is what she was. She'd been a childhood friend and a neighbor of his late father's properties, but they may as well have rotated in entirely different solar spheres. "You'll need to host a ball for her debut," Daphne said, shoving herself slowly up.

Daniel hopped to his feet and made to assist her, but she pointedly ignored his arm and, instead, reached for her cane. "Balls are costly." His mind tabulated all the funds that would go into such an event.

Daphne limped around her seat, coming so close, her arm brushed his. "If you can afford to host those wicked summer parties every July you can afford to throw your sister a proper ball."

Fair point. He followed her slow, painful march across his room. "Daphne," he called out when she reached for the handle. She looked back. "If you wish to attend one of those wicked parties, there is always an invitation for you."

Her lips tugged and she caught the plump flesh of the lower lip between her teeth. Her shoulders shook with her amusement and even with the length of the room between them, the light cast by the roaring fire in the hearth set her eyes aglow. "*Goodnight*, Daniel," she said with a wry amusement.

"Daph," he managed and, oddly, when he gave her a half-grin, it felt vastly different than the false one she'd taken umbrage to in the carriage ride.

CHAPTER 7

Thirty-three. Following her discussion with Daniel, Daphne had mastered those thirty-three miserable stairs once more.

She winced as she lurched forward down the hall. But for her brief foray into London all those years ago, she'd rarely ventured out of her family's modest cottage. There had been jaunts to the village and Sunday services, but there had not been long carriage rides or opulent estates or townhouses with more stairs than there really should be inside a home. Yet, in being here and navigating freely, if slowly, a sense of pride buoyed her. It proved her right and Mrs. Belden wrong. Proved that she could, even with her limited movement, work on her own imperfect legs.

Daphne reached her temporary chambers and shifted her cane to her opposite hand. She shoved the door open.

"Miss Smith," Alice said, hopping to her feet with such rapidity that a wave of envy assailed her. How very strange to remember moving with such speed and grace, that she could, in a moment, forget the very true state of her now mangled limb. "I hope you do not mind I came to wait. There was, *is* something I wished to speak with you on."

"Think nothing of it," she said gently. This room, after all, was far more Alice's and she nothing more than an interloper here. An interloper with a wicked past; a past that would certainly preclude her from securing employment at both Mrs. Belden's and Ladies of Hope. Shoving aside that kernel of unease, she limped forward. "And please, Daphne will suffice." A spasm wracked her leg and she briefly pressed her eyes closed. "I expect whatever has brought you here is of some import." She motioned to the bed, as more a desperate need for a seat.

Alice immediately settled into a graceful array at the edge. Daphne claimed the spot beside her. "May I be frank with you, Daphne?"

"I would be insulted if you are not." She admired the young woman's honesty. The ladies she'd had the misfortune of meeting during her Come Out had all been nasty, gossipy, and hurtful beings.

Her charge drew in a slow breath and then spoke on a rush. "I'm concerned about the whole matchmaking business."

She assessed Daniel's sister; different in coloring but so very alike in the spirit of her rakish brother. With Alice's flaxen hair, the color of spun-gold, and gently curved figure, she fit with all Society's standards of flawless English beauty. "I do not believe you have—"

"I am not like the other ladies," she cut in. "Or I wasn't like the ladies at Mrs. Belden's. I laugh loudly."

"As you should freely laugh." Even if Society disagreed.

"I speak my own mind." Alice stared on, a challenge in her eyes. Did she believe Daphne would condemn her for that important trait?

"Which is good and commendable," Daphne put in, tamping down a grin. In that fearlessness, Lady Alice was very much like her unrepentant brother.

Alice continued over that praise. "I have a brother who is a notorious rake." Yes, there was that. A dangerously seductive gentleman, far more perfect in looks than a man ought to be.

"I never had a mother with whom to discuss the ideal candidate for a husband," the girl said, hopping once more to her feet. "Or how to find *the* gentleman. Do they find you?" She cast a look at Daphne. If Daniel's sister hoped that Daphne had guidance or advice to give on finding *the* gentleman, then she was better off hoping for that fairy godmother, she'd read of in *The Girl With the Glass Slipper*. "I'm warned away from rakes." With good reason. "But some rogues make good husbands."

Yes, that was the twaddle they fed young ladies, to give them hope about those wicked lords. Dangerous, dangerous stuff, indeed. Lord Leopold traipsed through her mind, grinning and seductive. She balled her hands hard and thrust his vile visage back.

"Do you know who will make you the ideal match, Alice?" she asked softly. Daniel's sister whipped about to face her. "The gentleman who sees you for you. Who appreciates your spirit and doesn't wish to stifle it. The gentleman who will respect your name, but also defend your honor, if need be. The gentleman who doesn't wish to change you, but who helps you to see the greatness you are capable of. Trust your heart, listen to your mind, and you will find him." Those were the hopes she herself had once carried, that had also been buried in that trunk and tucked away where all dreams went to die.

Alice looked at Daphne with dewy eyes. Alice sank to a knee beside her. "That is beautiful," she breathed. "Have you ever known a gentleman such as that?"

I thought I did. Ultimately men of all stations, be they merchants or members of the peerage, with an appreciation for perfection would never look upon a woman so disfigured and see in her a match. Nor did they truly see anything in another like her; nothing beyond a charity case. "I haven't," she said quietly. "But that does not mean he does not exist," she added for the girl's benefit. In truth, she lied. At nearly thirty years of age, she'd long ago given up on the dream of the gentleman she'd described for Alice. Such dashing heroes existed in nothing more than the pages of books.

"I overheard what you said to my brother."

Daphne's mind raced. There had been the discussions in his carriage and back at Winterbourne Manor prior to their departure, and peppered within all those exchanges had been roguish innuendos and seductive comments from him that his sister had no place hearing. That no lady had any place hearing. "Uh…" She wet her lips.

"I know I should not listen at keyholes," the young girl said quickly, wholly misunderstanding the reason for her hesitation. "But I did and I heard what you said to Daniel about my happiness being important and reminding him that I am certainly not a ship."

She swallowed a groan. The girl had been listening belowstairs a short while ago. *Oh, please don't let her have heard all the talk about peignoirs and naughty parties.*

"I had feared Daniel would rush to wed me off as quickly as possible so he could resume his scandalous pursuits," Alice said. "As you said to him."

Oh, God, the girl had heard that. Daphne's cheeks burned hot. There was no doubt the young lady had listened in on too much. "Your brother will not do such a thing," she assured her charge.

"Do you believe that?" Alice retorted, eyeing her curiously.

"Yes," she said truthfully. Prior to their meeting in the library, that assurance would have been an empty one. But she'd witnessed his battle plans and his red neck and cheeks as she'd put her accusations to him. For the indifference he presented to the world, there was still some humanity left in Daniel Winterbourne. Something shifted in her chest. A lightness in knowing he'd not lost all of himself to wickedness.

"But for holidays and a handful of weeks in the summer, I see my brother not at all," Alice informed her. "I spent more time at Mrs. Belden's because Daniel didn't wish me underfoot." The sadness in those words tugged at Daphne. Alice would have never known Daniel as he'd been before Alistair's death. Joyful. Teasing. Loyal.

She held the young girl's gaze. "Given his rakish existence," short of abandoning his pursuits, which he never would, "sending you away was the honorable recourse."

"You know him better than I," Alice added casually.

Once she had. "Me?" No longer. A memory flitted in of her first ball; her seated on the sidelines among the wallflowers as he entered to the whispers and admiration of the crowd.

"The servants used to talk about how you and he were quite close." The girl's revelation snuffed out that remembrance.

They had been the *best* of friends. Again, time changed them all. Her heart pulled with the poignant reminder. "He was my friend," she said softly. "And it is how I know that despite your worries, your brother will not see you wed to the first suitor to come along." He was desperate to wed her off, but she could not believe he'd be one of those ruthless sorts. "He'll listen to your opinion." His asking her for help, when most gentlemen wouldn't humble themselves by revealing a weakness, was testament to that. "Now you should go rest."

As she herself desperately intended to, in the privacy of her thoughts without Daniel traipsing through her mind; of the way they'd once been and the dreams she'd once carried.

"Do you know," Alice said coming to her feet. "I agree, Daphne, and I also believe it is because of your influence. The servants would tell me about your friendship. Daniel will listen to you."

She managed a lopsided smile. The young lady gave her far more credit than was due where her rakish brother was concerned. After the girl had skipped from the room, leaving Daphne alone, yet again, she layered herself back onto the bed and closed her eyes. She wanted to sleep. She wanted to close her eyes and forget the precariousness of her situation that had found her in this unlikeliest of places. And more, to forget Daniel with his teasing eyes and naughty words who stirred a dangerous hungering deep inside.

Her eyes popped open and she stared overhead. The fire cast shadows upon that bucolic scene painted above. It was futile. The irony was not lost on her. All she'd wanted was to climb into bed and lose herself in sleep and forgetfulness and now her thoughts ran amok making such a feat impossible.

The truth was, not even two days ago, she would have possessed the same reservations about Daniel's intentions for and of his sister. Her one Season alone and the reports she'd read in the gossip columns, and the same gossip to follow him into the country, had proven he had gone from loyal, steadfast friend to cold, empty-hearted rake.

It had been easy to despise the life he lived and to disavow him and all he represented. By very nature of that title rake, the one he so prided himself on, he was very much Lord Leopold. Or so she would have said—two days ago.

But he had proven remarkably unlike anyone she'd known since that long ago fall. From servants to villagers to the lords and ladies in London, men and women who looked at her with varying degrees of pity, disgust, or not at all. By nature of her disfigurement, she'd found herself unwed, unemployable, existing on the fringe of the world for so long.

Until Daniel.

He'd offered her first real, *meaningful* employment, dismissing her disability and seeing her as more capable than any credited. Yes, desperation had driven that offer, but he was an earl—a powerful earl who still had the funds for wardrobes and balls, and surely there was coin enough for an appropriate companion. Nonetheless, he'd hired her and had called her belowstairs without thinking of the injury that plagued her. Because he still saw *her*. When no one truly saw her beyond the uselessness of her limb. A woman who had been coddled by her father and the handful of servants in his employ. And pitied by everyone else.

Yes, two days ago, she would have said she hated Daniel. Hated him for being a disloyal friend who'd not been there when she most needed him. Hated him for not having been the one beacon in a lonely London world for a girl relegated to the status of wall-flower. But he'd cast shadows and doubts upon everything she'd believed about the careless rake.

Mayhap there is still good in him...

As soon as the thought slid in, she slapped her hands over her face. "Do not be silly," she muttered into the quiet. She was making castles out of sand and, invariably, the rains always came. She would do well to remember that. Daniel might have offered her employment, but she should not lose sight of the necessity that had driven that request and his eagerness to be free of his responsibilities. Nor should she forget the danger in his pretty words.

Four gowns and a peignoir...

As though a gentleman who took wicked widows and glorious creatures to his bed would ever feel anything less than revulsion for her imperfect form. Not that she wished him to. She didn't.

Filled with a restlessness, Daphne flung her arms wide and stared up at the ceiling, attempting to shove Daniel from her mind.

...If you wish to attend one of those wicked parties, there is always an invitation for you...

A painful laugh escaped her. It was futile. There would be no sleep. And it was not fear of again seeing Lord Leopold, the bastard she'd gifted her virtue to. Or facing the *ton*, again. Or worry of what would become of her after this.

It was Daniel. It was always Daniel.

CHAPTER 8

¶IT WAS A UNIVERSAL TRUTH that every woman, regardless of station, status, or level of wit and beauty, enjoyed a visit to the modiste. Or, it had been a universal truth, until Daphne Smith had gone and shattered it.

The lady stood with her head tipped back, the sharp lines of her cheeks etched in planes of equal parts horror and terror as she gazed upon the establishment. She stole a frantic look down the street and, for a long moment, Daniel expected the lady to bolt in the opposite direction as far and as fast as her legs could carry her. With her determination, she could outpace any man should she so wish.

But now, given that horror, the last place she wished to be was here.

"Oh, how exciting," Alice piped in, the excitement in her tone contrasting sharply with Daphne's behavior. "Just so we are clear, I am not wearing white and ivory, Daniel."

He cuffed her under the chin. "I've no idea what is appropriate for a lady. We will have to defer to Miss Smith."

His words had the intended effect, springing Daphne into movement. "I don't—"

"Then, we shall defer to Madame Thoureaux," he offered up, instead.

She looked blankly at him and he favored her with a wink.

His sister rushed ahead, yanking the door open, and Daniel gestured for Daphne to enter. The lady wet her lips and cast a single, longing look back at his carriage. He dipped his head close to hers. "Miss Smith, they are gowns and shifts and chemises, not venomous snakes and spiders."

The fire in her eyes was enough to singe a man. "You cannot speak of a lady's undergarments in the street," she hissed, frantically searching her gaze about at the curious passersby staring on.

He motioned with his hand. "Then, come inside," he paused. It was unconscionable to deliberately bait her. "So we may discuss them in here." But he'd never been accused of having a conscience.

Daphne emitted a strangled, choking sound and hurried inside.

He closed the door behind them and as it closed in their wake, it set the tinny bell ajingle. Madame Thoureaux, the small, turban-wearing woman rushed forward, speaking in a hideous rendition of a French accent.

"My lord, I zee you have brought me," she jolted to a stop, flaring her eyes as they settled on Daphne, "another…" She passed a critical stare over the redhead, her gaze lingering on the wooden cane. The proprietress grimaced. "…*lovely* creature to attire."

Daphne stiffened and he stole a sideways glance. Her thin shoulders brought back, she elongated that long, graceful neck with a regal grace befitting a queen.

At the thinly veiled attempt at the modiste's disdain, fury stirred. He opened his mouth, but Daphne cut into the scathing comment on his lips with a pleading look. "Indeed," he said in clipped tones. "My sister," he motioned to Alice who stood assessing bolts of fabric. "And her companion, Miss Smith." The modiste swung her eyes back to Daphne and understanding dawned.

"*Of course*, she is zee *companion*."

Of course. Daniel stitched his eyebrows into a single line.

Madame Thoureaux clapped once. "I will see to zee young lady."

"Miss Smith will also require garments befitting her station as companion," he informed the woman. He could all but see her eyes counting the coins before she rushed off to aid his sister.

One of the woman's assistants came forward to collect Daphne, who made a sound of protest. Her desperate gaze found his, but he winked, studying her as the younger woman urged her over to the fabrics.

Daphne now occupied, he strolled over to the pillar at the center of the shop and continued to watch her. Periodically, the assistant would hold up a fabric and she would nod, her lips moving in a polite declination.

He folded his arms at his chest. The modiste had made the erroneous, though certainly not unfounded, conclusion about Daphne's status. On any day and any occasion, the last place he'd care to be was at a modiste with his sister. However, this was not solely his sister here—it was Daphne—and as such, he'd mustered the fraternal devotion and foregoing the pleasures of his clubs, had, instead, sought out more proper pursuits.

A slow grin that would have made any proper companion or mama fearful curved his lips. Daphne was not his lover and with her hideous chignon and ill-fitting garments, bore no hint of the stunning creatures he usually accompanied to this very shop. Given her status as his onetime friend, he'd not given much thought to more than her generous lips and long neck. Now he deepened his scrutiny. There was a restrained beauty to her that proved his reputation as rake. For he wanted to tug those pins out and allow her crimson curls to cascade about her in a waterfall. He roved an eye over her, taking her in with male appreciation.

When she'd stormed his home and demanded the return of that child's treasure she'd found long ago, he'd not assessed her with his usual rakish critiquing. Now, he rectified that failing. At five or so inches shorter than his own six-foot three-inch frame, she stood taller than most men. Even the cane she relied upon could not detract from her willowy grace. Small breasts. Narrow waist and intriguingly generous hips that fair begged for a man to sink his fingers in as he settled himself between her cream white thighs.

The object of his scrutiny glanced up from another bolt of yellow the assistant lifted for her inspection and their gazes collided. Those emerald eyes deepened to a rich jade. Did she sense the hungering running through him even now? To lay her down on the crimson satin fabric on display and make love to her as she so desperately needed?

Shoving away from the pillar, Daniel stalked forward, coming around the table to where she stood conversing with the assistant. The young woman stopped mid-sentence and looked to him. "Emerald satin," he directed. "The lady requires an emerald satin with a black lace overlay and Austrian crystals adorning the décolletage."

"Brown and grey will suffice," Daphne quickly countered, holding up one of those dreary fabrics.

Alas, a lord's word in these establishments may as well have belonged to God Almighty himself. Daniel inclined his head. "Greens and blues. Rich hues." He assessed her once more, lingering his gaze on her modest décolletage. "A daring neckline."

Daphne gasped, slapping her fingers over her mouth. He was the bastard all knew him to be, because a grin played on his lips at her outrage. The assistant rushed off to search for the respective fabrics. "This isn't appropriate, Dan...my lord," she said in hushed tones, as soon as they were alone.

It had always been one of his greatest joys as a youth, baiting and teasing Daphne Smith. "What is that?" The lure was just as strong, all these years later. "Me properly attiring my sister's very proper companion?"

The lady met his gaze. "A daring décolletage is never—" He winked at her and those words ended swiftly. She retreated a step.

"Ah, but a daring décolletage is always appropriate," he murmured, continuing his slow pursuit as she limped awkwardly away from him. Retreating, making her way down the aisle.

"Companions do not don gowns of emerald and sapphire with black lace overlay and daring décolletage."

Companions in his employ would. Particularly this one. He'd not have her covered up like an abbess in a nunnery. Not when he wished to see her willowy form displayed before him. "Tell me, Daphne," he whispered. "Why does a siren with crimson-kissed hair hide that beauty behind tight coiffures and ill-fitting garments?"

She wet her lips and his gaze took in that slight, seductive gesture. Blood surged to his shaft and he fought the hungering to dip his head ever so slightly and make love to her mouth. After all, a beautiful woman was a beautiful woman and what was the point unless he was kissing one. "There is neither the money nor the need for expensive garments, Daniel," she said with a matter-of-factness that dulled his desire. "I am a woman of nearly thirty years."

"You are eight and twenty." She started and he swiftly lowered his arms to his side, his heart thudding. He didn't know those personal details about a lady. Daniel drew in a breath and forced himself to calm. Of course, this was Daphne. Entirely different knowing things about her.

She paused alongside a table and trailed her fingertips over a shimmery orange material that harkened back to days spent watching sunrises with this woman then child, at his side. Yes, she was nearly thirty and, yet, how little she'd changed in some ways.

"You always hated dresses, Daphne Smith," he said bemusedly, starting as that remembrance was pulled from somewhere inside.

"Not always," she said softly, still smoothing her palm over the fabric with a loving caress. God, how he envied that bolt of material. "The girl you last knew didn't stay that same person. She grew up. *I* grew up," she amended. "You were just not around to see it." Was it his own desiring that accounted for his hearing the wistful regret there?

"No, I was not," he conceded. After Alistair's death and his mother's passing, the only person to remind him of his past, had been this tall, slender figure before him. As such, it had been easy to sever her thread from the fabric of his life. Or he believed it had been easy. He balled his hands. "Who did she become?" he asked softly.

"A silly dreamer." She stilled the distracted movements of her fingers and studied those long digits as though she could divine the meaning of life from them. An unexpected, inexplicable hungering to know what caused the ache of regret in that soft admission.

"We all begin as dreamers, Daphne," he said quietly as he, a self-absorbed bastard who'd not given a jot about anyone, sought to reassure. The same hold she'd had over him as a girl, remained, all these years later. There had always been an ease between them and time hadn't erased it. He motioned to the table and she followed that gesture with her gaze. "Wearing grey skirts and brown dresses cannot undo the regrets we carry." As soon as those words left his mouth, a frisson of disquiet went through him. He wasn't one of those gents with meaningful words for *anyone*.

Daphne raised her eyes to his, eyes that had always seen so much. "Neither will donning black jackets and false smiles. And yet, we each survive in our own way, don't we?" His body stilled under the piercing insight; words that suggested the life he lived was nothing more than a carefully crafted façade. "I'm no longer a dreamer," she said, that calm pragmatism at odds with the frisson of panic unfurling in his belly. "I'm a practical woman. Logical. And I wish to live a life of purpose."

A life of purpose. His very existence made a mockery of her goals; serving as an always present reminder of his father's words that he had made true with time. He gave her a slow, practiced grin, needing a protective space between them. He neither wanted, nor needed, Daphne rousing any feelings in him. "Do you know what I live for, Miss Smith?" he whispered, with that slight formality erecting that barrier. He continued approaching her.

Daphne gave her head a slight shake and God love that slight movement that dislodged her rotten chignon and freed a crimson strand as it was meant to be free.

"Pleasure," he purred.

She paled and her freckles stood stark in her cheeks. She backed up. "You're trying to shock me." There was a breathless quality to her accusation better suited for whispered endearments behind chamber doors.

"Yes," he whispered. "Is it working?"

"I wiped your tears when you cried after I bloodied your nose. I cannot be shocked by someone I've known that long, D–Daniel." That faint tremble made a lie of her bravado.

With every step, she moved deeper and deeper into the shop as he intended, pulling them away from the flurry of activity while his sister pored through fabrics with the modiste. Daphne's back knocked against a pillar, ending her retreat. She glanced about as he came to a stop before her.

Raising an arm, he rested his palm above her head, effectively trapping her, standing so close his chest brushed the soft flesh of her breasts. A wave of lust bolted through him as her eyes briefly clouded with passion. "If you cannot be shocked, then I'll tell you how I live for the blissful surcease that can only be found when you lose yourself in another body." For in those empty exchanges, where there was a moment of mindless ecstasy, he could then forget. Forget that everyone who loved him had died. His mother. His brother. And that of those who remained, was him, the Devil's spawn, as his father had dubbed him. "For everything melts away in the throes of lovemaking. Where you live for nothing but feeling."

"I am not one of your lightskirts," she whispered as he shielded her with his body.

"No," he conceded. "But…" *You could be.*

By the regret in her eyes, she braced for that improper offer.

He tried to push out the words intended to shock and hurt. To give them to her, the truest words; he'd like to lay her down and explore her body in every way, releasing her from the bonds that held her, until she exploded in climactic joy. What had become as a means to push her away and protect himself, now became something altogether more real, dark, and dangerous. *I want her…* Shock slammed into him. He, who reviled innocence and goodness, hungered for her.

As if the fates sought to remind him of exactly the kind of man he was, a soft, husky purr sounded over his shoulder. "Lord Montfort, I thought you'd never return from the countryside." He wheeled around. The Baroness Shelley, an overblown creature, a lady he'd taken as his lover on and off through the years stood there, regarding him through catlike eyes. Her smoky lashes lowered as she fingered the vast expanse of flesh spilling over her plunging neckline.

It was a sight that should inspire lust, if not at the very least, appreciation. Instead, a wave of annoyance hit him at her untimely interruption. "Baroness," he greeted smoothly, while Daphne slinked away. He positioned himself between the two women, but the baroness merely angled her head.

She surveyed Daphne for a brief moment and then, with a haughty flick of her head, sauntered closer to him.

He frowned. How easily this woman and the modiste dismissed Daphne. Yet, with the women side by side, he appreciated Daphne's understated beauty and elegance more. From over the wanton widow's shoulder, he followed Daphne's movements as she limped around the opposite side of the table and made her way to his sister's side.

Baroness Shelley layered herself to him, calling his attention, once more, up. "I often think of our night together." Her lips tilted up in a seductive, calculating grin. She trailed a searching hand up his leg, brushing him through his breeches.

His skin pricked with the feel of knowing eyes at the front of the shop. And by God, if he, Daniel Winterbourne, the Earl of

Montfort, didn't find himself with a hot neck for a second time in the course of a bloody day. He artfully disengaged the lady's glove-less hand and raised it to his mouth for a smooth, practiced, and deterring kiss. "Just the one?" he countered easily, with ease that only came from years as Society's most notorious rake.

She tossed her head back and an emotionless, husky laugh spilled past her lips. "I have thought of many of our nights together, but the night of your orgy, particularly," she whispered. The lady stretched up on tiptoes and pressed her lips close to his ear. "You've an invitation to my bed this evening, my lord." The rose fragrance that clung to her skin hung heavy and cloying, nearly choking him. So very different from the delicate scent liberally dabbed upon another lady's skin.

He glanced up. His and Daphne's gazes collided and cheeks afire, she swiftly returned her attention to a bolt of fabric held up for her inspection.

What in blazes was this fascination with Miss Daphne Smith and why did he not feel so much as a stirring of lust for the wanton creature against him, even now?

SHE SHOULD NOT BE SHOCKED. Nor scandalized. Nor even the faintest bit surprised that Daniel Winterbourne had gone from an ill-attempt at seducing her against a pillar in a modiste's to favoring a lush, stunning beauty courting his favors.

Of course, any attention he bestowed on any woman was a meaningless, artful attempt from a notorious rake. In every way, her imperfect body had earned her derision from those who'd not employ her to gentlemen who'd never noticed her to one noble-man who'd bedded her for no desire other than to add a *cripple* to his list of conquests.

But God help her… Daphne briefly pressed her eyes closed—for one breathless moment, with her back against that pillar and Daniel's body shielding their scandalous exchange from scrutiny, she'd felt very much a woman…a beautiful, desirous one, who yearned to know the passion and desire he spoke of.

For that act he so exquisitely painted was the manner of splen-dor she'd dreamed of and hoped for. In the end, there had been nothing but pain. A quick coupling with skirts yanked about her waist and a man who professed love, rutting between her legs and grunting, while she fought through the agony, seeking the very beauty Daniel had just described.

She forced her gaze back to him and his nameless beauty and allowed the truth of who he was and the truth of the mistakes she had made to sink in with the weight of her previous folly. Lest she become lost in the false defenses she provided his hopeful sister or lured by his easy charm, he was a rake. And ultimately, those rakes took their pleasures where and when they could. Be it against a pillar in a modiste's shop or against a wall inside a host's library with a virginal lady so desperate to know love. Her stomach twisted in remembrance of her own long-ago folly and she balled her hands. She'd not further risk her reputation and her chance of a future at Ladies of Hope.

"*She* looks scandalous." Alice's words penetrated the memories of that night made in folly. "The woman with Daniel," she whispered. "Is that the manner of woman gentlemen prefer?"

Midnight curls, breasts over-spilling the strained bodice of her gown, flawless, unfreckled skin, yes, Daphne rather thought that was precisely the manner of woman gentlemen preferred. Particularly rakes. "I expect some gentlemen," she settled for.

Alice grunted. "Well, I'd hoped Daniel had more discriminating tastes than to take on with that woman. Shamelessly throwing herself at him."

"My lady, I am ready for you," Madame Thoureaux called. The woman rushed over to gather Alice, once more.

Her charge gone, Daphne was left alone on the shop floor with the assistants bustling about, and Daniel and his…his…siren. Or lover. Or whatever they two, in fact, were. Nor did it bother her whether they were something or anything, or nothing. She stole another peek. Daniel still clung to the baroness' fingers. His sister had been incorrect. No throwing necessary. A pebble of jealousy, dark and niggling and very much unwanted, settled in her belly. That green-eyed emotion making a liar of her earlier thoughts.

After endless hours in the miserable shop with Daniel hovering in the corner, they'd finally concluded. Never was she more eager to be free of an establishment.

Holding the door open, Daniel allowed his sister and her companion to move ahead of him. Daphne deliberately held back and followed along at a slower pace behind brother and sister.

Her role in this family was that of servant and, as such, her place was behind them. Propriety dictated as much.

Liar. You just need distance from him. She needed an order over her senses and a restoration of logic, where she could quash his correctly whispered supposition about how she'd hidden herself away these years. What would he say if he knew of her dreams as a woman? A gentleman so driven by his own self-pleasures, he'd, no doubt, sneer and jeer a lady taking employment inside an institution for disabled women.

Staring at his broad shoulders as he lifted his hand in greeting to passing lords, Daphne marveled at the divergent direction their paths had taken. Once they'd danced along the same trail, but somewhere along the way, he'd moved along one where he was this revered, sought after gentleman, so wholly in his element among people of every station. And then there was her. Reserved. Quiet. Eager to shape and make her own way in the world.

But it hadn't always been that way. There had been a time she had thrilled at the adventure of Daniel's world. The balls and soirees, the slide of satin fabric as a maid had helped her into the extravagant piece. Time had proven how useless those scraps were. The immaterial mattering so very much more. And so when she'd left London with her own secret shame all those years ago, she'd been eager to put distance between herself and the mistake of her poor judgment. She'd not looked back with regret. In time, she'd built herself up on the hope and determination to *be* more, when the world insisted she could not.

Now, there was Daniel, the immovable rake, who, by the accountings of him, was nothing more than a shallow, selfish figure. And yet, he'd seen the lie she'd told herself for so many years. He'd looked close enough to see the regret there and that passion she secretly yearned to know.

As they moved over the pavement bustling with pedestrian traffic, Alice assessed the wares in shop windows. Daniel remained as aloof as he'd ever been, not even bothering to glance at Daphne.

"Montfort!" That greeting cut across her tumultuous musings and Daphne slowed her step behind Daniel and Alice. They had stopped to greet the owner of that booming baritone.

"Webb," Daniel returned, impatience lacing that exchange.

Tall, blond, and sporting a similarly cold smile as the one donned by Daniel, the other man's grin painted him as a rogue. But then, would he truly keep company with any other?

She hovered at a safe distance as the gentlemen exchanged slight bows and greetings. Alice dropped a curtsy and returned her attention to perusing the front, dusty window of a bookshop. Just then, the door opened with such alacrity, the wood panel slammed into Alice's hip and she gasped as a patron stepped outside.

Young, with pale blond hair, and a pair of spectacles perched on his nose, the gentleman took one look at Alice and blanched. "Egads, f-forgive me," he stammered, doffing his hat. "I did not—" The young man's words trailed off as he stared wide-eyed at the equally wide-eyed girl.

At the silent, but charged exchanged, Daphne cocked her head.

"Montfort, this graceless clod is my brother, Mr. Henry Pratt," his friend spoke in bored tones.

Mr. Pratt's neck went red and he jammed his hat back on. All the while, he lingered his gaze on Alice. A small blush marred her cheeks as she glanced down at her slippers. The young man shifted a wrapped package under his arm and sketched an awkward bow. "How do you do?" he murmured to Daniel, his stare wandering once more to Alice.

While the necessary introductions were made, Daphne stood a silent observer. The young pair eyed one another with equal interest. A potentially dangerous interest when shown to the wrong suitor, as she knew too well. And yet, where there was a feral glimmer in the man named Webb's eyes, this gentleman's sparkled with kindness. She looked to Daniel. He took in the silent exchange between Alice and Mr. Pratt with a frown.

"You are withholding introductions, chap," Webb chided and Daniel snapped his focus over to the other man who gawked at Daphne's cane.

She reflexively curled her hand hard over the head of her walking stick. Society had a bothersome and unwanted fascination with a disfigured person. Interesting enough to gape at but, by their standards, not worthy enough to hire. She tightened her hold on the wood. ...*you should be honored, Miss Smith. I've never rutted with a cripple before*... Bile burned in her throat and she briefly closed her eyes as the harsh laughter echoed around the chambers of her mind.

Daniel's voice reached across that horror, pulling her back. "May I present my sister's companion, Miss Smith. Miss Smith, Baron Webb, and his brother, Mr. Henry Pratt," he said, his smooth baritone forcing her eyes open. Curiosity wreathed the brothers' expressions.

She shoved aside those old, but still fresh memories. Daniel's brow dipped and he looked at her, a question in his brown eyes. A concern that was oddly harder to take from this man than the wicked glimmer of before. "My lord," she greeted. "Mr. Pratt," she added, dropping a hasty curtsy. She gasped as her leg buckled under the suddenness of her movement. Her cane slid along the ground. Her stomach lurched as she stumbled sideways.

"Miss Smith," Alice cried out.

Daniel instantly shot a hand around her, effortlessly catching her to him and her heart thumped hard as he spared her the indignity of crashing to the cobbles. The weight of his hand at her waist was strong, reassuring, and burning her with the heat of his palm.

"Thank you," she murmured, her face awash with humiliation as she sought to avoid his gaze.

The baron peeled his lip back in a derisive sneer that sent further shame burning through her. Mr. Pratt frowned at his brother and bent to retrieve her cane. "Miss Smith, it was a pleasure," he said gently. Alice's little sigh cut across the busy London street sounds.

Daphne accepted the walking stick and cleared her throat. "Thank you," she said quickly. Webb stole another mocking look at her. She was never more grateful than when the unlikely pair of brothers took themselves off and left her alone with the Winterbournes. As she limped, ahead her movements were met with further scrutiny. The stares from the shopkeepers, lords, and ladies were no less probing now than they'd been all those years ago. Other than an object of sick fascination, Society had little use for a woman such as her.

Daniel was so very wrong. There was nothing thrilling in London. And the sooner she was gone to begin the life she wanted for herself, the happier she would be.

CHAPTER 9

THAT AFTERNOON, DANIEL HAD EARNED so many reproachful sideways stares from Daphne that he began to think he'd be better just giving her those damned references she wished for and sending her on her way. The only reason he kept her on in her post was his own need of a companion for Alice.

He told himself that. Mayhap, if he repeated that mantra, he'd come to believe it.

Having tolerated enough of the lady's obvious letdown, Daniel had taken his leave quite gladly of his townhouse. Given the Baroness Shelley's offer that afternoon, there was only one place he should be. And on any other day, would be.

...I am not one of your lightskirts, Daniel...

Except, this night.

Not for the first time since his uncle's ultimatum, he cursed the old bastard whose orders for no scandals or wicked behaviors had seen him at White's, instead of his other wicked clubs. For if he hadn't cut off the remaining funds and, more importantly, Alice's tuition at finishing school, Daniel would even now be at Forbidden Pleasures with a whore, mayhap two, on his lap.

Or, in the baroness' bed.

And there would have been no Daphne Smith, the straitlaced, purse-mouthed lady in desperate need of several uninterrupted evenings of lovemaking and who retained a grip on his musings. For reasons that, for the first time with any woman, moved beyond a sexual hungering.

Such madness accounted for his presence at White's, the sole intention to forget his unwitting fascination with her.

By God, she was *Daphne*, the freckled girl who'd been at his side whenever he spent his days in the country. Only now, she was Daphne, the fiery-tempered siren, independent and strong. A fearless woman, who'd stormed his estate and demanded references. A woman who'd make her way in the world not by cheating others or selling parts of her soul the way he had—but through unwavering strength and, in that, wholly unlike any other lady he'd known before her.

There was something tantalizing about a woman who didn't preen or fawn or wished to be fawned over, but rather commanded control of her life.

He rolled his snifter of brandy back and forth between his hands. Why could Miss Daphne Smith not stay relegated to the corner of his mind where forgotten souls dwelled?

"Montfort."

He looked to the two gentlemen now interrupting his musings, grateful for the distraction. "Webb," he greeted jovially, gesturing to the open seat across from him. It was in bad form to drink and carouse alone. Surely there had to be some Parliamentary rule against it. If not, it certainly deserved a look in the House of Lords.

The baron commandeered one chair while Mr. Pratt hovered, shifting back and forth. That telling discomfort was at odds with the carefree gentlemen Daniel kept company with. Nor was Webb the devoted familial sort to drag his brother around. Curiosity piqued, Daniel gestured to the other vacant chair. With a hurried thanks, the young man plopped himself down.

A servant came over and quickly deposited tumblers before the other gentlemen and then, with a bow, took his leave.

Webb tipped back on the legs of his chair. "I could not fathom what God-awful business was keeping a gentleman who so despises the country away from London."

Daniel reached a hand out to shove the bottle across the mahogany table to the baron.

"But then I saw the *delightful* creature you're squiring about London and it became clear," the man finished.

Daniel tightened his mouth. "The delightful creature you refer to is, in fact, my sister." As such, even rakes had to adhere to some form of rules where at least their sisters were concerned.

Mr. Pratt frowned, a dull flush staining his cheeks. "Forgive my brother for his—"

His friend chuckled, cutting into the younger man's apology. "I referred to your Miss Smith. Quite an interest—" He grunted. "Did you kick me?" The younger man glared in return. The two shared an unspoken, lengthy look, and then Webb sighed. "My brother is interested in the *other* lady."

The other lady? Daniel cocked his head. Who in blazes was the other lady they referred—?

"Lady Alice," Mr. Pratt put forward in solemn tones.

Lady Alice? *My sister*? He rubbed his hands briefly over his ears. Surely he'd misheard the other man?

"My brother wants to court your sister," Webb interjected, confirming there was nothing, in fact, wrong with Daniel's hearing.

Both men stared at him. By their probing expressions, they sought a response. This was no bloody diversion from thoughts of Daphne. This was…well, the infernal rubbish he could do without. Society well-knew the Pratt family was in as dire financial straits as the Winterbournes. As second-son, Henry Pratt would have even less prospects and wealth than Webb. He wished to have Alice off his hands but into wealthy ones. Hands that could possibly benefit Daniel. Henry Pratt offered nothing to Daniel *or* Alice.

Mr. Pratt coughed into his fist. "I am a barrister." A barrister. In short, no wealth there. As though he'd followed Daniel's drawn conclusion, he continued on a rush. "I have recently built my own business and, though Lady Alice certainly could and should marry a titled man," a *wealthy* man., "I still seek permission to court her."

Daniel studied the eager-eyed, would-be suitor. *Court her.* An impoverished barrister without a farthing to his name? Nay, Alice would have a fat in the purse duke or marquess.

Webb looked back and forth between them. "You can be free of the girl and free to carry on with the companion," Webb reminded him with a cynical smile.

Daniel's fingers jerked and he knocked the crystal decanter over. Webb hopped to his feet, cursing softly, as the fine liquor spilled on the table and over the floor.

"Bloody hell, Montfort," Webb groused, while servants rushed over to tidy the mess. "A crime to waste good spirits."

At any other time, Daniel would have been in full agreement. He sighed and motioned for another bottle. Alas, such hopes of forgetting the minx now residing in his ramshackle townhouse were not to be.

"Granted she is not your usual tastes," Webb murmured as a servant came forward and set another bottle between them.

Mr. Pratt again coughed into his hand. "We were discussing Lady Alice."

"She is my sister's companion," Daniel continued over the other man. A woman who wasn't afraid to go toe-to-toe with him and challenge him at every turn. Annoyance went through him at how easily she'd slipped back into his thoughts.

"Yes, Lady Alice," the tenacious barrister neatly slipped in. "The young woman whom I wish to—"

The baron snorted and proceeded to pour himself a drink.

What in blazes did that bloody snort mean? "What?" Daniel snapped.

Webb kicked back on the hind legs of his chair and sipped his drink. "I would rather talk about the companion you're tupping than the proper miss my brother wishes to court."

Daniel gnashed his teeth. "I am not tupping her," he gritted out. *I want to.*

Webb chuckled. "You never met a creature you wouldn't bed."

Yes, that was true. So why did he want to bury his fist in the baron's nose for that matter-of-fact statement? "This woman is different." Even if he did want to make love to her until the words *proper* never left her lips again. Swiping his glass off the table, Daniel grimaced. By God, had he, in fact, uttered those words? And he, previously grateful for the other gentleman's interruption, wanted to send him to the Devil with all his talk of—

"Ah, of course. You do have more discriminating taste than to bed a cripple."

A seething haze of red rage descended over his vision. The tumbler cracked under the force of his grip.

"Good God," Webb groused as another stream of liquid poured onto the table. "You are already in your cups."

Actually, he had been nursing the same goddamn brandy for an hour, which if revealed or discovered would result in the demise of his reputation as whispered about reprobate. As such, he quite contentedly left the other man to his erroneously drawn opinion. "Get out," he said through tightly clenched teeth. "Both of you," he said, directing that to the young barrister whose cheeks had gone ashen. At least the man had the sense his brother was missing.

The baron scratched at his creased brow. "What?"

A shadow fell over the table and they looked up. Cedric Falcot, the Marquess of St. Albans, Daniel's closest friend, stood above them; the only figure between Webb and a bloody beating that would have seen him rid of his teeth.

"Get out. I'm meeting with St. Albans," he ordered.

"Webb," St. Albans greeted, as the baron rose to his feet with as much dignity as a man who'd just gotten ousted from the respective table. "Pratt."

Mr. Pratt reluctantly followed suit. Good, he was just as eager to be rid of the lovesick swain with designs upon Alice. The girl, at least, deserved a man with a fortune.

"St. Albans," the baron returned stiffly.

The gentlemen traded places, with Lord Webb and his brother stalking off.

"What was that about?" St. Albans drawled. Outside of Daphne, St. Albans had been the closest thing Daniel had known to a true friend. A friendship of which, after taking coin from the other man's sire to ferret information back and forth between son and father, Daniel was wholly undeserving of. Still, he was a selfish enough bastard that he'd gladly be rid of Webb for the familiarity of St. Albans.

"His presence grew tiresome," he muttered. Infuriating. Tiresome. All the same thing. First the younger, untitled chap wanting to wed Alice and then Webb... He growled. A servant came forward with a glass.

St. Albans held his hand up in declination and the liveried footman made to retreat.

"I will take that," Daniel mumbled, slipping the tumbler from the younger man's hands. Pouring himself another glass, he looked at his friend. "Difficulty with the wedded state?"

The other man offered a smile, one devoid of the sardonicism that had long been inherent in his grin. ... *That is not a smile, Daniel. That is an empty, dark expression that could never be disguised as anything good...* "Anything but," the marquess said softly. So that was the real smile Daphne spoke of. Who knew rakes, rogues, or scoundrels were capable of it? "Genevieve is expecting."

Kicking back on the legs of his chair, Daniel took a long swallow and then cradled his tumbler between his hands. "Expecting what?" he asked, furrowing his brow.

"A babe." Amusement curled St. Albans' lips up at the corners. "We are expecting a babe."

His chair teetered forward and landed on its fours. The abrupt movement sent liquid splashing over the rim of his glass. "A child?"

St. Albans chuckled. "You know, the manner of offspring born to the human sort."

As long as he'd known St. Albans, the other man had vowed to never become a father. With his own bastard of a sire, he'd commiserated, but Daniel had also well-accepted who he himself was. A useless rake, who killed all who loved him and, as such, he'd little need to ever propagate the world with heirs, bastards, or any other kind of babes. St. Albans' father must be triumphant. "So the Duke of Ravenscourt has won after all," he said slowly, giving his head a regretful shake.

His friend folded his arms. "I rather believe Genevieve and I have won."

Those protestations didn't fit with who St. Albans had been the whole of his life. "But, you never even wanted a bloody babe."

Another laugh rumbled from the marquess' lips and he leaned forward to pat Daniel on his arm. "As I told you last summer, I love my wife. I want a family with her. I expect someday you will—"

"What has torn you away from such marital bliss?" he smoothly interjected. Rakes didn't talk about matters of the heart. Hell, rakes didn't even posses the bloody organs. "At this late hour."

St. Albans studied Daniel's still nearly full decanter. Did he gauge how much he had consumed this evening? Yes, wedded bliss did odd things to a fellow. Swearing off brandy, smiling about babes... Daniel would sooner duel the Devil than walk that path. St. Albans fished around the inside of his jacket and tossed a thick ivory velum note onto the table. A familiar ivory velum. "I paid a visit to your residence, to see what the urgent matter requiring my assistance was, but found you, uh," St. Albans winged an eyebrow up, "otherwise absent to discuss said urgent matter."

Daniel cursed. Of course. Yes, there'd been the note sent 'round because he did really require help. The second bloody person he'd been forced to turn to. Daphne's flashing green eyes flitted through his vision and he swiped his glass up and took a drink.

"I did wait, before your butler directed me here." St. Albans paused. "*Not* Forbidden Pleasures."

"*Not* Forbidden Pleasures," Daniel grumbled, recalling the urgent matter that had led to the missive. Or rather, the other urgent matter that was not his unwitting fascination with the fiery-tempered Daphne. At the other man's questioning glance, he proceeded to inform him of Lord Claremont's demands that had resulted in Daniel's presence in the very proper club.

"I see," St. Albans murmured. "You can trust Genevieve and I will lend our support to Lady Alice." How free the other man was with that generosity, when Daniel had betrayed his confidence all for some coin handed him by St. Albans' father.

An unexpected guilt knotted his belly. "Thank you." He managed to force those two words out, when he used them sparingly to not at all.

"We are friends," the marquess said with a casual shrug.

Of which, St. Albans was the far better one.

The marquess drummed his fingertips on the table. "During my wait, I had the pleasure of meeting with Lady Alice." Had the two ever met before that? Odd, Daniel had known St. Albans nearly the whole of his life and couldn't recall such a meeting. "As well as her companion."

He stiffened, eyeing him warily. As a friend and rake, he'd no doubt view Daniel's lust for the spirited woman on his person. Instead, St. Albans continued to drum a staccato beat on the smooth, mahogany surface. When it became apparent the other man intended to say nothing more on it, Daniel let some of the tension from his shoulders. "Miss Daphne Smith." A long litany of black curses paraded through his mind. Of course, the other man wouldn't let the matter rest. "Yes. Miss Smith."

"The same Miss Daphne Smith whom you were friends with as a child."

As St. Albans words were more a statement than anything. Daniel continued sipping away at his drink.

"An *interesting* choice of a companion."

Did he imagine the suspicion underlying that casual observation? Daniel grunted. "It was mutually advantageous for the lady and me." And he'd say nothing more on it to this man or anyone.

His friend gave a casual nod. "Of course, you've never been one to do anything unless it was in some way beneficial to you."

Had there been rancor or condemnation, mayhap it would have been easier than St. Albans' absolute pragmatism. Daniel set his jaw. "Yes, well, I must see Alice launched," *She is not a ship, Daniel.* "Married off," he corrected. "And the sooner she makes a match," a worthwhile match. "the sooner—"

"You may return to your debauched ways?" This time, the healthy dose of disappointment there, he met St. Albans' eyes.

"Precisely." Daniel nodded and took another sip. He'd neither the time, care, nor inclination to indulge a censorious friend. Particularly one who'd spent more than a decade either rivaling or surpassing Daniel in the area of debauchery. He paused. And yet, he'd lived the whole of his adult life believing a rake could not be reformed—and certainly not happily. How singularly…*odd* to have St. Albans prove that long-held truth wrong. Unnerved, Daniel avoided the other man's eyes.

St. Albans remained quiet, looking about the crowded club, where gentlemen tossed away small fortunes all in a bid to feel something of life. "I am worried about you."

Daniel tightened his grip hard around his tumbler. "I assure you, there is nothing to worry about." Which was a lie. His country estates were crumbling. Creditors frequently called. Possessions required liquidating. "My uncle has dangled a fortune above my head, enough to temporarily reform even the staunchest rake, if even for a Season." The eight thousand would allow Daniel to carry on his depraved existence for several years. That thought should bring comfort. Instead, it heightened this odd restlessness churning in his gut.

"I'm not worried about your finances," St. Albans clarified.

"Splendidly loyal friend, chap," Daniel lifted his glass in mocking salute.

"I worry, that you're continuing down the same path to ruin."

At those charges, eerily reminiscent to Daphne's, the lady's sad, disapproving eyes and smile came to mind. He gritted his teeth. So there would be no forgetting Daphne Smith this day—or any day.

How much easier it had been when everyone had quite accepted him as an unrepentant rake. Now, Daphne had reentered his life, challenging him, nay worse, expecting him to be the same boy she remembered from their past. And here was St. Albans, come to do the same.

His patience snapped. Daniel planted his elbows on the table and leaned forward with such speed he spilled several droplets over the rim of his glass. "I do not need your worrying after me like a protective mama and I certainly do not require guidance on life from a man who lived the exact same existence for nearly his entire life," he hissed, spoiling for a fight.

"Of course." St. Albans proved again the better man and Daniel's annoyance stirred at that reminder. He'd far preferred it when they'd been equal in their rottenness. Remarkably cool, the marquess lifted his head in acknowledgement. "I will withhold my concerns, but trust Genevieve and I will support Lady Alice in any capacity she should require." The other man pushed back his chair. "If you'll excuse me, I'm home to my wife." He touched his fingertips to his forehead in a parting.

Daniel stiffly nodded. "Thank—"

"Again, there is no need to thank me. We are, after all, friends," the marquess spoke in solemn tones, so vastly different than the ones he'd adopted as a carefree scoundrel.

With that, St. Albans, *reformed* rake, took his leave. Daniel stared after him until he'd departed through the famous white doors at the front of the club. Then with a curse, Daniel tossed back the remainder of his drink and shoved to his feet. There was to be no peace anywhere. Not even his goddamned clubs, it would seem.

His gaze found the long-case clock at the side of the room. At this hour, the enticing Miss Smith would be in her chambers, doing…whatever it is proper ladies did at this hour. Which was, no doubt, sleep. Daniel stalked through the club, ignoring the greetings called out. He accepted his cloak and hat from the servant at the front and then stepped outside, gathering the reins for his mount.

He swung his leg over Satan and nudged the black gelding onward to his residence. He'd but a handful of months, at most, to suffer through proper clubs, dull events, and friendly lectures about his pursuit of wickedness. Alice would be wed, Daphne would be off for her post at the rotted finishing school, and he could continue doing what he'd done since he'd left university—nothing. Nothing, outside of whoring and carousing and drinking and wagering.

He nudged Satan at a quicker clip, frowning into the darkened London night. There should be some relief in thinking of what awaited him…and yet, there was this queer hollowness. "What in blazes is wrong with you?" he muttered, as he reined in his mount outside his Mayfair residence. Exhaustion. Ennui. There was no other accounting for it.

He dismounted and a waiting servant rushed outside to collect the reins. Daniel handed them over and then took the steps two at a time, sailing through the front door. He tossed his hat to the butler. "Tanner," he greeted and started for the stairway.

Under Tanner's bushy eyebrows, the butler's eyes formed perfect circles. "You are retiring *already*, my lord?" the older man blurted.

Daniel faltered and his neck went hot. "Uh, see that a bath is readied," he ordered. With the slack-jawed servant staring after him, he redirected his footsteps to his office and his well-stocked sideboard.

Couldn't a gentleman retire at—Daniel fished around for his watch fob and consulted the timepiece—he choked. Ten in the evening? And with the request for a bath like some aged dowager? Daniel cringed. No wonder his butler had been shocked into insolence. Daniel had not taken to his chambers at this hour in… he searched his mind…well, *ever*. Not the naughty child who'd snuck around his family's estates in the dead of night when none were the wiser. And not as a troublesome student at Eton and then Oxford. And most certainly never as a rake, living for his own amusements.

Daniel continued a brisk clip for his office, when he caught sight of the faint glow of light stretching from the open library doorway. He slowed his steps and peeked around the doorframe. Daphne reclined on the leather button sofa with a book resting on the table across from her.

Continue walking, Daniel Davidson Winterbourne. Continue walking…

Except, Tanner really was correct. It really *was* entirely too early for a chap to retire. And no decent rake worth his salt would seek

his rooms before his sister's proper, often-reprimanding companion.

   Abandoning his previous plans, he lingered at the doorway, eyeing her.

CHAPTER 10

cAT TEN O'CLOCK IN THE evening, a proper spinster, serving as a young lady's companion, would be tucked away inside her chambers.

But then, Daphne wasn't truly the proper lady that Daniel, and the world, took her to be. It was not, however, past wickedness that had her tucked away in the spacious library. Leaning against the arm of the leather button sofa, she stretched her arms forward and then winced as the knotted muscles clenched spasmodically.

Concentrating on her breathing, she laboriously shoved herself back into a reclining position and closed her eyes. In accepting Daniel's offer of employment and coming to London, she'd battled the fear of again facing Lord Leopold and having him reveal to the world that she was more whore than proper lady. She'd worried over entering Polite Society and suffering through their cold, mocking stares and pitying whispers.

But she'd not put proper thought into all the exertions that would be required of her. Thirty-three stairs, climbed countless times. Jaunts through the uneven London streets that were really feats of movement better fitted to the god Achilles. Climbing in a carriage. Climbing out. There was always movement. Constant movement that strained the limits of her body in ways that drew forth all her deepest regrets and frustrations. In dreaming of employment, where she helped formatively shape ladies into the strong figures they should and would become, Daphne had not allowed herself to think about how greatly her leg impaired her work.

She bit the inside of her cheek, despising herself that weakness, and briefly pressed her eyes closed. An unholy desire gripped her to be the carefree girl she'd once been, running through the countryside and not confined to a goddamned leather sofa because her leg was too useless to move. Certainly too useless to manage another thirty-three stairs this night.

Drawing in a slow breath, she again sat up and stretched her fingers toward her knotted calf. That's when the groaning floorboards penetrated the nighttime still. On a gasp, she whipped her gaze to the doorway. Her stomach promptly sank.

Bloody fantastic.

"Hullo, Daphne."

With her leg throbbing as a mocking testament to her own miserable lack of beauty, the last thing she cared to be presented with was the splendidly perfect Daniel Winterbourne with his languid steps and effortless grace.

He leaned one shoulder against the doorjamb. Must he be so smoothly elegant? "I'll give you a hint, Miss Smith," he said on a husky whisper. She damned her heart for tripling its beat. "This is where you return a greeting."

"My lord," she said, despising the breathless timbre to her voice. She gripped her skirts. *Mayhap he'd not heard it. Mayhap…*

His lips curled up in a feral grin better suited a hunter stalking its prey. He pushed away from the doorway. A fledgling hope stirred to life that he'd turn around and—he pulled the door closed. Of course, he'd closet them away. The bounder. "A good companion would, no doubt, rise and curtsy," he continued, slowly advancing.

"I never proclaimed to be a good companion," she muttered, covetously eyeing the wood panel between her and freedom. And there were also those too many steps and thirty-three stairs. She'd not forget those. "You are the one who put the demands to me. I simply wanted my references."

"Your *false* references," he pointed out.

"Given your less than honorable reputation," the one he took such delight in reminding her of, "I—" He stopped before her seat, bringing her gaze directly in line with his thickly corded thighs. Her mouth went dry. She'd scaled trees more narrow than their impressive breadth.

"You were saying?" Daniel drawled and she jerked her head up.

The knowing glint in his chocolate brown eyes sent heat rushing to her cheeks. What had she been saying? What was it…?

He flicked a hand. "Given my less than honorable reputation?"

Oh, yes! Daphne cleared her throat and with all the dignity a lady confined to a sofa for the better part of four hours could manage, proudly angled her chin. "I expected writing on behalf of a former friend was certainly not outside the realm of your moral culpabilities."

He layered his palms to the arm of the sofa. His gloveless fingers brushed the sensitive skin of her nape as he leaned forward. "I don't have any morals. Quite reprehensible, really." Then, he stroked the pad of his thumb along her right earlobe, bringing her eyelashes wildly fluttering. She gave thanks for the dimly lit space and his own positioning that protected her from that telling reaction to his careless caress.

A rake like Daniel had far more fiendish pursuits to attend than teasing her in a library. Alas…

He slid into the leather winged back chair closest to her and proceeded to drum his fingertips on the arms.

She sighed.

"Unable to sleep?" he hazarded.

Daphne forced herself around. She made to lower her legs on the floor, but the joint locked at the knee, suspending movement. Catching the flesh of her lower lip hard between her teeth, she smiled through the agony ripping through that limb.

He stared at her dubiously.

"Yes," she managed when she trusted herself to speak. "I am unable to sleep." Which wasn't altogether *untrue*. If she couldn't get herself abovestairs to her bed, then she certainly wasn't able to sleep. "I take it you do not have any other roguish—"

"Rakish," he neatly slid in.

"—pursuits, demanding your attention?"

Her question brought an immediate cessation to his drumming. "Do you know, Daphne?" he asked, stretching his legs out before him and hooking them at the ankles. "It occurs to me with your frequent questions and mention of my dissolute lifestyle, that you have an inordinate fascination with it."

She stared longingly at his crossed limbs. How easy it was for him. How simple and effortless. And it had once been that way for her, too. Then his words registered and she swiveled her head up to meet his hooded eyes. She snorted. "Do not be silly, Daniel." Despite the opinions he had of her as a straitlaced, virgin spinster, she was no innocent. She certainly knew what a rake's intentions were and where those seductive words and improper glances found a lady.

"Ah," he said, drawing out that syllable as he shoved himself up and dragged his seat closer to her. "So it is *me* you are so fascinated by?"

Daphne forced a laugh, but it emerged as a husky whisper of breath that sounded wicked to her own ears. "Your arrogance knows no bounds. And lest we forget, I am the one who taught you how to bait a hook." That reminder, harkening back to their past, came out more for her benefit than anything.

"But on matters of seduction—"

"You are shameless." She tossed her book at him and he easily caught it. Not bothering to steal a glance at the title, he set it aside.

"You judge me for being a rake," he said straightforwardly. "But at least I live." At his charge, she set her teeth. "What of you? How have you spent the past thirteen years?" Tucked away in her parents' house, reading, and embroidering. God, how she'd despised the tedium of that task she'd always been rubbish at and being confined to the cottage. And in this moment, she despised Daniel for being so bloody accurate. She went tight-lipped, refusing to let him bait her. "Hidden away in the country," he accurately supplied. "When was the last time you danced or swam or played shuttlecock?"

She'd been ten and he'd been almost thirteen. They'd played until the moon chased away the sun. "You know nothing of it," she groused. How dare he presume to know what she'd lost that long ago day and how it had shaped ever day thereafter? Her toes twitched, aching to take part in those long abandoned activities.

He inclined his head. "I gather it's been since your injury, then?" Damn him for being accurate.

People didn't speak of her leg. Instead, they offered pitying stares and low-expectations and, yet, Daniel did not. She appreciated that, but met that with stony silence, anyway.

"Very well," he sighed. "We shall cease all talks of the downcast lady *you've* become—"

"I am not downcast," she gritted out. "I am logical and practical."

"Ah, yes. You said that earlier. We shall also end all mention of my devilish reputation."

She studied him, welcoming the distraction from the pain radiating up her leg and from the too-personal charges he'd leveled. "Do you attach that word to any and every mention of your name to convince others that you are as wicked as the world believes you to be?"

But for a muscle that jumped at the corner of his eye, his body went motionless. "There is no convincing required," he drawled. "I assure you, I'm quite depraved." He fished a silver flask from his jacket, uncorked it, and toasted her. "Just as my father predicted."

She frowned. He'd not always been the immoral figure who thrilled at his own wickedness. Once, he'd been a loyal friend. The boy who'd carried her countless steps when she'd broken her leg. After Lord Alistair's drowning, Daniel had been forever changed— just as his entire family had. "Your father saw good in you," she said quietly. Or he had. Daniel had slowly retreated over the years, so the details of that relationship were now foreign ventures she only made.

Daniel changed positions and kicked his legs out, once again, hooking them at the ankles. "The boy who killed his only *worthy* son?"

His words wrung a painful gasp from her. Surely the once-loving, late earl had not leveled such hateful words on his sole living son? Then, grief did awful things to a person. It turned men into monsters and fiery girls into spiritless creatures. "You didn't kill your brother, Daniel," she said with a firm resolve.

His gaze moved to a point beyond her shoulder. "I couldn't save him." There was an eerie emptiness to his eyes, such agonized pain, that the air lodged in her chest.

Is that why he'd become this empty shell? Mayhap for her earlier charges, he did, in fact, know something about retreating within himself. "Sometimes accidents happen," she said softly, calling his focus back to her. "Sometimes there are wicked rainstorms that see little girls with a broken leg and sometimes young boys get carried away by a violent lake. There can be no undoing those moments."

No matter how much one tortured oneself with dreams of returning to an innocent past.

He gave a casual shrug and took another drink from his flask. "Mayhap, but I am still the dark scoundrel the world takes me for."

"If you have to say it as much as you do, then you are less corrupt than you believe." A lightness filled her at that obvious truth.

He snorted. "And if you believe *that*, then you are a naïve miss who'd do well to watch the rakes and rogues around you."

His words hit her like a fist to the belly and she glanced down at her skirts. Of course, he'd never dare countenance that she, the prim, proper spinster hired to aid his sister, had, in fact, been the naïve miss he accused her of being. And that naiveté had seen her stripped of her virginity in a night of folly. Daphne forced her gaze back to his and found him watching her; the harsh, angular planes of his face set in an inscrutable mask. "Tell me about your profligacy, then, Daniel. Tell me so I can know." And stop seeing good where there, in fact, was none.

He furrowed his brow. It was a remarkable slip in that impressive composure.

"Do you meet widows in alcoves?"

"Yes," he said instantly.

Why did her heart twist at the rapidity of his reply and the images evoked with that single syllable utterance? "Do you bed other men's wives?"

"Undoubtedly." He gave her one of those mirthless half-grins, his pearl white teeth flashing bright in the darkened room. "Sometimes two at the same time."

Disappointment flooded her, filling her with a regret she didn't wish to feel. "And do you dally with debutantes? Offer them pretty words so you might be the first to bed them?" she forced herself to ask.

Daniel chuckled. "I'd never be so gauche as to bother with a virgin." He winked. "Entirely too much work for me."

The tightness in her chest. Yes, Daniel was so quick to present himself as an unrepentant rake. While he might toss around flippant replies about virginal debutantes, his answer stood as proof. "I don't care what your father thought in his misery and grief, or what you've spent these years shaping yourself into. There is good in you," she said gently. Whether he chose to see it or failed to acknowledge it, it was there. And it gave her hope for the boy he'd once been and the man he could still be.

WHY HAD HE DIVULGED THOSE details about his father? Words he'd never shared with anyone.

Mayhap because when he was with her, Daphne didn't fawn or preen over him the way bored ladies of the *ton* did. Rather, she treated him as she *always* had, with a frank directness that knew no boundaries or bounds. And when was the last time anyone called Daniel Winterbourne, *good*?

Certainly not his father, who'd wished him dead too many times to count. Nor his departed mother, who had ceased *seeing* him after Alistair's drowning. Nor the rakes he kept company with. And yet, he'd found the last, solitary soul in the whole kingdom who believed there was good in him, insisted on it even after he'd admitted such scandalous things to her. Words not fit for any respectable lady's ears.

Foolish chit.

He'd even less of a desire to sit here, disabusing her of her foolish notions, than he had of a meaningful discussion on St. Albans' worries about him. Pocketing his flask, Daniel shoved to his feet. "I will allow you to your reading, madam," he said brusquely, sketching a bow. He'd rather lob off his left arm with a dull blade than sit here, resurrecting the memories of his youth.

Daphne inclined her head, but remained in repose. "My lord." She did not stand. Rather, she sat, precisely as she'd been since he'd poked his head in the room and found her here.

Just go, damn it. Go seek out your rooms and drink your brandy. He narrowed his eyes on her face, taking in details that had previously escaped him. The tense lines at the corner of her mouth. The strain around her eyes.

Then the truth slammed into him, briefly robbing him of breath.

She is hurt.

Even after her injury, he'd only ever seen her as the strong-willed girl he'd called friend. He'd never seen limitations because, well, there could never be limitations with Daphne Smith. Her spirit would never allow for it. Yet, here she sat, motionless from an old injury and he didn't know what to do with the realization.

Daphne angled her chin up another notch, all but daring him to voice that discovery aloud. She was as bold and proud as she'd been the day he'd come upon her at the edge of the lake, her leg broken.

With a sigh, Daniel reclaimed his seat.

"What are you—?"

"How long have you been down here?" he interrupted.

"I don't…" He leveled her with a single look and her words trailed off. "Several hours."

By God, she'd always been stubborn. "How many is several?" he asked impatiently.

Daphne lifted her shoulders in a shrug. "Four."

He cursed roundly.

"But I do enjoy your library," she said on a rush.

Daniel swiped her forgotten copy from the arm of the chair. "Oh, yes," he said dryly. "There is *so* much to enjoy." He wagged the aged leather volume before her face. "Colebrooke's, *A Grammar of the Sanskrit Language*, I take is quite riveting?" It remained one of the several hundred titles not carted off by the auctioneers who'd systematically emptied his library shelves.

She shifted in her seat. "It really *is* fascinating stuff."

"Even more so, if you read German," he said, his lips twitching. "Have you acquired a grasp of the German language since we last met?"

Daphne pressed her lips together. "No," she managed to push that denial out through them, anyway.

Setting aside all teasing, Daniel tossed the book aside where it landed on the floor with a loud thump. "You're hurt." Something in breathing aloud that somber charge, knifed at his chest.

"It is nothing," she said quickly.

He thinned his eyes all the more. She'd always been a rotted liar.

With an exasperated sigh, she hurled her arms up. "My leg hurts, is all."

He trailed his gaze down her slender frame and he lingered his stare on those lower limbs expertly concealed by her dress. A desire to tug the fabric back for reasons that moved beyond the sexual, gripped him.

"I promise, I am fine. I'll be able to see to my responsibilities in the morning," she rushed to assure him.

The air froze in his chest. "You believe I'd remove you from your responsibilities because of your leg?" He clenched his jaw. The fire's glow bathed her in light, emphasizing the color that filled her cheeks in a damning testament to that very fact. Hurt stabbed somewhere inside his chest. Hurt and a slow-building anger. He fixed on the anger, the anger was safer. "Hardly speaks to the good you still see in me," he sneered.

Her lips turned down at the corners. "Of course, I do not believe you'd send me away," she said with such matter-of-factness, she knocked him off-kilter. "Not without references." At that weak attempt at humor, she gave him a sheepish grin.

He sat there in mute silence and her smile faded. Why should it shock or surprise him that everyone, including this woman, had such an ill-opinion of him? They were right for those opinions. Yet it frayed on a jagged nerve he'd not known or felt—until now.

Daphne turned her palms up. "I believe in your effort to spare me from overexerting myself, you'd absolve me of certain tasks. I do not wish to be treated differently, Daniel. I want to be like every other companion, able to work without assistance. I want to be the way I was."

That person had died at the lakeside under the rain-dampened leaves, long, long ago, just as who he'd once been had ceased to exist. "You'll never be that woman, here," he said quietly, touching her legs. She jerked as though he'd struck her. Did she see herself as inferior? Having liked the man he was of his youth far more than the man he'd become, he could appreciate that. Daphne, however, had not changed. Not truly. "But you remain the same woman you always were here," he touched a fingertip to her forehead. "And here," he pressed a palm briefly to her heart and stilled. Of its own volition, his gaze fell to his hand upon her, with only the thin fabric of her gown a barrier between them. All he needed to do was move slightly and he'd cup that delicate—

"You don't know that." Her challenge emerged breathless. Her eyes turbulent with unidentified emotion cut across the haze of desire clogging his senses.

He yanked his fingers back. By God, if ever there was a doubt of his rakish reputation, lusting after Daphne was proof of his wickedness. "Don't I?" he challenged, winging an eyebrow up. "The girl who challenged me to races and fights is now a woman who'd storm my estate and demand I be a decent brother." An impossible task, as there was nothing decent about him. "And you're strong enough to make your way in the world." Of all the ladies of his acquaintance, she was the only one who'd beg for references and not baubles.

At the sudden adoration seeping from her expressive eyes, he recoiled, backing up a step, the moment too real. Unease filled him. He didn't know what to do with that sincerity. It went against everything and anything he knew or dealt in. To shatter the solemnity of the moment, he waggled his eyebrows. "Plus, I'd never send you away because I'm a selfish enough bastard that I'd never absolve you of your tasks when I have need of your assistance."

A shuddery sigh filtered from her lips. Despite his tumult, that whispery exhalation pulled an unwanted grin from him. Of course, only Daphne would react so to those pragmatic words, when every other woman he'd bedded wanted his praise of their beauty. He reached for her leg and she squeaked.

"What are you doing?" she demanded on a scandalized whisper, all dewy-eyed awe gone.

"Examining your leg," he said, easily disentangling her hand from his.

"You most certainly are not," she demanded, gripping him by the wrist.

He made to shrug her off once more, but something in her eyes held him back, froze him. A pleading. Since they'd met as children of five and eight, respectively, she'd been bold and demanding, just as she'd been the woman who'd stormed his manor and put demands to him. Through it all, she'd never been this figure with entreating eyes. "I will not look at it," he promised, in a gentled tone.

She eyed him warily and the clock ticked away a long stretch of silence. Then, she gave a slight nod.

With that, through the muslin fabric, Daniel ran a hand down the expanse of her lower leg.

Daphne gasped. "Wh-what are you doing? You said—"

"I promised not to look. I didn't say I would not touch," he murmured, stroking the taut, knotted muscles.

"You cannot... You should not..." Her protestations trailed off as he ran his knuckles in a circular rhythm over her upper thigh.

God, she must be in agony. It was a testament to that misery that she—now proper Daphne—did not resist his touch. Through the fabric of her out of fashion dress, he rubbed her calf until a little, throaty moan spilled past her lips. This was the first time in the whole of his life that he'd ever stroked or caressed a woman without sexual gratification being the ultimate goal to which they both sought. And oddly, there was a greater intimacy in this moment than any of the hot couplings he'd known.

"I have never felt anything so exquisite."

Did those words belong to Daphne or him? He glanced up from his task and momentarily froze. She sat, with her head hung back, eyes closed, the delicate planes of her face softened in a languid splendor. A bolt of desire worked through him; a hungering from a simple touch, through her frayed skirts, no less.

She opened her eyes and he swiftly yanked his attention back to her leg. He lifted her skirts ever so slightly and she jumped. "You said, you would not—"

"Let me rub your leg, Daphne."

Indecision raged in her eyes.

He'd been a rake far longer than he'd been a gentleman and, as such, a master of manipulation and words—it just had always been for his own personal gratification—until now. "Come," he cajoled. "I'm the same boy who swam naked with you in a lake. There is nothing I've not seen." A shame, he'd not had the proper appreciation to gaze upon her then.

She flared her eyes. "Daniel," she whispered, stealing a glance at the closed door. "We were children."

"There are no worries of disloyal servants," he assured. "The majority of my staff was let go due to lack of funds. All that remains are the oldest, who with their advancing years, are all abed, as well as their kin."

Daphne caught her lower lip between her teeth, worrying that flesh, and, by hell, if he wouldn't sell what was left of his black soul just then to taste the same succor. Then, she gave another slight nod.

Daniel gently raised her skirts, slowly, allowing her time to voice any objection. He lifted his gaze, questioningly. She remained motionless and he resumed his efforts, pushing the fabric up until her lower limb was exposed.

Silence fell on the room and agony squeezed his chest. The lower limb, improperly set, had left the entire portion below her knee twisted.

…I'll never ride again. Or curtsy. Or dance…

Her child's voice of long ago, wreathed in pain, echoed around the room as loud as though they were the words whispered in the copse where he'd found her. Had she done those things with the passage of time? Or did the old injury make those movements impossible?

His throat worked. She'd marched to Mrs. Belden's and then sought him out. And then marched back home with nothing more than a wooden cane to aid her. God, he was humbled by her strength.

Aware of her gaze burning a spot into his neck, he proceeded to rub the flesh, working the knots, and then continuing higher.

"D-Daniel, this is too intimate," she chided, her voice faintly breathless as she made to push her gown back into place.

"Bah," he interrupted. "This isn't intimate." He raised his eyes to hers and, never taking them from her face, said, "Touching you here," he brushed his palm higher up her thigh. The warmth of her leg burned his hand and killed all levity. He forced himself to finish the thought, his tone garbled. "That would be intimate." What had begun as an attempt at teasing, quickly faded as a charged undercurrent blazed to life. He lingered his hand on the smooth flesh of her thigh and worked his hand higher, stroking his fingertips over her searchingly.

Her breath hitched loudly as he came up slowly on his knees. His pulse pounded hard in his ears as he drew his hands out from under her skirts. Daphne's eyes, limpid with desire, searched his face. "Daniel," she whispered.

On a groan, he cupped a hand about her neck and availed himself to her lush lips as he'd ached to do since she'd pushed back her hood at Winterbourne Manor. Not bothering with gentility, he plunged his tongue inside her mouth, searching the hot cavern. A low, throaty moan spilled from her and he swallowed that testament of her need.

She twined her fingers in his hair, bringing her flush to his chest so her small breasts crushed against him. Emboldened, he reached a hand between them and caressed one. He tweaked the erect peak through the fabric of her dress and the bud pebbled all the more under his ministrations. His groan melded with her throaty whimper.

Fueled by a desperate hungering, Daniel slanted his lips over hers, drowning in the intoxicating taste of mint and chocolate. By God, she tasted of sweetness and innocence and he wanted to lose himself in her. He guided her down and shifted himself over her, never breaking contact with her lips. Working his hand up her legs, he cupped her mound and her hips bucked.

All these years, he'd disavowed innocence. With Daphne undulating into his hand while he rang little pleading sounds from her lips, he conceded that mayhap there was something to be said for innocence, after all.

CHAPTER 11

AT SEVENTEEN YEARS OF AGE, Daphne had turned her virginity over to a rogue. She'd known that man in the most intimate ways, joined together in a quick moment. That had seen her willingly divested of that thin bit of flesh and innocent no more.

And yet, never before, not even in Leopold's arms for that coupling had she felt...*this*. This exhilarating blend of pleasure-pain from Daniel's expert stroking. And more, as he caressed his lips down her cheek, blazing a hot trail with his mouth, lower to her neck, she felt—*beautiful*.

Her head fell back involuntarily as she opened herself to his searching. He nipped and sucked at the flesh, grazing his teeth lightly over her skin, as though he were a primitive warrior branding her as his. And God help her, with all the follies of her past, knowing the dangers in this seductive bliss, she wanted to belong to him.

"I have wanted to worship you here since you stood in my office," he breathed hotly against her skin that was moist from his ministrations. "I—"

Daphne twisted her fingers in his thick chestnut strands and met her mouth with his. She didn't want words from him. Words that reminded her of all that was wrong in allowing him, nay, needing him to touch her in these ways. She wanted this rapturous wonder to carry on into forever, where all she knew was this burn inside her veins.

They tangled their tongues in a volatile thrust and parry, exploring one another, and she cried out as he drew his mouth back, but he lowered his head to her chest.

With deft movements, he slid her bodice down. The night air slapped at her heated skin and a shuddery gasp exploded from her lips as he palmed her right breast. Daniel raised it to his mouth. He closed his lips around the taut, sensitized nipple, drawing it in and suckling.

"Daniel," she cried out softly, past the point of shame or fear of discovery.

Against her chest, his rumble of masculine approval increased her desperate fervor. In the single time she'd lain with a man, he'd given no consideration to her body. There had been only hasty caresses and a mouth used to silence her quiet cries of pain. This slow unfurling inside, that Daniel awakened her to, shattered every belief she'd had about lovemaking.

Daphne lifted her hips, searchingly, and he placed his hand on her mons. She bit her lower lip and thrust into him, besieged by the realization that he had, in fact, been correct—there was a vast difference between a rake and a rogue. This was it. This caress. This inspired a sense of beauty from a woman who was anything but.

Daniel palmed her center, with only her shift as the thin barrier between his touch and her body. And in that touch, she could almost believe, wanted to believe, she was...beautiful.

As though he heard that secret longing, he whispered against her breast, "You are so beautiful, love."

...You are so beautiful, love... I want to know you in every way...

Daphne jerked as Lord Leopold's whispered lies filtered into the moment. She bolted upright and the suddenness of her movement sent Daniel spilling onto the floor.

He grunted as he landed hard. "Bloody hell," he muttered.

She gasped and leaned over the edge of the sofa to where he lay sprawled. "I...I..." Daphne fell backward and slapped her hands over her face. *What have I done?* Her chest heaved with the force of her desires and a rapidly growing horror. By God, she was wicked and wanton and the same fool she'd been all those years ago, lured by pretty words. Nay, this, this was far worse. This was a heady, breathless desire that had consumed her like a conflagration.

Daniel's quiet, wholly unaffected voice cut across her spiraling panic. "Daphne."

She dropped her hands to her sides and quickly sat up. "We should not have done that." He opened his mouth. "*I* should not have done that. We cannot do that. Ever again.*" Even if it has been the single most erotic moment of my eight and twenty years.* "I—"

"Daphne," he interrupted firmly, coming up and perching himself on the edge of her seat. "It was a kiss. Nothing more." He may as well have spoken as casually as he would about his preference for tea or the unseasonably warm spring they'd been enjoying.

Nothing more? It had been so much more than a mere kiss. It had been the Vauxhall fireworks she'd watched shoot high above the London sky all those years ago, only tiny, colorful explosions inside.

Or, to her, it had.

Staring at him, his face an emotionless mask, reality intruded. This was Daniel, renowned rake. An embrace could never, would never be more to him. Regret stabbed at her chest, but was swiftly replaced by relief. "Of course," she said in steadying tones. "It cannot happen again, Daniel. I have my reputation and you…" Her words trailed off. For he was a rake and a nobleman rolled into one, and through that, he was permitted liberties that would mean the ruin of a lady.

He reached his left hand out and she stiffened as he trailed the pad of his thumb along her lower lip. "It *could* though." Her lashes fluttered wildly. *He is going to kiss me, again. And for my weak protestations, I want it and all it entails…* "If you wish it, Daphne."

If she wished it. His words brought her eyes open with a soberness that dulled all desire. This exchange, this fleeting passion, though toe-curling and magical to her, was no different than any other embrace he'd shared with countless women.

He might have scruples to not dally with an innocent, but neither would he ever be a gentleman to give his heart and his loyalty to only one woman. She would do well to remember it. Remember what came in trusting a rake. Even if it was a rake she'd swum naked with as a girl, as he'd pointed out earlier. "When I came to London all those years ago," she started slowly. "I was filled with excitement. How grand it all was. The gowns, the glittering balls, the unending nights." She paused and glanced past his shoulder, as memories intruded. "The promise and hope of a wild, thrilling love."

How very naïve she'd been. "You asked what I wished for. Do you know what I wish for now?"

He brushed a loose red curl back behind her ear. "Tell me," he commanded, touching his lips to her temple. She cursed the wild fluttering in her belly.

"I wish for stability," She spoke with a quiet solemnity that froze his movements. "I wish to have a respectable position where I have security and do not have to worry about funds or where I shall live." With tremulous fingers, Daphne reached inside her pocket and fished out her page. She handed it over to him. Daniel took the sheet and their fingers brushed, sending heated warmth shooting up her arm. "That is what I want," she murmured as he read the cut-out.

A lock fell over his brow and she ached to brush it back. He looked at her questioningly. "It is a place where young women, regardless of their disabilities or disfigurements, are welcomed and instructed." She jabbed the page. "I wish to go there." She paused. "As an instructor," she added and braced for his mockery, expecting it. Even wanting it, so he was not the insistent gentleman from moments ago who'd spoken of her strength and spirit.

"That is why you wish to work at Mrs. Belden's," he murmured quietly, as though he'd at last solved a complex riddle. "For experience."

"I want to present myself before the marchioness with experiences and references that I've earned, honorably."

He handed over her sheet and she quickly pocketed it. "And my references are inferior to Mrs. Belden's?"

Perhaps those jaded souls he interacted with now would have failed to hear the faint hurt underscoring that wry question, but she had known this man since they were children and she heard it. "You misunderstand," she said shaking her head emphatically. "References from you are merely an endorsement from one peer to the next." She lifted her palms. "You cannot speak to my ability to instruct or lead a classroom of ladies."

Daniel stared at her for a long while through thickly hooded lashes. "There is not another woman like you, Daphne Smith."

Not knowing what to make of that quiet utterance, spoken more to himself, she leaned over the arm of the sofa and gathered her cane.

He surged to his feet while she placed her weight on the walking stick, pushing herself upright. He slid an arm around her waist and bent down to scoop her up.

"What are you doing?" she squeaked.

He straightened. "Carrying you."

Warmth suffused her heart. Yes, to the *ton* he might always be an unscrupulous rake, but he would forever be the heroic friend she remembered. "You are always carrying me about." Through hills and uneven roads.

"Bah, I carried you but once. This will be the second time."

Once. But it had also been the darkest, most agonizing moment of her young life. The day that forever changed the course of her whole future. She smiled at him. "You are not carrying me, Daniel," she said with gentle insistence.

A dark scowl marred his features. "You always were too proud for your own good, Daphne Smith," he muttered.

With the aid of her cane, she shifted to face him, wanting him to understand. Nay, needing him to. "I'm not letting you because I am a cripple," he growled low in his throat, "but I am still, *more* than a cripple." Or she was determined to be. "And just as I've done for almost eighteen years, I'll walk every step and stair before I allow someone to carry me. Though I thank you for your gallantry."

He gave his head a bemused shake. "That is the first time I've ever been called gallant." A half-grin formed on his lips, dimpling his cheek. This was the real smile, the one that met his brown eyes.

...I am not putting you down... "Mayhap it was the first time you heard it, but it doesn't mean it was the first gallant act you've performed." Daphne began her slow, forward path, limping through the library with its near-empty shelves. She stopped at the door and he reached around her to push it open. "Thank you, Daniel," she said softly.

"For my offer to assist you?" He gave her one of his wolfish grins. "Or my kiss?"

He startled a laugh from her. "*Goodnight*, Daniel." She started down the corridor and then frowned. She glanced at him with his hands clasped at his back, matching her slow footsteps. "What are you doing?"

"Not carrying you."

Her lips pulled. "I see that. I meant—"

"I am walking with you." He stole a sideways glance at her. "And if you tell me I do not have to, I'm going to carry you."

A man, who by his own words lived for his own pleasures, why should he do that? His features remained a set mask revealing nothing, painting him as he'd professed himself to be—coolly unfeeling. And yet, with his offer to walk beside her, he threw that statement into contradiction. "Very well," she acquiesced. "But you must do something."

He eyed her warily. "Go on."

"I'll accept your company, if you pledge to curtail your drinking." He emitted a strangled, choking sound. "You drink too much, Daniel." Daphne lifted her walking stick slightly. "You use it as a greater crutch than the cane I use for walking." What demons did he seek to bury in those bottles and flasks?

She braced for his immediate rejection, for him to send her to the Devil for daring to suggest he limit his liquor consumption.

"Curtail," he said slowly, repeating that one word back. "As in cut off."

"As in reduce the amount, Daniel," she corrected. "There is nothing wrong with having a glass of brandy." She held a finger up. "There is something wrong with finishing off a decanter." With his dependency on spirits, he could bury away all thought and feeling. And never truly live. Not the way he once had.

He folded his arms at his chest. "And how will you know if I simply tell you what you wish to hear?" he challenged, as tenacious as the day he'd debated her use of his family's lake almost twenty-three years earlier.

"I'll know," she said softly. "Because when you drink you aren't really present. You are a ghost. Ghosts cannot feel pain. They cannot be touched. And they are not alive. Not really." She'd have him remember how much he loved simply being alive.

Something veiled dulled all hint of emotion from his eyes. "I do not need liquor," he said tightly. "I do not need anything or anyone." Yes, she suspected he *believed* as much.

They remained locked in a silent battle.

Of course, he'd reject her appeal. What grounds did he have to say yes? It would require him to put aside his own pleasures for—

A long sigh escaped him and then he held an arm out. Her heart jumped a beat. He'd agreed?

"Well?" he drawled in his usual charming tones when she continued to stare at him.

More than half-fearing he'd alter his mind and renege on that agreement struck, Daphne placed her left hand on his sleeve.

She sucked in a preparative breath and resumed the long trek. What had been interminable earlier became bearable with him at her side. Daphne concentrated on keeping one foot in front of the other. With each jarring movement, pain radiated up her leg and she fixed on that sharp tingling for it prevented her from focusing on forbidden kisses. A nearly impossible feat, given the tall, gloriously handsome gentleman at her side. She reached the end of the hall and paused. Moisture dotted her brow and she paused to dust away those droplets. "I expect you have any number of events to attend at this hour."

"I should," he muttered under his breath.

At the annoyance edging those two words, she lifted her gaze. "You may go, Daniel. I don't—"

"You misunderstand," he interrupted as they trailed down the hall past portraits of his distinguished relatives. "I am to be on my very best behavior."

Her skin burned with the heated memory of his touch. Did he even know what that meant?

"My uncle would have me rein in my rakish ways until my sister is properly wed." He chuckled. "I'm to avoid scandal and improprieties and at the Season's end, will be richly rewarded for my efforts."

Daphne stared quizzically at him.

"If I remain free of scandal, he will turn over eight thousand pounds entrusted to him by my mother," he clarified. "Those funds which require I find a proper companion for Alice." He grinned. "As you can see, your earlier worries were for naught. With the exception of my sister, you're the only proper lady of my acquaintance."

His words knocked into her with the force of a runaway phaeton. Daphne tripped and he shot an arm out, catching her to him.

"Staggering amount, isn't it?" he drawled, wholly misinterpreting the reason for her stumble. With his spare hand, he gestured to the places on the wall where paintings had once hung, those glaring reminders of his declining wealth. "Enough that even I can behave for." Eight thousand pounds? It was a fortune. The kind of funds that would see a family cared for and then their ancestors, long into the future. And yet, it was not those monies that would one day be Daniel's that robbed her of speech and breath.

...those funds require I find a proper companion for Alice... They reached the base of the stairs and she stared blankly at the bottom one. Ultimately, Daniel had drawn the same erroneous conclusion everyone had; a conclusion she'd been wholly content with the world keeping—that she was a proper, virginal miss. And why should they not see that? What gentleman would dally with or *care* to dally with a cripple?

Only, the life she'd lived was a lie far more fragile than she'd ever credited. Daniel's funds were dependent upon her good reputation and moral standing for his sister. And there was nothing good or decent about her. Her earlier wanton response to Daniel's touch and kiss in the library were proof of that.

"Daphne?" his gruff question slashed into her musings.

Blinking slowly, she looked up at him. "I do not require any further assistance," she said tightly. "I thank you for your company. If you'll excuse me?" Unable to meet his eyes, she started the long, slow ascent. Her neck burned with the intensity of Daniel's stare at her back.

And as she climbed his thirty-three stairs, she wished life had traveled along differently, and that she'd never fallen, and he'd never been a rake, and she'd never learned the perils in loving a rake, by throwing away her virginity to that man. Because then, mayhap things might have been very different and life would have matched those silly childhood dreams she'd once carried.

Now what?

CHAPTER 12

AFTER AN EVENING IN HIS arms, of knowing his touch and embrace, women invariably vied for, or pleaded for a return engagement. They did not studiously avoid or ignore him.

Except Daphne. She, however, did.

At first, the morning after their explosive embrace in the library, he'd credited her averted eyes and laconic silence to shyness. He hadn't a jot of an idea about innocent ladies, but he suspected Daphne's responses to him well fit with how any proper miss would be after such an exchange.

Nearly a week following their exchange in the library, the lady still would not fully meet his gaze. She was quick to leave a room whenever he entered, which given his deliberate entrance into the rooms where she happened to be, was really quite often.

Not that he should care either way how Daphne was in his presence. She'd a role within his household, as companion for Alice, and her devotion to his sister was truly all that should matter. It should.

And mayhap it would, if the lady didn't all but plaster herself to Alice's side when he was near.

"…Ahem…"

Blinking slowly, Daniel glanced up. His man-of-affairs seated in the chair opposite him, coughed into his hand. Furthermore, given the precarious state of his finances, he really had matters of far greater import than Daphne Smith. He thrust aside thoughts of the lady and attended Begum, the man he'd hired as soon as his father had passed and Daniel was made earl. That same greying figure now poured over the books laid out on the edge of his desk.

"As I was saying, my lord," Begum explained, his head bent over the books. "By these numbers here, in my estimation, the whole of Her Ladyship's Season will cost near one hundred pounds." The man scrunched his mouth, fixed on several inked lines in the ledger.

The clock ticked noisily in the background. Daniel reached for the decanter at the edge of his desk. ... *You drink too much, Daniel... You use it as a greater crutch than the cane I use for walking...* Curtail. She'd merely said curtail. Bloody hell. "Yes?" he asked impatiently, shoving aside the bottle.

Begum scratched at his always tousled, steel grey hair. "There are additional expenditures, my lord."

Payment to Madame Thoureaux's for five satin gowns and other...

His man-of-affairs pointed to the line.

"Is there a question?" Daniel prodded wryly.

With a frown, Begum removed his spectacles and sat back in his chair. "May I speak frankly, my lord?"

"Don't you always?" he countered. The unflinching honesty, when most servants, lords and ladies would prevaricate on matters of the weather, Begum had proven direct. He didn't tiptoe around his questions or statements and for that, he was worth his weight in gold as a servant.

"Your finances are as dire now as they were at the end of last Season, my lord."

Yes, the nearly depleted bookshelves and missing baubles were all testament to that.

"Mayhap more," Begum added, when Daniel still showed no outward reaction. "Between the cost of your wardrobe, and Her Ladyship's, as well as the upkeep of this residence, your coin is being stretched quite thin."

"There is plenty more to liquidate," he noted. And then there would be eight thousand pounds from which there would never stem another financial worry—until he squandered it all away again at the gaming tables.

"You've membership to Brook's, White's, the Devil's Den, Forbidden Pleasures, and the Hell and Sin Club, all payments nearly due. For a total payment of," Begum tapped his pen on each respective column. "Two hundred pounds, my lord," he said, looking up.

Well, this was bloody sobering stuff, indeed. Going through life for his own pleasures; the inventive mistresses and actresses he took to his bed, paid in coin and baubles. His clubs and the wicked parties he hosted, where vices were celebrated...all of those mindless pursuits allowed him to forget, at least, when he lived within those moments.

And then there was Begum. "Maintain membership at White's and Forbidden Pleasures," he muttered. Sad day, indeed, when a chap had to cut membership to his clubs. Damned Uncle Percival and his pinched purse. No doubt, the miserable bastard was bracing for his failure, anticipating it, and gleefully relishing the prospect of cutting him off from those desperately needed funds.

Begum set his pen down perpendicular on the middle of Daniel's ledger. With slow, methodical movements, he removed his spectacles, closed them, and set them alongside the pen. "As I have permission to speak frankly," he began, sitting back in his chair. "You can barely afford funds for Lady Alice's Season let alone a wardrobe and fineries for a mistress, my lord."

A mistress? Daniel furrowed his brow and followed Begum's point to that line in the middle of the page. "She is not my mistress." Though pairing Daphne with that word conjured delicious images of her spread out on soft satin sheets, her crimson curls draped about her naked body. Did the freckles still mar her shoulders and back as they had years earlier, when she was a girl baring herself in a lake without words like "proper" on her lips? "She is my sister's companion," he clarified, when Begum continued to sit there staring at him, perplexed. The same woman who'd asked him to limit his drinking and to whom he, for some reason he still couldn't rationalize, had agreed.

His man-of-affairs returned his attention to the page, assessing the purchases once more, but not before Daniel detected the skeptical glimmer in his eyes. "Uh, yes, well then, exorbitant purchases for any lady other than Lady Alice is, at this point, not a prudent use of your funds, my lord. I would rather encourage you to put your monies in safe investments to grow your wealth."

"Trade?" he asked bluntly.

The other man hesitated and then nodded.

Most members of the peerage sneered at lords, or any one really, dealing in trade. Daniel had never been one of those pompous, priggish sorts. He wasn't so arrogant that he'd look down at those who made their fortunes.

The truth of it was, he'd never worried after money. Those material matters always sorted themselves out. His uncle's proposition was testament of that. "I have eight thousand pounds coming to me when my sister marries, Begum. I expect we've little to worry after that."

"My lord?" Begum asked, as he came forward in his chair and searched through the ledgers for information that he'd not find there.

Daniel explained the funds that would be coming to the man who would be managing them. "As you can see, I but need to behave, allow Miss Smith to do her admirable work as companion, and," he dusted his palms together. "All will be well."

Begum removed a kerchief from inside his jacket and picked up his spectacles. He cleaned the lenses on that crisp white fabric, which Daniel had learned came to indicate the man was weighing his words. "I believe you'd still do well to at least consider the possibility of a steam—" A knock sounded at the door.

"Enter," Daniel called out, relieved by the interruption.

The door opened, revealing his butler on the other side. "My lord, you've a visitor. His—"

Oh, bloody hell. "I don't require a proper introduction," a familiar voice boomed. Daniel swallowed a groan as his uncle strode around Tanner and entered the room.

"The Viscount Claremont," the loyal servant offered anyway and then hurried out of the room.

"Uncle," Daniel greeted, tossing his arms wide. Two bloody visits in the course of a fortnight? This was bad, indeed. "A pleasure. First you pay me a *visit* in the country and now an unexpected morning one all the way in London, during the Season, no less? Why, despite your indications otherwise these years, I believe you do care."

His uncle snorted. "I'm not here for you, boy." Uninvited, as arrogant as if he was the owner of this townhouse himself, his uncle came forward. Begum kept his head down and hurriedly gathered up his ledgers and reports. He made to rise, but Uncle

Percival fell into the seat beside the man. "Going over your depleting coffers?"

Refusing to be baited, Daniel inclined his head. "Indeed."

The viscount passed assessing eyes over Begum as he stacked the leather folios. "You'd best be a wizard to help this boy."

Did he imagine the smile twitching on Begum's lips? Disloyal bastard. "That will be all," Daniel drawled. His man-of-affairs promptly smoothed his features, stood, and, with a bow for the viscount and Daniel, took his leave.

His uncle spent as much time in the country as Daniel did in London. Little drew him to the frivolities in Town which Daniel lived for. As such, he was not so naïve to believe this was anything but a calculated visit. "To what do I owe the pleasure of your esteemed company?"

"Do you truly believe I'm going to offer you eight thousand pounds and not oversee you this Season? That I'd be so foolish as to trust you at your word?"

Oversee him? Daniel choked. By God, his uncle spoke as though he were a green boy just out of university and not a man of thirty years. Still, his uncle proved himself the clever bastard he'd always been, with his rightful wariness. "Is it too much to hope you can't simply take your word from the gossip columns?"

Of which Daniel's name was invariably found.

His uncle laughed and his wide-shoulders shook with his amusement. "And you expect the gossips will have anything good to say about you this Season?"

Yes, fair point, there. Mayhap it was better to suffer through the occasional visit and the Season with his uncle in the same city. Daniel covetously eyed that brandy. A damned crutch she'd called it. It wasn't, but by God, if it didn't feel like Daphne was right, in this moment.

The viscount glanced around the office, searchingly. "I understand, you hired the girl a companion," his uncle said suddenly.

"Yes. Those *were* the terms you laid out, were they not?"

His uncle grunted. "Well?" He stretched his hand out and thumped the desk. "Where is she?"

So this is why he'd come? To make a judgment on Alice's companion. Alice's companion who was, in fact, Daphne Smith. Of course his uncle was right to question how he had wrangled up any suitable woman and so quickly. Nonetheless, he gritted his teeth at having to parade Daphne before him, for his *viscountly* approval, all because Daniel was dependent on the coins he'd hand over at the end of the Season. He gritted out a smile. "I'm afraid I do not keep her under my desk," he said with a sardonic edge.

Except, the mocking reply merely called forth wicked images of Daphne beneath his desk, on her knees. A wave of desire filled him.

"I'm certain it wouldn't be the first time you've had a woman under there," his uncle snapped, effectively dousing that delicious imagery.

It was one thing for Daniel to have those enticing musings of Daphne, quite another for his blasted uncle to disparage the lady's reputation. "I assure you," he offered coolly. "The lady is entirely appropriate and will fit with all the terms you've set forth and your expectations."

The viscount rested his palms on his knees and leaned forward. "I will be the judge of that."

DAPHNE HAD CONVINCED HERSELF THAT one mistake in her past did not matter to her serving as Alice's companion. As Daniel had said; he was a rake, with limited options.

And Daphne was a woman nearly eleven years removed from that wanton night in her past. Surely the man who'd debauched her, with her approval, would not dare breathe that story to light if their paths ever did again cross?

…you should be honored, Miss Smith. I've never rutted with a cripple before…

Seated beside her charge in the breakfast room, Daphne's stomach knotted. For after that night, she'd begged her father to leave London, never to know if Leopold had bragged of his conquest or whether whispers had surfaced. She absently stared at the untouched contents of her porcelain plate, hopelessly lost in those darkened memories and fears.

At her side, Alice nibbled at a piece of bread and pored over the copy of *The Times*. "They mention countless names," Alice observed, as she turned the page. "But not a single one of Mr.

Pratt."

Mr. Pratt. The kind-eyed gentleman from the street. Diverted from her own depressed musings, Daphne attended her charge.

The girl picked her head up. "Do you suppose that means he's not one of the scandalous sorts?"

Daphne fiddled with her fork. Actually, that is precisely what she'd make of it. Society fixed on rakes, rogues, and oddities. Lords and ladies who lived staid, respectable lives usually escaped whispers. *Usually.* "Does it matter whether or not he is one of those scandalous sorts?" she turned a gently spoken question, instead.

Alice's cheeks bloomed red. "I expect you'll find it silly that I should be captivated by a gentleman after a chance meeting in the street. But he came to your aid," she said on a rush, "and glowered at his foul-mannered rake of a brother."

So Daphne had been correct in her suspicions more than a week ago. Mayhap she was less wise all these years later than she'd hoped or believed. For instead of any disquiet at her charge's revelation, Daphne bit the inside of her cheek to keep from smiling. The girl had proven perceptive, seeing the obvious disparity between Daniel's friend and that man's brother.

"Not at all," Daphne assured. After all, she'd also once been young and romantic. She, however, had the bad judgment to seek excitement with a rake. She'd not have Alice make the same mistake. "There is no shame in dreaming of love." That elusive sentiment she'd so hoped for. She held Alice's gaze squarely. "It matters that you find a man *worthy* of that emotion."

"Daniel would never approve of him." The girl wrinkled her nose. Lowering her voice to a deep baritone, she did a spot-on impersonation of her brother. "Any wealthy gent will do. Don't go wasting your attention on anything less."

Both women locked gazes and laughed. When their mirth faded, Daphne stretched her hand out and briefly covered Alice's. "Your brother would not dissuade you from following your heart."

"Do you truly believe that?" Hope melded with doubt in the rightfully suspicious girl's eyes.

And yet for all the tales of Daniel's debauchery, she did. She'd seen proof of his goodness in his offering her employment. Just as she'd seen it again when he'd sought to carry her abovestairs. "I do," she said quietly. It was because of that goodness that she could not remain employed here.

Alice beamed and spoke with a renewed enthusiasm. "I read through the papers, hoping to see some mention of his name." She lifted the scandal sheet. "Wanting to know more. But then not wanting to see his name here, either."

No, because no good names or stories were ever mentioned on those pages. Reality intruded once more, ugly and unwelcome.

She gave silent thanks when Alice returned her attention to those pages.

Years earlier, she'd read through those same papers, with only one familiar name contained within. Lord Leopold.

The food in her mouth turned to ash and she forced herself to choke down the swallow. Somewhere between Daniel's revelation at the base of his thirty-three stairs and this very moment, she had come to accept the realization—she could not serve as Alice's companion. He had put the ultimatum to her so very quickly that she'd not had proper time to truly sort through all the ramification and implications that could visit his family if her past was to be revealed.

Liar. You thought of yourself and your security. You pardoned your actions, justifying them with the truth that Daniel was a rake.

But the truth remained. Gentlemen could be rakes and rogues and scoundrels. Society forgave them their wickedness, even lauded it. The desirability of those scandalous nobles rose because of their depravity. Ladies, however, were to be above reproach always and at every time. There was no allowance or pardoning of error. A lady's reputation is all she had and once it was gone, nothing remained, except for an uncertain future.

Stomach churning, Daphne set down her fork, unable to take another bite.

Alice sighed and tossed aside her paper. "I'm rather tired of reading about all the activities and events occurring. Vauxhall Gardens, the opera, balls, soirees, and we are…" She gestured wildly about the room. "Here." For which Daphne was eternally grateful. She'd rather waltz with the Devil in the bowels of hell than attend a single event.

And soon she would not have to. Why did that cause this ache inside her chest?

Alice let out a beleaguered sigh. "You would expect in having a rake for a brother, he'd care to show me…something."

"There is still the matter of formally introducing you before Society," Daphne gently reminded her. She'd no doubt when Alice was officially out, Daniel would usher his sister about Town, with the hope of coordinating the most advantageous match.

Alice plopped back in her chair and, with zeal, ripped a piece of bread with her teeth. "I really know nothing about it," she said around her mouthful. She swallowed her bite and then tossed the unfinished bread onto her plate. "I should, given Daniel's rare departure from London and his failure to miss any part of the Season."

Sadness pulled at Daphne's heart. Of course, with her mother having died shortly after she'd given birth to Alice, there had been no maternal guidance. With a rake of a brother, as she'd indicated, she should know something. "Did Mrs. Belden's not prepare you for the Season?"

The girl gave her a mischievous smile; a dangerous twinkle glinting in her gaze that marked her more Daniel's sister than even the deep brown of her eyes. "Oh, the instructors certainly prepared us about…" She paused and, squaring her shoulders, held up a stern finger and spoke in clipped tones the headmistress would be hard-pressed to not admire. "Propriety and decorum and politeness and Almack's and…" Alice dropped her head into her hands and made a snoring sound.

Despite her dread, Daphne joined the girl in laughter. Having been born an only child, other than Daniel's friendship when he was in the countryside, her existence had been largely a solitary one with only the servants and her parents for companionship. With Alice this past week, she'd found a joy in having another woman to speak to.

"Did you not have a Season, Daphne?" The question rolled from Alice's lips, easily reminding her as to why she could not stay.

"I did," she said softly.

"And?" the girl prodded with more of that raw honesty Daphne appreciated.

"There is something wondrous in the thrill of the orchestra, as you sit on the side of the ballroom and dancers twirl by in colorful gowns that put you in mind of a rainbow after a summer storm." Long ago memories surged forward, so the orchestra's strains played inside her mind. And she was that girl, Alice's age, fresh-eyed with excitement.

"Sit."

Daphne turned slowly to look at Daniel's sister.

"You said, sit," Alice clarified in gentle tones. "Not dance. Sit."

The lady was far too clever by half and observant.

"Yes, well, some ladies sit." The cripples. "And others will dance. You are one of the dancers. I promise you that." With her glorious golden curls and flawless skin and gently curved figure, Lady Alice Winterbourne possessed the beauty that found young women named Incomparables and Diamonds.

"Did you wish to dance?" Alice pressed, searching her face.

All ladies wished to dance. Didn't they? And run or walk or ride and jump. Any and all movement was glorious and freeing. Whereas Daphne's failed body held her soul trapped inside, where it had been since Daniel had turned her over to her father's arms all those years ago. ...*You judge me for being a rake... But at least I live... What of you, Daphne? How have you spent the past thirteen years...* "I did," she said quietly. "With the right partner." Instead, she'd picked a ruthless bastard who'd told her everything she'd longed to hear and she'd given him all for it. She'd not even had her dance.

Now, she'd also be without a post.

Brought 'round to the meeting she'd been putting off for the better part of five days, Daphne grabbed her cane and shoved to her feet. "I have a meeting with His Lordship," she explained to the question in Alice's eyes. An unannounced meeting where she'd tender her resignation. "If you'll excuse me?"

Alice gave a jaunty wave and then reached for her paper, losing herself in those sheets.

Lurching across the room, Daphne made her way down the corridors. With every step, she gave thanks for the first time for her lack of speed. She would convince him to release her of her obligations. Ask once more for those references, in the name of friendship, but she could not remain on here in London, a risk to his sister's reputation and the funds he so needed. There was Alice. And her reputation could not be thrown into question by a disreputable companion. In being here, she posed a risk to the young lady.

And Daniel, caring about nothing more than those eight thousand pounds, well, he'd surely be glad to be rid of her to protect that fortune awaiting him. What rake with a need for coin and his dissolute lifestyle would forfeit that on even the mere risk of a scandal?

Drawing in a slow, steadying breath, she took a step and then froze in the threshold of the open doorway. Daniel and an older gentleman, his fine attire a testament to his status, both sat staring at her. "Forgive me," she murmured and backed away. "I did not hear…I…forgive me," she said hastily.

As one, the two gentlemen climbed to their feet.

"Please," Daniel called. Coming around the desk, he motioned her forward. "Your presence was requested by my *esteemed* uncle, the Viscount Claremont."

Oh, God, his uncle wished to meet her. Daphne's stomach dropped. She was a cripple, but she was not hard of hearing, and she'd have to be deafer than a post to fail to hear the mocking edge threaded through that one slightly emphasized word. This was the uncle who'd saddled him with an unwanted companion and also the stern relation who'd come to judge her worth. Then, wasn't that the way of the world? A lady was judged as to her worth as a wife, a woman, an employee.

Daphne pulled her attention away from Daniel and looked to the stone-faced viscount. "How do you do, my lord?" Shifting her weight over the head of her cane, she sank into an awkward curtsy.

"Come closer, Miss Smith," he beckoned, in even tones that revealed little. "My wastrel nephew is, indeed, correct. I'm here to meet you."

She pursed her lips at that unfavorable opinion so carelessly voiced about Daniel. She stole a glance at Daniel. He wore his patently false grin. How did he feel about that blatant condemnation? On the surface, he exuded an indifference, but how much of that was real? Entering deeper into the room, she claimed the seat Lord Claremont motioned to.

Daniel followed suit.

The viscount stalked over to the well-stocked sideboard and poured himself a drink. He wasted little time with pleasantries. "I will be honest, Miss Smith, I am, of course, skeptical of any young woman my nephew could drum up so quickly for the respectable role of companion for my niece." The clink of crystal touching crystal, as he poured his brandy, filled the room.

He couldn't even deign to look at her. These noblemen. "Is there a question there, my lord?" Mayhap it was the truth that following this exchange, she'd no longer be in Daniel's employ. As such, she wouldn't subject herself to any stranger's judgment but that insolent retort sailed easily from her lips.

Daniel's grin widened and this was the true one of their childhood, filled with mirth and approval.

She scowled at him. *Do you think this is amusing?* she mouthed.

Daniel nodded. *Yes. I do,* he mouthed back, following that with a wink. He smoothed his features as the viscount wheeled around.

"Yes, there is a question there. Have you ever had a London Season, Miss Smith?"

"One," she demurred.

The viscount strolled over, the tension in his frame, belying his relaxed footsteps. "Was it a success?"

Daphne lifted her palms up. "It would depend upon one's definition of success." At his wrinkled brow, she expanded, "If a lady wished to avoid marriage and find herself a spinster, then yes. One might categorize it as a success."

Lord Claremont shot his eyebrows to his hairline.

Daniel folded his arms. "I believe Miss Smith has answered enough of your queries," he said tightly, all earlier traces of droll humor gone.

"I'll decide when the interview is concluded," the viscount snapped.

Daniel shoved to his feet and layered his palms to the surface of his desk. "Is that what this is? An interview?" he seethed and a volatile tension rolled off his frame.

Impossibly calm, the viscount reclaimed his seat. "Yes, this is an interview."

In short, he'd questioned his nephew's judgment. With Daniel's frustration a palpable force in the room, she was momentarily struck by a kindred connection with this man. Yes, Daniel was a rake and responsible for how the world now saw him, but they saw nothing more than a rake. Just as in her, they saw nothing more than a cripple. They were both relegated and restricted to Society's views of them. And sharing that with him stirred something inside her chest…an emotion she could neither identify nor name.

She met his gaze, an unspoken discourse passing between them. Emboldened, she returned her attention to the viscount. "What questions might I answer, my lord?" Either way, they were all irrelevant. Soon she'd be gone from this place. She curled her hands on her lap to keep from rubbing the dull ache in her chest.

"I'll be blunt then, Miss Smith," He hadn't been already? "Are you a respectable sort or one of my nephew's fancy pieces?"

She'd given her virginity to a bounder nearly eleven years ago. Therefore, by Society's standards, one would answer in the contrary.

"You go too far, my lord," Daniel barked.

Daphne quelled him with a look. She'd speak for herself. "My lord," she began coolly. "I am nearly thirty years old. I cannot move without the aid of a cane." With every concise declaration, Daniel's glower deepened. "I have looked in a bevel mirror enough times that I know precisely what I look like. As such, I hardly believe my virtue is in jeopardy with Lord Montfort," she said with a pragmatism that came from knowing who she was and accepting it. Crippled leg or no, she would have never been a grand beauty and it was more a matter of fact, than anything.

The viscount took her in with assessing eyes. Cradling his snifter in one hand, he captured his chin between his thumb and forefinger with the other. "Some might say you are too trusting of him."

Since she'd entered this godforsaken city eleven years ago, she'd been treated with disdain. An inferior interloper either beneath notice or deserving of pity. Her patience snapped. "And some might say you are too disparaging," Daphne said angling her chin up a notch. "It is all a matter of opinion."

The viscount's jaw fell open.

Daniel looked at her with more seriousness in his eyes than she remembered seeing in the whole of their lives together. He gave his head an imperceptible shake, but she ignored it, reserving her attention, instead, for his uncle.

Setting his snifter down on Daniel's desk, the viscount looked to her. "What do you think of rakes, Miss Smith?

"A lady need take care to avoid them," she answered with an automaticity that came from knowing the imprudence in not having a care.

Lord Claremont continued to pepper her. "But you take employment with one?"

Such cluelessness could only come from never having known
the struggles and obstacles posed to woman in their patriarchal
Society. "My lord, the opportunities and options for an unmarried
lady are limited. When presented with serving as companion for a
rake's sister or working in a less than respectable capacity, I would
invariably choose the former."

Silence hung in the room and then Lord Claremont smiled
slowly. With a guffawing laugh, he shook his head. "You will do,
Miss Smith. You will do." He spoke the way one might of the
Christmastide hog. "How did one such as you come to know a
rascal like this one?" He nudged his chin at Daniel.

"His Lordship's family and mine are—" She grimaced, for with
her father's passing, those properties had passed to a distant relative who'd *graciously* allowed her two years before he'd seized her
family's home.

"Neighbors," Daniel neatly slipped in, eyeing her peculiarly.
"Our families were neighbors."

"So you knew him when there was good in him?" the viscount
asked, coming to his feet.

Daniel immediately stood, with Daphne more slowly levering
herself up by the arms of the chair. "I trust you see good in him
still or you would not have put a test of morality to Lord Montfort." Shock marred the viscount's face and she immediately went
hot. She'd said too much, with those revealing words proving that
she knew more than any serviceable companion had a right to
know.

"I trust we are through here?" Daniel asked bluntly, his meaning
clear.

The viscount stuck a finger out. "You will be rid of me now, boy,
but I will continue to visit and be sure you're behaving yourself
and watching my niece." Turning, Lord Claremont dropped a bow.
"Miss Smith, it was a pleasure," he said, a ghost of a smile on his
lips.

She managed another curtsy. "My lord."

With strong, confident strides to rival his nephew, Lord Claremont took his leave.

They remained in like silence as the viscount's boot steps echoed down the hall and then faded altogether, leaving them—alone.

His disapproving uncle gone, Daniel propped his hip on the edge of his desk and gave her another one of his boyish smiles that set her heart dangerously racing. "Miss Daphne Smith," he stretched those four syllables out approvingly and clapped his hands. "That went well. You've managed the impossible—to impress my bastard of an uncle. I know I pledged to curtail my drinking. This, however, merits a toast." Picking up his uncle's discarded half-empty glass, Daniel saluted her and then downed the remaining contents. "Now, Daphne," he said, setting the snifter down with a thunk. "What pressing business brought you to my office?"

She fisted the top of her cane and straightening her spine. She spoke on a rush. "I have come to offer my resignation."

CHAPTER 13

SINCE DAPHNE HAD BEEN A girl of five, challenging him for the rights to his family's lake, she'd always shown a wicked delight in teasing him. At eight and twenty years, she was no different.

Daniel laughed, the sound emerging rusty from ill-use. "Oh?" he drawled and picked up his uncle's now empty snifter. As he came around his desk, starting for the sideboard, Daphne furrowed her brow. *Offering her resignation.* Reaching the mahogany piece stocked with liquor, he gave his head a wry shake. Then he registered the absolute silence blanketing the room. Bottle of brandy and glass in hand, he turned.

Daphne remained precisely where she'd stood since his uncle had taken his leave. Her freckles stood out stark against her pale cheeks. "This is no jest, Daniel," she said quietly. "I am offering my resignation."

At the somberness of her tone, a frisson of panic ran through him. The bottle shook in his hand and he steadied his grip on it. Leaving? Why should that thought rouse this frantic anxiety inside? *Because I've need of her for Alice, is all...* Yes, he required her presence and his uncle approved. No other lady would do for the post. That was all. Abandoning his glass and decanter on the sideboard, he gave a crooked grin. "Very well. Then, I am not accepting it." He leaned against the mahogany piece and winged a challenging eyebrow up.

She scrunched her mouth. He'd wager if she'd been a girl of

seven and not eight and twenty, she'd be stamping her foot. "You cannot, *not* allow me to resign."

"I can," He lifted his index finger. "*And* I did."

Daphne shifted her weight back and forth, and then she rested her palms on the back of the seat she'd previously occupied. "I'm leaving," she repeated, a determined glint in her eyes that sent his panic spiraling.

He called forth countless years' worth of rakish charm. "I understand you're no doubt displeased with me, love," he said in tones he'd often used with the skittish mare he'd been forced to sell off. As she should be. Daphne pursed her lips. Of course, she'd not be easy to cajole and win over like all the ladies before her. "Unpardonable for me to let my uncle question your honor," he added.

She clenched and unclenched the top of her seat. With sharp eyes, he took in the whiteness of her knuckles. "Don't you see? He *should* question her honor. He should question the honor of any woman who is entrusted with Alice's care."

He went still as understanding dawned. "This is because of our embrace." An embrace he'd very much like to repeat, here in his office, spread out on his desk. His blood fired hot.

Daphne shot a horrified gaze to the open door. In seven long strides, he was across the room, yanking the handle. As soon as he'd closed the door behind them, she shook her head. "This is not because of our embrace," she said, shaking her head. She took a faltering step toward him, and then lifted her palms. "You see, when I…" Her lips twisted. "Accepted the terms of your employment," employment he'd all but forced her into, "I did not know the agreement you'd struck with your uncle." She made an annoyed sound and slashed the air with one hand. "That, however, should have mattered less than Lady Alice. I am an," she wet her lips, "unsuitable companion for your sister."

Daniel snorted. "Why?" he asked, leaning against the wall. "Because my pompous uncle suggested as much?" With the exception of his sister, Daphne was the only proper and virtuous woman he knew—or *cared* to know. Of course, the sole reason being that he'd known her since they were children. *Liar.*

Always unrepentant, never uncertain, she glanced down at her ugly, serviceable boots. "I am scandalous." Her whisper barely reached his ears and yet…

He squinted, peering at her. Had she just said—?

Daphne lifted her head and their stares collided. "I am scandalous, Daniel," she repeated once more. Then, like a warrior princess, she tilted her chin at a defiant angle. "And companions must have sterling reputations and be above all reproach. Their *charges'* reputations are dependent upon it. As such, I cannot, in good conscience, remain but would instead ask you to provide me with letters of reference."

His riotous mind picked its way through those hasty ramblings before ultimately settling on one statement. *...I am scandalous...*

Another snorting laugh escaped him and he pushed away from the door. He took several steps toward her, then stopped. "If this is an attempt for me to free you from your responsibilities, I commend you on your cleverness." He dropped a bow. "But, you are the least scandalous lady I know."

"I do believe that," she mumbled, earning another grin from him. How easy it was to smile with her and around her. He'd believed himself unable to manage any real expressions of amusement. There was something freeing in it. Daphne gave her head a shake. "Nonetheless, my past precludes me from serving as Lady Alice's companion."

"*You* have a scandal in your past?" he parroted, incredulity slipping into his tone. What shocking deeds or acts could Miss Daphne Smith—?

"When I made my Come Out," she said, her shoulders back.

Incapable of a reply, he nudged his head in a silent urging for her to continue.

"There was a..." Her lips curved in a heartbreakingly empty smile. "...gentleman, and," she grimaced, "I'm no longer the virtuous lady you take me for."

Daniel went motionless as her quiet admission slammed into his gut like a blow he'd once taken from Gentleman Jackson himself. By God, she was Daphne, and, well, bloody hell, she was *Daphne*, and some bounder had put his hands on her? A loud humming filled his ears and he shook his head slowly. "Surely not."

She nodded succinctly. "Surely," she murmured.

His hands shook. To steady his trembling palms, he made tight fists, his nails digging into the flesh of his palms. Some bastard had robbed her of her virtue. Such a truth should not have shocked or ripped at the insides of an avowed rake and, yet, insidious thoughts slid forward. Daphne, a girl of seventeen, his sister's age, and some stranger robbed her of her virtue. "I will kill him." That seething whisper contained just an edge of the murderous rage ripping at him.

The hint of a smile hovered on her lips. "Do you think I was forced?"

He cocked his head. "You were not?" Which would mean Daphne had *given* herself to another. That she'd known desire for another. Why did he want to rip even this faceless stranger apart with his bare hands?

She collected her cane and fiddled with the top of it. "Oh, Daniel, no. He was a charming rake, who told me everything I wished to hear. And for that, I *gave* him my virtue. I am no virgin. No proper miss. I'm a person. Jaded and wary, just like you."

That admission hung in the room. They were nothing alike. She had a purity of soul that had long been absent on his worthless one. Of course, it was the height of hypocrisy to expect any lady, regardless of age or station or status, to be virtuous…and yet, she was not just any woman. This was *Daphne*. And there had been some bastard who'd lain with her. Who'd taken her virginity and left her unwed.

He forced his thoughts into a semblance of calm that belied the tumult roiling through him. "Do you believe I, of all people, would condemn you for laying with someone?" He, who'd had countless lovers, many times simultaneously. Except, even uttering that question burned like acid in his mouth. Another man had known her, in every way. Daphne Smith, the girl who'd been his friend and the woman…*the woman I didn't even bother with when she came to London for her Season.*

"Daniel," she continued her reasoning over the tightness squeezing at his chest. "There are your funds to consider."

My funds? Of course, his funds.

The eight thousand pounds dangled over his head, as the great hope from his dire financial straits. The same funds he'd not thought of until she'd raised the reminder. She stood, her carriage proud and strong, as she bared her secrets before him…a man who had no right to them. Yes, given his priggish uncle's terms, he should give her those damnable references and send her on her way. Even the hint of scandal would prove calamitous.

So why did he not send her away as she urged? *Because I cannot. I need her.* He started. Needed her? For entirely selfish reasons. Yes, of course, it was nothing more. Yet those unspoken protestations only felt like another grand lie where Daphne was concerned.

"Daniel," she prodded.

"My uncle already approves of you," he said, startled back to the moment.

Daphne sighed. "He'd be a good deal less approving if he were to learn about my past."

Her past. A past which, included some bounder who'd rutted between her legs and known the satiny smoothness of her skin. He longingly eyed his sideboard. His lips pulled in a grimace. The fates must be laughing, that he stood here, London's most notorious rake, burning with a hunger to fell the man who'd claimed her innocence. "Regardless, Daphne, I've no intention of setting you free." He could not let her go. Shock lit her emerald green eyes. "By your own admission, the gentleman was a rake." *Just as I am.* A vise squeezed about his lungs at that silent likening to the man who'd deflowered her. "As such, I assure you he'll not be at Almack's or any other polite event. So if your efforts in revealing your past are to be relieved of your role as Alice's companion, they are for naught."

Why is he doing this?

The man who'd not bothered to so much as call when she'd made her Come Out, and who'd lived for his own vices and pleasures, didn't put others' interests before his own. He was a rake who threw wicked parties. He was a man who forgot his sister, and dallied with village widows, and came down to the foyer to make outrageous advances of a lady waiting to speak to him.

Or that was the safe, neat way in which she'd filed Daniel Winterbourne away, because he'd earned his place into that spot. Just as his uncle had seen a reprobate in his nephew, so too had Daphne, because that's the image he presented to the world.

Now, the same man who earlier in the week had praised her spirit and her strength, stood with fury rolling off his form in waves, offering her position still, even at the possible risk of his forfeiture of those funds. That went against everything she *thought* she'd known about him and proved him to be so very different than the self-absorbed figure he presented to Society. A dangerous warmth unfurled inside her heart.

"Who was he?" he asked with a casual boredom.

He'd be so flippant in his motives and then probe her with that searching question? She shook her head trying to muddle through who, in fact, Daniel Winterbourne was—diffident rake or honorable friend. "By your earlier claim, as he was a rake and unlikely to attend the same events as your sister, it's unlikely we'll meet again." It was a lie. They both knew it. The likelihood of moving among the same Social events as Lord Leopold was great and, yet, she would be on the sidelines with the hired companions, invisible to him, just as she'd been invisible as anything more than a conquest to that same dastard years earlier. "And the alternative is the gentleman is married. As such, I doubt he'll be in the habit of raising attention to past conquests he might have made."

Long ago, she'd ceased to feel anything but a stinging hatred for the cruel man who'd taken her in his arms.

Daniel took slow, smooth steps toward her. "Then you still have not learned the proper wariness, madam." No, her body's heated awareness of this man even now and the burn of his kiss on her lips was proof of that. He came to stop, so close that their boots touched. For the sliver of a moment, she believed he'd dip his head and claim her mouth as he had in his library five days earlier.

And God help her, how she wanted that kiss. She concentrated on her breathing, but only inhaled the deep sandalwood scent that clung to him.

"What if I say I wish to know his name for reasons that have nothing to do with your role as companion?" he posed, brushing his knuckle down her cheek. His touch was as delicate as a butterfly's caress. "What if I wish to know as a friend?" Something stormy and volatile turned his dark eyes nearly a shade of black.

A friend, he said. And yet, his eyes were those of a stranger. His careless words better suited the rake than the gentleman who confounded her with his words of concern and his defensiveness on her part. She stared at his rumpled white cravat, needing to build a barrier for this one-time friend, now seductive rake who made her want to risk all again in ways that would invariably result in her being hurt—again. "Is that what we are, Daniel?" she asked softly. "After all these years, friends, still?" For as much time as she'd spent as a young girl, hating him for having abandoned her, he'd been the only friend she'd ever known and he would, no matter what life and fate shaped them into, exist in that role.

Holding her gaze with his, he palmed her cheek. "I rather thought we were, Daphne." She curled her hands hard. Friendship is all they'd once known and, yet, with him now, there was a hungering for dreams she'd long ago abandoned. He slid his stare to a point over the top of her head. "Or rather, that we could be again," he murmured, more to himself.

Sadness assailed her. Of course, Daniel who received the world as though it was his due, would think nothing of picking up as the ten and almost thirteen-year-old children, they'd been. The difference being the ultimatum he'd give her, holding ransom those references that would set her free. "When I first arrived in London all those years ago," she began hesitantly. "I sat inside a stranger's household, who'd taken me in as a request from your father, looking out the window, waiting for you to come."

His body coiled tight.

"You never came," she said, stating the obvious as a reminder to herself. No one had. No one, except one suitor, who'd won her affections and her virtue. It was a testament to her own desperation. "I was in London for more than three months and not once did you visit. Were you too busy?"

A muscle leapt at the corner of his eye. "I…" That gruff single syllable went nowhere.

"It is fine," she said softly, taking a step away from him and resurrecting the much needed barriers. "We were friends, Daniel, and you will always hold a place here," she touched her chest and his gaze followed that slight movement. "But let us not pretend we're the same children racing across the lake." The girl she had been died in the copse with him at her side. When had his world been irrevocably changed? With Alistair's passing? Or his mother's? Or mayhap it had been a culmination of all the miseries he'd known. She gentled her tone. "We've grown up. Become different people whose lives have traveled divergent paths. I told you about Lord—" He thinned his eyes into narrow slits. "I told you what I did," she swiftly amended, "because I am a servant in your employ and, as such, you require the truth."

He firmed his jaw and that hard glint sharpened in his eyes. Had her words hurt him? Daniel, a man who'd prided himself on being incapable of suffering? "Of course, madam," he said crisply. "You are correct. I have hired your services and you're here with the sole intention of looking after my sister. As such, I will allow you to return to your responsibilities." He drew the door open and, with that unbending divide firmly erected between them, Daphne limped forward.

When he closed the door behind her, she leaned against the opposite wall and borrowed strength from the surface. This was for the best—this safe distance. Because for his question about friendship, Daniel was something wholly dangerous—a rake—and what was more, a rake who'd proven himself to be an honorable gentleman not condemning her for her past, the way most of the *ton* would.

With that loyalty and honorability, he posed a far greater danger than any rake ever could. For she was still the same, hopeful girl clinging to childhood dreams about Daniel and a future with him in it. And there could never be a future with Daniel Winterbourne. Ever.

No matter how much she might wish it.

CHAPTER 14

ALL WAS RIGHT WITH THE world.

Or those were the words that had been printed in the paper about Daniel Winterbourne, the Earl of Montfort, and his peculiar departure from depravity and sin, into a seeming calm of respectability.

Having spent the past three nights at his tables at Forbidden Pleasures, he had shattered all confusion about his true character. Of which there could be no mistaking—corruptible, dark, selfish, and all things black, he lived for his own gratification.

… We've grown up. Become different people whose lives have traveled divergent paths…

He downed his third tumbler of whiskey and stared into the empty glass. His path had been solidified long, long ago, when he'd raced Alistair across the turbulent lake in the middle of a summer rainstorm.

…grab my fingers… I said grab my fingers, Alistair, please…

He'd resisted thinking of his brother for more years than he could remember. Mayhap it was Daphne's reentry into his life that brought everything rushing forward. But he was tired of battling back his past. He'd spent nearly his whole life running from the young man he'd been and the pressing weight of guilt. Only, doing so hadn't made the pain of loss disappear.

Now he allowed the memories in.

Memories long buried. Of failings and loss. Of a brother who'd only stepped into that water because of his taunting, and then his parents' keening misery at finding their son dead because of Daniel's inability to save him.

Having entered into the world but twelve minutes behind his brother, he had always striven to prove his worth. To prove he was better than Alistair in *some* way. But for swimming, Alistair had excelled in everything. So desperate to prove his own worth, he'd raced Alistair, and his brother, the weak swimmer that he was, had been carried away by a violent current. If not for Daniel's inherent need to be better at something, his brother would even now be alive and his family would have never fallen apart as they had.

Drawing in a slow breath, he stared at the lone drop of whiskey that clung to the glass like a teardrop. Bile stung his throat as he glared into his glass. But to blast his deceased father's memory, he'd not thought of his family in too many years to remember. He'd not thought of how his family had once been smiling and his parents equally proud of him and Alistair. Until that dark night when no boys should have been outside the lofty walls of their estate, when everything changed.

He briefly squeezed his eyes closed.

In the darkest days after Alistair's death, his own culpability and his father's shouts, rightfully blaming Daniel, there had been one person there with him, through it all—Daphne. She'd been steadfast in her devotion. When he'd wept with guilt and the agony of losing his twin, she'd held him. When he'd engaged in riskier and riskier pursuits to gain his family's notice, she'd attempted to talk him out of his wickedness. It was just one of the reasons why he'd cut her out.

I was not there for her.

Through the raucous din of laughter and coin striking coin upon the gaming tables, Daniel firmed his jaw. Bloody hell, in his advancing years, he was turning into a maudlin bastard. He swiped his bottle from the table. Damn and blast Daphne for not staying buried. She, with her expressive eyes filled with disappointment one moment and hunger in the next.

The lady was right to take him to task for thirteen years of neglect. But for the rogues and rakes he kept company with in London and the beauties he took to his bed, he'd kept the world insularly out. That had been the easiest course and he had been a man who'd long proven he only ever took that particular route.

From the day his mother died trying to birth a better child than him, he had vowed to never again care or let anyone in. Not the babe his mother had left behind. Not the girl he'd once called friend. No one. That was, no one except the miserable blighters like himself. Those wastrel lords, who didn't give a frig. And so he'd retreated from the world, descending more and more into a level of sin and debauchery from which there could be no coming back.

...I was in London for more than three months and not once did you visit. Were you too busy...?

Yes, he had been too busy. Whoring. Cavorting with unhappily married women. Bedding both sad and joyfully free widows. Attending orgies. Hosting orgies. All of it, dark acts committed by a coldhearted rake. And through it, she'd been waiting for a visit. He winced as an image trickled in of Daphne as she would have been, a girl of seventeen, at the window. Alone in a world she'd never been part of, one that he had been wholly born to. In the end, she'd been an easy quarry for a rake who preyed on her innocence and earned her virginity.

His stomach churned and with unsteady fingers, he set the glass aside. Too much bloody drink. There was no other accounting for it.

"You look to be in need of company."

Daniel abruptly glanced up at the Marquess of Tennyson.

Both were former spares to the heirs who'd found themselves ascended to the ranks of nobility. Rivaling Daniel in depravity, they got on famously well since Oxford and, more importantly, Tennyson wasn't the happily married blighter St. Albans had become. Rather, this marquess was a ruthless bastard in the market for an heiress. Daniel motioned to the vacant seat and the marquess plopped his tall, wiry frame into the chair.

"You have been absent from Town," the other man remarked, as he claimed a seat.

He gave a wave of his hand. "I have the additional responsibilities of a sister now," Daniel reminded him.

"Ah, yes, that is right," Tennyson said, layering his hands on the arms of his chair.

With neither sisters nor brothers underfoot, the marquess didn't know a thing about those responsibilities. Not that Daniel did, either. Not truly. He just knew of late with his well-ordered life now thrown on its ear by his miserable uncle.

"So you've become a devoted brother, then?" By the mocking smile on Tennyson's lips, he believed that as much as Lord Claremont.

Daniel snorted. "Hardly. My uncle is ransoming eight thousand pounds left me by my mother, if I *behave*."

The marquess went still and then tossed his head back, howling with laughter until tears seeped from the corners of his eyes. "Oh, this is rich. And here, members of the *ton* befuddled by it all. Of course, you'd only ever be driven by a wager."

"Of course," he repeated tightly. Had the other man always been this bloody aggravating? Mayhap Daniel would rather do with St. Albans' concerned probing than this prig's taunting. He took a long sip.

"There have been wagers placed," Tennyson said without preamble. How many times had he planted information to aid Daniel in a bet placed at White's or Brook's? He'd long been without the moral scruples to feel humility at cheating another lord.

In the past, it had filled Daniel with a thrill of certain wicked victory. Now, it left him oddly bitter. "Wagers?" he drawled because really, something was expected of him.

"About you," the marquess clarified, motioning over a scantily clad beauty with red hair and crimson lips.

He gritted his teeth. Must the woman have goddamned red hair? "Oh?" he forced that reply out in bored tones.

"About the young woman you've hired." Tennyson accepted the glass from the lush creature and tugged her unceremoniously onto his lap. She let out a little squeal and then promptly layered herself to the young lord, nuzzling his neck while she worked her hands over his body.

Bloody hell. Now Tennyson would drag Daphne through his thoughts. With a scowl, he poured himself another whiskey and took a quick drink.

The marquess shoved the whore off his knee and then swatted her on the backside, sending her off. He sighed. "The wagers are rich on how soon you'll debauch your sister's companion and where."

Daniel inhaled his swallow and dissolved into a fit, strangling on his spirits until tears flooded his eyes. He set his glass down hard and liquid sloshed over the rim of the glass.

The marquess sat sipping away, indifferent to his gasping, heaving attempts for breath. The *ton* was well within their right to question Daniel's intentions toward any young woman, but having Daphne's name thrown about cast a haze of red over his vision.

After he managed to draw in a shuddery breath, Tennyson dragged his chair closer. He stole a glance about. "Eight thousand pounds is a near fortune, *but*," he dangled that one word. "We can manipulate the wagering to secure you a sizeable sum that doesn't require you to *behave*." The other man waggled his blond eyebrows. "Anything but." Of course, with the other man being an equal wastrel also with depleting coffers, he'd stand to earn nothing from Daniel honoring the terms set forth by his uncle. It was no secret to Society that Tennyson had entered the Marriage Market in search of a biddable miss with a fat dowry.

"You'd have me throw away eight thousand pounds to secure you a few hundred?"

The marquess slapped his hand to his chest. "I'm insulted, chap. I'd wager far more than a few hundred pounds on a sure bet."

Daniel had influenced more wagers than most bookkeepers could properly track. Odd, he had never felt any compunction about a bet; neither the type, nor amount, nor persons involved.

Until now.

Tennyson and the *ton* would turn him into the very man who'd once ruined Daphne. And, mayhap, he had some good left in his soul after all, because even as he wanted to bury himself between her welcoming thighs, he could never be the man to ruin her on a wager. To keep from burying his fist in the marquess' blasted face, Daniel balled his hands tight. "I am not debauching my sister's companion," he said icily. Even breathing the possibility of it aloud sent nausea roiling through him in waves.

Understanding registered in Tennyson's cold blue eyes. "Ah, I see."

Do not ask. Do not ask. Let the matter die...

"What do you see?" he snapped.

"She is long in the tooth."

"She is not—" Daniel snapped his mouth closed so quickly, his jaw ached. He'd said too much and the hard grin on the marquess' lips said as much.

"Then, I suspect eight thousand pounds is an exorbitant amount to throw away on a straitlaced spinster. Though, there is something," he smacked his lips, "*delicious* in breaking those ladies free of their constraints, isn't there?"

Actually, he couldn't say. He'd never bothered with the reproachful ladies and their disapproving eyes. "I am sorry to disappoint," he said with a droll edge, setting down his glass. "But I've no intention of corrupting my sister's companion, nor accepting any wager that would compromise," Daphne's reputation, "my uncle's funds," he settled for. "Now, if you'll pardon me," he said, shoving to his feet before the other man could launch a series of comments or questions about Daphne that would earn him a fist in the face.

Tennyson inclined his head, but he'd already shifted his attention to the nearby whore, sauntering by.

Daniel stalked through the crowded hell. The disreputable club was heavy with the thick plume of smoke from too many cheroots. The acrid smell blended with the pungent odor of floral fragrances worn by the women working the floors. Such scents had never bothered him before. Now, they invaded his senses so that he increased his stride, eager to step out the doors and draw in a cleansing breath.

He gathered his hat from a servant and jammed it atop his head. Then, shrugging into his cloak, he fastened it at his throat. The guard at the front held the door open in anticipation of Daniel's exit and he stepped outside. He paused, blinking to adjust his eyes to the darkened London streets. Filled with a restiveness, he motioned to the street urchin waiting with his mount. The boy rushed over and handed over the reins. Daniel fished around inside his jacket and withdrew a guinea. He held the coin out, when his gaze snagged on the emblazoned George III. Tucking it back inside, he reached for another.

The boy coughed loudly, holding his fingers out.

Daniel dropped the different coin into his palm and climbed astride his mount. Perhaps it was the impending financial doom which hovered, only just now really acknowledged by him. Or mayhap, it was the tiresome company of Lords Tennyson and Webb, discussing the same wicked topics, seeking out the same wanton pleasures, but with each stride that carried him farther and farther away from the unfashionable end of London, which had always been home, some of the tension eased in his chest.

For the first time, *ever*, as he reined in Satan, there was a greater ease in being at his white stucco townhouse than his clubs. Daniel dismounted and a waiting servant came to gather the reins. Cloak whipping wildly at his ankles, he strode up the steps and through the doors opened by his butler. "Tanner," he greeted, turning over his cloak and hat to the tired-eyed servant.

"My lord."

Dismissing the aged servant for the night, Daniel briefly eyed the top of the stairs. Alas, after a lifetime of living on no sleep with only sin and spirits to sustain him, retiring at the eleven o'clock hour was as possible as having the power to manipulate time. He strode down the corridor, seeking out his offices. No doubt, Daphne had long retired by this late hour. After three evenings spent at his clubs and various *ton* functions, but for glimpses of her and Alice during the day, he'd had little interaction with her.

Given the vicious wagers being bandied about Town, it was for the best. Nor, with the charges she'd leveled at him of disloyal friend, of which he most decidedly was, did she care to see him, nor should he wish to see her. He'd long existed for nothing outside his own comforts and happiness and, as such, was not in the habit of suffering through the company of people who didn't desire his presence.

Why should she desire my presence? He'd all but forgotten her existence, abandoned her during her Season, and coerced her into assisting Alice, withholding letters of reference she desperately required. The greatest crime, however, had been the inadvertent one—the one that had found her prey to a rake, when he, with his own unscrupulous experience, could have watched for those other ruthless bastards.

His stomach muscles clenched reflexively and he paused at the corridor leading to his office. Then, something pulled him away from that room, where he'd do nothing more than continue his path to inebriation. He wandered down the hall and stopped beside the open doors that spilled out to the ballroom.

Tomorrow evening, would be the beginning of the end to Daphne's tenure. Alice would make her official entry into Society and from there Almack's. Then there would be an endless parade of infernal affairs until she found a husband. A fortnight ago, he'd wanted nothing more than to be rid of his sister and free to resume his carousing. Now, hovering outside the room, he wanted to freeze time, keep it still, where there was Daphne, unafraid to tease him, scold him, or talk with any real freeness. Or rather, discourse that didn't begin and end with the ultimate goal of sexual gratification.

He yanked his silver flask from inside his jacket and uncorking it, raised it to his lips. ... *When you drink, you aren't really present. You are a ghost...* With a curse he recorked and pocketed his flask. Good God, he must be tired. Or insane. Or mayhap both. He, Daniel Winterbourne, the Earl of Montfort, rightly feared by all proper mamas, waxed on in silent maudlin thought for Daphne's inevitable departure. Not even a healthy dose of liquor would help this madness. Daniel started to turn, but froze mid-movement.

Moonlight streamed through the floor-length window down the left wall of the ballroom, bathing the cavernous space in a soft glow. The bluish-white rays danced upon the neat row of chairs positioned at the far corner of the room. A lone figure sat perched on the edge of the middle seat, her hands folded on her lap, and her cane resting on the adjacent chair.

He should leave. Pretend he'd not seen her tucked away in the corner. Then, he had never done what he was supposed to—not as a mischievous boy and certainly not as a rakish man.

M AYHAP HE DIDN'T SEE HER. Mayhap, he'd turn on his heel, that silver flask in hand, and lose himself in spirits, as rogues and rakes often did.

"Miss Smith." His quiet baritone echoed in the empty ballroom.

She sighed. Daniel had never done what was expected of him. Then, neither had she.

"My lord," she greeted, struggling to her feet.

He held a hand up. "There is no need to stand on my account," he assured, stalking forward. Daphne studied him as he took strong, confident strides, easily closing the space between them. She had been without proper use of her left leg for so many years that she no longer recalled whether such movements came as natural gifts of elegance or rather were something one strove toward.

So many times, envy gripped her when presented with such ease. But staring at Daniel's assured steps, her mouth went dry with an appreciation that stirred low in her belly.

In one fluid movement, he settled into the seat directly beside hers and stretched his legs out, hooking them at the ankles. He draped his arm along the back of her seat, brushing her nape with his fingers. Dangerous shivers radiated from the point of his absent touch.

Rakes were men who filled voids of silence with empty talk and clever words. Daniel, however, just sat staring out, his gaze fixed on the pillar directly across from them, draped in garland made of ivory and white hydrangea. The fragrant floral scent permeated the ballroom and Daphne inhaled deep.

Three days ago, she'd resurrected the needed barriers between them. For as she'd said, he was no longer a friend, but a rake, dangerous in what he made her feel, longing she'd not even known with Leopold. But this was Daniel and she would never, ever be able to truly shut him out. "It is beautiful," she said wistfully.

He glanced around, perplexed.

She motioned to the ballroom, adorned in boughs and garlands of white and green hydrangea. Grabbing her cane, she pushed to her feet and limped to the middle of the dance floor. "How very empty and silent it is now. Tomorrow, it will be ablaze with life and music and laughter." A wistful smile played on her lips. In a way, she rather preferred it with only they two here and the hum of silence their only music.

"Did you enjoy it?"

She looked to him.

"Your Season," he clarified, his gaze, even in the dimly lit space, radiating a somberness so different than the charmer he was.

"When I was a girl, when I arrived in London, all I wanted was to attend my first ball. I had dreams of how it would be." She motioned to the empty dais where the orchestra would be set tomorrow evening. "There would be haunting waltzes and lively reels." She closed her eyes to the music playing in her mind. "When I came to London," she said, losing herself in that remembrance. "I was filled with such excitement, I didn't allow myself to think about how it would be." As a cripple. She let those words go unsaid. Daniel watched her so closely, her skin pricked with the intensity of the gaze he trained on her face.

"I'm sorry," he said quietly and heat flooded her cheeks.

She'd not have his pity. "For one month, I was lonely. Miserable. Wanting to go back to my father's cottage." She pivoted around to where he still lounged. The tightness around his hard lips belied his relaxed repose. "I sat in those chairs." She smiled. "Well, not those chairs, but wherever the neat row was set up for forgotten ladies were the ones I occupied. I did not dance one set," she murmured, her gaze unseeing, fixed on the gold candelabra behind him. "Not one." She lifted her shoulders in a shrug. "But then, I forced myself to explore the world around me, a place I'd never been, and came to appreciate the museums and parks." Daphne smiled, recalling the moment she'd stepped outside the townhouse, determined to command her happiness.

Daniel shoved slowly to his feet. "I should have been there," he said, his tone gruff as he came closer.

She offered him a half-smile. "Yes, you should have."

"If I had been there, where you were…" She'd not have had her innocence so calculatedly stolen.

Sadness assailed her. "Many times you were."

He started.

She looked away, staring out at the orchestra's dais once more. That long ago night flitted forward. The first glimpse she'd caught of Daniel upon arriving in London. How gloriously handsome he'd been in his impeccable black garments and wearing a half-grin on his face. "We attended many of the same events."

"Surely not?" he demanded, hoarsely.

"Surely," she countered. "You just…did not see me, Daniel. You were too busy." Flirting on the sidelines with gloriously clad beauties and voluptuous creatures with rouged lips and eyes. How she'd despised those ladies for having replaced her and earned Daniel's affection in ways she'd only dreamed. "I sat in those seats, in awe of your confidence amongst the *ton*." She chuckled. "I spent so many nights hating you for your ease."

Daniel caressed his knuckles down her cheek in a whispery soft touch. "I am so sorry." He stilled. Then, as long as she'd known him, he'd never been one to apologize. He'd often found a roundabout way of distracting a person from any crime he'd been guilty of before uttering them.

She frowned at him. "Don't you dare go pitying me." Not wanting that pulling emotion, Daphne stepped away, wandering deeper into the ballroom. "It was not all bad." For a time, it had been gloriously wonderful. Ultimately, she'd paid the price for that excitement. She stopped in the middle of the dance floor, under the enormous chandelier. "After a month of misery, I met him." She tilted her head and stared at those crystal teardrops dangling from that grand piece.

"Did you love him?" Daniel called behind her, bringing her attention back.

The flippant words on her lips about rakes not knowing of or believing in love faded with the somber set to his chiseled features. "I loved what he told me," she said, in truth. "I loved how he made me feel and the excitement that came with a man such as him ever wanting…" *A woman such as me.* She grimaced. With a woman's eyes, she now saw what easy prey she'd been for a man like Lord Leopold Dunlop. The second son of a powerful nobleman, he'd been untitled, but that truth had never mattered. She'd been so desperate for affection she'd given him a gift he'd never deserved. In the days after his betrayal, she'd resolved to never be a weak, pathetic woman dependent on any gentleman. She straightened and then gasped, finding Daniel a handful of steps away. Her heart thumped hard at his nearness. "Do you know how many times he danced with me?"

He gave his head a slight shake, dislodging a chestnut lock. "How many?" His was a harsh demand.

Daphne stretched her fingertips and brushed the loose strand back; luxuriant like satin. Unlike Lord Leopold's who'd caked his hair in thick oil. "Not once, Daniel," she murmured. "Through the whole of my Season, we didn't dance even one set. I told myself it was because he loved me and didn't wish me to humiliate myself. I later learned different." Never before had she breathed word of Lord Leopold Dunlop to anyone. He existed as nothing more than a past mistake, one she didn't allow herself to think on. In speaking of those three months to someone, there was something freeing that left her with a lightness in her chest. Of course, it should be Daniel. There had only ever been him in her life. Terror battered at her senses. For there could never be anything between her and Daniel. Nothing, honorable.

An animalistic growl rumbled deep in his chest. With the fiery rage burning from within the depths of his eyes, he was the boy who'd beat one of the villagers' sons for having stolen a kiss from her when she'd been a girl of ten. "No wonder you hate me. It was my fault."

She puzzled her brow.

He slashed the air with his hand. "If I had been there—"

Her small bark of laughter cut into his misplaced guilt. "The arrogance of you, Daniel Winterbourne, taking ownership of my mistake." She looked him squarely in the eye. "It was *my* mistake and you being my friend would have never undone it."

A thick silence descended on the ballroom.

Daphne shattered it. "I should return to my—" Her words ended on a gasp as he shot an arm out and curved it about her waist. With his spare hand, he tossed aside her cane, where it landed with a noisy clatter upon the marble. She eyed the brown stick and then swiveled her gaze up to Daniel's. "What are you doing?" she asked, breathless from the press of his hand through the fabric of her dress.

He lowered his lips close to her ears and the hint of brandy and cinnamon, an intoxicating blend of strong and sweet, filled her senses. "Eighteen years is entirely too long to not dance or swim or ride. I'm dancing with you, Daphne." How many times during her Season had she secretly wished to be waltzed about by him? "The bastard who stole your virtue was a bloody fool, without a jot of sense to see the treasure he held."

And God help her for the folly from which she would never recover from, Daphne fell deeper in love with him, there amidst the empty ballroom with the London stars twinkling outside the crystal windows as her witness. It was folly and dangerous, and far worse than any mistake she'd made with Lord Leopold and, yet, it had always been Daniel. With her mind churning slowly, he guided her through the first step.

"Relax, Daphne," he whispered, against her ear. "I'll not bite." He flashed another one of his seductive grins. "Unless you wish it." And just like that, the panic dissipated and she laughed. Relaxing in his arms, she turned herself over to this moment.

She'd loved Daniel Winterbourne since he'd carried her across the countryside. And she loved him for being a man who didn't see her disfigurement…a man who saw she was capable and not an object to be pitied. And a man who made her feel alive. In ways she'd never had in the whole of her life. There would never be more, could never be more. With his love for wickedness, Daniel would never be constant and she could never be with a rake. But there would be this and it would be enough.

Liar. I want all of him… Daphne faltered and he gripped her, deepening this relentless hold he'd managed. "I am falling all over you," she said, under her breath.

Daniel gave her a slow, wicked wink. "I am accustomed to it, love," he purred, startling another laugh from her. He joined her, that deep rumbling from his chest was unfettered and deep, pure in his joy. And how beautifully wonderful it was to share in his unfettered abandon.

"You are hopelessly arrogant, Daniel Winterbourne," she said, after their like amusement had faded. Handsome. Clever. Charming. He was nearly everything most ladies aspired to. *Nearly.* He'd never be faithful and, for that, there could not be anything with him. Her heart paused. Of course there couldn't. To him, she'd only ever be the girl he'd once been friends with and, now, was a companion for his sister. His gentle caress and tender embrace were no different than anything he'd given to so many women before her.

Daniel guided her in a small circle and she tripped again. He easily caught her to him, angling her so her weight shifted over to her right leg. She winced, as her muscles strained in protest to the foreign movements. As though in concert with her body, Daniel drew her close and anchored her to him while he twirled her in slow circles. He touched his lips to her temple and she slid her eyes closed in response. "You deserved a waltz to an orchestra's hum."

That hoarse declaration squeezed at her heart. *This is all I ever needed.* A wave of regret clenched at her with a vicious tenacity—a useless wish that he'd been anything but a rake. With his gaze, he roved a path over her face. Slowly, he brought them to a slow stop beside the dais.

Daphne's chest heaved with the force of emotion. Just over a week ago, he'd called her spiritless, but ultimately, he'd opened her eyes to the truth. In the eighteen years since she'd fallen, she had not truly been alive. She'd existed, but not truly lived. The one time she'd dipped her toes in the water of living, it had ended in folly. A folly that had made her retreat within herself. *I don't want to run anymore.* She wetted her lips and his gaze went to her mouth. "Daniel," she whispered.

He briefly closed his eyes and his mouth moved, as though in prayer. "You should go, Daphne," those words emerged garbled.

"Why?" She brushed her palm over the tense muscles of his cheek.

Daniel sucked in a slow, jagged breath. "Because I want to kiss you. I want to do a whole lot more with you and I'm trying to be honorable." His chest rose and fell quickly, and tenderness unfurled within her at his struggle.

A war raged within his brown eyes. Warmth filled her chest. The world saw only a rake and, yet, for all his efforts to prove the contrary, there was a gentleman alive within him. "I want you to kiss me." She wanted his embrace once more and would not feel guilt or shame. Nearly thirty, a woman grown, she'd know his kiss, if he let her.

"You don't understand," he rasped, dropping his brow to hers. "There are wagers and questions, and everyone believes I'll ruin you. And I *want* to debauch you, more than I've ever wanted another."

Her lips twitched at that rambling entreaty. "I expect you've far more *charming* words than 'I wish to debauch you'," she teased.

"Precisely. Normally I would." Daniel nodded jerkily, knocking her forehead. She winced. "Nor would I ever bump a woman in the head, until you, Daphne. What have you done—?"

She leaned up and kissed him. His entire body turned to stone against her and she braced for him to pull away.

With a groan he covered her mouth with his and there was nothing gentle about the meeting. He scooped her buttocks in his hand, anchoring her close, as their mouths met over and over again. He parted her lips and the taste of him flooded her senses. It tore a keening moan from deep inside where her greatest hungering for this heady passion lived.

Never breaking contact, Daniel guided her down, lowering her upon the dais, and coming over her. He dragged his mouth from hers and her soft cry of protest rang from the rafters. But he only moved his lips lower, finding the soft flesh where her pulse beat hard.

He suckled the flesh and she arched her head back, opening herself to his ministrations. He reached between them and shoved her bodice lower. The cool air slapped at her exposed skin and her nipples puckered.

At his absolute silence, her eyes fluttered open. He remained motionless, his gaze on her small breasts. She curled her toes as reality intruded. How many women had he taken to his bed? Beauties with abundant curves and, certainly, flesh that wasn't so freckled. Daphne fluttered her hands up to cover herself from his silent inspection, but Daniel captured her wrists, staying those movements.

Their gazes locked and the thick haze of passion clouding his eyes robbed her of breath. "Do not," he ordered. He touched his fingertip to the smattering of freckles between her breasts. "I wondered whether you'd still have these marks here."

"Alas, even without swimming n-naked in the lake under the summer sun, I'm still hopelessly freckled." All hopes of levity were lost by the faint tremor to that breathless admission.

"You are so beautiful," he whispered, touching his lips to the smattering of specks. Heat pooled at her center, filling her with a restless yearning.

She wasn't. But when he looked upon her with his molten hot gaze, she could believe those words spoken in his husky baritone.

He drew his mouth away and she mourned the loss of that tender caress. But then a soft cry escaped her as he closed his lips around the tip of her right breast and suckled that flesh. Toying with it. Teasing it, until she existed as nothing more than a bundle of throbbing nerve endings. Daphne moaned, arching her hips, desperate for his touch on that sensitive area he'd stirred to life.

Reaching between them, he tugged her skirts up. *I should not do this...* And yet, she was a woman, in control of her life. There would be no marriage or suitors, but there would be this. If he stopped, she'd be left with a dark, hollow emptiness, an unfulfilled ache. He palmed her mound and she gasped. "Daniel," she pleaded, needing more.

With strong fingers, he began to stroke her, toying with her nub, and she grew wet between her thighs. He claimed her mouth again for a searing meeting and he thrust his tongue inside to the rhythm he set with his fingers. His touch drawing her higher and higher, up an impossible climb. Her undulations grew frantic, taking on a pace driven by a frantic yearning for more. "Come for me, love," he pleaded against her mouth, quickening his strokes. She hovered on a precipice, hanging suspended.

He closed his lips around a nipple, drawing the bud deep into his mouth, while his fingers continue to work her and she shattered. A low tortured moan of agonized bliss spilled from her lips as she lifted her hips in a frenzied undulation, into his touch, coming on wave after wave, until she collapsed.

Eyes closed, Daphne lay there, her body humming and sated. Daniel came down beside her and draped an arm around her waist. His breath stirred the strands of curls at her ear that had come loose from her exertions. He placed a kiss there with such tenderness that tears pricked at her lashes.

"I am so s—"

"Daniel Winterbourne, if you apologize to me," she said breathlessly, "I'm going to bloody your nose."

A grin danced at the corners of his lips.

"I have never felt anything like that." How very inadequate those words were to capture the explosive bliss that had left her body weak, still. "Thank you," she whispered. For the first time in her life, she'd known passion that had touched her soul. And how right it was that Daniel had been the man to awaken her body to the power of lovemaking.

Wordless, he touched his lips to her temple and drew her back against him. "I love you," she said quietly. Against her ear, she detected the frantic rhythm of his heart. "I did not tell you that because I expect anything, Daniel," she said on a rush, when he remained frozen in silence. "I told you…" *Why did I tell him?* "Because I needed you to know how I feel," she finished lamely.

And she knew the precise moment she'd severed the connection with him.

He edged away from her. "You don't know me, Daphne. I'm not a good man."

She shifted in his arms, blocking his retreat. "I'd wager I know you better than you know your own self."

"I am a rake," he said, panic in his eyes. "You've confused what we've done here as love."

"I may have little use of my leg, but I know my mind," she shot back. Poor Daniel, how long he'd gone without any love or good in his life. She gentled her tone. "This is not about what's happened here. This is about a man who doesn't see me as nothing more than a cripple. A man who didn't laugh at my dreams of finding employment and encouraged me to make those dreams real," she finished as he swung his long legs over the edge of the dais, settling his feet on the floor.

"Do you love the man who forgot you existed for thirteen years?" His words sucked the air from her lungs and she battled back the onslaught of hurt.

When she and Daniel had been children, they'd come across a wild cat that had caught his paw in a hunter's snare. The creature had snapped and hissed, lashing out in his pain. How very much he was like that wounded creature. She slowly eased over to where he sat on the edge of the dais. "You let your father in here," she touched her fingertips to his forehead. "And it has scarred you here, Daniel." She lowered her palm to his chest, where his heart pounded wildly. "You have to trust that you deserve love and are capable of giving it." Until he did, he would never be free of his past.

His throat worked and there was a softening of his tense features. And then as quickly as it had come, the cool mask was back in place. Daniel disentangled her hand from his person. "Because there can never be more with me," he said succinctly. "I am incapable of giving you more."

And with that cold reminder, he stalked out of the room, leaving her alone—once more.

CHAPTER 15

SHE LOVED HIM.

Daphne's whispered words set off a firestorm of panic and terror that clutched at his mind, threatening his sanity.

People did not love him. Which was good. Which was how he wanted life. He'd been responsible for the suffering of all those who'd loved him: his mother, his brother. Now, Daphne had flipped his world upside down with talk of that very sentiment he'd avoided the whole of his life. His heart knocked painfully against his ribcage.

Still, with her hurt expression as he'd swiftly retreated last evening still fresh, he proved the ultimate selfish bastard—for he'd not undo that moment in her arms, last night, even if he could.

Never again would he look upon the dais in his ballroom without seeing in his mind the image of her spread upon it, arching into his hand and crying out her release. It did, however, make it far more bearable suffering through the tedium that was hosting his first—he shuddered—polite event.

From the front of the finally dwindling receiving line, Daniel stared over the heads of dance partners performing the steps of a godforsaken quadrille to that slight rise to where the orchestra played. Given all the whispers and wagers flying about Town, if he were an honorable gentleman, he'd at least feel some compunction at having taken her in his arms. But he was no gentleman, nor had he ever proclaimed to be, wished to be, or ever miraculously transformed into.

At his side, his sister shifted on her feet. "I certainly see why you are a rake," she groused under her breath, effectively dousing all wicked musings of Daphne Smith. "I'd far prefer attending wicked clubs and placing scandalous wagers to this infernal line."

Daniel frowned. "What do you know of wicked clubs and scandalous wagers?"

His sister flashed him a grin that was not at all innocent and entirely too mischievous and—he flared his eyes—by God, it was *his* smile, which given his own life, hinted at wickedness. "I asked—?" The next guests, Lord and Lady Buckingham, came forward and the question went unfinished as necessary introductions were made. "I asked what you know of wicked clubs and scandalous wagers," he repeated, as soon as the older couple left and they were alone.

Alice let out a beleaguered sigh. "Really, Daniel. You needn't sound disapproving like some worried papa." A worried papa? "Or protective brother."

He tugged at his suddenly too-tight cravat. *Damn it all.* "I am most certainly not a concerned papa."

"I said worried papa," his sister retorted. "Then, very well, you needn't be a protective brother."

A protective brother? He, who'd not allowed himself to think of Alice but for the handful of times he saw her through the years, was…was… He cursed, earning horrified stares from the couple who'd not made their full descent. They could go to hell with their shock. "You are my responsibility," he said out the side of his mouth.

Alice gave a roll of her eyes. "I'm a woman of seventeen years. Not a girl of seven. The time for elderly brother responsibilities came and went at least five birthdays ago."

Regret sliced through him like a dulled knife. And this time, when the next guest arrived, he gave thanks for the interruption that saved him from formulating a reply he didn't have and answering for the crimes of his absence.

After Alistair's drowning in the family lake, his father had foisted another child on his wife to "give him another child he could at least be proud of" as he'd snapped at Daniel the day he'd informed him of the impending birth. Then there had come his mother's death shortly after Alice had entered the world and the reminder, once more, from his devastated papa that Daniel was responsible for the death of all those he'd loved. That was one of the last times he'd spoken to his father. Instead, they'd both spiraled into a rapid descent of ruin—his father, in his misery, all but drinking himself to death and wagering away his life and Daniel...following in those same footsteps on the path of destruction.

In the end, he'd reckoned himself to be just like his father.

"You needn't frown, Daniel," his sister said gently. "I did not mean to give you hurt feelings."

Hurt feelings, now? He searched around for a servant. Would drinking a glass of champagne at the front of one's receiving line disqualify him from the terms set forth by his uncle? ... *You drink too much, Daniel... You use it as a greater crutch than the cane I use for walking...*

"And I should thank you," his sister continued, patting his arm. "You gave me an appreciation for finding adventure and thumbing my nose at Society's conventions."

Christ. "You are certainly not thumbing your nose at Society," he hissed.

"Smile, Daniel, people are staring."

He continued over her interruption. "You are going to find an honorable, respectable," dull and proper, "husband."

She lifted a hand and the card dangling from her wrist danced on the string. "By your admission, such a gentleman does not exist."

"Then you won't marry," he muttered. Not when the bloody alternative was to see her married to a man like Tennyson or Webb or worse, a man like Daniel himself. Feeling her stare on him, he whipped his head sideways. Alice eyed him as though she'd discovered a new genus of human. "What?" he snapped.

"You wanted to launch me like a ship, so you could then carry on your reckless ways."

Was there a question there? Then, as the orchestra concluded their set and couples left the dance floor, politely clapping, a horrifying realization trickled in. *Good God.* She'd listened at the keyhole during his discussion with Daphne. His mind raced. *Bloody hell.* What else had she heard? "Yes, well, no launching. I'm certain there are some decent chaps," he said belatedly to her questioning look. Daniel eyed the dance floor. There was, Lord... Or Lord...

Christ, yes, there was no one.

"And wealthy. He must be wealthy you said."

Because funds would make her life easier and, yet, her happiness mattered most. "I would have you wed a man who makes you smile," he said at last.

"Do you know what I believe, Daniel?" his sister asked softly. "I think Miss Smith has been a good influence on you and reminds you of who you once were." A sad smile hovered on her lips, reaching all the way to her eyes, and hit him like a gut-punch. "I just wish I had known you then."

His throat constricted and he made a clearing noise, coughing into his hand. He'd spent his lifetime proving his father's accusations right and never was his success truer than when presented with Alice's regretful words. Now, she spoke of him being a better person because of Daphne. Involuntarily, he sought her out. She sat primly on the edge of her seat, shoulders erect, head forward, unmoving. A glorious crimson Athena in an ice blue gown. With her regal demeanor she was the perfect companion. She shouldn't be seated there. She didn't belong hiding in the corner, just as she hadn't belonged on the sidelines of a ballroom all those years ago.

Alice jammed an elbow into his side and he grunted, looking to the next pair of guests who came forward. The Marquess and Marchioness of Guilford warmly greeted her and then the marquess leveled Daniel with a black glare.

"Montfort," the marquess said tightly. Yes, given his attempted seduction of the other man's wife, that dark look was certainly called for.

Daniel dropped a bow. "A pleasure." He shifted his attention to the dark-haired marchioness. "Lady Guilford." He stared after her a long moment, this woman he'd once attempted to bed. A woman who'd established an institution for young ladies with disabilities, a place Daphne dreamed of working. *Introductions.* She would desire an introduction to the distinguished marchioness. And yet, God help him for being a bastard who didn't want to arrange it for fear of what it would entail. Daphne cheerfully off to seek employment elsewhere—

Alice jammed her elbow in his side and he grunted again. His neck heated at the hard glint in the marquess' eyes. Yes, given his reputation, the man was certainly deserving of his suspicious opinion of Daniel's staring.

The couple started down the stairs.

"Did you tup his wife?" Alice whispered.

Daniel scrubbed a hand over his face and looked anywhere but at his sister and her far too clever eyes. By God, this was to be his penance. A sister who knew entirely too much and craved wickedness. "Have a care in what you say," he demanded in hushed tones, for her ears alone. "Your reputation—"

Alice snorted. "Come. Surely you see the hilarity in counseling me on proper behavior? Well, did you? Bed that gentleman's wife?"

Damn her for being correct. He was certainly the last person in the realm to be schooling anyone on matters of propriety. His feet twitched with the urge to flee and he again found Daphne with his gaze. She'd know how to handle this and what to say... There would be no help there. "No," he bit out. "I did not bed the lady." Certainly not for a lack of trying.

"But I expect you tried," Alice said and then turned to greet the next pair through.

Oh, saints be praised. "St. Albans, Lady St. Albans," Daniel said quickly, besieged with relief at the arrival of actual friends. Well, one friend and his wife, now eyeing him with rightfully wary eyes. Daniel's neck went hot and, not for the first time since his world had been upended these past weeks, embarrassment gripped him. After all, the lady had crashed one of his orgies and found her husband in attendance.

"Lady Alice," St. Albans greeted, sketching a bow. After he added his name to her nearly full dance card, he said, "May I present my wife, Lady St. Albans."

"How do you do?" the lady murmured softly. It did not escape Daniel's notice the manner in which she angled her body away from him. "Are you enjoying your first ball, my lady?"

Alice snorted. "Hardly. I've already mentioned to my brother that I'd welcome the diversions he himself so enjoys."

Lady St. Albans flared her eyes and then buried her smile behind her hand.

St. Albans emitted a strangled laugh, his hilarity only deepening at Daniel's glower.

"I've assured her that she is in no way to enjoy any such amusements," Daniel mumbled.

"And I assured him that he's become quite respectable since I've come to London."

The marquess' mirth faded to a grin. "Indeed?" he drawled. "Montfort, a respectable, doting brother?" There was a probing curiosity there and Daniel shifted. It wasn't well done of a friend to strip a rake of his reputation at the front of a crowded ballroom.

Lady St. Albans shot her husband a faintly reproachful glance, but he only widened his smile.

"I suspect it is Miss Smith's doing," Alice piped in.

And amidst the din of the orchestra and buzz of whispers and discourse, a silence fell among their quartet. *Bloody hell*. St. Albans and his wife eyed him with renewed curiosity. "My sister suspects a good many things." Daniel infused a deliberate nonchalance into that drawl, praying for any distraction that might spare him from that scrutiny. It was the first time in the whole of his life he'd given a jot at being so studied.

Several moments later, the happily wedded couple walked off and Daniel stared at their retreating frames. How wholly different a man St. Albans had become. Spending time in the country with his wife, the marquess no longer visited his wicked clubs or brothels. Immediately following their marriage, Daniel had pitied the poor bugger. As St. Albans dipped his lips close to his wife's ear and said something that roused a robust laugh from the lady, a twinge of envy plucked at him.

"Never tell me you attempted to seduce your friend's wife?" his sister said on a horrified whisper.

He sputtered. "Good God, no!" The denial was ripped from him. Not that he'd ever been with moral scruples, but a man still had to draw the proverbial line somewhere.

"Thank goodness," Alice muttered. "I'm sure it is in bad form to—"

"It is." He scowled. "As is speaking about your brother or any gentleman's pursuits."

Alice folded her arms at her chest and arched an eyebrow. "If one shouldn't speak of those pursuits, then one shouldn't take part in them, either."

Clever girl.

"The Viscount Claremont."

And a rotted day only went from bad to worse with his servant's announcement.

Before his name was even finished being called, the viscount was already moving. "You look lovely, gel," their uncle said gruffly to Alice. "The vision of your mother."

The mother who'd only given birth to a babe to take the place of the child Daniel had failed to save that long ago day. His gut knotted. But then, if there had been no late in life childbirth, there would have been no Alice. A girl he'd spent seventeen years avoiding, only now finding, with her spirit and wit, was really...rather fun to be about. A smile tugged at his lips.

"Has your brother seen you properly cultured with trips to the museums?" the viscount pressed her, pulling Daniel back to the moment.

He stiffened. Of course, the bloody bastard would fix on the one end of the agreement he'd not yet honored.

"My companion and I have a visit planned tomorrow," Alice put in smoothly.

Their uncle peered at him for hint of the lie there. From the corner of his eye, Daniel detected Alice's wink. *Tomorrow*, she mouthed. Additional loyalty he didn't deserve.

"Hmph," Lord Claremont grunted. He shifted his attention, once more, to Alice. "And is your brother behaving?"

"Better than I'd ever believed him capable of," Alice said, rousing another laugh from their usually stern relation. "I believe it is Miss—"

"This is your first set," Daniel said hurriedly, before she attributed any of her false perceptions of him to a woman whose suitability his uncle had already questioned. Quickly gathering her hand, he settled it on his sleeve and started down the hall. The irony was not lost that he, Society's most notorious rake, was hosting a Come Out ball for a debutante just out on the Market.

"Yes," Alice whispered as they started down the stairs. "I rather believe it wise not to mention Miss Smith to Uncle Percival." Wise, indeed. "He would only assume something improper is occurring if I mention her influence."

Something improper had occurred and, God help him, he wished for it to happen again...and more. His eyes strayed to the dais.

"Are you blushing? Your cheeks are all mottled, Daniel."

"I do not blush." Just as he did not host, attend, or talk about proper events. Until now.

The orchestra struck up the chords of Alice's first set and her partner, St. Albans, came forward to escort Daniel's sister into the center of the ballroom.

Alice gone, he stood on the sidelines, arms clasped at his back, eyeing the dancers performing the steps of the quadrille. The lords and ladies in attendance were the most proper ones he could drum up given his reputation. The people in Daniel's usual company studiously avoided such dull affairs, as he himself had. He'd reveled in the dissolute friends and lovers he'd kept, for there were no meaningful connections or emotions. There were no lowered expectations, because those expectations had already been lowered years and years ago. As such, it perfectly suited the empty life of pleasure he wished to live.

Only…since Daphne had reentered his life, and forced him to smile, and challenged him on who he was as a person, he'd not sought out his usual pleasures. Not solely for the funds dangled over his head by his uncle, but because he'd not given those events a thought.

It is because of Daphne.

The thrill of each meeting, with whatever challenge she'd utter and scolding she might dole out, was more riveting than the monotony of the rakish existence he'd lived for so long. Good Christ, he needed a drink. Daniel swiped a flute of champagne from a passing servant. The silver tray wobbled in the footman's hands and the young man hurriedly righted it, before continuing on. With the need of liquid fortitude, he tipped his glass back and drank deep, concentrating on something safer. Something duller. And something less dangerous than catching a damn case of emotions.

As the set concluded and St. Albans turned her over to her next partner, Mr. Pratt, Daniel stared at his bright-eyed sister with her flushed cheeks as they performed the intricate steps of the reel. He froze. Had he ever been so innocent that something as simple as a dance could bring such visible joy?

…Through the whole of my Season, he didn't dance even one set with me…

Daniel tightened his grip involuntarily on the stem of his glass and found Daphne with his gaze.

She studied the dancers, a wistful smile on her lips that robbed his lungs of air. She deserved to dance. Not to the strains of an imagined orchestra in an empty ballroom, but bold and unrepentant in a fine satin gown with a smile on her crimson lips. One of the true smiles she'd spoken of. Not forced. Not sad or longing. And a hungering as powerful as the need for sustenance coursed through him to be the one to guide her through those steps.

Daphne stilled and shifted her gaze over the dance floor until she found him. Her eyes locked on his.

He inclined his head imperceptibly in a slight greeting. An unrestrained grin replaced the earlier one. The cacophony of the ballroom sounds melted away as he saw just that smile. And her.

Fingers curled around his forearm, shattering the charged connection, and he whipped his attention down. "There is something very tempting about slipping away from polite events and taking your pleasures outside the ballroom with the thrill of discovery, isn't there, my lord?" Baroness Shelley wrapped that invitation in a husky purr that promised sex and sin.

He passed his gaze over her, assessingly. The gold creation she wore featured a plunging décolletage that the rouged tips of her breasts faintly crested over. The satin fabric with a lace overlay clung to abundant hips and generous buttocks. She was a veritable feast, of which he'd have gladly availed himself to. Oddly, this time, he remained unmoved. Daniel carefully disentangled her grip from his sleeve. "Alas, madam, I am to play host tonight. You will have to seek your pleasures elsewhere."

Shock rounded her eyes; the dark charcoal making the violet depths a stark purple in her face. Then, she swiftly schooled her features and, with a slight pout, sauntered off.

Daniel closed his eyes a moment. What in the hell was wrong with him? Sending off an inventive creature who'd fulfill a man's every carnal wish? Except… He knew.

It was a fiery-haired siren with expressive eyes and who, through her presence alone, reminded him that once, long ago, he'd been an entirely different man than the one he'd become.

SEATED ON THE FRINGE OF the ballroom, Daphne sat perched

on the edge of her chair, searching desperately through the throng of lords and ladies for a particular one announced.

She was here—the Marchioness of Guilford.

A guest of Daniel's. He knew the lady and had made no mention of that connection. In the crowd, she caught glimpse of the lady speaking with her husband and then a couple moved into Daphne's line of vision, blocking her view. Sinking back in her chair, she moved her gaze elsewhere and her stare collided with Daniel's tall, elegant figure. That twinge in her chest ached as a beautiful creature sauntered off, flashing him an invitation with her eyes. Resplendent in midnight finery, that showcased his impressive, broad strength, he exuded a commanding strength that was hard to not admire.

For any woman.

From the debutantes to dowagers present, they all covetously eyed him. That unrestrained appreciation roused unwanted jealousy. He'd never be a man who belonged to one woman. Instead, she, just like many others before her, would dream of and hope for—more with him. From him.

She returned her attention to the young couple he now spoke to; how free he was with his laughter and discourse for the Marquess and Marchioness of St. Albans. Vague remembrances slipped in, of Lord St. Albans who'd occasionally visited Spelthorne.

Taller and broader than when Daniel had first introduced them all those years ago, that meeting rushed forward with such clarity, they may as well have been children in the copse. The anger, fear, and sense of betrayal at having a new friend added to their mix.

…I promise he will never replace you, Daph. He's my friend at Eton. But you'll be my forever friend…

Pressure squeezed at her heart. And yet, his bond with the marquess remained strong enough that they were friends even still. Whereas Daphne had been severed from his life like a thread dangling from his sleeve. As they continued speaking, she studied their exchange.

Given the station difference between her and Daniel, it should come as no great shock that they'd invariably drifted apart. It was the way of their world. He belonged amongst the powerful peers who now danced within his ballroom. And she belonged on the sidelines, serving his sister, and then after Alice, hopefully other young ladies. Young ladies, who'd someday step out into this, or another ballroom and enter Polite Society.

Where Mrs. Belden's had represented hope, the idea of her future without Daniel left her bereft.

As though she felt his eyes on her, Daniel had sought her out. Even with the stretch of the floor between them, his concern reached across the room. He frowned, a question in his gaze. She mustered a smile she did not feel for his benefit.

"There you are, Miss Smith."

Daphne shrieked at the unexpected interruption, earning stares from the other companions seated beside her. "Alice," she greeted and quickly grabbed for her cane, awkwardly shoving herself to her feet. She grimaced. With her fascination and distraction with her employer, mayhap Mrs. Belden had been correct after all, and Daphne would make a rotten companion.

Alice's eyes twinkled with a knowing gleam that sent panic mounting. Surely she had not been so very obvious in her thoughts? "Come," the girl said, looping her arm through Daphne's. "Stroll with me." Daphne adored the young lady for believing she could stroll anywhere. "I would have a moment away from the crush of guests." They started toward one of the curtained alcoves off the corner of the ballroom. It did not escape her notice that Alice slowed her stride to accommodate Daphne's uneven, awkward gait.

Self-absorbed in her own hungerings and fears, she'd not given proper thought to why her charge sought her out. "Is everything all right?" she asked, as Alice ushered her into the alcove and the curtains fluttered shut behind them.

The younger lady plopped onto one of the chairs set up against the wall and tugged her slippers off. "Oh, fine. Fine," Alice waved her slipper about. "With the exception of some pinched toes." A dreamy expression lit her eyes. "But I swear I feel no pain. We danced," she said, layering her head against the wall. "Mr. Pratt and I danced," she repeated. "He wishes to court me."

A joyous smile hovered on Alice's lips and at that tangible happiness, Daphne's maudlin thoughts about Daniel from before briefly lifted. For so long, she had been bitter and broken in the loss of her own innocence. Seeing it alive in Alice now, didn't fill her with fear or envy, but rather an equal happiness for what *could* be. She collected one of Alice's hands and gave a light squeeze. "Listen to your heart and mind in equal measure. And be certain he is worthy of you."

From outside the alcove, the orchestra's quadrille came to a stop. Daphne looked to the front of the curtain. "We should return," she said and made to stand.

Alice shot a hand out, staying her movements. "Are you enjoying yourself, Miss Smith?"

At the unexpected question, Daphne blinked slowly. The events were as infernal now as they'd been eleven years ago. "Quite," she said belatedly.

Daniel's sister snorted. "*Quite* tedious. But for my dance with Mr. Pratt, the whole affair has been boring," she said, wiggling her feet back into her slippers. "And like my brother, you are a dreadful liar, Miss Smith." At that likening to Daniel, Daphne's cheeks warmed and she gave thanks for the dimly lit space. Her charge sent her a probing sideways glance. "No doubt that tedium is why Daniel became a rake."

It was not Daphne's place to explain that, at one time, he'd been an altogether different person and only after her brother and mother's death had he slowly become a figure she no longer recognized. "Life changes us all," she offered, instead.

"Do you know, Miss Smith?" her charge began, as casually as though they spoke of the weather and not intimate details about Daphne's employer. "As a girl, I was often alone." Her heart tugged. Daphne had mourned her own mother's passing when she'd been a girl of thirteen. What had it been like for Alice to never know that special relationship? It should have been the Countess of Montfort beside her even now. "I never knew my mother and Daniel was…" She rolled her eyes. "You *know*, Daniel." Yes, Daphne did very well know. "And my father…" Alice's expression took on a distant quality. "My father didn't know whether I was a servant or daughter."

How grief had ravaged the Winterbournes. After their son's passing, the once smiling, loving Earl and Countess of Montfort's entire family had withdrawn from Society.

"I am sorry," Daphne said softly.

Alice waved off that useless apology. "It allowed me much time to observe the world around me. He wasn't always that way, was he, Miss Smith?"

Surely there was more Daniel's sister cared to do than hover on the sidelines discussing her brother's past? She opened her mouth to say as much, but caught the uncharacteristically solemn glint in Alice's eyes and ended the flippant reply. "No. He wasn't," she said quietly. In fact, but for those three months in London where she'd witnessed hints of his wickedness, she'd only known him to be the loyal, laughing friend.

"What was he like?" Alice pressed.

Through the slight crack in the curtains, Daphne searched for a glimpse of him. Couples twirled by in a kaleidoscope of vibrant colors, briefly parting to reveal Daniel. He remained engrossed in conversation with the Marquess of St. Albans and the lovely lady at his side. "He was clever," she said, pulling her gaze away. *He still is.* "Competitive." He'd raced her on land and lake and never let her win. "Funny." He'd had her laughing until a stitch had formed in her side. Invariably, life dulled the purity of that joyous sound. "Heroic," she said softly, more to herself, finding him once more.

Alice snorted. "Given his reputation and his absence these years, it's hard to see Daniel as anything other than a rake, and certainly not a hero."

There was, of course, merit to that well-deserved charge. Yet, time changed them all. Made a person into someone other than they'd been. In her case, it had seen her crippled. In Daniel's, he'd become a wicked scoundrel. There was no excusing his transformation, but rather an acceptance to how life had ultimately marked them. Wanting Alice to at least know there had been a time when he'd been a different person, Daphne displayed her cane and then settled it on the floor. "Do you know how I was crippled, Alice?"

Her charge shook her head. Curiosity piqued in her expression. "I was racing through a copse," *chasing treasures.* "It had been raining. I fell." Her leg burned in remembrance of that long ago agony. Her voice was hoarse from screaming and crying, until she'd lain there and simply waited to die. Or be discovered. "I was there for hours, alone. Your brother found me. And he carried me the mile to my home."

Alice's lips parted in surprise and her eyes went soft. "All I ever knew were Daniel's wicked pursuits and the scandalous gossip printed of him in the papers." Of which there had undoubtedly been much. "But you see more in him, don't you?"

...It allowed me much time to observe the world around me...

The determined light now filling Alice's brown irises sent off the first warning bells. Daphne wetted her lips and glanced about.

Alice pounced. "I see the way you are with one another." Daphne's stomach sank to her toes and she gave her head a frantic shake. This is what the girl was about? What Lady Alice spoke of would mean the ruin of Daphne's reputation as a companion. "How you look at one another. And I do believe, mayhap, Daniel could be one of those reformed rakes."

Daphne fluttered a hand about her throat, skittering her gaze about. The girl was wrong. Except upon the pages of sweeping love stories and gothic tales, rakes and rogues could not be reformed.

"You do not need to say anything, Miss Smith," Alice said, patting her hand. "I must return. I have another set coming with Mr. Pratt." Then the girl stood and marched off, perfectly cool, after she'd yanked the rug out from under Daphne's feet.

She closed her eyes and sank back in her seat. Her heart beat a double-time to the orchestra's too slow strands of a waltz. She'd been so transparent that a seventeen-year-old girl had seen all. Seen, when Daphne herself had only just realized her love for Daniel. He was a man who beautiful ladies in daring gowns layered themselves against.

A vicious envy for the cloying beauty she'd spied earlier at his side took hold. Despite his sister's naiveté about her brother, Daphne did not delude herself into thinking that any woman would truly matter to Daniel Winterbourne. When she left, his life would continue as it had for the past thirteen years, with countless women there to warm his bed. Her heart spasmed.

Enough.

Daniel did not factor into her future. Ladies of Hope did. A future with purpose did. By Society's standards, a lady could not have both, nor was it a possibility with Daniel, anyway. Even if her heart wished it. Then, he was a gentleman who'd thumb his nose at Society and allow his wife to march scantily clad through Hyde Park if she so wished it.

Pushing to her feet, Daphne retrieved her cane and limped from the alcove. She made her way back to her chair. With each faltering, lurching footstep, her skin pricked with the stares leveled on her. She'd long become accustomed to those stares. Invariably, people were drawn to that which was different, including people, though not always in kind ways. She stumbled and caught herself with her cane.

Loud sniggering ensued at her back. Squaring her shoulders, she turned and challenged the stranger with her eyes. "Do hush," a pretty blonde lady beside her scolded. "You should be kind to a lowly cripple."

Time had proven, even those attempting kindness, offered pitying words. *Say nothing. You are here not as a guest, but as a servant.* She'd never been the obedient sort. "There are different manners of low," she interjected softly. "The worst being those who fail to see the worth in all others, regardless of their handicap."

The two young women gasped and then, with matching frowns for Daphne, stalked off.

"That was beautifully said," an unexpected voice sounded softly from over her shoulder.

Daphne wheeled toward the owner of it, so quickly she stumbled once more. Her heart thumped hard. The Marchioness of Guilford. "My lady," she greeted belatedly, sinking into a horrid curtsy.

How many others had waved off that effort on her part, to *spare* her the exertions? The lovely woman with her midnight curls and soft eyes merely smiled. "I often tell myself it is not Society's fault that they speak without the proper words or respond in the right way."

The lady spoke as one who knew. Which was an impossibility; flawlessly beautiful and elegant in her movements, she exuded ladylike perfection.

"It just means you try to teach them the right ones," the marchioness said with a smile.

A young lady with golden curls rushed over, capturing the marchioness' arm, commanding her notice. Daphne retreated, watching the other woman until she disappeared among the other guests.

She'd earlier thought that a woman could not have love and a purpose outside of the household, but had been incorrect. The Marchioness of Guilford was proof that a woman could have love, purpose, and family.

Daphne sought Daniel out again with her gaze. There would never be that complete dream, as long as Daniel failed to see more.

CHAPTER 16

The TOWNHOUSE AT LAST EMPTY and quiet ringing in the halls, Daniel strolled through the corridors. In his hands he carried a bottle of brandy and glass.

By the terms set forth by his uncle, tonight had been a resounding success. He had rebuffed the advances of several eager widows. Widows who at any other time, he would have gladly *entertained* and buried himself between their welcoming thighs, as Polite Society carried on their proper events, just out of ear-shot.

His sister had danced every set. Those honorable gentlemen who'd partnered her, as dull as the plaster on his walls, men whom Daniel would never keep company.

There had been no scandals.

If all continued along this placid trajectory, Alice would be married off, he would be free—and Daphne gone. A pit formed in his belly.

Daniel paused and drew a long pull from the bottle, shaking his head with a grimace at the fiery trail it blazed. He reached the ballroom, the flower garland draped about the pillars now wilted and petals littered the floor like floral teardrops.

His gaze instantly found her, perched on the edge of the rise. Where she, of course, should be. How harmonious they'd been in thought as children and, now, even after the passage of time, those thoughts were the same still. Yet, how was a gentleman to act around a lady after she'd professed her love and he'd run like the Devil was nipping at his heels? "Miss Smith," he called out, his quiet greeting echoed around the room.

"My lord," she returned. It may as well have been last evening, when he'd lain her on that very surface and wrung cries of ecstasy from her full lips.

Strolling with bottle in hand, Daniel came forward. With a slower, deliberate stride, he allowed her time to stand and make a proper exit.

Instead, she fixed on his every movement, until he came to a stop beside her. Her eyes briefly went to his decanter. He braced for her stinging rejection of his company or her abrupt departure. Alas, this was Daphne—unlike any other woman he'd ever known. She ran guarded eyes over his person; lingering her stare on his chest. "You are missing some garments, my lord," she drawled, the wariness in her gaze made a mockery of that casual tone.

He despised her being guarded. He preferred her as she'd always been—his friend. Just…the friend he now also wanted to take as his lover. Daniel hitched himself up onto the seat beside her and she scooted over, making space for him. "Bah, cravats are over-rated." He abandoned his bottle, setting it on the dais next to him. In this moment, he didn't want to be soused or numbed. He just wanted to be with her, remembering what it was to laugh and tease.

A smile played on her lips and just like that, the easy calm they'd always enjoyed was restored. "I take it you are of like opinion on jackets and shoes?" She tipped her chin meaningfully at his white shirtsleeves and stockinged feet.

"Oh, certainly. Those, too." He angled his mouth close to her ear. "And breeches."

She snorted. "You'd have us walk around like Adam and Eve, in a veritable Garden of Eden, then."

Her vivid words conjured a tantalizing vision, an image more tempting than the apple those first sinners had thrown away para-dise for, of him and Daphne naked, twined in one another's arms, with her hair cascading about them. It was a sin that she should tuck those strands away so tightly and leave him to wonder about their length and feel and—

Daphne shot him a questioning look. "Are you unable to sleep, Daniel?" she asked. A wave of desire went through him at how effortlessly she wrapped his name in her husky contralto.

"Sleep?" He yanked out his timepiece. "It's entirely too early to be abed."

"Daniel," she chided, yanking the watch fob from his hand. She peered at the numbers. "It is nearly thirty minutes past four."

He waggled his eyebrows. "As I said, entirely too early."

She released the chain. Her startled laugh, clear and bell-like, pealed around the ballroom. A laugh wholly pure and unjaded like those false chuckles from the cynical women he bedded. He closed his eyes and breathed of her soft lilac scent, filling his lungs with it. And God, he would have traded all those other meaningless exchanges to have Daphne Smith under him right now. Her laughter subsided and she settled her palms behind her, leaning her slender weight back, away from him. The delicate planes of her face settled into a contemplative mask and with her distracted gaze trained on the mural overhead, he used it as an opportunity to study her.

He'd never given thought to what a woman was thinking. All that mattered was the feeling of mutual bliss that came in mindless sexual surrender. Meaningless couplings that, in a fraction of time, allowed a man to forget the emptiness that his life, in fact, was. The emptiness he'd allowed it to become. Here, beside Daphne, with her total lack of artifice, he wanted to know what she was thinking.

She turned slightly, looking at him. "What is it?"

"I want to know what you're thinking." What she was feeling? What caused the little glimmer of worry in her eyes, or made her nibble at her lower lip as she did now?

Daphne propelled herself upright. "And here I thought a rake didn't much care about anything beyond his own self-interests and desires." God, how in concert they'd always been.

"No," he murmured. "Generally, they do not."

She fell silent. For several moments, he expected she'd ignore his inquiry. "It will be nearly eleven years. Eleven years since I last attended a ball. Lord and Lady Ackerland's and what a grand event it was. There were so many guests, a person could scarcely move." Daphne trained her gaze on the pillar wrapped in ivory hydrangea and he hated that she saw in her mind's eyes a time he'd never been part of.

Daniel drew his legs up and wrapped his arms loosely about his knees. "The night was memorable enough that you remember it so clear," he murmured, desperate to bring her back to him and the present.

She grabbed her cane and tapped the marble floor in a broken rhythm. "A lady generally recalls the night she gave away her virtue."

His body coiled tight and he had the feel of a serpent poised and eager to strike. A hungering for the name of the bastard who'd robbed her of that gift filled him. Lowering his feet to the floor, he opened his mouth to speak but caught her sad eyes. He'd long shied away from any in-depth conversations, preferring talks of wagers, whores, and disreputable events. By that, he should grab his bottle, climb to his feet, and run as far and as fast as his legs could carry him.

But she needed to speak of that long ago night. It was written in the beautiful freckled planes of her face. So he waited.

"I wanted to dance." She spoke so quietly. Was the admission spoken for herself, for him? "Instead, he asked me to meet him in our host's library. Of course, I did not think of all the rooms and doors I'd have to open or the danger to my reputation," she spoke so quickly, her words tumbled over one another. "I just felt this…" She turned one hand up. "Excitement. How thrilling it was. He wanted to meet *me*." A high-pitched laugh bubbled past her lips. "It was wicked and clandestine, and unlike anything I'd ever done. Unlike anything, any gentleman wished for me to do."

And Daniel proved the soulless bastard he truly was and always had been. Because with that break in her telling, he wanted to silence her story. Wanted her to end it so he didn't know what had transpired between her and some nameless blackguard. Didn't want to think of his Daphne, a girl of seventeen, sneaking around a stranger's townhouse, to meet a man who ultimately became her lover. God, how he despised himself. For having failed her. For having failed to be there *for* her.

"He took me in his arms," she went on softly. A burning, biting hatred stuck in his throat and he struggled to swallow past it. "He promised to show me far grander pleasures than dancing." If Daniel was a proper rake, he'd be bored by a telling he already knew the end to. The rotters he kept company with bragged of their conquests and wagered on their next bed sport. Daphne lifted ravaged eyes to his and she may as well have splayed him open with the old broadsword that hung above his office at Winterbourne Manor. "He took me against a wall, with my skirts up like a whore."

His stomach roiled and he struggled to draw in an even breath. The image of her painted so real, it crept forward, insidious like poison; seeping into every corner of his being, threatening to consume him. "Daphne." He didn't even recognize that hoarsened voice as belonging to him. It was the gruff, gravelly sound of a stranger, with rage pumping through his veins.

"When it was over," she went on as though he'd not spoken, her words curiously hollow. "He grinned, this cold, empty smile." *That is not a smile, Daniel. That is an empty, dark expression that could never be disguised as anything good…* Oh, God, how he despised himself. "He said…" She shook her head.

Don't ask. It does not matter. "What did he say?" he demanded.

She wetted her lips and stole a glance about. "'You should be honored, Miss Smith. I've never rutted with a cripple before.'"

A black rage fell over his vision, momentarily blinding him, so all he saw, tasted, and smelled was the death of the man who'd broken her heart, used her body, and shattered her innocence.

"That was the last ball I attended." Daphne folded her arms at her chest, in a lonely embrace. He wanted to take her in his arms and drive back that dark solitariness that he knew only too well. She snuck a peek at him. "I'm surely scandalous to even speak of it. Especially with you," she said, swinging her legs back and forth slightly over the edge of the dais.

"Daphne Smith, you could not be scandalous if you ran through the king's palace naked as the day you were born."

His admission startled a laugh from her and a lightness suffused his chest at being the person to bring back her smile. "You believe I jest?" A loose curl popped free of her chignon and he leaned over and brushed it back, deliberately grazing his fingertips over her cheek. Her breath hitched and he lost himself briefly in the green of her eyes. He caressed his knuckles over the satiny soft flesh. "One scandal does not make a person scandalous, Daphne. It makes you a person who made a mistake." Whereas he, with a lifetime of sins attached to his dark soul, wore his deviltry as a second skin. Mayhap it was the late hour, but he was besieged with moroseness. Daniel absently picked up the bottle beside him, studying it.

Daphne took it from him and their fingers brushed; a sharp charge like the one that lingered in the air during a lightning strike passed between them. Then, Daphne drew back and trailed her finger around the rim of the bottle. "You recently told me about the wonders that come from losing yourself in another body." He winced. "I didn't know that wonder. It was painful and awkward and I stood there looking at the door, waiting for it to end. There was no ecstasy, Daniel. No bliss."

He closed his eyes. There could never be any mistaking Daniel Winterbourne as a gentleman. With his vices and darkness, he was not a man to duel another. Instead, if he found the bastard's name, he would tear him apart with his bloody hands and dance a jig upon his dead body with glee. Drawing in a steadying breath, Daniel faced her. "That is not how it has to be, Daphne." That is not how it should be.

She nodded jerkily. "You have said as much." She briefly dipped her gaze to the gap in his shirt and then slowly lifted her eyes to his. "And now I want you to show me."

A dull humming buzzed in his ears like the swarm of bees they'd knocked from a hive, all those years ago. His heart paused its beat. Surely he'd misheard her. Surely with his lust-filled dreams, waking and sleeping ones, he'd conjured that breathy appeal in his mind.

Daphne set aside the decanter and reached for his hand, twining their fingers together. She drew his hand close to her chest. "I want you to make love to me, Daniel."

PROPER YOUNG LADIES DID NOT ask a notorious rake to make love to them.

But Daphne was no longer a young lady. She was a woman. A woman who ached to know more than the glimpse Daniel had shown her last evening. Ached to know him in every way. To know the bliss he painted with his words and to block out the memories of that other time. To cleanse them from her and only know the beauty of Daniel's embrace.

"Daphne," he said hoarsely, slipping his hand from hers. She went cold, mourning the loss of his touch. "I cannot."

All the greatest humiliations of that night in Lord Leopold's arms ripped through her and her heart lurched. Of course. Gentlemen didn't desire her. The man she'd given her heart and virtue to had only wanted it as a twisted game of conquest that came in bedding an oddity. Daniel would have too many scruples to shame her in that way, but neither could he bring himself to find the bliss he so spoke of in her arms. Her entire body was afire with mortified shame. Daphne reached for her cane. "I see," she said, her voice hollow as she struggled to always unsteady feet. "Forgive me. I will allow you your spirits." Never more had she wished for the full functional use of legs to carry her far and fast away from this humiliation. She took a step and Daniel shot a hand around her wrist, staying her movements.

"What do you think you see?" he demanded.

Glancing down at his fingers, she looked to him, and proudly met his gaze. "I am no beauty, Daniel," she spoke with a pragmatism that came in knowing who she was and having accepted it. "I'm not a woman you'd take to your bed." Unlike that gloriously lush figure from Madam Thoureaux's who'd sidled up to him this evening; the pair of them, the picture of beauty personified.

"Is that what you believe?" he asked gruffly. Never loosening his grip, he drew her slowly closer until only a handbreadth of space divided them.

Heat poured from his broadly muscled frame, stealing her thoughts. Her mouth went dry. "I-Is it not true?" she managed, when she trusted herself to speak.

Daniel filled his hands with her buttocks and dragging her close he pressed her against the vee between his legs so that his shaft prodded her lower belly. Her breathing grew shallow. "Make no mistake, Daphne Delilah Smith, I want you." That husky avowal set off a wicked fluttering low inside. His brandy-tinged breath wafted over her; purely masculine and wicked, and wholly him.

"Then make love to me." Surely that sultry whisper did not belong to her?

He sucked in an audible breath and his flesh sprung harder than ever. Mayhap she was more than just a little bit wicked, because a thrill of feminine triumph raged through her at his obvious desire—a desire for her. Her in all her flaws and imperfections. But then, he released her so quickly she stumbled, quickly righting herself with her cane.

Daniel retreated a step, holding his hands up, as if to ward her off. "Damn it, Daphne, I'm trying to be honorable."

Warmth unfurled in her heart. At the furious and frustrated glimmer hardening his eyes, she fell even more in love with him. Yes, she would one day leave London and him…and they would carry on with their own separate lives as they once had. He'd marry and give another woman children. Grief scissored her heart. But she would have this from him. This moment, without apology or regret, just the pleasure he'd spoken of. Daphne limped forward. "I do not want you to be honorable. I want you to make love to me."

An agonized groan spilled from him. He closed his eyes tightly and his lips moved silently, as though in prayer. "You don't know what you are saying. You have romantic dreams—"

"Stop telling me what I feel or how I feel." Capturing his hand, she drew it to her breast and he instantly cupped the small mound. A harsh groan rumbled in his chest. "This is what I want, Daniel," she said resolutely, meeting his gaze. "One night of the pleasure you spoke of. I'm not asking for you to love me. I'm asking you to show me passion."

He stilled. Desire glazed over his eyes and then he caught her to him. The cane slipped from her fingers as he devoured her mouth. There was no hint of yesterday's gentleness. His was the kiss of a man who sought to brand her as his. Parting her lips, he thrust his tongue inside.

Daphne whimpered and met his movements with wild abandon, the heady taste of brandy and cinnamon swamping her senses. Retrieving her cane, he swept Daphne into his arms and she cried out as he broke the kiss. *He is stopping?* Her body screamed in protest. "What—?"

"I'm not going to take you on a ballroom floor or against a wall," he said on a silken whisper. "I am going to have you in your bed, spread before me, as I've ached to since you stormed my foyer." He searched his gaze quickly over her face. "Do you want to stop? Tell me now."

She wrapped her arms about his neck and kissed him, letting

her desire serve as her answer. They mated with their mouths in a primal dance until wetness pooled at her core. Daphne moaned in the pleasure-pain of his embrace. Yanking away, Daniel started swiftly through the ballroom. "Someone may see us," she whispered against his chest.

"They are all sleeping," he said instantly, his voice gravelly from unfulfilled desire. He caressed the swell of her buttocks, toying with the flesh through her gown, until he'd worked another breathless whimper from her lips. "Take pride in your pleasures," he commanded. "Let the world judge, for they do not know the wonder."

She marveled at his long-legged strides, those graceful, yet hurried steps that found them abovestairs so effortlessly. Not pausing, he pressed the handle of her door and closed it quietly behind them. He set her cane against the wall and continued over to the bed. Then, as though he handled the queen's crown, he gently set Daphne down in the center of the bed.

Daphne shoved up onto her elbows. He yanked his shirt over his head and tossed it aside, baring his naked chest to her gaze. Another bolt of desire raced through her. Broadly muscled, he was a chiseled masterpiece, sprinkled with tightly coiled chestnut curls. He lowered his hands to his waist. She should be shocked and scandalized and shy and look away, but God help her, she wanted to see all of him.

Unfastening his breeches, he shoved them down, kicked the pair aside so that he stood resplendent before her, a model of masculine perfection. His oak-hard thighs and taut buttocks all bespoke a gentleman accustomed to the saddle. His shaft jutted high and proud from a thatch of chestnut curls.

Her mouth went dry. He was everything beautiful…hard in places where she was soft. And perfect in ways she could never be. All the oldest insecurities came rushing forward, reminding her, once more, of her own inadequacies. Her throat worked painfully and she averted her gaze.

The bed dipped as he climbed upon it. On all fours, he came toward her. "Look at me," he ordered on a command that managed to be both hard and soft all at the same time; a demand no lady could deny. Daphne lifted her head and her heart tripled its beat at the passion burning from within his brown eyes. "I have never wanted another the way I've wanted you, Daphne Smith. You are beautiful and I'm going to show you tonight just how beautiful you are." Then he covered her mouth with his and he swept his tongue inside. The taste of him, the burn left as he palmed her breast through her dress, melted away all reservations.

He kissed her until her core throbbed, aching for his touch. Then, he rolled over and took her with him. He yanked the long row of buttons down the back of her gown, rending the fabric. Tiny pearls popped free and sprayed the bed and floor, landing with soft pings. She gasped. "Daniel, the cost—" Her words ended on a shuddery moan as he slid the fabric down to her waist. Her shift followed and then her breasts were exposed to the cool night air and his worship.

"You are so beautiful," he breathed, palming the small mounds. He pressed them together and thrummed the rosy tips of her nipples, wringing a tortured plea from her lips.

Then, he lifted his head and suckled first one of the aching buds and then the next. Daphne hissed through her teeth and arched her hips frantically, her hunger spiraling, as he raised her higher and higher up on a level of mindless desire.

Daniel continued his special torture. He flicked his tongue back and forth between her nipples, laving them, suckling them. She thrashed her head back and forth on the coverlet. "Please," she entreated, her hips undulating on a rhythm set by his touch. He stopped and she cried out at the loss of him. With his long, steady fingers, he shoved her gown lower and lower down over her hips. The reality slid forth, unwanted but unrelenting. *He will see all of me.* He would expose her damaged limb and make love to her broken body. "Wait," she whispered, resting her hand on his.

With his breath coming hard and fast, he looked questioningly at her.

"Leave it on. I'd not have you…" Her cheeks warmed, which was madness to blush so when she lay with Daniel in all his naked splendor. "See…" *My leg.* "Me."

Hooding his thick, chestnut eyes, Daniel pierced her with the desire reflected there. "I want to worship *all* of you, Daphne." Then, he slid her dress down her legs. Her shift followed, until she lay before him, naked and exposed in every possible way. She went motionless, as he shifted onto his side and worked his eyes over her. He touched every part of her skin with his hungry gaze, burning her as though it were a physical caress he bestowed.

He lingered on her left leg and she bit the inside of her cheek as her desire slipped. Daniel glided down the bed and caught her calf in his hand. "What are you...?" Her words ended on a shuddery whisper as he touched his lips to the oddly angled limb.

"So perfect," he whispered and tears blurred her vision. His breath tickled her skin as he trailed a path of kisses higher up her leg to the inside of her thigh. He palmed her center and she slid her eyes closed on a hiss, his touch sending a forbidden thrill through her.

Daniel pressed the heel of his powerful palm into her core. She bit her lower lip and tangled her fingers in his luxuriant chestnut strands. With a groan, he slid his fingers inside and began to work her. "Oh, Daniel," she cried out, bucking into his hand.

His breath came hard and fast in time to her own. And then he removed his hand, replacing it with his mouth. Of their own volition, her hips shot up as his hot breath fanned her center. She lifted into him, aching for...for the wickedness he held forth. A soft keening cry burst from her lips as he teased the pleasure nub, flicking it with his tongue and then drawing it into his mouth. She bit hard on her lower lip, scrabbling at Daniel's shoulders.

An agonized groan ripped from deep within her as he stopped, and shifted his weight over her. His hair damp with perspiration, she brushed the longer strands back behind his ears and splayed her legs open for him. Daniel settled himself between her thighs, resting his shaft at the entrance of her still throbbing womanhood. "Please," she begged.

He pushed inside her, inch by agonizing inch, and the drenched walls of her cavern smoothed his entry. His breath came raspy and harsh, and then with a hoarse shout, he lunged forward, filling her completely. She cried out and wrapped her arms about him, hanging on, as he set a slow rhythm and then gradually increasing the pace he'd set.

Panting, Daphne angled her hips, matching his movements. "Oh, God," he whispered, dropping his brow to hers as he continued his deep strokes that touched her to the quick. "You are so tight."

"I have never hungered for anything like this, Daniel."

A low growl of masculine satisfaction purred from his lips. As she caressed his cheek, he turned his head quickly and gently nipped at the soft flesh of her palm, teasing it with a kiss. "I'm going to show you the stars, love," he whispered and then quickened his thrusts.

Their hips rose and fell in harmony. Each time he filled her, Daphne arched her body, crying out as she crested that beautiful summit once more.

"That is it, love. Come with me," he ordered on a guttural groan.

Uncaring that it might rouse anyone else who shared that floor, Daphne tumbled over the edge on an eternal scream that reached the rafters. And with an echoing shout, Daniel followed, spilling his hot seed inside her and wringing every last ounce of breath and pleasure from her.

Daphne collapsed into the feather mattress. With great, gasping breaths, he came down above her, catching his weight on his elbows. Their chests rose and fell together and they remained, bodies flush, until their breathing settled into a smooth, even pattern. Daniel rolled onto his side and drew her against his chest. He smoothed his palm over her belly, in slow languid circles that brought her lashes fluttering closed.

After her fall, Daphne, as she'd once been, had ceased to exist for the world. All anyone had ever seen from thereafter was a cripple, dependent upon the charity and kindness of others. An object to be pitied. Less than a woman for the bend of her leg.

Everyone, except for him. Daniel who'd treated her as a woman of strength, capable to fill a role as companion when no other lord, lady, or gentry folk would.

The words tumbled to the edge of her lips, words that needed to be spoken, when his soft, bleating snore filled the quiet. Rolling onto her side, Daphne propped her head on her hand and studied him in sleep. The harsh planes of his face bore no hint of the jaded bitterness that he wore as a flawless mask. Stretching out her other palm, she caressed his cheek.

She'd told herself one night with him was all she would need to sustain her through the long, lonely life that awaited her as a spinster working at Mrs. Belden's. Lying beside him, her body still heated from his touch, she found out too late that she'd only lied to herself.

One night would never be enough with Daniel Winterbourne.

CHAPTER 17

AFTER MAKING LOVE TO DAPHNE, as he'd slipped from her chambers and sought out his rooms, Daniel had cemented a well-known fact—he was a worthless rake.

Such a truth would have never mattered before. Now, it had him hiding, trying to sort through the tumult of his tired thoughts. Hiding in the billiards room, to be precise, a wholly masculine sanctuary Daphne had no place passing or visiting, as such, a room where he could have some much needed distance from her and her siren-like grip over him.

Daniel arranged the balls on the table and grabbed his cue. He'd never been the manner of gentlemen to bed members of his staff, but Daphne was no mere servant—she was a friend of his youth and, as such, what transpired early that morn, should never have happened for that reason alone. He should be riddled with remorse and regret for it.

He stared blankly at the table. Where the same glass of brandy he'd poured earlier rested, untouched. Alas, he was a blackguard to his core. For he'd have forfeited his worthless life before giving up that time in her arms.

With any other woman, that carnal bliss would have exercised this inexplicable hungering he had of her. *What hold do you have over me, Daphne Smith?* How many times must he join his body with hers to sate his lust? *It will never be enough.* The idea held him paralyzed. Because that is all it was. Lust. It could not, nor ever would be more. And if he told himself that enough times, he may even very well come to believe it.

Footsteps sounded in the hall and his heart sped up in anticipation. Disappointment filled him. Tanner appeared, not with the fiery-haired siren who commanded Daniel's thoughts, but rather a gentleman. "The Marquess of Tennyson." Or rather, a rake.

Tennyson did an up and down look of him and then chuckled. "Good God, man, you look like hell. Imbibed, too much?"

"Indeed," Daniel muttered. Imbibed on thoughts of Daphne, and the pleasure of her body, and… He tamped down a groan and tossed his cue over to the other man. Tennyson easily caught it in his fingers. Grateful for the diversion, Daniel fetched another stick from the wall and returned to the table.

"After your proper affair last evening, I rather expected to see you at your clubs this morning," Tennyson remarked casually, perching his hip on the edge of the table.

With the marquess' assessing eyes on him, Daniel concentrated his attentions on the table. Not for the first time, irritated with the man's probing, he took his first shot and the crack of his stick striking the ball echoed in the room.

The marquess snorted and folded his arms at his chest, so the stick rested at his shoulder. "The *ton* is talking about you."

"The *ton* is always talking about me," Daniel drawled, as he leaned over the table and positioned his cue. Talk which was invariably unfavorable, scathing, and not at all good. He drew his arm back to take his shot.

"Yes," the marquess conceded. "But now, the gossips are trying to determine whether or not you've reformed your rakish ways or whether you're too busy to attend your old haunts because you're tupping your sister's companion."

Daniel's stick jammed into the top of the velvet table, sending his shot wide.

Tennyson laughed and availed himself to Daniel's snifter. Then setting it down, he studied his next move. "I had the same reaction to the outlandish idea that a fellow like you would ever abandon his rakish ways." Fortunately, he attended the remaining balls scattered about the table, mumbling to himself.

He'd ceased to care about Society's whisperings of him. But this was different. This was Daphne. Fury pounded away at him.

"Your shot," Tennyson said, motioning to the table. His words snapped Daniel back into movement.

He lined up his stick with his next shot, when the marquess spoke, halting his movement. "The papers have labeled your sister an Incomparable."

Christ. Daniel gritted his teeth so hard, pain radiated along his jawline. He completed his shot and the ball sailed wide. "Have they?" his counter-question emerged tightly. Of course, given his desire to return to his own enjoyments without the care of another person charged him. He should be elated at the words printed of Alice in the paper. But Incomparables were sought after and courted by lecherous and noble lords alike. He swiped a hand over his face. His madness was spreading to every corner of his brain. There was no other accounting for it.

"There is talk a sizeable dowry has been assigned the lady by your uncle," Tennyson said breezily. Too breezily. And as a rake himself who'd perfected the art of mellow indifference, he easily recognized it in the other man.

"And what of it?" If the marquess had a bloody brain in his head, he'd have detected the lethal edge to Daniel's tone.

But rakes and rogues were driven so much by their own greed, they oftentimes failed to see anything beyond that avarice—and desperation. Tennyson set his cue down on the edge of the table. "I'm thinking, it would be mutually advantageous to both of us." He gestured back and forth between them.

Daniel furrowed his brow. What was the other man on about?

The marquess glanced at the open doorway and then dropped his voice to a low whisper. "You are eager to be rid of your sister. I am in need of a bride with a fat purse." Tennyson lifted his palms. "You know how it is for a rake. Most proper mamas and papas have no interest in penniless lords with our reputations." It was an ideal solution dangled by the other man that should appeal to a ruthless bastard like Daniel. But being deservedly lumped in any category with this man left him feeling ill. "If I wed her, you'll be rich with your uncle's eight thousand pounds. I will be rich with her fat purse." Lord Tennyson grinned as though he'd conquered the kingdom. "And then, we may each carry on as we always have."

The man wanted to marry Alice. Nay, Tennyson wanted him to sell her like a whore. A fortnight ago, he'd have possessed not a single compunction about such a ruthless pawn. Alice had been a stranger, more burden than sister, who'd presented a distraction to his carousing.

Now, she was a young woman who saw too much. A woman with a refreshing sense of humor and clever wit. And he was *enjoying* the budding relationship with his younger sister. Where that truth would have once wrought horror, now he found himself welcoming the prospect of making a difference in someone's life. He tightened his mouth. He'd sooner see Tennyson dead than wed to her. Alice deserved more. She deserved a happy life and a family, like theirs had once been. A life she'd never known. And if it was Mr. Pratt, the impoverished barrister, then so be it. Suddenly, tired of the marquess' cynical company, Daniel returned his stick to the rack. "I've other plans for Alice." Ones that included her finding happiness with a gentleman who was not at all like himself or Tennyson or Webb.

The marquess' wrinkled brow hinted at his befuddlement. "But she's underfoot," he blurted.

Annoyed at the tenacity he'd once admired, Daniel clenched his jaw. "I am afraid I have business to attend, Tennyson. If you'll excuse me?" He'd just conveniently leave off that such matters included joining Daphne and Alice at the museum. Of course, his accompanying them was driven by a need to be rid of Tennyson and his own uncle's demands. And…

…*You are a rotten liar, Daniel*… Daphne's pain-filled words from that long ago day filtered through his memory.

"Of course." The marquess sprang into movement and hurried to match his stride to Daniel's. "Perhaps, I might first secure an introduction to your sister so—"

"The lady is out," Daniel said curtly. Or she soon would be. "With her companion." He'd duel the Devil in hell on Sunday before he let Alice near this rake…or any rake, rogue, or scoundrel. Unfortunate for Tennyson, he had discovered the last kernel of honorability left in his soul and, by damned, if he didn't feel different than the rake he'd been all these years. He walked briskly through the halls, with the long-legged marquess easily keeping up. With each step, fury licked at Daniel's insides, fueling his movement. Tennyson was the manner of bastard who was not above ruining Alice. However, there would be little reason the two should even meet. The marquess lived for his vices the way he did and spent his days and nights courting sin.

They reached the end of the corridor when Alice's bell-like laughter filtered from the intersecting hall.

Christ. Daniel cursed as his sister and Daphne all but collided with them and the ladies gasped in unison.

"Forgive me," Tennyson murmured, reaching a hand out to steady Alice.

Daniel narrowed his gaze on the other man's grip.

"Montfort, will you not perform…" The marquess' words trailed off as he looked to Daphne. Surprise stamped his features and then his coldly mocking eyes lingered on her cane.

Bloodlust pumped through him at the unspoken condemnation. Struggling to rein in his volatile emotion, he performed the necessary introductions. "Tennyson, allow me to introduce my sister, Lady Alice Winterbourne. Alice, the Marquess of Tennyson."

Alice dropped a curtsy. "My lord." She spoke with an inherent boredom in that unimpressed greeting and pride stirred in his chest. Clever girl.

With the ghost of a smile, Daniel completed introductions, eager to be rid of the other man. "Tennyson, may I also present my sister's companion—"

"Miss Smith," Tennyson neatly interjected, reaching for Daphne's fingers. "How do you do?"

Miss Smith? Daniel searched his mind. Had he mentioned Daphne to the marquess?

Her hand still clasped in Tennyson's, Daphne stood frozen like the ornate statues outside his townhouse steps. Her freckles stood out as vivid marks in her ashen cheeks, raising a frown from him.

"It is a pleasure." Tennyson's purr exuded an improper familiarity that made the lady yank free of his grip.

He alternated his gaze between the pair and faint warning bells sounded at the back of his mind. An insidious thought, born of nothing but a stilted exchange. Tennyson's possession of her name, Daphne's ashen pallor.

Then, Daphne stumbled a step, burying her fingers in the folds of her skirt and the other hand gripped the cane hard. "M-My lord. If you will excuse me," she said and, avoiding Daniel's probing stare, she limped off.

Then, Tennyson said something to Alice, commanding his attention once more.

Oh, God. He is here.

By the introduction, he'd found himself in possession of a new rank and title. He went by a new name but he was the same man he'd been all those years ago.

She had always known the possibility existed that Daniel, being a rake, kept like company as Lord Leopold. Somehow seeing it. Witnessing it. And knowing it made it real in ways that gutted her.

As Daphne lurched down the hallway, putting more and more distance between her and the man who'd betrayed her all those years ago, she pressed her eyes closed tight. And worse…he was friends with Daniel. A tortured moan lodged in her throat and she quickened her stride.

Of course she'd known it possible their paths might cross. Had mentally prepared for what that encounter would be like. But in all her greatest horrors and nightmarish imaginings, Lord Leopold had never, ever been friend to Daniel. Because he was not the manner of man who would dare even speak with a blackguard like Lord Leopold.

Only he was. For Daniel, had shaped himself into that, embraced that rakish existence. Her stomach revolted and she pressed her hand to her mouth. She reached the stairs, damning her useless leg as she made the long, slow climb. Damning the injury that had been the single most formative moment in her life. It had shaped her dreams of who she was. It had shattered her romantic hopes for a happily ever after with a loving husband. Seen her dependent on the mercy of a relative and then seeking employment when that mercy ran out. And it had brought Lord Leopold into her life.

At last, Daphne reached the landing. Increasing her stride, she used her cane to bear her weight as she dragged her leg along. Panting from her exertions, she found her rooms and limped inside. Closing the door, she took several steps.

Her leg, strained from her exertions, gave out, and she crumpled, quickly catching herself. Numb inside, she ambled over to the bed and sank onto the edge.

After she'd left London and returned to Spelthorne, she had lived her life in alternating states of emotion—humiliated shame for the mistake she'd made in trusting Lord Leopold and hatred for a blackguard who'd toyed with her heart. A blackguard, who'd correctly identified her as a weak, pathetic creature. A woman desperate to be loved, he gave her those very words she was searching for.

Having the greatest mistake of her life thrown into her face, roused the oldest, still fresh humiliation.

...I've never rutted with a cripple...

She pressed shaking palms over her eyes. "He is friends with him," she whispered into the silence, needing to breathe the words aloud and give them life. And she wanted it to not matter the company Daniel had kept all these years. Wanted it not to matter that when she left, he'd pick up and carry on as he had for thirteen years. Tears pooled in her eyes, blurring her vision. For it did matter.

Heavy footsteps sounded on the opposite side of the oak door, muffled by the wood paneling. But there could be no doubting those commanding steps that paused outside her door.

Daniel shoved it open and, commandeering the room, closed it behind him. "What is it?" he demanded without preamble.

Daphne ran regretful eyes over him, a person who called Lord Leopold friend. The agony of that truth chipped away at her heart. She gave her head a slight shake. "I cannot stay here."

Shock cracked the hard, immobile planes of his face. Questions whirred in his eyes and then he took a step toward her. "You know Tennyson." His was a curt statement, more than anything, but Daphne nodded once. Daniel took another step, his eyes narrowing. "*How* do you know Tennyson?"

He knows. For the image he'd established amongst the *ton*, Daniel had been clever and quick-witted, equally capable with words and numbers when Daphne hadn't.

Tension spilled from Daniel's frame. "I asked how you know him."

She sank her teeth into her lower lip. It was one thing to pardon her foolish actions from eleven years ago. It was, however, an altogether different thing, when that man who'd deceived her was, in fact, friend to the man who'd stolen her heart. Daphne skittered her gaze about, seeking escape. Words. A proper reply.

"Daphne," he demanded gruffly. The floorboards creaked as he moved.

Just that one word, her name, infused her spine with strength and she picked her head up. She'd not remain in this world, but neither would she make apologies for her past. Their gazes collided and an indefinable flash sparked in his eyes.

"It was him, wasn't it?"

There was a faint plea in those words. Not pretending to misunderstand, Daphne managed a slight nod.

He froze and then slowly sank to his haunches. Burying his face in his hands, he unleashed a string of black, inventive curses that turned her cheeks warm. "Oh, God." The air left his lips on a sharp hiss.

She stared at his bent head, strangely hollow. "You are friends with him, then."

Daniel shot his head up, his brown eyes riddled with frenzied emotion. He surged to his feet and joined her at the edge of the bed, sinking to a knee. "I..." His throat worked. "He... I am a rake."

A sad smile turned her lips. "Yes." He'd taken great care to remind her and remind her often. But still, he'd always existed as Daniel and, for his wicked reputation, he would always be the friend who'd carried her across the countryside. Now, he also happened to be the man who kept company with the scoundrel who'd betrayed her.

A pang struck deep inside her chest.

"If I knew," he began in ragged tones. "I would have never..." The column of his throat worked. At her arched eyebrow, he finished. "I would have beat him within an inch of his life for you."

Tears sprang to her eyes and she blinked them back. "But these are the people you have chosen, Daniel. You turned your back on me and Alice, and who you once were." She touched her fingers to his chest, where his heart pounded hard. "In here." She let her hand fall to her lap. "I have seen good in you, where you cannot see it in yourself. But I cannot remain in your employ." Or in any part of his life. "If these are the people who fill your world." No, she could not. Not if she hoped to spare herself the eventual heartache that came in loving Daniel Winterbourne.

Yet, how was there to account for the frenzied, half-mad glimmer in his eyes if he were that dissolute gentleman who was friends with men like Tennyson? He pressed his hands over his face, briefly, and then spoke in more somber tones than she'd ever recalled. "After my mother's passing, my father reminded me how I destroyed all who I came in contact with. My mother. Alistair." He paused and his features contorted. "You." Her. Daphne's heart hitched. Those hateful words, with her used as leverage against him, would have come when he was just fourteen… at a time when he'd still smiled, and laughed, and been a friend. From then, he'd gradually retreated, until he'd left for university and disappeared from her life.

"That is why you ceased coming around," she said softly, as at last it became clear. And why he avoided Alice. Her heart wrenched all the more.

He gave a brusque nod, faint panic in his eyes. What must it be for this man who'd perfected an artificial smile and indifferent mask, to let her inside this way? Daniel looked beyond her shoulder, studiously avoiding her eyes. "I found people like me."

Daphne touched his chin and forced his gaze back to hers. "Do you truly believe you are like the Marquess of Tennyson?"

His Adam's apple bobbed. "I know I am."

She challenged him with her gaze. "Have you seduced a young woman out of her virtue, just so you might add her as a conquest?"

"No," the answer emerged sharp. She'd not believed even with his dissolute lifestyle, he'd have descended into that level of sin. There had been good in Daniel Winterbourne. That good didn't fully die. It just faded and was lost deep inside, waiting for him to acknowledge it. He leapt to his feet and began to pace. "But there have been other conquests," he said, his voice hoarse. "Women I've bedded on wagers. Unhappy wives, sad widows, actresses." Each methodical accounting of the women who'd come before her, struck like well-placed arrows, serving as a reminder that she could never be enough for him.

Daphne hugged her arms about her waist, his words merely serving as a reminder of something she already knew. Jaded as he'd become over the years, Daniel could never, would never be the man to give her everything she dreamed of and for—a marriage built on love and trust like the one known by her parents.

Or children. There would never be children. Her throat worked. Remaining on in the post with Alice, once an inconvenience, then a joy, now became an impossibility. Her tongue heavy in her mouth, she managed to speak. "I cannot remain here, Daniel."

His entire body jerked as though she'd struck him. "I will never see Tennyson again," he rasped.

This was about so much more than the Marquess of Tennyson. This was about her. And Alice. And Daniel. Restless, Daphne struggled to stand and limped away, putting distance between them. "If he…" She grimaced. "Reveals my past—"

Daniel swiftly moved, placing himself in her path. "I'll not send you away," he said, his tone harsh. A panicky light glimmered in his eyes and then was gone, so all that remained was the customary hardness that so often dwelled in their depths.

Daphne fiddled with her cane. "Lord Tennyson—"

"Tennyson will say nothing," he snapped impatiently. She eyed him warily. How could he be so confident of that man's integrity? Or did he merely delude himself? "He requires an heiress. And as such, he'll not be eager to bandy about his…." Splotches of red appeared in his cheeks.

Daniel Winterbourne was still capable of blushing. Not a single gossip or member of the peerage would dare believe it.

"Escapades?" she supplied quietly when he said nothing more.

"Do not," he bit out.

"Not speaking those words doesn't undo what happened between me and Lord Tennyson," she reminded him.

His body coiled tight like a serpent poised to strike. "He will say nothing. I promise you."

"But what if he does?" she pressed, refusing to abandon the point. Serving as the voice of reason when he would not. "There is your sister's reputation. If Lord Tennyson breathed a word about our night, Alice would suffer. There is no room for question with a companion's honor. I'll never receive employment at Ladies of Hope, Daniel," she said, willing him to understand.

"I could marry you."

Daphne and Daniel both went stock-still. For an instant, her heart lifted. Then she registered the panicked horror wreathing his features and that same foolishly hopeful organ crashed to her feet. It was the same sharp pain as when she'd come down wrong on her leg and snapped that bone all those years ago.

She slowly removed her hand from his person. "Was that an observation or a proposal, Daniel?"

"It could be either," he said gruffly. "You could marry me."

Having loved him since she was a girl, she selfishly wanted to make those words into the offer she wanted it to be. And loving him as she did, she desperately sought to convince herself that his offer was something more. "Why?"

He cocked his head at an endearing angle that gave him a boyish look, melting away the jaded edge that he wore so easily.

"Why would you marry me?"

Daniel opened and closed his mouth several times. "We are friends," he said at last. "Which is a good deal more than most marriages are based on. We get on well. I require help with Alice," he spoke with a military precision. "You'll be free to carry on whichever ventures you so wish."

Despite her splintering heart, she laughed and stepped into his arms. He immediately folded her in an embrace. "Oh, Daniel," she said, layering her cheek against his jacket and inhaling the sandalwood scent that clung to him.

He'd not immediately gone to the eight thousand pounds awaiting him, or his need for an heir or companion for his sister, but rather...their lifelong friendship. And even as her heart convulsed with regret for what it wasn't, it rejoiced for what it was—him, doing the honorable thing, when he believed himself incapable of it. "What manner of friend would I be if I let you do that?"

He tipped her chin up and the passion blazing from within his eyes scorched her, leaving her breathless. "Do you believe all I feel for you is friendship?" He lowered his mouth to hers. She turned her head and his kiss grazed her cheek.

"No," she said softly. "I believe you desire me." She paused. "As you desire many women. That is not anything to base a marriage on." She forced herself out of his arms.

"You are rejecting my offer, then?" Daniel demanded with a shocked arrogance only a man of his rakish reputation could manage.

Daphne laughed and amusement mingled with the pain of regret. "Only you could present a statement as a proposal and find yourself offended at my rejection. Yes," she confirmed, her smile dying.

"Though I am grateful," she added. That Daniel would abandon his bachelorhood for a woman who offered him no dowry and no connections, made her love him all the more and spoke to who he truly was. "What manner of friend would I be if I allowed you to give up your future for me?"

A tick pulsed at the corner of his mouth. "It is my decision," he squeezed out through tight lips.

She sighed. Did that resolve come from his lofty station? "No, Daniel. It is both of ours." Daphne slid her gaze over to her small valise tucked in the corner. "I'll not marry where there is not love. And you are not capable of giving me that emotion. I wish to leave, Daniel. I require references. I ask, as you are my friend, to please give them to me."

For a moment, she thought he would resist, force her to remain on in her post, and suffer through the pain of loving him and the torture of this Season. Daniel nodded; the motion jarring and jerky. "Of course," he said, his voice flat. "I…" Her heart sped up with a fragile hope. "I would ask you to remain on in your post until a suitable replacement is found."

"Of course," she parroted, nodding quickly. "I'd not abandon Alice." She held her palms up.

A heavy silence descended and their gazes were locked. Daniel cleared his throat. "I will leave you, madam." With his effortless strides, he turned on his heel and marched for the door. Then he paused to look back. "If you should change your mind and accept my offer, it remains, Daphne."

Pain flooded her chest and she forced a smile that pained her cheek muscles. "Thank you, Daniel."

With that, he left.

CHAPTER 18

DANIEL NUDGED HIS MOUNT THROUGH the crowded London streets at a risky clip that earned shouts and furious looks from passersby. He, Daniel Winterbourne, 5th Earl of Montfort, notorious rake, reprobate, and scoundrel had offered to marry Daphne. Well, an almost offer.

...Only you could present a statement as a proposal and find yourself offended at my rejection...

And given that and the lady's ultimate, if wise, rejection of that offer, his mind remained in tumult from all she'd revealed—Tennyson.

He tightened his hold on his reins and urged Satan on, faster. Tennyson had been the blackguard who'd robbed Daphne of her virginity. The man who'd identified a hopeful romantic and punished that innocence by taking her against a wall like a whore on the streets. Should he be truly shocked, given his own dark deeds and wicked soul? And yet, as he dismounted outside White's and stalked up the steps, he could not see past the thick haze of rage threatening to blind him.

He fixed on that hatred and fury. Far easier than thinking of his impulsive offer, which hadn't really been an offer, to marry Daphne Smith.

Ignoring the greetings called out to him, Daniel strode through the club. As he walked, he earned glares and glowers from men he'd made cuckolds of.

…But these are the people you have chosen, Daniel. You turned your back on me and Alice, and who you once were…

Who he once was. He was a man who'd cut, first, Alice from his life. And then Daphne. A friend who he hadn't bothered to look after her when she'd made her Come Out. Even as he knew what perils awaited a young girl from the country and the rakes who would be lying in wait. A tortured groan lodged in his throat. He yanked out one of the chairs at his table and sinking into the hard contours, motioned for a servant. For it, she'd given her virginity to a man who'd never had a right to that gift.

Agony sluiced away at his insides, blended with a blinding rage. Rage that Tennyson had known her as only he should have. That she had loved the other man, if even the thought of him. That Daniel had kept company with the blackguard. Oh, God. He'd had him as a guest in his home and in the country. They'd shared women and drinks.

I'm going to be ill…

Yanking the stopper from his bottle, Daniel poured a tall glass of brandy, paused, and then filled it to the rim. He raised it to his mouth and took a long swallow, welcoming the fiery trail it blazed down the back of his throat. This was his penance. For his sins and the reckless life he'd lived. Now he would live with the knowing that he'd failed the one person who'd been constant in his life. He'd failed her. In every way.

The lady preferred employment at a miserable finishing school, to life as his countess. Why should she wish to marry a bastard like him? Not that he truly wished to marry Daphne or anyone. He'd no desire to bring about another person's pain and suffering. Still, her rejection chafed. For it reminded him of his failings.

And what I threw away…

If his life had followed a different trajectory, he would have been the young man waiting for her in London, courting her, and ultimately wedding her. By the time, she'd arrived in Town, however, Daniel had been beyond the point of no return, firmly entrenched in his dissolute lifestyle, long past respectability, and even further past deserving a woman like Daphne Smith.

"I see the important business called you away." That hated voice, the devil's baritone cut into his turbulent musings. And with fury pumping through his veins, Daniel looked up. "You should have let me know and I would have joined you." Lord Tennyson didn't bother to await an invite. He drew out a seat and, motioning for a glass, availed himself to Daniel's bottle.

With each casual movement made by the bastard across from him, Daniel's muscles went taut.

...You should be honored, Miss Smith. I've never rutted with a cripple...

His glass splintered under the weight of his grip and he set it down. As Tennyson looked through bored eyes out at the guests about the floor, Daniel studied him. Smug. Self-assured. Ruthless. Arrogant. And in Tennyson, God help him, he saw himself. Saw each crime and sin laid out. All the men whose wives he'd bedded and the shameful events where he'd poured the remaining wealth left by his father. By God, he had even betrayed St. Albans. A man who'd been loyal and confided his greatest fears about marriage and siring a child. Daniel, with a ruthless disregard, had turned those secrets over to the other man's father.

It was a rather humbling moment, to look at himself, truly look at himself, and find he didn't much like what he saw. That he didn't like himself at all. His stomach muscles clenched.

For her faith in him all these years, Daphne was wrong. There was no good in him. "You bastard," he said quietly, the words reserved for both him and the man seated across from him.

Tennyson slowly returned his attention forward. "What—?"

"I know what you did," Daniel cut in.

Then a slow understanding dawned in the other man's eyes. "Oh, you must mean Miss Smith." He flicked a hand. "Yes, yes. Bad form bedding your sister's companion. It was a long time ago and I couldn't know she'd become her companion." He waggled his eyebrows. "In truth, it would not have stopped me from tupping her." Tennyson laughed uproariously, his shoulders shaking from his mirth.

Gripped by rage, Daniel propelled forward. He shot an arm out knocking the glass from the marquess' hands. "Montfort," the other man's cry ended on a squeak as Daniel curled his hand around his neck.

"You bloody bastard," he seethed, fire pumped through him, scorching him with hatred. "I could kill you." *I want to kill him for having broken Daphne's heart and for having known her body and...* The buzz of whispers ricocheted about the club, dimly penetrating his fury. With alacrity, he released Tennyson suddenly and the black-guard collapsed in his seat, sucking in great, gasping breaths.

"By God, Montfort, you've gone mad," the marquess, rasped, rubbing his neck. "Is this because you wanted to have her first? I know there is an appeal to bedding a virgin and a cripple." He grabbed Daniel's decanter and took a drink. "But trust me, the lady was rubbish." A buzzing filled his ears as the marquess' words came as though down a long corridor. "You should thank me for properly breaking her—"

With a roar, Daniel launched himself across the table, taking Tennyson down. The other man cried out as Daniel buried his fist in his nose. His fingers slippery from the other man's blood, he continued to pummel Tennyson, punching him over and over. In his mind's eye, he saw Daphne with this man rutting between her legs. Touching her. Mocking her. He drew back his arm, when someone caught it hard and yanked Daniel away. Driven by blood-lust, he wrestled against the hold.

"You're going to kill the man, Montfort," Lord Guilford's cool tones cut across the momentary haze of madness.

Then Daniel registered the absolute silence. All the patrons stared with their faces wreathed in shock and horror. Breathing heavily, he shrugged free of Guilford. He stepped over the prone body of a moaning Tennyson and stalked through the club. Whispers followed in his wake.

He jerked to a stop beside the famed betting book. Glancing down, he immediately found his name. An entire page's worth of wagers, all including Daphne's name.

Nausea roiled in his belly and, in one swift movement, he ripped the piece from the book. The rending loud in the near quiet of the club. Then, the whispers took on a frenzied tenor as Daniel stalked over to a nearby sconce and touched the edge of the page to the candle. The orange flame licked at the corners, curling it back, and then the fire consumed it.

Daniel dropped it to the carpeted floor and stalked away.

As he reached the door, frantic shouts went up and he stepped outside.

There was no escaping Daphne, anywhere.

There never had been.

FOUR MONTHS.

Daphne was seated on the sidelines of Lord and Lady Waverly's ballroom. Four months were all Daphne calculated as the absolute greatest amount of time she had for the glittering world of Polite Society.

She skimmed her gaze over the ballroom to where her charge stood, surrounded by a swarm of gentlemen. Daniel hovered close; a stony-eyed gaze fixed on those men. A wistful smile pulled at her lips. How very much he'd changed in these nearly three weeks. He'd gone from a brother who didn't wish to be bothered with a sister underfoot to a scowling, protective father-like figure.

Her smile withered. Given the endless barrage of suitors and the steady stream of lemonade fetched, Daphne had even less time for London.

…You could marry me…

That offer Daniel had made; an offer that was not really an offer, flitted through her thoughts.

After she'd left London, she'd never wanted to set foot amongst Polite Society gatherings. Not because she despised Town. For she didn't. A girl who'd never left Spelthorne, but for those three months, she'd reveled in a world outside.

Rather, she'd not wanted to come back because it was easier to hide away than be presented with a daily reminder of her greatest mistake. Her idiocy. With the passage of time, she'd challenged the limitations imposed on women such as her. Believed that, even though marriage might not exist for imperfect women with crippled bodies, there were honorable pursuits and ventures that gave one purpose.

Daniel, however, had shown her she was more than that one night with Lord Tennyson. He had proven that, despite Tennyson's words to the contrary, she was, in fact, a woman capable of passion; a woman defined by more than the bend of her leg.

The orchestra plucked the strands of the next set and Mr. Pratt escorted Alice onto the dance floor. As they took their places, Daniel remained fixed to his spot; shoulder propped against a pillar, a flute of champagne dangled between his fingers.

Impossibly cool. Elegantly attired in his midnight jacket and black fitted breeches. It was that primitive beauty that commanded the legions of women. From over the heads of the dancers, their gazes collided. Her breath lodged painfully in her chest. He lifted his head in an imperceptible greeting and she forced her eyes away. To acknowledge even that slight movement would rouse whispers and rumors about a woman in Daniel Winterbourne's employ.

"Dreadful affair, isn't it?"

At the too-loud question, Daphne started. She glanced to the woman seated two seats over. The Marchioness of Guilford sat, patiently smiling. She gasped. "My lady." She grabbed her cane and made to rise.

"Please do not stand," the lady quickly interrupted. "Not because I believe you incapable of that movement, but because it's a rather silly bit of pomp and circumstance that presents one as more important than another."

And for the first time since Daniel's empty offer of marriage, a real smile turned her lips.

"Dreadful affair, isn't it?" the woman repeated.

"Yes," Daphne answered instantly, earning another grin from the marchioness. "Though, twirling around a dance floor is a good deal less tiresome than sitting on the edge of a ballroom *watching*." After all, as one on the sidelines, she well-knew.

"I'm here because of my sister-in-law." The delicate lady angled her head toward a couple going through the steps of the set. Daphne widened her eyes and swung her gaze over to the host and hostess.

Oh, blast. "I—"

"My sister-in-law being the hostess doesn't make the event any less tedious." They stared out at the twirling dancers. "I do not recall seeing you."

"I have not been to London in eleven years," Daphne explained. "And then, I was here for but three months."

"Fortunate," the marchioness muttered and a bark of laughter escaped Daphne.

They shared a smile. Yet, the lady spent her time in London. Was it her husband who insisted on attending *ton* functions? Her curiosity stirred.

"You are in the Earl of Montfort's employ," the young marchioness said quietly, unexpectedly. "What is a kind young lady such as you doing with a rake like him?" She searched her gaze over Daphne's face.

Disappointment warred with annoyance. The woman knew nothing of Daphne and only what the gossips said about Daniel. She'd had greater expectations for a woman who'd opened an institution for disabled ladies, that she'd not pass judgment on others. Of course, he'd earned that reputation, deserved it. But he'd also seen more in her than her disfigurement and, as such, he would never be, could never be the shallow bastard Society took him for. "Even rakes require help, my lady," Daphne said crisply. "I believe we all do." *Including myself.*

"Some more than others," the other woman murmured. "Especially Lord Montfort, I gather."

Most women would be properly deferential and say nothing in the presence of a marchioness' criticism; particularly a woman who she one day sought employment from. Daphne, however, would not stay silent because of a person's rank alone. "He may be a rake, my lady, but he hired me," she said quietly. To suit his own purposes, but nonetheless he had offered her work without even a mention of her disfigurement. "And in a world where people can't see past a disability, he saw me as capable of something more. I believe that says more about his character than all the rakish deeds reported in those gossip pages."

The lady gave her head a slow, approving nod, as though Daphne had passed some unspoken test. "Brava, Miss Smith. You don't fear anyone, do you?"

"What good would fear do me?" she returned. With first her injury and then the death of her mother and eventually her father, the challenges had become greater and greater. "If I'd spent my life fixed on my troubles, I'd be at the mercy of a relative who'd inherited my father's properties, instead of this ballroom."

The marchioness fiddled with a heart pendant at her neck, bringing Daphne's attention to that gold filigree piece. "Ahh, so that is how you came to be with the earl. Desperation."

Yes, one could certainly have said she had been driven into the role of companion because she'd been literally and figuratively without options. But how much had come of it. She'd found peace in who she was and an acceptance, at last, that her disfigurement only defined her as she allowed it to. And Daniel. She'd found him, once more. Pain squeezed at her heart. For unless he found himself, her love was destined to die.

"Where will you go when Lord Montfort's sister weds?"

That unwitting reminder that Daphne's time with Daniel would soon end, squeezed at her lungs like a vise. She'd spent the past eleven years silent and somber, and he'd teased her and drew her back to the living in ways that she'd not known she'd been deadened. "I'll seek employment at Mrs. Belden's Finishing School," she said at last. She'd carry her letters of reference to Mrs. Belden's on the hopes that those letters from Daniel were enough to secure her a post, but even that was not a certainty.

The other lady blanched. "Egads, whyever would you do that?"

Folding her hands on her lap, Daphne drew a breath. "May I speak frankly, my lady?"

The other woman lifted her head. "Please."

"Ultimately, I wish to seek employment at your institution." Surprise flared in the other woman's eyes. "I have great respect and admiration for a place that would welcome girls deemed unfit by Society, but I also have an equal respect that you'd hire only the most distinguished, worthy instructors for them."

"You are seeking employment at Mrs. Belden's in order to attain references," she spoke those words as a statement she'd already determined the answer to.

Daphne nodded anyway.

"I see," the marchioness said, when she remained silent. "Why don't you come accept employment with me?"

She blinked slowly. Had the woman said—?

"I will find a place for you at Ladies of Hope."

Daphne's mind raced. The marchioness offered her the very thing she craved—security. She'd have employment and control of her own fate. It was a gift held forth by a stranger, when the world had proven itself remarkably cold, thus far. She should be grateful and, yet, it felt hollow. Handed her as a token gesture, more than anything. "You do not even know me," she said flatly.

The marchioness leaned back in her chair. "You believe I've offered you a place at my institution because of your leg," she said with a bluntness Daphne appreciated.

She managed a slight nod and Lady Guilford leaned forward. "I've offered you a post because you're unafraid of standing up

to ladies who'd wrongfully pity you. Because you rightfully challenged me when I spoke disparagingly of Lord Montfort." The
marchioness proceeded to tick off on her fingers. "You're honest.
You speak freely to me, when most others pick their way around
words the way one might move a piece around the chessboard."
Daphne smiled. "And because of my daughter."

Daphne furrowed her brow.

"Many know about Ladies of Hope and call me the odd bluestocking marchioness, but they do not know why I established the
institution." The marchioness touched the right side of her face.
"My daughter is without hearing in one ear."

That is why the lady knew. Her daughter, too, by Society's standards was one of those imperfect sorts, like Daphne.

The marchioness spoke in impassioned tones. "I want a world of
people who see her and not her differences. I want her to move
through life with dignity and strength." She held Daphne's gaze.
"But sometimes, by your own admission, we all need help. And if
it is offered to my daughter when she needs it, I hope she has the
humility to take it."

Daphne's throat worked. She'd spent the whole of her life wanting to be seen as more than her injured leg. Daniel had proven that
she was so much more than that largely useless limb and now this
woman, too.

"I've need of an instructor now to work with the young ladies
who've limited use of their legs, Miss Smith. At present, I have a
doctor advising them. I would rather they receive guidance from
one who knows more than information listed in a medical journal."

The other woman dangled forth everything she had dreamed
of. *I will have to leave Daniel…* "I…" She fought for the words that
would make that coveted post her own.

The marchioness patted her hand. "You do not need to answer
now. Think on it." She looked across the ballroom. "People are
eyeing me." She sighed and levered herself upright. "Now, let me
go and assure them that I'm having a perfectly wonderful time."
She rolled her eyes skyward.

Daphne climbed to her feet with some effort. Shifting her cane,
she made to curtsy, but the marchioness wagged a finger.

"Curtsies are for emphasizing a divide and I vowed to never be one of those ladies respected for her title alone."

Daphne again smiled. "I assure you, my lady, no one would dare respect you for anything less than your strength and character."

She captured Daphne's spare hand and squeezed. "And remember, whenever you have need for employment, you may come to me." Waving off her rushed word of thanks, the marchioness swept off with the sure footsteps of a boldly confident woman.

As the marchioness strode through the ballroom, Daphne stared after her. With one chance meeting, a future had been dangled before her. One that included the very thing she'd dreamed of—security in a world that was uncertain for all women. It represented a practical future.

Sitting there, on the side of the ballroom, staring absently at the dancers assembling for the next set, she discovered she craved something more, something she'd abandoned hope for long ago—love.

Nay, Daniel's love.

Daphne drew in a shuddery breath. She'd but a Season left with him. It would be enough. It had to be.

Or else she was making yet another mistake in London.

One that was far more dangerous than that decision eleven years earlier.

CHAPTER 19

"WHERE IN BLOODY HELL IS my nephew."

Seated in his office poring over the paperwork his man-of-affairs had brought 'round earlier that morning, Daniel sighed and closed the books. He'd learned long ago the nature of that tone. And also the reason for unexpected visits. He picked his head up just as Tanner opened the door, revealing his uncle. "His Lord—"

"No need for introductions," Lord Claremont commanded, brandishing a newspaper. "The boy knows who I am," he said, stalking forward. "Get out," he ordered, not looking back.

Tanner quickly pulled the door shut, leaving them alone.

"Uncle," Daniel drawled. "To what do I owe the—?"

"Stuff it, boy," he bellowed, jabbing the gossip columns in his hand. "This isn't a social visit," he thundered, as he settled his large frame into the chair opposite Daniel's desk. The viscount hurled the paper across the desk and it whacked Daniel in the chest, falling with a noisy thump atop his ledgers.

Daniel shoved them from his work. He didn't need to look at those pages to know the words stamped in ink there. Just as words of his actions at White's had been whispered about in his ballroom last evening and printed on every paper to land on lords and ladies' breakfast tables that morning. His uncle stared furiously back and Daniel winged a single eyebrow up, tauntingly.

The viscount leaned forward and thumped the desk hard with the flat of his hand. "I told you no scandals." His uncle pursed his mouth. "And you burn down White's?" An act that had seen Daniel's membership forever revoked to that great, estimable club.

Reclining in his seat, he kicked his heels up on the edge of his desk. "Bah. By the papers reporting, it was just a table and some carpeting," he said in mocking tones that sent his uncle's brow lowering. But he would have unrepentantly set the entire club ablaze for the ugly wagers placed on Daphne. Fury thrummed inside him all over again.

His uncle lingered his gaze on the soles of Daniel's boots. "Everything has always been a game with you."

"Yes," he conceded, his agreement only a half-truth. Since the passing of his mother and brother that had been the state Daniel had allowed himself to live in. Until now. Nay, until Daphne. She'd challenged that rakish existence and forced him to truly look at the life he lived…and reminded him of how it once had been.

Lord Claremont peered at him. "You do not care what this means for your eight thousand pounds?"

The muscles of his belly clenched. Yes, he had. Seeing the stories printed in the papers, Daniel had well known what it portended.

"You'll have to marry an heiress or sell the remaining unentailed properties you have," his uncle said, plucking the very thoughts from Daniel's head.

And where saddling himself with an equally cold and ruthless heiress would have been the only path he wished to travel, now it left him feeling sick inside. "I've options," he said, forcing a bored yawn. Options, which included stretching his finances and dipping his toes in trade, which he should have and could have done years earlier. All that had once failed to matter, now did.

"I might have forgiven the scandal at White's," his uncle said, with a grunt. "But I cannot forgive you two."

Daniel looked back perplexedly.

Reaching inside his jacket, Lord Claremont withdrew a thick folded note and tossed it down on Daniel's desk. "Here."

Picking it up, he unfolded the page and his stomach sank. The words blurred together and he forced them into focus, reading the damning note signed by Tennyson.

"You need to pick better friends," his uncle mocked.

Bile climbed in his throat and stung like acid. He'd told Tennyson everything about his uncle's requirements and, as such, he'd neatly, if inadvertently, handed over the perfect revenge. Tennyson's reputation in deflowering an innocent all those years ago would never be revealed and ruin his prospects with an heiress. But Daniel's uncle would know and the funds promised would go up in flame more easily than that page at White's. Daniel briefly closed his eyes.

"He's not a friend," he said tightly, carefully refolding the sheet. He tossed it back to his uncle who caught it with two hands. There had only ever been one true friend, who'd known everything about who he was, and who he'd wished to be in life, and ultimately who he'd become.

Lord Claremont snorted as he tucked the page back inside his jacket. "Then you should use greater discretion in what you bandy about to enemies."

"Tennyson deserved a beating." The lady had been deceived by a scoundrel and for that act that had shattered her heart and innocence, his uncle and Polite Society would hang her upon a cross and turn the proverbial cheek on the man responsible for those crimes.

"I do not disagree with you there. Never liked his father, either. Pompous bastard." His uncle lifted one shoulder in a lazy shrug. "Nonetheless, the lady was ruined by him."

The lady was ruined by him...

The lady was also the same girl who'd skipped stones beside him in a lake. Who, despite the struggle presented by her leg, walked to Mrs. Belden's for a post and then marched all the way to his estate to spare his sister hurt. At every score, she'd boldly challenged the existence he'd lived. And with her worth, she was far better than the whole of the peerage rolled into one.

His uncle spoke, slashing into his thoughts. "I'll allow you one more opportunity to earn the eight thousand pounds." He folded his hands and dropped the interlocked digits on his belly.

"You wish us to wed?" He started, his own surprise reflected in the viscount's eyes. Where had that question come from? And why, with each passing moment, did the possibility of being joined to Daphne fill him with this lightness.

"See you wed?" His uncle gave his head a bemused shake. "Quite the opposite."

Daniel eyed his uncle with a wariness that came from too many lectures and games from this man over the years.

"I want her out," his uncle said quietly. His usual rancor was gone, the solemnity in its place far more threatening.

Daniel's body turned to stone. "What?"

"Your Miss Smith," his uncle clarified. "If Tennyson breathes a hint of a word about her scandal, your sister's virtue will be called into question. I'll not have Alice's reputation compromised."

Turn Daphne out. Send her on her way with the references, as she'd asked for not even a day ago. Where she'd return to the country and that would be the last he saw of Daphne Smith. He curled his hands. "I cannot," he said quietly, firming his mouth.

His uncle drummed his pinky fingers together. "For eight thousand pounds, a man can do anything," He looked at him meaningfully. "Particularly a bounder like you."

Almost three weeks ago, Daniel would have sold his soul to the Devil for even a chance at the monies promised him by his uncle. Funds that would see his debts paid and able to resume his wicked pursuits.

"Well, what is it going to be, boy?"

SEATED IN THE PARLOR WITH Colebrooke's work on her lap, Daphne attended that German translation because it was a good deal easier than noting the stack of gossip columns littering the rose-inlaid table.

"Oh, dear." Alas, her charge made the task impossible. "Have you read this, Miss Smith?" Alice called, forcing her attention to the girl. A copy of *The Times* in her hand, Alice stared questioningly back.

"I…" Had read them when they'd arrived and had been battling a constant state of nausea since.

"This cannot be good for Daniel," Alice muttered, no answer clearly required from her. She tossed down the reputable paper and picked up one of the more scandalous sheets. The girl's eyes formed moons and she gasped. "They say he burned down White's."

"I'm certain he did not burn down the *whole* of White's," she said, with a conviction she did not feel. But still, surely the reporting from *The Times* about the fate of that distinguished club would not prove erroneous.

"And he beat Lord Tennyson." Alice made a tsking sound with her tongue.

Oh, God. Her stomach muscles knotted. Forcing her intent gaze away from her book, Daphne stole a peek at Alice. Did the girl suspect…? Finding her attention solely diverted on those gossip sheets, Daphne struggled for calm.

Alice hurled down the paper and reached for another. "I venture I know the reason for the dispute." By the accounting in the papers, it had been a violent beating that had seen the man escorted home by several other gentlemen. Daphne, however, wouldn't contradict the girl her word choice. Alice nibbled at her nail. "Do you suppose it was over a wager?"

Of course, Alice could never begin to suspect the truth. Daphne forced her tone into a semblance of calm. "I couldn't begin to suspect the merits of their argument," she lied and guilt assailed her. For she well-knew the reason for that beating doled out and the burning of that page in the White's betting book, and now… the inevitable forfeiture of the funds promised him by his uncle.

Daphne closed her eyes a moment. *I am going to be ill.* Why would he do this? A true rake would not have found fault with Lord Tennyson's actions in those long ago days and a true rake certainly wouldn't have taken him to task for it eleven years after the fact. With her charge prattling on about the scandal of the Season, as it had been marked in papers, she opened her eyes. She took in the details so very telling about this family's circumstances: the fraying brocaded curtains. The pulls in the fabric of the upholstery. The bright paint bearing the imprint of frames, from where portraits once hung. All testaments to Daniel and Alice's need for funds.

If he had not already been disqualified from the terms laid forth by his uncle, Daphne still only served as an impediment between him and his eight thousand pounds. Once, she had been a naïve girl with an optimistic view of the world. She was a woman grown now and, as such, she accepted the truth—there could never be love with Daniel. He'd stated as much too many times now for her to even hope. Her heart twisted.

There had always been friendship, however. The scandal pages had detailed his violent beating of Lord Tennyson, proving once more Daniel's loyalty and regard as a *friend*.

It was all she would ever have from him.

But in humiliating the marquess, as long as Daphne remained in London, she'd serve as a potential pawn for that dastard. She could not, nay would not, allow him to use her against the Winterbournes.

Coward that she was, she wished to go, without ever having a goodbye with Daniel's sister who'd come to mean so much to her. Before her courage deserted her, she spoke quickly. "I must leave."

Alice stopped speaking mid-sentence and tipped her head. "Would you like company?" she asked perplexedly, starting to rise.

Daphne stayed her. Having been an only child, there had been a dearth of friendship or companionship, particularly when Daniel had been away at school. *How I am going to miss this family.* She took a slow breath. "I must leave my post here," she clarified.

Alice's smile fell. "What?" she blurted. "You *mustn't* do anything. Unless you *wish* to, but you did not allude to as much. Which leads me to believe you feel you *have* to."

With her quick-wit, Lady Alice missed nothing.

Daphne curled her toes into the soles of her slippers. How to go about explaining to an innocent the circumstances of Daphne's past? With the same impressive fortitude as her brother, Alice met Daphne's gaze squarely, a demonstration of the girl's strength and directness. Yes, Alice deserved some explanation. "I have to leave," she repeated. "There is, *was* a situation that makes it impossible for me to remain."

Pursing her lips, the other lady folded her arms. "Does this have anything to do with my brother nearly burning down White's and beating Lord Tennyson to a pulp?"

She swallowed hard. "I…"

Alice collected her hand. "You needn't answer that, unless you wish." Which at this moment, with this woman, she did not. Daniel's sister went on. "I do not know what transpired that resulted in the scandal my brother brought about at White's, but I have no doubt that Lord Tennyson deserved that beating." She jutted out her chin. "And I also know my brother and I would never have you leave." She paused. "For any reason. Unless you wished it."

The young lady spoke with the innocence only a girl was capable of. For the world's ill regard for the Winterbourne family, they'd been grossly wrong in their opinions. There was no more loyal pair than Daniel and his sister. "Thank you, Alice," she said softly. Outside of her parents, Daphne had existed with nothing more than either disinterest or pity from Society and, yet, in these two she'd found people who saw the woman and not the disability. "I, however, would not forgive myself if I remained." And ruined Alice's future. No, Daphne could not repay their kindness with selfishness.

"But—"

"If you'll excuse me, Alice?" she asked, shoving to her feet. "I must meet with His Lordship." Daphne made a slow exit and started down the hall. She kept her gaze trained forward, purpose driving her footsteps. This was for the best. Now, mayhap if she told herself that enough, she could almost believe it. She reached his office and raised her hand to knock, when voices inside carried out into the hall, faintly muffled.

"…I am not turning her out…" Her stomach reflexively knotted at Daniel's furious declaration and she borrowed support from the cane. *I should go. I have no place listening at keyholes.* Yet after stealing a glance about the empty hall, Daphne took a step closer and, as if she were a girl again, pressed her ear to the panel.

"What will you do for income without my funds, Daniel?" Lord Claremont's bold challenge was met with silence.

"I'll sell off—"

"You are running out of items to sell," his uncle interjected. "And if you manage to see a return on any investments, it would still require the leniency of your creditors."

A tense quiet stretched out into the corridor and Daphne held her breath so long her chest ached. She didn't want the reminder of Daniel's circumstances, which were a product of his lifestyle, these past years. Ones that merited an heiress or cooperation with his uncle's terms. She touched her forehead to the door; the wood was cool on her heated skin.

"You have no choice, Daniel." There was a finality to that pronouncement issued by the viscount. "There have already been whispers and rumors that you are bedding your sister's companion. If Tennyson's involvement with the lady comes to light, it will only cement those whispers."

Of course, Lord Tennyson would have revealed her past.

Her throat worked and where once there had been shame at her folly, now she held her shoulders with stiff rigidity. Her mistake was hers and she owned it, but it only defined her as much as she allowed it. And if she remained in Daniel's employ, it would be all anyone saw in her.

"If I marry her…" The remaining words were lost to the door panel and his lowered voice. She captured her lower lip between her teeth. Despite his uncle's and Society's ill opinions, Daniel was more than the rake he presented. He'd still, with the threats made by his uncle, offer his name, anyway. She fell even more in love with him. All of her heart would forever belong to him.

"If you marry her, you'll never see a pound," his uncle said bluntly. There was the shuffle of footsteps from within the room and heart in her throat, she staggered back. "We are done here."

The door opened, leaving her exposed in the hallway with embarrassment burning a path from her feet to the roots of her hair.

The viscount looked at her, shock registering in his eyes. A dull flush mottled his cheeks and he yanked hard at his cravat.

"Daph…Miss Smith," Daniel swiftly corrected, coming forward.

"My lord," she greeted succinctly, managing a curtsy for the viscount. "Forgive me," she said to Daniel. "There was, *is* a matter of import, I'd speak with you on."

"Lord Claremont was just leaving," he said tightly, stepping aside so she might enter.

His cheeks ruddy, the viscount dipped a bow. "Of course." He fixed Daniel with a final stare. "I would have you think on what I said to you, boy."

As soon as the viscount had taken his leave, Daniel pushed the door shut, closeting them away. They faced one another with an uncharacteristic silence hanging awkward between them. He spoke quietly. "I am sorry you had to hear that," he said curtly.

She shook her head. "It is fine." She'd not hold him accountable for his uncle's opinions. "He didn't speak anything that was not true, Daniel." Surely he knew that?

By the white lines that formed at the corners of his tense lips, he did. "He can go to hell," he said tightly, stalking over to his sideboard. He swiped the bottle closest to his fingertips and poured himself a tumbler of whiskey. "I'm not sending you away because he ordered it." When he turned back, a muscle pulsed violently near his jaw.

"What of your funds?" she countered, taking a step toward him.

That muscle worked all the more. "I will find a way." *I always do.* Those words hung in the air, as real as if they'd been spoken.

She closed her eyes as a slow, painful laugh bubbled past her lips. Daphne buried the sound in her fingers. "Oh, Daniel," she murmured, joining him at the sideboard. "How confident you've always been. You've been that way since you were a boy. Sometimes, in life, there are no options. No matter what you do, your circumstances are your own." Just as his financial state belonged to him, from a lifetime of dissolute living. "I have to go," she said gently. "You know that."

He jerked, as though she'd run him through. "Don't leave." There was a faint entreaty that ran all the way through her.

"Why do you want me to stay?"

Panic flared in his eyes and he searched about. Daphne came over to him in a soft whir of skirts. She touched her fingers to his lips. Silencing him. "I don't care that the *ton* thinks me inferior because of my birthright and leg or even my damaged reputation. I don't care how many pounds you have or don't have to your name. I care about what you *can't* give me." She let her arm fall to her side. "I want love, Daniel. I always did. I'll not settle for less."

He pulled his hand free, a frantic light glinting in his eyes, and dragged his fingers through his hair. "I've been a rake so long, I don't know how to separate that from who I am. All I know is I do not want you to leave." There was a hoarse desperation there that made her want to stay. For selfish reasons. To have him, in any way she could.

Yet, if she gave up on the offer made by the Marchioness of Guilford, just for a few fleeting months with Daniel, Daphne would lose all of herself.

She backed up a step. "If you defied your uncle and lost those funds, you would grow to resent me." And that she would never be able to bear.

Pain sparked in his eyes. "You think so little of me," he whispered.

"You misunderstand." Daphne shook her head. "It is because I think so much of you that I'm leaving. You've offered me marriage, vowed to defy your uncle, without considering that, in doing so, you'd forfeit your future." The opportunity to find love. And she was so very selfish and dark, because she despised the woman who would one day own his heart. "I was offered employment."

His lips moved, but no words came out.

"The Marchioness of Guilford and I spoke. She offered me a post at her institution." She paused. "And I am accepting it. For you and Alice." Daphne drew in a breath. "And *me,* Daniel. I must do this for me. For eighteen years of my life, people have pitied me."

"I have never pitied you." That denial ripped harsh from his throat.

Her heart tugged. "No." Then there had never been anyone in her life like Daniel. Her friend and one-time champion. The boy, then man who'd seen a woman of wit and strength, and had not imposed limitations upon her because of Society's perception on perfection. "But there is only one reason for me to stay." *You.* "And a thousand reasons for me to go. You told me that I am the same person here," Daphne touched her fingertips to her head and then her heart. "I need to do this."

Some indefinable emotion glinted in his eyes and then, much like the hardened gentleman whose foyer she'd stormed, he peeled his lip back in a sneer. "You'll just leave, then. *You,*" he spat that word as a vile epithet, "who accused me of using alcohol as a crutch and hiding myself away, will run."

His words found an unerring mark. She scrabbled with her skirts. "I am not running."

"Bah," he shot back, scraping the air with his hand. "You're no different than I am. I may have become a rake to protect myself, but going to Lady Guilford's, you'll be protecting yourself from the world just the same."

His words held her frozen and she pressed her eyes closed. In this moment, she hated him. Hated him for being right. But more, she hated herself for having a gift proffered by the marchioness and wanting more. For in all her weeks with Daniel and his sister, thoughts of Ladies of Hope had barely been a thought.

She forced her eyes open. Security at Lady Guilford's institution was the next best dream Daphne could hope for. "Not every girl or woman like me has the advantage of believing in themselves or having someone like you who believes in them." Love for this man filled every corner of her being. For Daniel had never treated her differently. Not as a girl with an intact limb and not as a woman with a disfigured leg. "I need to be there, Daniel," she said softly, needing him to understand.

He tensed his shoulders. "Do you know what I believe?" He didn't allow her a chance to respond. "You are using your purpose as a way to hide." Had he been snapping and snarling, that challenge would have been less painful than his quiet rebuke.

Tears blurred her vision and, unable to meet Daniel's defiant gaze, she stepped around him.

"Daphne, wait," he entreated. For a fraction of a moment where hope dwelled, she thought he would give her the words that would keep her here. He dragged a hand through his hair. "I have spent so much time keeping the world out," his voice emerged ragged. "I don't know how to let anyone in…or *how* to feel." His admission emerged as an apology.

She sucked in a shuddery breath. "I want it all, Daniel. Love, a family, a purpose outside of a proper household, and in the absence of those other dreams, I will take at least one of those dreams that is presented before me." With his silence and her heart splintering apart inside her chest, Daphne left.

CHAPTER 20

One week later
London, England

ONE WEEK.

It had been seven days since Daniel's scandal at White's had landed on the front of every scandal sheet. A veritable lifetime where a rake such as he was concerned. Since then, there hadn't been a hint of a whisper of impropriety or wickedness. Not so much as a naughty actress, scandalous soiree, not even an irate husband. In all, he should be thrilled with the triumph. He was waiting on a fortune about to fall into his lap, which would set him free of the financial strains created with his own careless hand.

There was still the matter of marrying Alice off, which might pose a bit trickier given the dearth of honorable gents in the whole of England and, more, the absolute absence of invitations to polite *ton* events. But ultimately, Alice would be gone as well as Daphne, and he would be alone, just as he wished his life to be. Or as he'd wished it to be. Now it was all so bloody jumbled. For, seated on the dais on the corner of his ballroom, he'd never been more miserable. Picking up the decanter at his side, he raised the bottle to his lips and froze.

...You drink too much, Daniel... You use it as a greater crutch than the cane I use for walking...

Daphne had been right. His drinking was a crutch. He slowly

lowered the bottle to his side. He'd spent years attempting to numb himself, with whores, and wagers and liquor, because a part deep inside of him had been broken. She'd seen that truth and called him out for it. But she'd also seen good in him. Even as he hadn't seen it in himself.

And she is gone.

He stared blankly forward. Then, what reasons had she to stay? What had he to offer her? Certainly not the love she deserved. He would ultimately destroy it and, in the process, her, and that he could not bear. For with her courage and conviction and strength, she was unlike all others. His throat worked and he damned the fates for having made a liar of him in his assurances all those long ago days.

"Daniel." That unexpected greeting brought his head up. His sister stood at the entrance of the ballroom. He hopped up. "Alice," he called, his voice echoing around the empty, cavernous space.

She sailed over and stopped before him. She ran her gaze over his wrinkled cravat and jacket. "Tsk, tsk, Daniel. It is bad form to drink alone," she scolded as she hitched herself onto the dais. He didn't bother to correct her likely supposition. Instead, he reclaimed his vacated seat. Alice picked up the decanter and took a long swallow.

Daniel swiped a hand over his face. By hell, if she could take a drink like that she'd had some experience. She was going to turn him grey. "A lady shouldn't…" And the hypocrisy of offering any lessons on propriety or decorum promptly silenced him. He claimed the bottle from her and set it out of her reach.

His sister stole a sharp sideways looks at him. The lady was deserving of her resentment. The moment she'd entered the world and his mother had slipped out of it, Daniel had retreated, rejecting the small babe, Daphne, and all he'd once been. And because of who he was and, more importantly, who he could not be, Daphne had been forced out of Alice's life. Regret filled him. *…I am still that man…*

Alice dragged her knees to her chest. She looped her arms around them. "Father hated you," she said softly, unexpectedly.

His entire body jerked, as with those three words Alice ripped bandages off a wound he'd believed long healed. *…you've allowed him in here…*

"But do you know what, Daniel?" she asked.

"What?" he forced himself to reply, the single syllable utterance emerging ragged. Daphne and Alice together had shattered the armor he'd worn all these years. They'd left him exposed and battling more emotions and sentiments than he had in the whole course of his life.

"He hated me, too." He whipped his head sideways, but Alice's attention remained fixed on the opposite wall as she rubbed her chin back and forth over her skirts. "He hated the servants. He hated guests who came to call. All I knew was his hate."

The late earl had not always been that way and, with that, an ever-growing shame continued to grip him. For Daniel had mourned the loss of a life he'd lost, but this empty, dark world of hate and sadness Alice painted was all she'd ever known. "He was once happy," he forced himself to say. Until Daniel's grip had slackened and his efforts to fight a current proved futile, and their family was the same, no more.

And yet, there would have never been Alice if there hadn't been the grief-stricken parents determined to bring another child into the world. This quirky, spirited, and romantic girl who dreamed of love and desired a barrister over a duke. Now he couldn't imagine a life without her in it.

"Yes, the servants would tell me as much," Alice said, ceasing her distracted movements. "He wanted me underfoot even less than you," she said, flashing him a wry smile. Only, there was so much heartache contained within that pained attempt at humor that the bandage ripped once more. He'd failed Daphne and he'd failed Alice. In his bid to safeguard himself, he'd only brought hurt to the people who should have had his protection. Nor had his own hurt been healed by the debauched path he'd traveled. It had only left him... *empty.*

"You'd be wrong on that score," he said, throwing an arm around her shoulders and giving her a slight, awkward hug. He could not undo a lifetime of neglect, but he would show her the affection he'd long withheld.

"No, you would be," she said with a maturity far greater than her seventeen years. "I was the child, the unwanted *girl* child, who reminded him every day with my presence that his beloved wife was lost giving me life."

She spoke those words as one who'd heard them uttered too many times. His gut clenched reflexively. "Our mother wanted you desperately," he said quietly. In those days when the late countess had learned she was expecting, Daniel had still been a child. "For almost eight months while she was carrying you, she smiled," he said softly, looking out. "When she hadn't smiled in the whole year before that." For with Alistair's passing, the light had gone out in the countess, only to be briefly reignited.

"They wished for a boy," Alice said bluntly. Her mouth twisted in a macabre rendition of a smile. "Father spent a good deal of time telling me as much."

"No child would have been good enough for him," Daniel answered with an automaticity of truth that came from a place deep inside. He accepted that truth at last and, in it, found a peace. Their father had been shattered and there would have never been any putting him back together into so much as a semblance of the man he'd once been. Those issues, however, had been the late earl's. They were not a result of anything Daniel had done or could have done. It had only taken the whole of his adult life to acknowledge that. "The day Alistair died..." How odd, a sibling who'd never even known her eldest brother. A sheen misted his vision and he blinked it back. By God, what had become of him?

And yet, there was no shame or annoyance in this resurgence of emotions.

When Alice lifted questioning eyes to him, he forced himself to continue. "The day he died, Father's very reason for being died as well. No person could have ever eased that hurt." Only now, seventeen years of his brother being gone, Daniel at last realized that truth. Accepted it, and a great weight was lifted. Freeing and healing. He'd spent years being the useless, worthless man his father accused him of being, ultimately fulfilling that prophecy laid out for him. He'd allowed it to define the person he'd become. Until Daphne.

His sister stared on expectantly.

"Given my," his neck heated, "deplorable..." Good God, it was bloody torture humbling oneself in this way *and* talking about ones feelings. "...treatment of you these years," he settled for, when she winged up an eyebrow. "You're deserving of any resentment you hold for me." His gaze drifted across the ballroom. "But I am sorry," he said softly, futile words that proved useless when there could be no undoing them.

"We both allowed him control here, Daniel," his sister replied, touching her forehead. "And as long as he does, neither of us will know happiness." She paused. "Your sending Miss Smith away is testament of that."

Sent her away. His throat worked. "I didn't—" He fell silent. Daphne had ultimately left. She'd gone to protect his eight thousand pounds and Alice's reputation, and for herself. She'd gone to have a life with purpose.

Goddamn you, Daphne. How dare you reenter my life, and make me feel, and want to be a different man. And then leave.

A viselike pressure squeezed at his lungs and he drew in a ragged breath. She'd breathed life back into him and it was bloody agonizing.

"Go to her, Daniel." Did that urging belong to his sister or did it exist in his own mind?

Footsteps sounded in the hall and they both glanced to the entrance of the room. The Marquess of St. Albans filled the doorway. "I told Tanner I'd show myself here," the other man called. He came forward and bowed to Alice. "Lady Alice."

"Lord St. Albans," she returned. "I'll allow you both your visit." She gave Daniel a lingering look, as though she wished to say more, but then hopped down from the dais and skipped out with the exuberance of her youth.

His friend claimed the spot just vacated by her. "So you've managed to not burn down Brook's. I'd call that a successful week," St. Albans drawled with high-sarcasm.

"Not yet," he said with forced humor, handing over the decanter he'd yanked from Alice's fingers.

The marquess accepted it, his earlier mirth gone. "You look terrible," he said.

As it was an observation, Daniel opted to say nothing. When Daphne had packed her meager belongings, boarded his carriage, and rode several streets onward to another residence, he'd known he would miss her. He'd never anticipated…this…great, gaping hole inside where his heart had been. A hole that had left him empty in ways he'd never been. He rubbed his hand over the ache in his chest. To no avail. The agony persisted; vicious, sharp and unyielding.

In the end, she'd gone. All that remained was a stark reminder of how cold his existence had been the thirteen years without her. For three fleeting weeks, he'd smiled and laughed and lived. And with her gone, despair and pain sucked at him, holding him trapped in his misery. Another wave of despair slammed into him.

St. Albans set aside the untouched bottle. "Your sister sent 'round a letter, urging me to pay you a visit."

Daniel's neck heated. The traitor.

"I understand Miss Smith has taken employment elsewhere," St. Albans said quietly.

His shoulders went rigid. "Yes well, my wicked household is really no place for a lady," he said, his gaze unfocused. Particularly a lady of strength and integrity like her. In the past, he'd exercised little discretion and no uttered word was spared from sharing. God, what a bastard he'd been.

Taking care to leave out the most intimate details, he proceeded to fill St. Albans in on his uncle's discontent with Daphne as a companion, neatly and intricately sidestepping Tennyson's treachery against Daphne all those years earlier…and again, these eleven years later.

"Ah, so the lady had no choice but to seek employment elsewhere." St. Albans said when he'd concluded his telling. The other man spoke with the ease of one who'd worked through a particularly challenging riddle. He kicked his feet out in front of him. "It is an uncertain world for a woman without a husband. Few options."

"I offered her marriage." The admission slipped out and Daniel silently cursed, wanting to call it back. He'd let more people in these past weeks than he ever had before. Still, sharing that piece, Daphne's rejection, with St. Albans was entirely too personal.

The marquess stared back, flummoxed. "What?"

Skin hot, Daniel briefly eyed the bottle. "She needn't have left." Of all the times to abandon spirits. He'd picked the bloody worst time to develop a sense of morality. "I offered her marriage and she…declined." Not once. But twice.

What reason had she to say yes? That taunting voice whispered around his mind. *She wanted love, deserved it, and you did not give it to her.*

St. Albans again puzzled his brow. "So, instead of sacking the lady, you offered her marriage. And she said no. You should be elated."

Yes, he should be. "You are absolved of any obligation for—"

"It wasn't about obligation," he thundered, jumping to his feet. The abrupt movement sent the decanter toppling over. St. Albans shot a hand out and righted it. An absolute stillness fell over the room.

The marquess edged away from the spilled liquor. "What was it then, Montfort?"

It is about her. And me. And us together. Unable to meet the other man's assessing eyes, he set his snifter down and wandered over to the hearth. Laying his palms upon the smooth marble, he stared down at the cool, metal grate. "She chose to leave." And every day he woke up with her not in his home, the ache in his chest deepened. His heart spasmed.

"Did you give her a reason to stay?" the other man asked quietly.

He scoffed, shaking his head. "What do I have to offer her?"

"Do you love her?" the other man asked bluntly. Those words held Daniel motionless, as they invariably did. Just as they had when Daphne had breathed them into his ear, after he'd brought her to climax.

He turned slowly back to face his friend. "I don't love anyone." He forced that long held truth out past tight lips.

The marquess inclined his head. "Then you should be grateful she declined, because now you are free."

Free. Squeezing his eyes shut, St. Albans' words crashed into him, made a mockery of the past thirteen empty years he'd lived. For there was nothing freeing in Daphne being gone from his life. It was raw. Agonizing. And gutted worse than any blade taken to his person. He struggled to draw in a breath through the pain knifing away at his insides but the agony persisted. The heartache, spread to every corner of his being so all he knew was a desolate misery. So this was love.

Love? He had rejected feeling anything for anyone. And yet...

I cannot live without her.

Oh, God.

I love her. Daniel shot his hands out, catching himself against the fireplace. He loved her courage and her strength and her convictions. He loved her delight in simple things. He'd *always* loved her.

First as the girl who'd been a steadfast friend at his side through life's greatest joy and miseries, and now as a woman who'd braved all life had thrown at her.

"Yes," St. Albans put in gently, as he came to his feet. "Invariably, that emotion has such an effect on a man." A grin twitched at the other man's lips. "Especially a rake now trodding a different path."

Daniel struggled to reconcile a lifetime of wickedness with everything he now hungered for. Nay, not everything. Rather, a family. He wished to be a family with Daphne. And Alice. Though long past the point of being a brother worthy of her, he wanted to be a family with her now. "I've spent too many years being a rake to ever change." His voice emerged hoarse to his own ears.

The marquess slapped him on the back. "If that were true, you'd not be in an empty ballroom, thinking about a woman who rejected your suit," he reminded him. "The man you once were wouldn't give a jot about his uncle's orders and would be busy at his clubs drinking himself into a stupor." He snorted. "And you certainly wouldn't destroy a good bottle of brandy."

His world too unsteady to manage the customary grin that wry response should have elicited, Daniel frantically lifted his gaze to the other man. His pulse hammered loudly in his ears, deafening. "Now what?" he whispered. Now more than ever, he needed a friend. Even a friend he'd previously wronged.

St. Albans widened his smile. "Why, you go win the lady's heart."

Win the lady's heart. He braced for the panic those words should bring...panic that did not come. He'd been a rake, a rogue, a scoundrel, wholly undeserving of her, but he wanted to be deserving of her now. He wanted to be the man she saw, when he himself hadn't. He had so little to offer her, not the treasures she deserved—His heart thumped slowly. By God, that organ coming back to life hurt like the bloody devil. Daniel touched a hand to his chest. His fingers collided with the hard coin inside his jacket pocket.

Now, to convince Daphne to abandon the treasure she'd been searching for her whole life and risk it all on a rake.

CHAPTER 21

"HER LADYSHIP REQUESTS YOUR PRESENCE in her office."

Seated in her small office at Ladies of Hope, Daphne glanced up at the servant, Melanie, a young girl with limited vision who used a stick to guide her way through the institution. Daphne furrowed her brow. She wasn't set to meet with the marchioness and review her responsibilities until Friday.

Melanie cleared her throat and that sprung Daphne into movement. She exited the room behind the servant. The click of their canes echoed along the marble corridors, while Daphne made her way slowly to the Marchioness of Guilford's offices.

As she walked, she looked around at her new *home*. For all the grandeur and opulence of Daniel's residence and country estate, Ladies of Hope may as well have been a study in the Palace of Versailles Daphne had seen depicted on the pages of a book long ago.

The vibrancy of the pale pink satin wallpaper spoke to its newness. The elaborate carving in the mahogany Chippendale furniture bore the markings of wealth. In short, it was a veritable palace, far more fitting a queen, than an institution for young women with few options in life. And yet, Daphne had never aspired to such grandeur. Certainly not as a girl and not as a woman fresh to London.

When she had been a girl, she'd had dreams of how her life would be. Those dreams had been unrestrained as the movements of her legs had once been. Even after her injury, she'd not truly recognized the extent to which her future had been altered. She had allowed herself the dream of a husband, children—love. Love, with only one man—Daniel.

With the passage of time, those dreams had slowly died, leaving in their place, alternate hopes: Security. A roof over her head. Food in her belly.

The charges he'd hurled at her just prior to her leaving echoed around her mind. He'd accused her of running and hiding and those words had stung. How dare he question her aspirations?

Working inside Ladies of Hope and in possession of those three gifts to which all unwed women sought, she acknowledged the truth—he had been correct. Daphne had never felt emptier. She wanted a life of purpose and work…but she also wanted love. His love.

She'd lived thirteen years without Daniel Winterbourne in her life and, yet, she'd been away from him a week now and the hollowness in not seeing him, being with him, baiting him, was greater than all those years combined.

Drawing in a shuddery breath, she stopped outside the marchioness' office.

The young woman immediately looked up from the journal on her neat desktop; an ever-present smile on her pretty face. "Miss Smith," she greeted happily, jumping to her feet. With both palms, she motioned Daphne forward. "Come, come," she urged. "How are you getting on, Miss Smith?" the marchioness asked as they claimed seats across from one another.

"Well," she answered, the lie springing easily to her lips.

"You are adjusting to being away from…the Earl of Montfort?" The question emerged hesitantly.

Daphne choked on her swallow. Surely the other woman did not suspect? "I don't—"

"It was nigh impossible to miss the manner in which you studied one another," the marchioness said with a gentle smile. "The pages linked you two together. Wagers were taken about whether he'd ruin you," she continued. "It is one of the reasons I hoped you'd accept my offer of employment. I'd not see any lady ruined."

He hadn't ruined her. He'd helped her redefine her worth beyond her bent leg. "The gossips know nothing," Daphne said resolutely and the other woman nodded her agreement. "Dan…"

The marchioness narrowed her eyes. "His Lordship and I were childhood friends." And for a fleeting time, lovers. "His offer of employment stemmed from that connection." And somewhere along the way, he'd upended her world and opened her heart in ways it had never been.

"That is all there is between you, then?" The marchioness dropped her chin into her hands. "For, in seeing you here, I've come to suspect that, mayhap, his intentions were not the dishonorable sort and that, mayhap, your feelings were mutually engaged."

That aching organ inside her chest, clenched. "There were... feelings," Daphne murmured, admitting those words for the first time aloud to another soul. "But it requires two hearts to realize and form a complete one together." By his admission, Daniel was incapable of reform, wanting a future, capable of a future without her in it.

A commotion sounded in the hall with heavy footsteps and loud cries going up.

Daphne jumped and swung her gaze to the closed door. "What...?"

The loud bang of doors being slammed echoed from the hall. "Her Ladyship does not receive visitors, without an appointment," a servant shouted.

The marchioness rounded her eyes. "What in blazes?" She peered at the front of the room just as the door burst open. Daniel's tall, commanding figure stood on the other side of that panel. He shot his hand out to keep the door from hitting him in the face. He swept his piercing gaze over the parlor, instantly finding Daphne with his eyes and the burning intensity there robbed her breath.

Daphne cocked her head. "Daniel," she whispered. *Oh, God, he is here.* Her heart skipped several beats. *What is he doing here?*

He moved his gaze over her person, the way a person might when trying to memorize another. "Daphne," he said, his deep voice gruff with some unnamed emotion. She'd never heard that from him and his mellifluous baritone washed over her, leaving her warm in ways she'd been cold since their parting.

Gasping for breath, the butler skidded into the room. "I-I said H-Her Ladyship is not receiving visitors," he cried, clutching at his side. "Your Ladyship," the servant entreated. "I have summoned the footmen. I informed the gentleman you were not receiving visitors—"

"It is all right," the marchioness said in soothing tones as she sat back in her chair. "It is not every day a rake storms my offices." A smile plucked at the corners of the other woman's lips.

Daniel blinked slowly and moved his gaze from Daphne over to the woman, sprawled in her chair. "I am not here for you." He turned to Daphne. "I am here for *you*."

At the husky quality to that statement, butterflies danced in her belly. Daphne wetted her lips. "Are you unable to find a companion for Lady Alice?" she asked, hesitantly.

With long, languid steps he advanced. "I am not here because of my sister," he said to her, his low tone revealing nothing. He continued coming, until the rose-inlaid table halted his forward movement. That mahogany piece stood a small barrier between them.

Two footmen came rushing into the room, but the marchioness held a staying hand up.

Daniel moved around the table, so only a handbreadth separated them. He palmed her cheek and she leaned into his touch. "I am here for *you*."

"I don't under—"

"I love you," he interrupted hoarsely.

The cane slipped from Daphne's fingers, bounced off the table, and clattered to the floor. The marchioness promptly stood and quickly exited the room, closing the door behind her. His words sang through Daphne, filling her. She touched her fingertips to her lips. *He loves me?*

He spared a glance at the closed door and shook his head. "It took me time to realize it," he said, gathering her hands. He raised them to his mouth, one at a time. The delicate brush of his lips on her skin brought her eyes briefly closed. "It took me thirteen years." The column of his throat moved. "Mayhap my whole life, to see that which was always in front of me." He released her hands and she mourned the loss of his touch. "I love you. I've loved you since you were a freckle-faced girl searching for treasures at the lake." Pain glazed his eyes. "I spent my life running from that love…from any sort of feelings because I was so convinced I did not deserve it. I believed everything good that came to me was destroyed. I became what my father told me I was." A broken laugh burst from his lips. "And because of that, I certainly didn't deserve you."

That self-doubt had kept them apart. She never wanted to be without him, again. "You do," she whispered, taking his hands once more. Tears clogged her throat and she swallowed hard. "You always did. You just never believed it."

"I don't want to run from you anymore, Daphne," he said, his voice hoarse with emotion. All beautiful unrestrained devotion, adoration...and love. "I want you to be my wife and I want to have fiery-haired girls with your spirit and strength. I want you to continue working here, if that is what you so desire."

Tears flooded her eyes, blurring his visage. How many gentlemen would support their wives in that endeavor? A single drop streaked down her cheek, followed by another. And another. Daniel caught one tear with the pad of his thumb and brushed it away.

"I am in dun territory. I don't have a fortune to offer you," he said, stepping away. He reached inside his jacket and withdrew a coin. "I only have a treasure and if you marry me, it is yours." Daniel held up a rusted coin with a lightning crack down the center of the King George III's face.

"Daniel?" she swung her gaze between him and that cherished coin. All sound melted away so that a humming filled her ears. *Impossible.* He pressed the rusted metal, warm from being inside his jacket into her palm. Automatically, Daphne closed her fingers around it and then she forced them open, staring down at the coin found all those years ago. He'd kept it. That small treasure unearthed in the mud beside their lake and he'd held onto it. She shook her head and lifted stunned eyes to his, once more. "But you said...you said you did not keep it," her words emerged softly.

Daniel shook his head. "You assumed I'd wagered it away. I merely said that was a likely assumption." He flashed her a half-grin. "It also proved to be the incorrect one. I always kept it here," he said quietly, touching his chest. "You were always here."

Her hand fell quavering to her side. "Oh, Daniel."

His smile died. "As I said, I don't have a fortune to offer. My uncle has cut me off, but you and I can carve out a life together." He sank to a knee, wringing a gasp from her. "Daphne Smith, will you marry m—oomph?"

She hurled herself into his arms, knocking him back. Daniel

came down hard with her atop him. "Yes," Daphne breathed. Capturing his face between her hands, she touched her mouth to his in a gentle meeting. "But I was wrong," she said when they broke the kiss. His eyebrows dipped, in question. "I didn't find a treasure all those years ago." A small, quivering smile turned her lips. "I found love, with you."

Daniel guided them back to their feet and flashed another grin. "And you do know what they say about reformed rakes?"

She shook her head slowly, unable to sort through the joy, love, and giddy lightness dancing inside. "What is that?"

He flashed her a crooked grin. "We make the best husbands."

"You are wrong, Daniel." Daphne smiled. "They make the best heroes."

EPILOGUE

One month later
London, England

"WHAT DOES HE WANT?" DANIEL gritted out.

Tanner shifted back and forth on his heels, looking between him and Daphne. "Uh...?" He cast an imploring glance at his mistress.

"Tell him to go to hell," Daniel muttered, attending the ledger on his lap. He'd far more interest in: one, making love to his wife, two, attending the investments Begum had vetted for him, and three, well, really anything else than accepting his uncle's company.

Seated at his side, Daphne, who'd previously been evaluating her notes for Ladies of Hope, nudged him, earning a grunt.

Daniel scowled. "I am not—"

"He is your family," she reminded him gently.

He well knew who the bastard was and he'd not have in his household a single bloody person who disparaged his wife. "Tell him to go to—"

"Sending me to hell now are you, boy?"

Daniel snapped his teeth together so hard, pain shot to his temple. Tanner shot his employer an apologetic glance and Daniel waved it off. He'd learned through the years, the viscount's tenacity was a skill that could be taught to battlefield soldiers.

Daphne came to her feet and when he remained insolently sitting, she glared at him.

A silent battle ensued. With a sigh, he shoved to his feet.

"Your wife has far greater manners than you ever did," his uncle observed, needlessly.

"My lord," Daphne murmured, putting a hand on Daniel's arm.

He flexed his jaw. "What do you want?" he demanded, not wasting any time with pleasantries.

Uninvited, the viscount claimed a chair and motioned to the sofa. "Please, please."

By God, the high-handedness of the bastard. He opened his mouth to deliver a stinging diatribe, but Daphne caught his gaze.

Do not, she mouthed.

"By the accounts in the gossip sheets, congratulations are in order," Lord Claremont said crisply as he tugged off his gloves and stuffed them inside his jacket. "Your sister is betrothed to the Pratt boy. A poor barrister, but a good man."

When Daniel remained stoically silent, Daphne cleared her throat and spoke for them. "She is happy and that matters most."

He flicked his stare over her a moment, lingering on her cane, and then with eyes that revealed nothing, looked to Daniel. "I warned you, that should you wed Miss Smith, you'd never see a pence." He pursed his mouth. "You did it anyway."

"I love my wife," Daniel said, his voice a steely avowal. He slid his gaze over to Daphne and their eyes locked. His throat constricted. He'd let her walk out of his life too many times. He'd never again let her go. No matter the size of the fortune the viscount had dangled before him. "I'd burn your eight thousand pounds before I gave her up," he said, returning his attention to his uncle.

His uncle chuckled. "Given your antics at White's, I well believe that." The viscount withdrew his gloves and tossed them down onto the table. They landed with a quiet thwack. He again reached inside his jacket and fished around. He extracted a thick sheet of folded velum. "Though, burning eight thousand pounds would be a waste of good funds," he said, handing over the page.

Daniel stared at the ivory sheet.

"Go on, take it," his uncle urged.

With stiff fingers, Daniel unfolded the sheet and skimmed the page. He furrowed his brow and then whipped his head up. "What game do you play?" Daphne plucked the page from his hands and from the corner of his eye, he detected her racing gaze over the words inked there.

The viscount reclined in his seat. "No games. You forfeited eight thousand pounds when you gainsaid my wishes and married the woman you loved. But it secured you twenty-thousand," his uncle said with a small grin.

His fingers shaking, Daniel accepted the note from Daphne and re-read it. "I do not understand," he said gruffly.

His uncle settled his elbows on his knees and leaned forward. "Daniel, I've known you since you were a babe chasing shadows on the walls with your eyes. Do you believe I truly couldn't see good in you?" Regret filled the viscount's gaze and he touched his fingers to an imagined brim as he looked at Daphne. "I'd ask you to forgive me for suggesting you were less than appropriate as a match for my nephew. The moment you stepped into his office and challenged me, I knew you were the only one who could reform this one."

His wife favored the viscount with a soft smile. That sincere, tender expression caused a lightness in Daniel's chest. How had he spent his life hiding from that joy? "It was an equitable match. I may have reformed your nephew, but he reminded me of the joy in living."

Pride filled Daniel. Pride in her strength and courage and wit. Her generous heart. And the truth that she belonged to him just as much as he belonged to her. He forced his attention back to his uncle. When Daniel spoke, his voice emerged hoarse. "I don't know what to—"

"Don't say anything," his uncle interrupted. "I don't seek repayment. Nor do I have any more demands for you. You've made me proud, Daniel."

Those words, ones his own father had not even had for him, gripped him, and he swallowed hard. His wife slid her fingers into his other hand and squeezed.

"Make good with the funds, boy," his uncle said gently. He shoved to his feet. "But seeing the wife you had the good sense to marry, I expect you'll do just fine."

Daniel looked to his wife. "I assure you," he said, lingering his gaze on Daphne's freckled face. "I will do far better than 'just fine', Uncle." Together, he and Daphne would know happiness and love and, in that, there would be nothing more they needed.

A twinkle lit the older man's eyes. "I do not doubt that, my boy." Much like he'd done when Daniel had been a small boy, his uncle patted him on the back hard and then left.

As soon as he'd gone, Daphne wrapped her arms about Daniel's waist. When she lifted her gaze to his, merriment danced within her eyes. "It would seem *you've* found your treasure, now."

"You're wrong," he murmured, lowering his brow to hers. "We both found it twenty-three years, ago, together, when we first met." Only now they were joined together forever, as they were always meant to be.

She collected his hand and brought it to her flat belly. "And now we've found one more."

His heart started and he went still. Was she saying…? Were they…? His mind sought to work through that veiled insinuation. She dangled forth the hint of a dream. One she'd shown him he desperately wanted—a family with her. "What?" he demanded hoarsely.

She wrinkled her nose. "Though, if one wishes to be truly accurate, we've created him together."

Daniel collected her by the shoulders and searched her eyes, needing the words from her. "What are you saying?"

That twinkle deepened in her expressive eyes. "We are going to have a babe, Daniel."

A babe. Emotion surged through him, sucking his lungs of air and leaving Daniel frozen. Where he once would have scoffed and sneered and ran from the swell of joy and love that now gripped him, now he turned himself wholly over to it. He let it fill him, healing and euphoric. There would be a child with Daphne's smile and spirit and strength. He struggled to swallow past a tightened throat.

His wife's smile dipped as indecision flared in her eyes. "Are you not—?"

"A girl," he rasped. "It will be a girl like you."

Her features softened. "You do realize there will also be rakes and rogues and—"

"Over my bloody body." He growled, battling back rage at the imagined scoundrel courting any future daughter's favors. "A boy," he bit out. "It *will* be a boy."

With Daphne's laughter filtering about the room, Daniel swung her in his arms and joined in.

THE END

OTHER BOOKS BY
CHRISTI CALDWELL

TO ENCHANT A WICKED DUKE
Book 13 in the "Heart of a Duke" Series by Christi Caldwell

A Devil in Disguise

Years ago, when Nick Tallings, the recent Duke of Huntly, watched his family destroyed at the hands of a merciless nobleman, he vowed revenge. But his efforts had been futile, as his enemy, Lord Rutland is without weakness.

Until now…

With his rival finally happily married, Nick is able to set his ruthless scheme into motion. His plot hinges upon Lord Rutland's innocent, empty-headed sister-in-law, Justina Barrett. Nick will ruin her, marry her, and then leave her brokenhearted.

A Lady Dreaming of Love

From the moment Justina Barrett makes her Come Out, she is labeled a Diamond. Even with her ruthless father determined to sell her off to the highest bidder, Justina never gives up on her hope for a good, honorable gentleman who values her wit more than her looks.

A Not-So-Chance Meeting

Nick's ploy to ensnare Justina falls neatly into place in the streets of London. With each carefully orchestrated encounter, he slips further and further inside the lady's heart, never anticipating that Justina, with her quick wit and strength, will break down his own defenses. As Nick's plans begins to unravel, he's left to determine which is more important—Justina's love or his vow for vengeance. But can Justina ever forgive the duke who deceived her?

ONE WINTER WITH A BARON
Book 12 in the "Heart of a Duke" Series by Christi Caldwell

A clever spinster:

Content with her spinster lifestyle, Miss Sybil Cunning wants to prove that a future as an unmarried woman is the only life for her. As a bluestocking who values hard, empirical data, Sybil needs help with her research. Nolan Pratt, Baron Webb, one of society's most scandalous rakes, is the perfect gentleman to help her. After all, he inspires fear in proper mothers and desire within their daughters.

A notorious rake:

Society may be aware of Nolan Pratt, Baron's Webb's wicked ways, but what he has carefully hidden is his miserable handling of his family's finances. When Sybil presents him the opportunity to earn much-needed funds, he can't refuse.

A winter to remember:

However, what begins as a business arrangement becomes something more and with every meeting, Sybil slips inside his heart. Can this clever woman look beneath the veneer of a coldhearted rake to see the man Nolan truly is?

TO REDEEM A RAKE
Book 11 in the "Heart of a Duke" Series by Christi Caldwell

He's spent years scandalizing society.
Now, this rake must change his ways.

Society's most infamous scoundrel, Daniel Winterbourne, the Earl of Montfort, has been promised a small fortune if he can relinquish his wayward, carousing lifestyle. And behaving means he must also help find a respectable companion for his youngest sister—someone who will guide her and whom she can emulate. However, Daniel knows no such woman. But when he encounters a childhood friend, Daniel believes she may just be the answer to all of his problems.

Having been secretly humiliated by an unscrupulous blackguard years earlier, Miss Daphne Smith dreams of finding work at Ladies of Hope, an institution that provides an education for disabled women. With her sordid past and a disfigured leg, few opportunities arise for a woman such as she. Knowing Daniel's history, she wishes to avoid him, but working for his sister is exactly the stepping stone she needs.

Their attraction intensifies as Daniel and Daphne grow closer, preparing his sister for the London Season. But Daniel must resist his desire for a woman tarnished by scandal while Daphne is reminded of the boy she once knew. Can society's most notorious rake redeem his reputation and become the man Daphne deserves?

TO WOO A WIDOW
Book 10 in the "Heart of a Duke" Series by Christi Caldwell

They see a brokenhearted widow.
She's far from shattered.

Lady Philippa Winston is never marrying again. After her late husband's cruelty that she kept so well hidden, she has no desire to search for love.

Years ago, Miles Brookfield, the Marquess of Guilford, made a frivolous vow he never thought would come to fruition—he promised to marry his mother's goddaughter if he was unwed by the age of thirty. Now, to his dismay, he's faced with honoring that pledge. But when he encounters the beautiful and intriguing Lady Philippa, Miles knows his true path in life. It's up to him to break down every belief Philippa carries about gentlemen, proving that not only is love real, but that he is the man deserving of her sheltered heart.

Will Philippa let down her guard and allow Miles to woo a widow in desperate need of his love?

The Lure of a Rake
Book 9 in the "Heart of a Duke" Series by Christi Caldwell

A Lady Dreaming of Love

Lady Genevieve Farendale has a scandalous past. Jilted at the altar years earlier and exiled by her family, she's now returned to London to prove she can be a proper lady. Even though she's not given up on the hope of marrying for love, she's wary of trusting again. Then she meets Cedric Falcot, the Marquess of St. Albans whose seductive ways set her heart aflutter. But with her sordid history, Genevieve knows a rake can also easily destroy her.

An Unlikely Pairing

What begins as a chance encounter between Cedric and Genevieve becomes something more. As they continue to meet, passions stir. But with Genevieve's hope for true love, she fears Cedric will be unable to give up his wayward lifestyle. After all, Cedric has spent years protecting his heart, and keeping everyone out. Slowly, she chips away at all the walls he's built, but when he falters, Genevieve can't offer him redemption. Now, it's up to Cedric to prove to Genevieve that the love of a man is far more powerful than the lure of a rake.

To Trust a Rogue
Book 8 in the "Heart of a Duke" Series by Christi Caldwell

A rogue

Marcus, the Viscount Wessex has carefully crafted the image of rogue and charmer for Polite Society. Under that façade, however, dwells a man whose dreams were shattered almost eight years earlier by a young lady who captured his heart, pledged her love, and then left him, with nothing more than a curt note.

A widow

Eight years earlier, faced with no other choice, Mrs. Eleanor Collins, fled London and the only man she ever loved, Marcus, Viscount Wessex. She has now returned to serve as a companion for her elderly aunt with a daughter in tow. Even though they're next door neighbors, there is little reason for her to move in the same circles as Marcus, just in case, she vows to avoid him, for he reminds her of all she lost when she left.

Reunited

As their paths continue to cross, Marcus finds his desire for Eleanor just as strong, but he learned long ago she's not to be trusted. He will offer her a place in his bed, but not anything more. Only, Eleanor has no interest in this new, roguish man. The more time they spend together, the protective wall they've constructed to keep the other out, begin to break. With all the betrayals and secrets between them, Marcus has to open his heart again. And Eleanor must decide if it's ever safe to trust a rogue.

To Wed His Christmas Lady
Book 7 in the "Heart of a Duke" Series by Christi Caldwell

She's longing to be loved:

Lady Cara Falcot has only served one purpose to her loathsome father—to increase his power through a marriage to the future Duke of Billingsley. As such, she's built protective walls about her heart, and presents an icy facade to the world around her. Journeying home from her finishing school for the Christmas holidays, Cara's carriage is stranded during a winter storm. She's forced to tarry at a ramshackle inn, where she immediately antagonizes another patron—William.

He's avoiding his duty in favor of one last adventure:

William Hargrove, the Marquess of Grafton has wanted only one thing in life—to avoid the future match his parents would have him make to a cold, duke's daughter. He's returning home from a blissful eight years of traveling the world to see to his responsibilities. But when a winter storm interrupts his trip and lands him at a falling-down inn, he's forced to share company with a commanding Lady Cara who initially reminds him exactly of the woman he so desperately wants to avoid.

A Christmas snowstorm ushers in the spirit of the season:

At the holiday time, these two people who despise each other due to first perceptions are offered renewed beginnings and fresh starts. As this gruff stranger breaks down the walls she's built about herself, Cara has to determine whether she can truly open her heart to trusting that any man is capable of good and that she herself is capable of love. And William has to set aside all previous thoughts he's carried of the polished ladies like Cara, to be the man to show her that love.

THE HEART OF A SCOUNDREL
Book 6 in the "Heart of a Duke" Series by Christi Caldwell

Ruthless, wicked, and dark, the Marquess of Rutland rouses terror in the breast of ladies and nobleman alike. All Edmund wants in life is power. After he was publically humiliated by his one love Lady Margaret, he vowed vengeance, using Margaret's niece, as his pawn. Except, he's thwarted by another, more enticing target— Miss Phoebe Barrett.

Miss Phoebe Barrett knows precisely the shame she's been born to. Because her father is a shocking letch she's learned to form her own opinions on a person's worth. After a chance meeting with the Marquess of Rutland, she is captivated by the mysterious man. He, too, is a victim of society's scorn, but the more encounters she has with Edmund, the more she knows there is powerful depth and emotion to the jaded marquess.

The lady wreaks havoc on Edmund's plans for revenge and he finds he wants Phoebe, at all costs. As she's drawn into the darkness of his world, Phoebe risks being destroyed by Edmund's ruthlessness. And Phoebe who desires love at all costs, has to determine if she can ever truly trust the heart of a scoundrel.

TO LOVE A LORD
Book 5 in the "Heart of a Duke" Series by Christi Caldwell

All she wants is security:

The last place finishing school instructor Mrs. Jane Munroe belongs, is in polite Society. Vowing to never wed, she's been scuttled around from post to post. Now she finds herself in the Marquess of Waverly's household. She's never met a nobleman she liked, and when she meets the pompous, arrogant marquess, she remembers why. But soon, she discovers Gabriel is unlike any gentleman she's ever known.

All he wants is a companion for his sister:

What Gabriel finds himself with instead, is a fiery spirited, bespectacled woman who entices him at every corner and challenges his age-old vow to never trust his heart to a woman. But... there is something suspicious about his sister's companion. And he is determined to find out just what it is.

All they need is each other:

As Gabriel and Jane confront the truth of their feelings, the lies and secrets between them begin to unravel. And Jane is left to decide whether or not it is ever truly safe to love a lord.

LOVED BY A DUKE
Book 4 in the "Heart of a Duke" Series by Christi Caldwell

For ten years, Lady Daisy Meadows has been in love with Auric, the Duke of Crawford. Ever since his gallant rescue years earlier, Daisy knew she was destined to be his Duchess. Unfortunately, Auric sees her as his best friend's sister and nothing more. But perhaps, if she can manage to find the fabled heart of a duke pendant, she will win over the heart of her duke.

Auric, the Duke of Crawford enjoys Daisy's company. The last thing he is interested in however, is pursuing a romance with a woman he's known since she was in leading strings. This season, Daisy is turning up in the oddest places and he cannot help but notice that she is no longer a girl. But Auric wouldn't do something as foolhardy as to fall in love with Daisy. He couldn't. Not with the guilt he carries over his past sins… Not when he has no right to her heart…But perhaps, just perhaps, she can forgive the past and trust that he'd forever cherish her heart—but will she let him?

THE LOVE OF A ROGUE
Book 3 in the "Heart of a Duke" Series by Christi Caldwell

Lady Imogen Moore hasn't had an easy time of it since she made her Come Out. With her betrothed, a powerful duke breaking it off to wed her sister, she's become the *tons* favorite piece of gossip. Never again wanting to experience the pain of a broken heart, she's resolved to make a match with a polite, respectable gentleman. The last thing she wants is another reckless rogue.

Lord Alex Edgerton has a problem. His brother, tired of Alex's carousing has charged him with chaperoning their remaining, unwed sister about *ton* events. Shopping? No, thank you. Attending the theatre? He'd rather be at Forbidden Pleasures with a scantily clad beauty upon his lap. The task of *chaperone* becomes even more of a bother when his sister drags along her dearest friend, Lady Imogen to social functions. The last thing he wants in his life is a young, innocent English miss.

Except, as Alex and Imogen are thrown together, passions flare and Alex comes to find he not only wants Imogen in his bed, but also in his heart. Yet now he must convince Imogen to risk all, on the heart of a rogue.

More Than a Duke
Book 2 in the "Heart of a Duke" Series by Christi Caldwell

Polite Society doesn't take Lady Anne Adamson seriously. How-ever, Anne isn't just another pretty young miss. When she discovers her father betrayed her mother's love and her family descended into poverty, Anne comes up with a plan to marry a respectable, powerful, and honorable gentleman—a man nothing like her phi-landering father.

Armed with the heart of a duke pendant, fabled to land the wearer a duke's heart, she decides to enlist the aid of the notorious Harry, 6th Earl of Stanhope. A scoundrel with a scandalous past, he is the last gentleman she'd ever wed…however, his reputation marks him the perfect man to school her in the art of seduction so she might ensnare the illustrious Duke of Crawford.

Harry, the Earl of Stanhope is a jaded, cynical rogue who lives for his own pleasures. Having been thrown over by the only woman he ever loved so she could wed a duke, he's not at all surprised when Lady Anne approaches him with her scheme to capture another duke's affection. He's come to appreciate that all women are in fact greedy, title-grasping, self-indulgent creatures. And with Anne's history of grating on his every last nerve, she is the last woman he'd ever agree to school in the art of seduction. Only his friendship with the lady's sister compels him to help.

What begins as a pretend courtship, born of lessons on seduc-tion, becomes something more leaving Anne to decide if she can give her heart to a reckless rogue, and Harry must decide if he's willing to again trust in a lady's love.

FOR LOVE OF THE DUKE
First Full-Length Book in the "Heart of a Duke" Series
by Christi Caldwell

After the tragic death of his wife, Jasper, the 8th Duke of Bainbridge buried himself away in the dark cold walls of his home, Castle Blackwood. When he's coaxed out of his self-imposed exile to attend the amusements of the Frost Fair, his life is irrevocably changed by his fateful meeting with Lady Katherine Adamson.

With her tight brown ringlets and silly white-ruffled gowns, Lady Katherine Adamson has found her dance card empty for two Seasons. After her father's passing, Katherine learned the unreliability of men, and is determined to depend on no one, except herself. Until she meets Jasper…

In a desperate bid to avoid a match arranged by her family, Katherine makes the Duke of Bainbridge a shocking proposition—one that he accepts.

Only, as Katherine begins to love Jasper, she finds the arrangement agreed upon is not enough. And Jasper is left to decide if protecting his heart is more important than fighting for Katherine's love.

IN NEED OF A DUKE
A Prequel Novella to "The Heart of a Duke" Series
by Christi Caldwell

In Need of a Duke: (Author's Note: This is a prequel novella to "The Heart of a Duke" series by Christi Caldwell. It was originally available in "The Heart of a Duke" Collection and is now being published as an individual novella.

~★~

It features a new prologue and epilogue.

Years earlier, a gypsy woman passed to Lady Aldora Adamson and her friends a heart pendant that promised them each the heart of a duke.

Now, a young lady, with her family facing ruin and scandal, Lady Aldora doesn't have time for mythical stories about cheap baubles. She needs to save her sisters and brother by marrying a titled gentleman with wealth and power to his name. She sets her bespectacled sights upon the Marquess of St. James.

Turned out by his father after a tragic scandal, Lord Michael Knightly has grown into a powerful, but self-made man. With the whispers and stares that still follow him, he would rather be anywhere but London…

Until he meets Lady Aldora, a young woman who mistakes him for his brother, the Marquess of St. James. The connection between Aldora and Michael is immediate and as they come to know one another, Aldora's feelings for Michael war with her sisterly responsibilities. With her family's dire situation, a man of Michael's scandalous past will never do.

Ultimately, Aldora must choose between her responsibilities as a sister and her love for Michael.

ONCE A WALLFLOWER, AT LAST HIS LOVE
Book 6 in the Scandalous Seasons Series

Responsible, practical Miss Hermione Rogers, has been crafting stories as the notorious Mr. Michael Michaelmas and selling them for a meager wage to support her siblings. The only real way to ensure her family's ruinous debts are paid, however, is to marry. Tall, thin, and plain, she has no expectation of success. In London for her first Season she seizes the chance to write the tale of a brooding duke. In her research, she finds Sebastian Fitzhugh, the 5th Duke of Mallen, who unfortunately is perfectly affable, charming, and so nicely… configured… he takes her breath away. He lacks all the character traits she needs for her story, but alas, any duke will have to do.

Sebastian Fitzhugh, the 5th Duke of Mallen has been deceived so many times during the high-stakes game of courtship, he's lost faith in Society women. Yet, after a chance encounter with Hermione, he finds himself intrigued. Not a woman he'd normally consider beautiful, the young lady's practical bent, her forthright nature and her tendency to turn up in the oddest places has his interests... roused. He'd like to trust her, he'd like to do a whole lot more with her too, but should he?

A Marquess For Christmas
Book 5 in the Scandalous Seasons Series

Lady Patrina Tidemore gave up on the ridiculous notion of true love after having her heart shattered and her trust destroyed by a black-hearted cad. Used as a pawn in a game of revenge against her brother, Patrina returns to London from a failed elopement with a tattered reputation and little hope for a respectable match. The only peace she finds is in her solitude on the cold winter days at Hyde Park. And even that is yanked from her by two little hellions who just happen to have a devastatingly handsome, but coldly aloof father, the Marquess of Beaufort. Something about the lord stirs the dreams she'd once carried for an honorable gentleman's love.

Weston Aldridge, the 4th Marquess of Beaufort was deceived and betrayed by his late wife. In her faithlessness, he's come to view women as self-serving, indulgent creatures. Except, after a series of chance encounters with Patrina, he comes to appreciate how uniquely different she is than all women he's ever known.

At the Christmastide season, a time of hope and new beginnings, Patrina and Weston, unexpectedly learn true love in one another. However, as Patrina's scandalous past threatens their future and the happiness of his children, they are both left to determine if love is enough.

ALWAYS A ROGUE, FOREVER HER LOVE
Book 4 in the Scandalous Seasons Series

Miss Juliet Marshville is spitting mad. With one guardian missing, and the other singularly uninterested in her fate, she is at the mercy of her wastrel brother who loses her beloved childhood home to a man known as Sin. Determined to reclaim control of Rosecliff Cottage and her own fate, Juliet arranges a meeting with the notorious rogue and demands the return of her property.

Jonathan Tidemore, 5th Earl of Sinclair, known to the *ton* as Sin, is exceptionally lucky in life and at the gaming tables. He has just one problem. Well…four, really. His incorrigible sisters have driven off yet another governess. This time, however, his mother demands he find an appropriate replacement.

When Miss Juliet Marshville boldly demands the return of her precious cottage, he takes advantage of his sudden good fortune and puts an offer to her; turn his sisters into proper English ladies, and he'll return Rosecliff Cottage to Juliet's possession.

Jonathan comes to appreciate Juliet's spirit, courage, and clever wit, and decides to claim the fiery beauty as his mistress. Juliet, however, will be mistress for no man. Nor could she ever love a man who callously stole her home in a game of cards. As Jonathan begins to see Juliet as more than a spirited beauty to warm his bed, he realizes she could be a lady he could love the rest of his life, if only he can convince the proud Juliet that he's worthy of her hand and heart.

ALWAYS PROPER, SUDDENLY SCANDALOUS
Book 3 in the Scandalous Seasons Series

Geoffrey Winters, Viscount Redbrooke was not always the hard, unrelenting lord driven by propriety. After a tragic mistake, he resolved to honor his responsibility to the Redbrooke line and live a life, free of scandal. Knowing his duty is to wed a proper, respectable English miss, he selects Lady Beatrice Dennington, daughter of the Duke of Somerset, the perfect woman for him. Until he meets Miss Abigail Stone…

To distance herself from a personal scandal, Abigail Stone flees America to visit her uncle, the Duke of Somerset. Determined to never trust a man again, she is helplessly intrigued by the hard, too-proper Geoffrey. With his strict appreciation for decorum and order, he is nothing like the man' she's always dreamed of.

Abigail is everything Geoffrey does not need. She upends his carefully ordered world at every encounter. As they begin to care for one another, Abigail carefully guards the secret that resulted in her journey to England.

Only, if Geoffrey learns the truth about Abigail, he must decide which he holds most dear: his place in Society or Abigail's place in his heart.

NEVER COURTED, SUDDENLY WED
Book 2 in the Scandalous Seasons Series

Christopher Ansley, Earl of Waxham, has constructed a perfect image for the *ton*–the ladies love him and his company is desired by all. Only two people know the truth about Waxham's secret. Unfortunately, one of them is Miss Sophie Winters.

Sophie Winters has known Christopher since she was in leading strings. As children, they delighted in tormenting each other. Now at two and twenty, she still has a tendency to find herself in scrapes, and her marital prospects are slim.

When his father threatens to expose his shame to the *ton*, unless he weds Sophie for her dowry, Christopher concocts a plan to remain a bachelor. What he didn't plan on was falling in love with the lively, impetuous Sophie. As secrets are exposed, will Christopher's love be enough when she discovers his role in his father's scheme?

FOREVER BETROTHED, NEVER THE BRIDE
Book 1 in the Scandalous Seasons Series

Hopeless romantic Lady Emmaline Fitzhugh is tired of sitting with the wallflowers, waiting for her betrothed to come to his senses and marry her. When Emmaline reads one too many reports of his scandalous liaisons in the gossip rags, she takes matters into her own hands.

War-torn veteran Lord Drake devotes himself to forgetting his days on the Peninsula through an endless round of meaningless associations. He no longer wants to feel anything, but Lady Emmaline is making it hard to maintain a state of numbness. With her zest for life, she awakens his passion and desire for love.

The one woman Drake has spent the better part of his life avoiding is now the only woman he needs, but he is no longer a man worthy of his Emmaline. It is up to her to show him the healing power of love.

A SEASON OF HOPE
A Danby Novella

Five years ago when her love, Marcus Wheatley, failed to return from fighting Napoleon's forces, Lady Olivia Foster buried her heart. Unable to betray Marcus's memory, Olivia has gone out of her way to run off prospective suitors. At three and twenty she considers herself firmly on the shelf. Her father, however, disagrees and accepts an offer for Olivia's hand in marriage. Yet it's Christmas, when anything can happen…

Olivia receives a well-timed summons from her grandfather, the Duke of Danby, and eagerly embraces the reprieve from her betrothal.

Only, when Olivia arrives at Danby Castle she realizes the Christmas season represents hope, second chances, and even miracles.

"Winning a Lady's Heart"
A Danby Novella

Author's Note: This is a novella that was originally available in A Summons From The Castle (The Regency Christmas Summons Collection). It is being published as an individual novella.

~★~

For Lady Alexandra, being the source of a cold, calculated wager is bad enough…but when it is waged by Nathaniel Michael Winters, 5th Earl of Pembroke, the man she's in love with, it results in a broken heart, the scandal of the season, and a summons from her grandfather – the Duke of Danby.

To escape Society's gossip, she hurries to her meeting with the duke, determined to put memories of the earl far behind. Except the duke has other plans for Alexandra…plans which include the 5th Earl of Pembroke!

Tempted by a Lady's Smile
Book 4 in the "Lords of Honor" Series

Richard Jonas has loved but one woman—a woman who belongs to his brother. Refusing to suffer any longer, he evades his family in order to barricade his heart from unrequited love. While attending a friend's summer party, Richard's approach to love is changed after sharing a passionate and life-altering kiss with a vibrant and mysterious woman. Believing he was incapable of loving again, Richard finds himself tempted by a young lady determined to marry his best friend.

Gemma Reed has not been treated kindly by the *ton*. Often disregarded for her appearance and interests unlike those of a proper lady, Gemma heads to house party to win the heart of Lord Westfield, the man she's loved for years. But her plan is set off course by the tempting and intriguing, Richard Jonas.

A chance meeting creates a new path for Richard and Gemma to forage—but can two people, scorned and shunned by those they've loved from afar, let down their guards to find true happiness?

"RESCUED BY A LADY'S LOVE"
Book 3 in the "Lords of Honor" Series

Destitute and determined to finally be free of any man's shackles, Lily Benedict sets out to salvage her honor. With no choice but to commit a crime that will save her from her past, she enters the home of the recluse, Derek Winters, the new Duke of Blackthorne. But entering the "Beast of Blackthorne's" lair proves more threatening than she ever imagined.

With half a face and a mangled leg, Derek—once rugged and charming—only exists within the confines of his home. Shunned by society, Derek is leery of the hauntingly beautiful Lily Benedict. As time passes, she slips past his defenses, reminding him how to live again. But when Lily's sordid past comes back, threatening her life, it's up to Derek to find the strength to become the hero he once was. Can they overcome the darkness of their sins to find a life of love and redemption?

CAPTIVATED BY A LADY'S CHARM
Book 2 in the "Lords of Honor" Series

In need of a wife…
Christian Villiers, the Marquess of St. Cyr, despises the role he's been cast into as fortune hunter but requires the funds to keep his marquisate solvent. Yet, the sins of his past cloud his future, preventing him from seeing beyond his fateful actions at the Battle of Toulouse. For he knows inevitably it will catch up with him, and everyone will remember his actions on the battlefield that cost so many so much—particularly his best friend.

In want of a husband…

Lady Prudence Tidemore's life is plagued by familial scandals, which makes her own marital prospects rather grim. Surely there is one gentleman of the ton who can look past her family and see just her and all she has to offer?

When Prudence runs into Christian on a London street, the charming, roguish gentleman immediately captures her attention. But then a chance meeting becomes a waltz, and now…

A Perfect Match…

All she must do is convince Christian to forget the cold requirements he has for his future marchioness. But the demons in his past prevent him from turning himself over to love. One thing is certain—Prudence wants the marquess and is determined to have him in her life, now and forever. It's just a matter of convincing Christian he wants the same.

ᶜSEDUCED ʙY A ʟADY'S ʜEART
Book 1 in the "Lords of Honor" Series

You met Lieutenant Lucien Jones in "Forever Betrothed, Never the Bride" when he was a broken soldier returned from fighting Boney's forces. This is his story of triumph and happily-ever-after!

~★~

Lieutenant Lucien Jones, son of a viscount, returned from war, to find his wife and child dead. Blaming his father for the commission that sent him off to fight Boney's forces, he was content to languish at London Hospital… until offered employment on the Marquess of Drake's staff. Through his position, Lucien found purpose in life and is content to keep his past buried.

Lady Eloise Yardley has loved Lucien since they were children. Having long ago given up on the dream of him, she married another. Years later, she is a young, lonely widow who does not fit in with the ton. When Lucien's family enlists her aid to reunite father and son, she leaps at the opportunity to not only aid her former friend, but to also escape London.

Lucien doesn't know what scheme Eloise has concocted, but

knowing her as he does, when she pays a visit to his employer, he knows she's up to something. The last thing he wants is the temptation that this new, older, mature Eloise presents; a tantalizing reminder of happier times and peace.

Yet Eloise is determined to win Lucien's love once and for all... if only Lucien can set aside the pain of his past and risk all on a lady's heart.

Only For Their Love
Book 3 in the "The Theodosia Sword" Series

Miss Carol Cresswall bore witness to her parents' loveless union and is determined to avoid that same miserable fate. Her mother has altogether different plans—plans that include a match between Carol and Lord Gregory Renshaw. Despite his wealth and power, Carol has no interest in marrying a pompous man who goes out of his way to ignore her. Now, with their families coming together for the Christmastide season it's her mother's last-ditch effort to get them together. And Carol plans to avoid Gregory at all costs.

Lord Gregory Renshaw has no intentions of falling prey to his mother's schemes to marry him off to a proper debutante she's picked out. Over the years, he has carefully sidestepped all endeavors to be matched with any of the grasping ladies.

But a sudden Christmastide Scandal has the potential show Carol and Gregory that they've spent years running from the one thing they've always needed.

Only For Her Honor
Book 2 in the "The Theodosia Sword" Series

A wounded soldier:

When Captain Lucas Rayne returned from fighting Boney's forces, he was a shell of a man. A recluse who doesn't leave his family's estate, he's content to shut himself away. Until he meets Eve...

A woman alone in the world:

Eve Ormond spent most of her life following the drum alongside her late father. When his shameful actions bring death and pain to English soldiers, Eve is forced back to England, an outcast. With no family or marital prospects she needs employment and finds it in Captain Lucas Rayne's home. A man whose life was ruined by her father, Eve has no place inside his household. With few options available, however, Eve takes the post. What she never anticipates is how with their every meeting, this honorable, hurting soldier slips inside her heart.

The Secrets Between Them:

The more time Lucas spends with Eve, he remembers what it is to be alive and he lets the walls protecting his heart down. When the secrets between them come to light will their love be enough? Or are they two destined for heartbreak?

Only For His Lady
Book 1 in the "The Theodosia Sword" Series

A curse. A sword. And the thief who stole her heart.

The Rayne family is trapped in a rut of bad luck. And now, it's up to Lady Theodosia Rayne to steal back the Theodosia sword, a gladius that was pilfered by the rival, loathed Renshaw family. Hopefully, recovering the stolen sword will break the cycle and reverse her family's fate.

Damian Renshaw, the Duke of Devlin, is feared by all—all, that is, except Lady Theodosia, the brazen spitfire who enters his home and wrestles an ancient relic from his wall. Intrigued by the vivacious woman, Devlin has no intentions of relinquishing the sword to her.

As Theodosia and Damian battle for ownership, passion ignites. Now, they are torn between their age-old feud and the fire that burns between them. Can two forbidden lovers find a way to make amends before their families' war tears them apart?

MY LADY OF DECEPTION
Book 1 in the "Brethren of the Lords" Series

This dark, sweeping Regency novel was previously only offered as part of the limited edition box sets: "From the Ballroom and Beyond", "Romancing the Rogue", and "Dark Deceptions". Now, available for the first time on its own, exclusively through Amazon is "My Lady of Deception".

~★~

Everybody has a secret. Some are more dangerous than others.

For Georgina Wilcox, only child of the notorious traitor known as "The Fox", there are too many secrets to count. However, after her interference results in great tragedy, she resolves to never help another… until she meets Adam Markham.

Lord Adam Markham is captured by The Fox. Imprisoned, Adam loses everything he holds dear. As his days in captivity grow, he finds himself fascinated by the young maid, Georgina, who cares for him.

When the carefully crafted lies she's built between them begin to crumble, Georgina realizes she will do anything to prove her love and loyalty to Adam—even it means at the expense of her own life.

NON-FICTION WORKS BY
CHRISTI CALDWELL

Uninterrupted Joy: Memoir: My Journey through Infertility, Pregnancy, and Special Needs

The following journey was never intended for publication. It was written from a mother, to her unborn child. The words detailed her struggle through infertility and the joy of finally being pregnant. A stunning revelation at her son's birth opened a world of both fear and discovery. This is the story of one mother's love and hope and…her quest for uninterrupted joy.

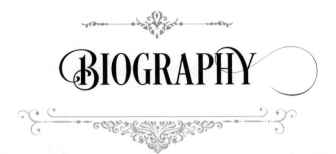

BIOGRAPHY

Christi Caldwell is the bestselling author of historical romance novels set in the Regency era. Christi blames Judith McNaught's "Whitney, My Love," for luring her into the world of historical romance. While sitting in her graduate school apartment at the University of Connecticut, Christi decided to set aside her notes and try her hand at writing romance. She believes the most perfect heroes and heroines have imperfections and rather enjoys tormenting them before crafting a well-deserved happily ever after!

When Christi isn't writing the stories of flawed heroes and heroines, she can be found in her Southern Connecticut home chasing around her eight-year-old son, and caring for twin princesses-in-training!

Visit *www.christicaldwellauthor.com* to learn more about what Christi is working on, or join her on Facebook at Christi Caldwell Author, and Twitter *@ChristiCaldwell*